LEGEND

ROSEWOOD HIGH #7

TRACY LORRAINE

Andy & Amelia x

Edited by My Brother's Editor

Proofreading by Sisters Get Lit(erary) Author Services

1

———

KYLE

"So how does it feel?" Kane asks as I drop down into his passenger seat after throwing the few belongings I had into the trunk.

"It's been about thirty seconds, bro."

"I know." He shrugs. "I just thought you might feel different."

"Relief?" I ask, glancing over at him.

"Fuck, bro," he growls, running his hand down his face and resting his head back on the headrest. "I'm so fucking sorry you had to go through that."

"It's not your fault," I mutter, looking out the window at the building and the barbed wire-topped fences I'm about to finally break free from.

"I should have been there. I could have stopped it." Regret laces his voice, and I know why. He thinks this happened because he got distracted and left me alone at that party. But it can only be my fault. It was my decision. It was my mistake. It's time he lets it go and moves on.

"It's okay, Kane. I don't blame you for this. It's just... it's over. Time to move on."

"Speaking of... I've got a surprise for you."

I raise a brow, waiting for him to spill the beans. I'm sure there are going to be a lot of surprises waiting for me, seeing as I mostly checked out on real life for the past twelve months.

"Go on," I encourage, already getting impatient for him to just put his car into drive and take me away from this place and the memories that I already know are going to haunt me for the rest of my life.

"What's the one thing we used to dream of?"

"Err... become millionaires and move to LA?" I ask with a laugh, knowing that there's no way he's achieved that without me knowing.

"Close, but no."

"Just tell me," I sigh, my head falling back in defeat. I'm so fucking tired. All I want to do is go home and crawl into a semi-comfortable bed for a month. My eyes fall closed and I relax for what feels like the first time in just over a year. It's a weird feeling.

"We've left Harrow Creek."

I let a second pass for him to tell me that he's joking, but when he doesn't, I rip my eyes open once more and stare straight at him.

"For real?" I ask, more hope than is probably necessary filling my voice. He's not wrong that we used to dream of leaving that shithole on almost a daily basis. But without money, and seeing as we were only kids, there was no way of that happening. Although, I didn't think it would be right now either.

"For real. I got us a new place."

"Where?"

I swear some of the color drains from his face at my question and a little guilt flickers through his eyes.

"Kane?" I warn, already assuming what's about to fall from his lips. "Don't tell me that you've—"

"Rosewood."

That one word is like a bullet to my chest. All the air drains from my lungs and my shoulders sag.

"Why, Kane? Why would you do that to me... to us? Of all the places."

He stares at me, his brow wrinkling in concern. "It wasn't very easy, and I needed help, a lot of help. We didn't have that many options, so it was Rosewood or stay in the Creek and that was not happening. After..." He gestures to the building behind me. "You needed a fresh start, and I've done everything I can to give you one. I know you might not like it, but you've got a year to make the best of it before you can go to college."

I hate that my first reaction to what he's done is anger, but I can't help it. I know I should be grateful, and I am. Not going back to the Creek is the best news I could have wished for. But going to Rosewood. The place the one person I never want to see again lives, that's not exactly what I wished for upon release from that hellhole.

She was the one that put me in there, I sure as hell don't want to see her the second I come out. My fists curl, my nails digging into the worn leather of Kane's passenger seat as I try to contain the anger she ignites within me.

"Rosewood is a big town, Kyle. You probably won't even see..." He trails off, correctly guessing where my head is at.

"Kane, this is a really fucking bad idea," I warn.

"I've got us our own house, I've got you a place at Rosewood High so you can graduate, and hopefully, we'll keep social services off our back until you turn eighteen in a few weeks."

"Yeah, then I can leave," I mutter.

"Kyle," Kane warns, his voice low and menacing. It might work on others, they might think it's scary, but I know him too well to be scared of him. He's my big brother. My best friend. The one I've always relied on, trusted with everything. I fear that I might just have to put everything I'm feeling right now aside and do those things once again.

"Fuck... Rosewood, really?"

"I've pulled a lot of fucking strings to make this work for us, bro. I need you on board."

I stare at my brother. The one person I've looked up to all my life. There's no way I can say no to him now. Not after he's supported me through this and apparently done everything in his power to help me start over.

"I guess you'd better take me home then."

The corner of Kane's mouth twitches up into a smile. "It's not much but—"

"It'll be perfect. I'm sure a huge improvement from where I've been."

Kane flashes a look back over his shoulder, but I don't. I'm done with the place, it's time to move forward, even if that has to be in Rosewood with the girl that condemned me to hell in the first place.

I keep my eyes focused out of the window as Kane takes us to our new home. Being out here, everything just feels... strange. I might have hated that place, my cell, the guys who I was forced to live with. But after so long it became normal of sorts. Being out in the open... it's weird.

"What's the first thing you want to do?"

I don't even have to think about it and the words fall from my lips in a heartbeat. "Sleep in a comfortable bed."

"Huh, and here I was thinking you'd want a girl, or even a walk on the beach."

"They can come after. Sleep and a hot shower... alone."

"Damn, I was going to come and watch as well," he mutters with a laugh as he takes a left at an intersection I've never seen before but he seems to know well.

"You're still weird, I see."

"Would you want me any other way?"

"I guess not."

It's almost two hours after we left that place that I never want to think about again when he pulls into a quiet neighborhood and then onto a driveway.

"Wow, this is... cute."

"I never promised you a mansion, Ky."

"No, but this looks like a grandmother should live inside. It's not exactly party central." My heart constricts at the mention of a grandparent. That's just one more thing that I'll never forgive *her* for.

"A good thing seeing as we're going to have a social worker on our back for the next few weeks along with your parole officer."

I twist in my seat and look at my brother where he's still holding the wheel and staring up at our blue and white bungalow.

"Thank you," I say sincerely.

I surely didn't expect any of this, and I may have sounded somewhat ungrateful when he first mentioned this place but I really do appreciate what he's trying to do.

"It's not just for you, bro."

"I-I know. I can't imagine what you've had to do to secure all this. How are you even paying for it?"

"Gran left us a bit of money, and like I said, I had some good help."

"Who the hell wanted to help us? Two scumbags from the Creek."

"Someone who understands. Shall we?" he asks, cutting off any more questions I might have.

He shoulders the door of his old Nissan Skyline and jumps out. I guess some things never change.

Following suit, I climb out and grab my stuff from the trunk.

I trail behind Kane as he heads up the stairs to the porch. There's a swing seat at the other end and a coffee table with an ashtray in the middle.

"Smoking outside only."

"Sure thing, *Mom*," I say with a laugh but as his shoulders tense before me, I realize it might have been the wrong thing to say.

He spins and pins me with a hard look.

I've never been scared of Kane... okay, maybe a few times when I was younger but I know I can hold my own now, especially after the amount of time I've spent working out and fighting off assholes in the past year but still, the look on his face makes me swallow somewhat nervously.

"All it takes is for that social worker to turn up and get a sniff of weed in this place and all of this is going to come crashing down around our feet, Ky. You think they were happy about giving me guardianship of you, even if it is for a few weeks? Let me answer that for you... No, no, they fucking didn't. I might be older than you, but not by much and my rep isn't exactly squeaky fucking clean. This," he says, holding his hands out to gesture to our granny house. "Is a fucking miracle. So for a few weeks, just a few weeks, you need to do what the fuck you're told or I'll send you back into that place myself for fucking up all my hard work. You got that, little bro."

I have to clench my jaw to stop me from saying anything in response to his patronizing tone.

"You got it," I say in the end. "Point me in the direction of my bed."

"It's not even lunchtime yet."

"I don't give a shit."

"Okay. Well, Bea is coming at four to make sure you've settled in so you need to be awake and showered and looking respectful by then."

I drop my eyes to his exposed inked arms, his ripped jeans, and battered boots. Respectful, right.

"You know what I mean," he mutters before pulling the screen open, unlocking the front door and dragging it open.

Inside is a mostly empty living space. There are two old couches with a coffee table in the middle. There's a dining table in front of what can only be described as vintage kitchen units and a couple of mismatched chairs. It's... interesting. But a hell of a lot better than where I've come from.

"You get yourself a job and hopefully we'll be able to get some better shit."

"It's fine, K."

He glances at me but he refrains from pointing out that we don't even have a TV right now. "This is your room." He swings the door open and I find something that makes me sigh in relief. A queen-size bed with what looks like fresh sheets. Heaven.

Dropping my bag, I jump on the bed and starfish in the middle of it.

"My room's at the other end of the hall. The bathroom is in between us. I bought you a new cell and a laptop with the money I had left over." He nods to the dresser where the boxes sit.

"Kane, you didn't—"

"I did. I told her that I'd take care of you, give you a fresh start. That's what I'm doing."

"But... what about you?"

"Me?" he asks with a humorless laugh. "We're out of the Creek, Ky. I'm good."

"But what about work? What about..."

"That doesn't matter right now." Walking over to the dresser, he picks up the cell phone box and throws it at me. "Maybe set an alarm, yeah?" Then he walks out and closes the door without saying another word.

His footsteps get quieter before the front screen at the front door rattles and the house falls silent.

I stare at the room I'm sitting in. It's not much to write home about. The walls are a dirty cream color, the woodwork is chipped, the floor is stained, and the window is cracked. But... it's mine.

There's one single dresser along with a nightstand beside the bed, and a door that I can only assume is a closet.

Pushing from the bed, I kick my sneakers off and pad over. Pulling it open, I find a few of my old clothes hanging inside.

I haven't seen them for a year and I'd forgotten they even existed.

I pull each of the drawers open finding brand new boxers and socks and a few new t-shirts and sweats.

Dragging a couple out, I tuck them under my arm and head out to find the bathroom. I might want to sleep, but before that happens, I need to wash the smell of that place off me.

The bathroom is... well, it's blue. Really fucking blue.

But none of that matters because the water is hot and I'm the only one in the room, in the house actually, seeing as I saw a trail of smoke in front of one of the windows as I walked here.

A lot might have changed in a year, but Kane isn't one of them. He's still as unreadable as ever. I have no clue if he's happy about this or not. I know he wants me back. That's not in question. But does he really want to be in Rosewood? He hates those who did this to us as much as I do. Of all the places in this country. Why here?

Steam billows from the stream of water and after stripping down, I stand under the torrent.

It's so hot it burns, but I relish in it. After having to wash in lukewarm water for a year, I'll take the pain. It isn't like I haven't felt worse. I drop my hand to the scar on my side, remembering the pain of the knife but I quickly push it aside, that's all in the past now and all this is, is a reminder of why I'm never going back there.

I stand there so long the water begins to run cold. I make

quick work of washing with the shower gel on the side before getting out and drying off with a towel that is thicker than I've felt in a long time.

I find a brand new toothbrush in the cupboard that I make use of. There's also a new razor and shaving gel but I can't be bothered with that. Those new bedsheets are calling.

The second I step into the hallway dressed in just a pair of sweats I find Kane heading this way.

His eyes go from mine and to my body, zeroing in on the scar for a beat.

"Whoa, where'd my little brother go?"

"He went to fucking juvie, bro."

A smirk curls at his lips.

"Jailbait and cut. You're gonna be fighting the Rosewood pussy off," he jokes.

I want to join him but the second he mentions pussy, only one girl pops into my mind.

I shake my head and turn toward my room.

"What? Don't tell me they turned you in there. You still want pussy, right?"

I flip him off before I slam my door closed.

Pulling the sheets back, I fall into them, loving the feeling of the crisp, cool cotton against my skin.

———

"Okay, everything looks good here," Bea says, closing her folder and looking up at me with a soft smile playing on her lips.

Turns out this afternoon isn't the first time I've met my social worker. She'd been to visit me inside a couple of times. I've had so many people try to 'help' me over the past year that I stopped paying attention to who everyone was after a few months. I didn't need help. I just needed to get out and pay the girl, who put me there in the first place, a visit.

"Do you need anything else from us?" Kane asks almost nervously. It's weird seeing him take control of this situation like an adult. He's always been my fun, slightly insane older brother, seeing him act the part of my guardian, even if it is just for Bea's benefit is weird.

"Yes, you've done a great job here, Kane. I know it's not been easy but hopefully, everything will go smoothly over the next few weeks and you'll be free to continue your lives without me breathing down your neck. Have you heard from your parole officer yet?"

I nod, remembering the meeting we had before I left.

"Okay, good. I spoke to Principal Hartmann earlier, everything is ready for you to start at Rosewood High on Wednesday."

"Wednesday?" I ask, assuming that I'd at least get a week to myself.

"Yes, we thought it best you get into your new routine as soon as possible. I spoke to him about being on the team and your previous experience with tutoring."

"Great," I mutter, glaring at Kane. I really don't need any more on my plate than just restarting my life.

"It'll be fantastic, Kyle. Rosewood High is a great school with a fantastic football team should you decide to join. It'll give you fantastic opportunities for the future."

I blow out a long breath. My future. I have no idea what that looks like for me now. I'm a Harrow Creek trailer park kid with a record. Not exactly the thing dreams are made of.

"Yeah, we'll see."

"Well, you've got time to figure stuff out."

"Okay well, if that's everything, I'll see myself out. Here's my card." She slides it across the table toward me. "I'll be in touch on Wednesday evening to see how school went but if you need me in the meantime, I'm always available on my cell."

"Thanks," I mutter, glancing down at her card.

She smiles at both of us before tucking her chair away and letting herself out as she said she would.

Silence surrounds us long after the shutter has crashed shut.

I have no idea what she really thought of the whole situation but I guess it doesn't really matter. She's happy enough with it to allow it to continue.

"I met with Principal Hartmann last week," Kane says after a few minutes of silence once the shutter door had slammed shut.

"Okay."

"Bea is right. It's a good school. Nothing like Harrow Creek High."

"Is anywhere as bad as Harrow Creek High?" I ask with a laugh, stretching my legs out and slumping down in the chair a little.

"You've got me there. I know it's a lot, but the team won state last year. All their best players are about to graduate, they'd be crazy not to want you."

"I don't know, K. So much has changed."

"Has it though? Football was our thing, our way out."

I nod at him because I always allowed him to think that it was our thing, when really, it was his. He's always been so much better than me. I swear if we were lucky enough to be born somewhere different he'd already have the NFL after him. He is *that* good. But as it is, our life was—is—shit, and those kinds of opportunities don't just appear for kids like us.

They happen for Rosewood kids, not Harrow Creek kids.

"We'll see," I mutter, pushing to stand and pulling the refrigerator open to grab a soda.

"We're gonna have futures, Ky. I'm going to make sure

of it."

"I'm just happy to be free. I'll worry about the rest later."

"Talking about being free... you need to get changed."

"Why?"

"Why? Because we're celebrating tonight."

"That's okay. I don't need—" He pins me with a look that cuts off my argument.

"The guys will be here in an hour or so, the girls too..." He wiggles his brows at me.

"Kane, I don't need—" I try again.

"Humor me. I want to celebrate. This is a new start for us, kid. Things can only get better from here on out."

He scrubs his hand on the top of my head like he used to when we were kids, only I'm not so small anymore. I almost match his six-foot-three and after the muscle I've gained in juvie I might even have a few pounds on him right now.

"Fine," I say. "But is it a good idea with Bea breathing down our necks?"

"She's good, she's happy. Let's enjoy ourselves for just one night, eh?"

"Okay, fine."

———

I wake with what feels like a drum pounding in my head.

Fucking Kane.

I roll over with a groan, hoping that my stomach stays settled and bump into a person.

My eyes fly open and my heart jumps into my throat when I find not one but two half-naked girls in my bed.

Jesus, fucking hell.

What happened last night?

Lifting the covers, I find that I'm still wearing my boxers.

"Get the fuck out," I bark, my voice rough from a lack of sleep and a raging hangover.

I shake both of the girls awake.

"Get the fuck out of my bed."

They both look as rough as I feel as they do as they're told and drag their bodies from my bed before stumbling across the room toward the door.

The sight of them with makeup down their faces, their dresses twisted up around their waists and their tits half hanging out does nothing for me and I briefly wonder if that's just because of who they are or because I got my fill last night.

I don't remember anything past drinking straight from a bottle of vodka while Kane passed me a blunt to celebrate my release. I don't know who those girls were, when they arrived or how we even all ended up in here.

"Fucking hell," I mutter, pulling the covers over my head and allowing myself to drift back off.

When I come back to hours later, it's to the sound of my brother kicking people out of our house. I have no idea who's out there but I don't care enough to go and see.

There's movement for about ten minutes before the voices fade and the footsteps disappear before engines start and fade into the distance.

"Ky, you up?" Kane asks after knocking on my bedroom door.

"Go away," I bark, rolling onto my back.

"You want food?"

I want to say no, but my stomach growls at the thought of something decent to eat and I find myself throwing the covers back and dragging on a clean pair of sweats.

"Whoa, aren't you a sight for sore eyes."

"Fuck off," I grunt, pushing past him where he's blocking my doorway and marching for the bathroom.

"You're welcome, by the way," he says with a laugh as I slam the door behind me and immediately reach for my toothbrush.

I don't look up as I take care of my mouth, hoping that as I rid myself of the putrid taste, I can remove the hangover and lack of memories from last night. But the second I'm done and I lift my eyes to the mirror, I can't help but gasp.

I've got girl's lipstick fucking everywhere.

"Fucking hell."

I scrub my hand down my face and push my hair back before turning the shower on and stripping down.

"Good night, eh?" Kane asks when I drop down to the table while he fries bacon at the stove.

"Can we not talk about it?" I slide down the chair until I can rest my head back and close my eyes as the sound of his deep chuckle fills the room.

"Tell me that you at least remember it."

Feeling his stare burning into my skin, I drag my eyes open and stare at him.

"No, I have no fucking clue what happened, although the lipstick trail was a good indication."

The fuck actually fucking belly laughs at me.

"I told you to lay off the vodka after a year off."

"Whatever. At least I don't remember most of the mistakes."

"Who says they were mistakes? Two girls are never a mistake, Ky."

"Whatever you say. That ready yet?"

He drops a plate down in front of me and my mouth waters.

"Don't get used to it. I might have sorted us a house but I'm not your keeper," he mutters, pulling out his own chair.

"Wouldn't have expected you to be."

"I have today off, but after tomorrow, you won't see me much."

"What are you doing?" I ask, thinking of the less than legal shit we both did for money before I went away. Surely he must have a better job now to even stand a chance of getting me here.

"Doesn't matter," he mutters, stuffing a piece of bacon into his mouth. *Or maybe not then.* "You should probably spend more time worrying about yourself than me. You're heading back to high school tomorrow." He winks and my stomach twists.

I want to graduate, I have always wanted to but the second I got thrown in the back of that cop car a little over a year ago, I knew that the chance was even slimmer than it was already. Not that many kids leave Harrow Creek High with a diploma, the odds were already against me, despite my ability.

"Can't wait." The enthusiasm in my tone says it all about how I feel about returning to school. I should be finishing up senior year right now, yet here I am about to start it a year later than I should have. Although I can't deny that it's all my fault.

"Just do something for me." The serious tone in his voice has me looking up at him.

"Sure."

"Stay away from *her*."

I snort. "You're kidding, right?"

"No. I promised... uh... I just had to promise you'd put your head down and focus on your education. No going after revenge." His brow lifts.

"You're fucking kidding me," I repeat, not believing that he can ask that of me after everything.

He shrugs and all it does is piss me off further.

"Just stay away from her."

His plate clatters into the sink before he stalks to his bedroom.

"Is that what you'll do when you see *her* again?" I call after him but he doesn't respond aside from slamming his door hard enough for the entire house to shake.

2

___

HARLEY

"Who's Nathan?" Ashton, my best friend's boyfriend asks, as we walk toward English lit.

I can't help the wide smile that pulls at my lips as I think of him.

I haven't seen him since he took me out Sunday night but we've messaged almost every moment since.

He's sweet. Really freaking sweet. And he treats me like I'm something special, something worthwhile. It's nice. Especially as both of my best friends now have boys and I'm playing the odd one out.

"A guy from Maddison Prep that Harley met at Ethan's party. They've had a few dates," Ruby answers for me while I relive my time with him.

"Ah, dating a prep boy, eh? I hear they don't put out until at least the tenth date." My breathing falters at his comment.

We kissed, he's run his hand up my thigh and wrapped it around my waist, but that's where we've stopped so far.

"Shut up, you idiot. He's a good guy. Right, Har?"

I'm lost in my own head as we walk into our class. My thoughts back on Nathan as he kissed me goodbye on Sunday night. It was... nice.

I look up at the last minute knowing I'm about to weave my way through the desks to locate my own at the back when my world comes crashing down around my feet.

I stop dead on the spot and Ruby slams into my back as my heart jumps into my throat and I swear it damn near stops beating.

"Har?" Ruby asks, concern lacing her voice as she walks around to see my face.

She gasps at whatever she finds on my face but her reaction to this isn't the one that affects me.

"Are you okay?" I rip my eyes from him to find Ruby staring right at him with a scowl on her face.

I want to laugh. She's so small and so sweet yet she stares at him like she's about to walk over there and rip him a new one.

"W-who's that?" she asks, looking back at me and taking in my tear-filled eyes.

My lips part but it takes a second for any words to come out.

"Y-you remember Kane, the guy from my house on Sunday?" I whisper, ensuring no one but the two of them can hear.

The image of walking home to find him in my house Sunday night hits me and I feel the sting of betrayal from my mother having anything to do with the Legend brothers after what happened twists my insides once more.

I know she likes to help kids who seem to be a lost cause, but I never thought she'd stoop so low to help them.

No wonder she looked so sheepish when we discovered them.

"Yeah." She nods and then looks back to him.

I do the same and find what I already know, his light blue eyes are trained right on me. Although the happy-go-lucky look I remember from our childhoods is long gone. In its place is hate like I've never witnessed before.

I swallow nervously.

I did that to him.

"That's his little brother, Kyle." My voice cracks on his name and I hate it.

What I did was right. Okay, maybe frowned upon where we grew up, and I certainly never intended for Kyle to take the rap for it, but he was still in the wrong.

"Okay. And why does he look like he wants to kill you?"

"Probably because he does."

I swallow down my fear, my nerves and suck in a stealing breath.

My instinct is to run. To get as far away from his cold, evil eyes and hide anywhere I can find where I'm safe.

But what's the point in that?

He's here, and something tells me that he'll find me no matter where I go.

"Are you going in or what?" Someone barks from the hallway, bringing me back to reality and reminding me that I stopped right in the doorway.

"Yeah, sorry," Ruby mutters, dragging me to the side a little so the others can pass. "What are you going to do?"

"I'm going to sit my ass down and do my work, Ruby. What are you going to do?" I don't mean to snap at her but I can't help it. My emotions are currently being put through a blender.

"Are you sure? If you want to sk—"

"No," I cut her off, assuming where she's going. "I'm not running from him."

A proud smile pulls at Ruby's lips.

"Good for you, Har. Let's do this."

"You want me to beat his ass, just let me know," Ashton offers, startling me. I'd forgotten he was witness to this.

"Morning everyone. Please find your seats and let's pick up where we left off last lesson," our teacher calls out over the chatter filling the room.

The three of us move toward the back of the room. The closer I get to Kyle, the harder it becomes to breathe. It's like he literally sucks the air from my lungs. I know he probably wants me dead, but I'd have put money on him making it much more painful than this.

His calculating eyes follow me as I pass him and it's not until I'm a few feet away that I finally suck in a huge breath.

Running would have been so easy. But it would only last for so long because eventually, I'd be right back here.

I find my seat beside Ruby and pull my books out.

I know she's watching my every move. I can feel her burning stare, but she doesn't say anything. Not yet.

I hoped I'd got away with putting off explaining my reaction to Kane's appearance in my house. I thought it was going to be a one-off thing and we'd all move on and forget about it. But it seems I was wrong because it wasn't a one-off. It was a warning sign. A sign that my entire life is about to turn upside down.

I wish I knew... If I thought anything like this was about to happen then I'd have... What would you have done?

I blow out a breath.

There was nothing to do.

My past. My decisions. My mistakes. They're just catching up with me in the form of a smoking hot Kyle Legend.

I run my eyes over the backward cap he's wearing. His blond hair poking out from beneath it. I take in his shoulders, which are so much wider than I ever remember them being and down his exposed arms that are hanging down beside the chair. His fists are curled in frustration causing muscles to pull his forearms tight and for his veins to pop out.

This version of Kyle Legend is definitely different to the one I remember.

My stomach twists as reality hits me.

Kyle isn't a bad person. Actually, he was always a pretty awesome person. And despite the issue between us, I'm pretty sure everyone here is going to love him.

He and Zayn were always tight, well, until we moved and carved out a better life for ourselves.

It makes me wonder what the relationship might be like between them now after what I did.

Will Kyle take it out on him too, or is his wrath going to be solely aimed at me?

———

Every second of English lit this morning was as painful as the moment I walked in and saw him. The only good thing about it was that we were kept busy the entire time and Ruby was unable to unload the million and one questions I could see behind her eyes.

I get two more hours of relief as we had different classes, but I know my time is running out because lunch is approaching and there's no way, no matter where I hide, that she won't find me and try to drag every single bit of information out about what happened.

Dread sits heavy in my stomach as the bell rings and kids start filing out of class toward the cafeteria. It's not until I'm out of the door that the whispers register.

I've been so lost in my own head this morning that it could have been going on for hours, but it's only now I take notice.

"I heard he went in for attempted murder."

"And only served a year. Puh-lease. That's bullshit. It was just assault."

I shake my head at the group of girls as I pass them.

"He's so fucking hot. Have you seen the size of his arms?"

"Yeah, I'd let him throw me over his shoulder any day."

Rolling my eyes, I continue as the trail of whispers get

worse and even more unbelievable until I get to the cafeteria.

Ruby is already here, and I have to swallow down a groan as she jumps up and runs over to me.

I know she's only trying to help but right now, all I want to do is disappear.

"Are you okay?" she asks, looking me up and down.

"Of course."

"Have you seen him again?"

I shake my head as I follow her over to our tables. "It's only a matter of time. Have you seen Zayn?"

"Not yet. I'm sure he'll be here in a bit."

I look around the cafeteria as I sit down beside her, trying to see if he's here.

"So I'm hearing all kinds of crazy shit about this guy. Most of which I don't believe for a second. But... do you feel like telling me what I should know?" She pins me with a look and raises a brow.

"Not really," I mutter. I look to the line forming for food. Part of me wants to join it just so I've got something to do but I already know that I'm not going to be able to eat anything.

"Har," she sighs, sympathy filling her eyes as she wraps her fingers around my hand. "Let me help you."

"It's not that I don't want that. I do. I just... I really don't want to have to think about it, let alone talk about it."

"I get it." She squeezes my hand tighter "I'm here, whenever you're ready. But can I ask just one question?"

"Sure."

"He didn't actually... kill anyone, did he?"

I can't help the laugh that bubbles up my throat at the thought of Kyle actually killing anyone.

"No, Rubes. As far as I'm aware, he's never killed anyone."

"He went to juvie though, right?"

"That's two questions," I point out. "But yeah, he's done a year."

"Right, and—" I raise a brow at her in amusement that her one question is now turning into three but her words are cut off when everyone around us falls silent. "Shit," she breathes.

My entire body tenses, my temperature increases a few degrees and my need to run almost gets the better of me once more.

It's only been a few hours and he's already getting under my skin. And I swear he's not even trying.

Swallowing down my apprehension, I suck in a breath and lift my eyes.

My brother is standing before us with none other than Kyle fucking Legend by his side.

My teeth grind as the two of them stand together as if the years haven't passed and they're still close. I swear to God, if he knew about this, I'll fucking kill him. If he knew and didn't warn me. If he knew and... and is okay with this then..." My fists curl, my nails digging into my palms until it hurts so much, I'm convinced I've drawn blood.

"Guys, this is Kyle. He's a fucking kick-ass running back." He directs his words to Jake, but I don't miss his eyes very briefly flick to me. "He's starting as a junior. You're going to want him on the team next year."

"Legend, yeah, I know all about your performance," Jake says, his eyes lighting up with excitement. It's no secret that he's worried about the team who are going to proceed him and the rest of the seniors that are about to graduate.

"This is bullshit, Zayn," I snap, standing from my seat before my brain has even processed what's just happened.

Zayn's concerned eyes turn on me at the same time Kyle's amused ones do.

"Har, it's okay."

"Are you fucking kidding me? Did you know about this?" I fume as tears burn the backs of my eyes.

"No, I had no idea until this morning."

"You know Mom did this, right?"

"Do you really want to do this here?" he asks me quietly, glancing at the crowd around us.

"I can't believe you." My lips curl in disgust that he's happily accepting Kyle into his life, his team, this easily.

"You're making a bigger deal out of this than there needs to be." My jaw drops as I hear his voice for the first time since that night.

My eyes snap to his light blue ones and my teeth grind. My chest heaves as we stare at each other. Something crackles between us, something I remember from that night, but I force it aside. Nothing good came of that night and nothing will now.

"This is bullshit, Zayn. But it's good to know where your loyalties lie."

"Harley, wait," Zayn calls as I finally do what I've wanted to do all day. I run.

"Harley, what's—" I dodge Poppy as she tries to intercept my escape from the cafeteria and bolt down the half-empty hallway.

I have no idea where I'm going, but that's not important now. I just need to get away from him and my memories of that night.

It was just supposed to be a party like all the others I'd been to in Harrow Creek. Maybe it was naïve of us to think we could turn up once we've moved and to be treated like we always were... like one of them.

The main door to the football stadium is open when I get there.

The entire place is deserted, just as I hoped as I climb the steps between the bleachers and find myself a seat at the top.

I drop my ass to one of the red plastic seats and lower my head into my hands.

The tears I've been fighting all morning finally come.

He isn't supposed to be here, and my own mother shouldn't have been the one to help it happen.

Betrayal wraps around my chest, making it hard to breathe.

None of this is my fault. I was the victim that night, I still shouldn't be the one suffering now.

But it *wasn't* his fault either, was it? a little voice in my head screams. Yet, he paid the ultimate price.

By some miracle, no one finds me before the bell rings.

Math.

The last place in the world I want to be. The only thing that would make it worse would be having him in class.

Groaning, I pull a compact mirror from my purse and set about fixing my makeup.

By the time I push open my classroom door, I'm late.

All eyes turn on me but I keep my stare on the floor as I mutter my apologies to Mr. Wilson and make my way to my desk.

I pull out my books and get started on the instructions that are on the board for us without looking at or talking to anyone.

I stare at the equation in the textbook that I'm supposed to be solving and all the numbers, letters, and symbols start swirling around the page as my head begins to spin.

I fucking hate math.

I try. I try as hard as I can until my only reaction is to want to curl up in a ball and admit defeat.

I hate that I can't do this. Everyone else around me makes it seem so easy. Zayn and my older sister Letty, both make it seem so easy. I always feel like the stupid young one when we're all together.

They've both always got top grades in everything, seemingly without even trying yet I work my butt off and I'm still borderline failing.

I sigh, resting back in my chair and closing my eyes.

I hate feeling like a failure. It makes me feel weak, and I'm not weak.

Finally, after Mr. Wilson gives us all an insane amount of homework the bell rings and everyone begins to pack up their stuff and leave.

"Harley, could I speak with you a moment?" he calls across the room before I manage to escape.

The knot in my stomach grows as I walk toward him.

"What's up, sir?"

"We need to talk about your latest test." All the air whooshes from my lungs.

"That good, huh?"

"Harley, we both know you've been struggling all year. I know you hate the idea of it, but I really think you need to get some extra help."

The words I always say to him when he brings this up fall from my lips. "I'm fine, thank you."

"Harley," he sighs, sitting back in his chair and crossing one leg over the other. "That wasn't a suggestion. I'm putting your name in for tutoring. I've got some fantastic students in my AP statistics classes that would be great for you."

"It's okay. Zayn can help."

"Harley," he says a little more sternly than before. "You need some help. This is only going to get harder as we move into senior year. You can't wait any longer."

"But—"

"You'll get an invitation to meet whoever you are matched with in a few days. You can organize between yourselves how often, when and where you meet, but rest assured, I will be checking that you do so, and I will be expecting to see an improvement in this." He presses two fingers against last week's test paper that's on his desk and he slides it my way.

I try to swallow over the huge lump in my throat as I stare down at the huge F on the front right by my name.

As much as I want to argue with him right now, I know

that I don't have a leg to stand on. And if Mom finds out about me failing a test, I really won't have a choice. She's offered to get me a paid tutor time and time again, but I always manage to put her off. I fear that my struggles and my avoidance is about to bite me in the ass with a sharp pair of teeth.

"I won't let you down," I mutter as I snatch up my test and bolt to the door.

"You're a good student, Harley. Don't let one grade drag you down."

His words ring out in my ears as I walk away and out to the parking lot.

We usually have cheer practice now, but seeing as we've got the week off, I make my escape knowing that everyone will probably want to go to Aces, and right now, I really don't want to be around anyone, and I certainly don't want to see my brother as he shoves his old best friend into the middle of our new lives.

Mom's car is in the driveway when I pull up, the sight of it is almost enough to make me turn around and go elsewhere but I know I can't put this off forever. It seems she may have already been keeping secrets for a little too long.

I slam the front door harder than necessary to announce my arrival and within seconds, I hear her soft footsteps on the hardwood.

The moment she rounds the corner, I close the distance between us.

"Why didn't you tell me?" I seethe, my blood boiling beneath my skin. "Why didn't you tell me you were helping him? Why? Why would you let me walk in blind to that situation?"

"Harley," she says softly, pissing me off even more. "You know I can't discuss clients with you."

"Bullshit, Mom," I spit, much to her irritation. "This is my life. Screw your job."

"Harley, I understand you're annoyed but—"

"Annoyed? Annoyed? That doesn't even come close, Mom. I walked into English lit and there he was. No freaking warning whatsoever."

"In my defense, I thought he was starting next week."

"Convenient," I mutter, spinning away from her and pulling my red hair back from my face.

"It's true. Now that Kane has guardianship, I'm not involved. Bea has taken over his case. I'm sorry, Harley."

"No," I say, staring into her dark eyes. "No. Not good enough. Why did you even agree to help them?"

"Because it's the right thing to do and you know it. You said it yourself that Kyle didn't do anything wrong that night so why wouldn't I help when Kane came to me?"

"You knew that he'd hate me when he got out. You knew that he'd blame me for ruining his life." While he may not have been the one to cause my pain that night, he was still there. He knew what was going on and he let it happen nonetheless.

She swallows as guilt passes across her face.

"It wasn't your fault, Harley."

"You think I don't know that? I'm the one who has to live with the memories of that night. He has every right to hate me."

"I'm sure he doesn't—"

"Were you there? Did you see the way he looked at me?"

"Well, no."

"This was the wrong thing to do, Mom. I know you want to save every kid out there with a messed-up life, but you should have stayed clear of this one. Does Letty know you've been helping Kane?"

She swallows nervously once more.

"Great, so at least I can rest easy knowing that you've been lying to all three of us. You need to tell her. She deserves to know as much as I did that the Legends have moved to Rosewood."

"It doesn't matter to Letty. She's off at college enjoying herself."

I shake my head at her. "If you really believe that then maybe you're not as smart as you make out."

"Harley," Mom snaps, hurt clear in her voice.

My mom has always been my hero, the only person I've ever looked up to. What she's achieved, it's... incredible. But right now, I'm struggling to even look at her.

"I'll be in my room," I mutter, stalking toward the stairs.

I throw myself on my bed after kicking my sneakers off and bury my face in my pillow to muffle the scream that rips from my throat.

Memories of that night hit me. I can smell the heavy mix of weed and cigarette smoke as if I'm right back there. I remember his hands on me and how his touch burned my skin. I remember how the room spun around me before everything started to get totally out of control. I remember the other pair of hands, the panic, the exact moment the desire thrumming beneath my skin turned into something else entirely. I remember how desperately I wanted to get away but Letty was no longer in sight and no matter how much I wanted to scream for help, I couldn't because I was losing control.

I knew making that phone call would be a death wish. People who live in Harrow Creek don't call the police. We don't rely on others—even the law—to fight our battles. So the second I hit dial, I knew it was the beginning of the end. I just wish they got the right guy.

It's not until a knock rattles my bedroom door a while later that I realize that I must have fallen asleep. So much for the homework sitting in my bag.

I flip onto my back and look up at the ceiling as Zayn calls out.

"Har? Can I come in?"

The sound of his deep voice has everything that's happened today slamming back into me.

Kyle Legend is once again part of my life.

I slam my head back against the pillow and squeeze my eyes shut.

"Yeah, come in," I shout back reluctantly.

The door cracks open and he slips inside before closing it again.

"I had no idea, Har. I swear."

I blow out a breath and continue staring at the ceiling, refusing to look at him.

"You could have fooled me the way you hyped him up to the team."

"What would you rather I did, ignore him? Kyle's not a bad person and you know it."

"Do I?"

"Har," he warns, walking closer and sitting on the edge of my bed. "He's just spent a year in juvie."

"I know," I spit. "I put him there, remember?"

"No, I'm pretty sure the blow in his pockets was what put him there," he mutters.

"I was the one who made the call. I set the events of that night into motion."

"No," he says, reaching for my hand but I snatch it away. I don't want his support or comfort right now. I just want to be alone. "None of that was your fault."

"Try telling Kyle that."

"He's fine about it, Har. He just wants to get on with his life."

My shock at his words has my eyes snapping to his.

"You're shitting me. Did you see the way he looked at me earlier?"

"He told me, Harley. He doesn't hold any of this against you."

"Then he's lying. Ask Ruby and Ashton. They'll tell you exactly how he looked at me."

"He was probably just shocked. He just wants to start over. Graduate. Move on. You need to do the same thing."

With him giving me death stares every time I see him? Yeah, *I'm* sure *that'll* be easy.

"Fine," I sigh, knowing that it's pointless arguing with him.

3

KYLE

I sit in the middle of a diner surrounded by members of the Rosewood High Bears and sitting next to my old best friend, Zayn Hunter.

When he walked over earlier with a wide smile on his face, I wasn't sure if it was a joke.

The night I ended up in the back of a cop car... he has every right to hate me for what went down before I was carted away.

That's if he knows what actually happened, of course.

But it seems it was genuine because no sooner had he accepted me into his new life, then he introduced me to the team and ensured I got my ass to their conditioning session after school.

I know Kane had talked about me joining the team, but I just wanted to keep my head down and get on with graduating, seems that isn't what's going to be happening because I've been thrust right into the center of Rosewood's royal circle.

"So you just got out of juvie?" a guy with dark hair and even darker eyes sitting opposite me asks. Everyone else has kept the gossiping about me behind my back today, although not very discreetly. But this guy doesn't seem to give a shit about beating around the bush.

"Yeah. I did a year," I say.

He nods in understanding, and I'm relieved when I find no judgment there.

"I'm Ash. I only started here on Monday."

"So I'm not the only one in this group to be adopted recently then," I say with a smirk.

"Think they'd befriend anyone who can throw a ball right now."

"Way to make me feel special," I mutter much to his amusement.

"So what's the deal with you and Harley then?" he asks, shocking the fuck out of me.

"Uh..."

"Ruby, her best friend, she's my girl." He nods toward where the cheer squad are sitting at another table and a small brunette girl's eyes light up the second she sees him.

I want to say I recognize her, but I've seen so many new people today that all the faces are blurring into one, the only clear one in my mind is hers. It's the same one I've focused on for a fucking year.

I was looking after her that night. I never would have let anything happen to her, yet she called the cops anyway and screwed me over.

"We've got history," I say with a shrug, dragging my soda closer and taking a swig.

"As in exes?"

I almost spray him with my drink. "No, nothing like that." Not really.

Images from that night before the shit hit the fan fill my mind and I shift in my seat as my cock swells at the memory of her sitting astride my lap.

Harley's beautiful, I've never been able to deny that. But

more importantly, she was always my boy's little sister. Off-limits, no matter what.

But then they left, and she and Letty turned up that night and things just got a little out of control without her big brother there as the reminder I needed that I wasn't allowed to touch.

"Okay, so did she kill your cat or something because you looked like you wanted to slit her throat for whatever it was."

"Nah, it's not like that. I was just surprised to see her again," I lie. "So what's your story? Where did you move here from?"

He chats briefly about moving from Seattle, but he doesn't give me much to go on, although it's impossible to miss the shadows lingering in his eyes.

"So, what do you think?" Zayn says, dropping into the seat beside me. "You think you've still got what it takes on the field?"

"Fuck you, Hunter. Legend by name, Legend by nature."

"Always were a big-headed motherfucker," he deadpans, slugging me in the shoulder. "I gotta bounce, my girl is waiting on me. It's good to have you back, man. I think you're going to like it here."

"Yeah? I've definitely experienced worse."

He chuckles, I'm sure thinking about the hellhole that is Harrow Creek High but that place was like paradise compared to juvie and the motherfuckers I was forced to spend my time with.

"Harley..." he says somewhat hesitantly.

"It's fine, man. What's done is done. Time for us all to move on."

He claps me on the shoulder. "You got it, man. You need anything, you know where I am."

I don't. I have no fucking clue where he lives, but I'm sure it won't take me too long to find out.

Thoughts of the girl he shares a house with fill my mind. Maybe I should find out sooner rather than later.

"Sure. Thanks for today." I nod to the guys surrounding me. I wasn't expecting this, but I sure do appreciate it. I had a feeling I was going to walk into Rosewood High with a huge target printed on my back, but it seems I didn't need to worry... or maybe I still should because it's clear Zayn doesn't know the whole truth.

"Anytime. I'm glad you're here. We'll catch up for real soon. J's having a party Saturday night," he says, pointing at another of the guys sitting at the other end of the table. "You're coming, right?"

"Hell yeah."

"Sweet." He nods once more before turning his back and walking out of the diner.

"So a history with Harley and best buds with Zayn. This doesn't have disaster written all over it at all."

I narrow my eyes at Ash. I'm not sure if I'm annoyed with him or just impressed that he doesn't beat around the bush.

"Watch yourself, man. Things could get messy."

He laughs to himself and shakes his head. "Allow me to let you into a little secret." He leans over the table so he can whisper something to me, and I'm powerless but to move closer. "Those girls..." He looks to the squad again. "They might look sweet, sexy... easy to play with. But let me tell you, they've got fucking claws, man." He sits back, his face a mask of seriousness until his lips curl at the edges. "I've got the scratch marks to prove it." He winks and I can't help but laugh.

"That much fun, huh?"

"Man, you have no idea."

"And Harley is one of them?"

"My girl? She's about to become captain, and Harley is her right-hand woman. You want to go there after everything that's gone down between you, then all I can do is wish you luck, man."

"I'm not sure if this little chat is turning me on or scaring the shit out of me."

Ashton throws his head back and laughs. "Seeing as you've just spent a year locked up with a bunch of dudes, I'd bet money on the former." He reaches for his soda and downs it before pushing to stand. "I'm out, got a date with my girl." He winks. "I'll see you tomorrow."

I nod at him and watch as he turns his stare on his girl. Something swirls within me as he prowls toward her and swoops her up in his arms. I tell myself it's just been a really, really long time. My eyes scan around the rest of the cheer squad until I land on a dark pair of eyes. They're not the ones I want to stare into sure, but they're better than nothing.

A shy smile curls at her lips before her cheeks redden as I push to stand and walk over.

"Hey, I don't think I saw you around today," I say, dropping into the seat Ruby vacated beside her. "I know I'd remember if I did." I cringe at my line but as her smile gets wider, I realize it's worked a charm.

"I'm Aria, and you're..."

"Lonely."

She chuckles, her hand resting on my upper arm as I rest it around the back of her chair.

"The guys not making you feel welcome?" she asks, her fingers walking up to my shoulder. I glance at her long talons and Ashton's warning repeats in my ears.

My own smile twitches at my lips. The Creek girls of my past make these girls look like teddy bears. I'm pretty sure I can handle a Rosewood cheer slut.

"Not in the way I need," I growl. Leaning into her, I get close enough that my breath caresses her ear and she shivers. "You down for showing me around town... alone?" I whisper so no one else at the table can hear me.

"That sounds—"

"Aria," another girl snaps.

We both look over and my eyes almost pop out of my head when I find a dark-haired girl standing, staring daggers at Aria with her hands on her hips and one very round belly.

Holy shit.

"Yeah, I'm pregnant, asshole. What of it?" she barks at me when she notices what's holding my attention.

"Uh...n-nothing."

"Aria, we're going. I suggest you put jailbait down."

"Excuse me?" I ask, my brows lifting in shock.

"You heard me."

"Down, Chels." One of the guys who was sitting at the table with me only moments ago steps up behind her and slides his hands over her growing belly.

"Good to know the Bears don't shoot blanks," I deadpan.

Chels—I assume Chelsea—turns beet red, her entire body locking up in anger while the guy—who I'm sure I've been introduced to but don't remember, throws his head back.

"Damn straight, man. We're not fucking champs for nothing."

"Shane," she gasps.

"What, baby? Just having a laugh with the new boy."

My teeth grind at being called that. It's a nickname I remember all too well from when I was first locked inside that place. A shudder rolls through me at the memories from my 'initiation' by some of the longer residents who thought they owned that place.

"Whatever," she mutters, taking a step forward and out of his hold. "Stay away from my girls." Her finger points right at me before she uses it to indicate her squad, her eyes narrowed in anger.

"It looks like you've got enough on your plate, you don't need to worry about me. I'll make sure I'm gentle... ish."

She growls, actually growls at me.

"Alright, momma bear." The guy wraps his arms around her tighter and presses his lips to her neck but her hard eyes never leave mine, even as they begin to shutter with pleasure.

"Stay away from my girls," she warns again as she's directed out of the diner by her boy.

"So," Aria says, turning back to me. "What were you saying about showing you around?" Her eyes land on me and where I should probably feel some excitement about the possibility of spending time with her, I feel nothing.

"Another time maybe?" I push to stand and disappointment crosses her face.

I look over to the team but they're all lost in their own conversation.

Unnoticed, I slip out of the diner and look out at the ocean beyond.

As a kid, I always dreamed of moving to Rosewood so that we could go to the beach every day. We've driven through once and I remember looking out at the glistening ocean and seeing the happy families playing on the sand. It looked incredible, and at six or seven it was everything I wanted my life to be.

We might have had both our parents in our lives at that point, but things were far from perfect. If I'd have known just how bad things were going to get then maybe I wouldn't have been staring out the window that day hoping for better, I'd have just been happy that the four of us were together. We weren't going to get too many more chances.

With a sigh, I turn toward the parking lot.

It turns out that it wasn't only the girls I didn't remember from Kane's little party the other night because when I step out onto the porch later that afternoon, I find my car waiting for me. Clearly, I walked straight past it in my desperation to start at Rosewood High this morning. I roll my eyes at myself.

I hadn't thought much about it. I assumed that maybe Kane had sold it, I certainly didn't expect to see it again, that's for sure.

My black VW Golf looks exactly the same as the day I left her. Kane even made sure she was delivered back to me clean.

I walk over, taking in her black matte wheels and the sport bumpers I fitted in the months before I went away.

It feels like a lifetime ago now.

I tap her hood, a smile pulling at my lips although I feel pretty pathetic that I walk out of juvie and all I've got is my brother and my car waiting for me.

Aside from Kane's friends who came to the house on Monday night, I haven't seen any of the guys I used to hang around with.

I know why. I don't need to put much thought into the reason they're probably less than thrilled that I'm out but it still kind of stings to know that they really didn't give a shit. I'd grown up with those motherfuckers. Did all sorts of shit for them, hence why I found myself locked up.

I hated it when Zayn moved away. He was the only one who got me in that place.

I drop into my car and rest my head back.

I wish I could confidently say that they'll all stay away, but I know that I'm on borrowed time. When I was arrested, it wasn't just me they took. It was the majority of Gray's stash that was in my pockets.

He's not going to let that go with a stint in juvie. I owe him, and it's only a matter of time until he turns up wanting payment.

My fingers grip the wheel until my knuckles turn white.

I don't want anything to do with any of them. I might not be thrilled about being here, near her, but it's a hell of a lot better than being back in that shithole.

Kane's car isn't in the driveway when I get home. He's still not told me what he's doing but he did tell me not to expect him around much.

I find enough food to make a sandwich. I place that and a can of soda on the table before pulling out the books I was given today and making a start on my homework.

I was given tests from every single class I attended, and not just the standard homework the others got, helpfully each teacher supplied me with catch up work too.

I get it, I've got a lot to prove.

They'll have seen my reports from Harrow Creek no doubt but even I know they don't exactly fit the stereotype of a Creek kid. While everyone else was failing and set on a future without a high school diploma, my grades were always A's.

I worked hard. Harder than anyone else around me. I had a dream and staying in that hellhole and dealing either drugs, weapons or people wasn't where my interests laid.

I shake my head thinking that everyone I know from back there is probably still doing the exact same thing they were a year ago.

That creek is a place of ruin. There aren't many that get out and make anything of their lives. It seems the Hunters— and hopefully us—might be an exception to the rule.

I do the statistics work first. It's the easiest after all, then I set about doing the rest.

It's dark out by the time I've finished, and Kane still isn't home.

Packing everything away ready for another day at Rosewood High, I head for a shower then to bed.

As I lie there staring at the ceiling, the only thing I can see is her panic-filled eyes as she stared at me from the doorway.

She had no idea I was going to be there, that much was

obvious. What I don't understand is why, because it seems that it was Jada Hunter who helped Kane set all of this up. Why wouldn't she warn Harley that I was going to suddenly be a part of her life once again? Surely a heads up would have been nice, although, I must admit, I did love her shock.

4

———

HARLEY

Nathan: I've got a surprise for you.

Excitement flutters in my belly as I stare down at his message. We've spoken every day since he dropped me home after our meal on Sunday night but I have yet to see him again and I'm desperate to. I hate that he's all the way in Maddison County.

"What are you smiling about?" Ruby asks as her and Poppy join me on the bench I'm sitting on.

"Message from Nathan."

"Oooh," Ruby sings, her brows wiggling.

"You seeing him this weekend?" Poppy asks.

"I think so. He says he's got a surprise." I shrug.

"He so wants to get between your legs," Ruby jokes.

"It's only been a few weeks," I argue, although I wonder if the words are more for me than them.

"Time doesn't matter. If it's right then it's right." Ruby shrugs.

"I'm just going with the flow," I tell them although I can't help the knot that forms in my stomach.

The first night we met, things between us were electric

and when he kissed me... whoa. I'd only felt anything like that once before in my life and I latched onto it, that along with the fact he's clearly a really nice person.

He's perfect in pretty much every way, he's everything I said I wanted but as time goes on I can't help thinking something just isn't right. I keep telling myself that it's because we haven't had any time alone. We've either been at a party or in a movie theater or restaurant. What I really want is it to be just us away from prying eyes and other people. I want to get to know him properly. See if that spark that was there at the party reappears when we're alone.

Harley: I can't wait. x

"He'll be at Justin's party tomorrow night, right?" Ruby asks.

"Err... I have no idea. I'm not..." I trail off, knowing that they're not going to like what I want to say next.

"You're not what?" Ruby asks, her brow quirked.

"I don't think I'm going to go."

"What? Why not? Especially if Nathan is going to be there."

"It's not him. It's—"

"Kyle."

"Can we not?" I beg.

"What happened, Har?" Poppy asks, her warm hand landing on my thigh.

"I... uh... I was the one who had him put in juvie," I admit, staring at the concrete beneath my feet but their lack of response has me looking up at them.

"We kinda assumed that, Har."

"Oh."

"I didn't actually call the cops on him. He just happened to be there. I didn't even know he was in possession of anything. I totally screwed him over," I admit.

"You didn't know."

"I shouldn't have called the cops. It's not how things are done where we're from." They both stare at me like I have two heads. I understand why. Poppy might have been with us to Harrow Creek, she understands a little about what it's like there, but only people who live there really get it.

"You must have had a good reason to do it."

"Y-yeah, I thought so. But things didn't go as they were supposed to."

"That's not on you."

"It doesn't matter. I blame myself anyway. He didn't deserve that."

"Have you spoken to him?"

I shake my head.

"Maybe you should. Get it all out in the open. Zayn seems to think he's okay about everything. He certainly doesn't seem angry," Poppy says.

"You didn't see how he looked at me yesterday morning," I mutter.

"She's right. It was brutal," Ruby agrees.

"He was just surprised. He said so himself."

"You seem to have fallen onto Team Kyle pretty fast, Pops."

"Not at all. I've got your back always, you know that. I'm just telling you what I've seen and heard from both him and Zayn. He seems like a decent guy."

"Yeah, he was." My mind wanders back to a simpler time. A time where my biggest issue was having the most insane crush on my brother's best friend.

"OMG, you have a crush on him, don't you?" Ruby almost squeals.

"What? No. Why would you even say that?" I argue a little too insistently.

"Um... because it's obvious that you do. I mean, he's hot. I can see why you'd want him but—"

"He hates me. With good reason, I might add."

"Nothing a little blow job wouldn't fix, I'm sure."

"What?" I shriek. "Ruby, you did not just suggest that."

"She's got a point. It's amazing what you can convince a guy to do with a good su—" I hold my hand up to Poppy.

"Do not go there," I warn. "I don't need to know what gets you on your knees for my brother." I shudder at the thought.

"Just try talking to him, Har," Ruby says. "It was what you told me to do about a million times with Ash, remember? And it worked."

"You ended up in bed with him," I point out helpfully.

"See," Poppy says. "It's the answer."

"You two are no help. I need new single friends," I whine, not for the first time.

"Aw, you love it."

"Do I? Do I really?" I roll my eyes at the pair of them.

Thankfully, the bell rings before they can try convincing me to talk to him or drag me inside where I know he's hanging out with the team.

Only a few days in and he's already found his place in this school. It's not lost on me that as he fits right in, I feel like I'm losing my grip on my place.

"I've got volleyball. At least I can pretend the ball is his head."

They both laugh at me before waving me off as they head in the opposite direction to their classes.

At least in the gym with the girls, I know I'm safe from bumping into him. It's only been a day and I'm putting more thought into my every step than I have in my entire time here at Rosewood High.

We haven't shared another class yet, but I know it's only a matter of time before I walk into a classroom and find him there waiting for me.

"You okay?" Stella asks me as she holds the locker room door open for me.

"Yeah," I mutter, but my voice is obviously lacking its usual spark.

"We missed you at Ace's last night."

"I had a ton of homework to do."

"Riiight."

"What's that supposed to mean."

"Harley, I'm not an idiot. I've heard the rumors."

"Of course you have," I breathe. "No, he didn't kill anyone, or even threaten to kill anyone."

"Oh, I didn't mean that. I meant that the two of you have history."

My head snaps up so fast I'm surprised it doesn't roll off my neck. "W-what? What's being said?"

"Nothing much but the way you're suddenly avoiding the team, him. It's been noticed and people are jumping to conclusions."

"The squad, you mean?" We all know what a bunch of gossiping bitches the seniors are. If they don't have a cock between their lips then they're spreading around some bullshit.

"There's nothing between us."

"You all grew up together though, right? And you are avoiding him?"

"Yes, yes. Stella, I—" Another group of girls come stumbling into the locker room, chatting and laughing away as they pass us. Stella waits, her eyes trained on me. "Kyle was Zayn's best friend until we all moved here. We grew up together, and I was there the night he was... he was arrested. That's all you need to know."

"Sure thing, Harley."

"Stella, I—"

"It's fine, Harley. I get it. But if you want to talk, I'm here, okay? I've been to a lot of schools over the years, I've seen a lot of shit. You need an unbiased opinion. I'm here."

"Thank you. I really appreciate it."

She nods at me and we begin getting changed.

"So, you ready for cheer to start up again next week?" she asks me, thankfully steering the conversation to something I'm happier talking about.

"Yes. I never thought I'd say it after all those crazy hours before nationals, but I miss it."

"Auditions are going to be brutal though, aren't they? Chelsea is such a perfectionist."

"Yep. But I get it, she wants to leave a good squad behind her. We've got big shoes to fill."

"That we do."

———

I feel a little better after expelling some of my pent-up energy during volleyball. I hadn't realized how much stopping all my exercise quite so abruptly after nationals had affected me. As I get dressed, ready to head home, I tell myself that I'm going to reset my alarm for the morning and go for a run before school. Hopefully a bit of fresh morning air will also help clear my head.

"Harley," Mr. Wilson shouts the second he spots me in the hallway.

I just about manage to bite back my groan of frustration as I make my way over.

"Yes, sir?" I say politely.

"I thought you'd want to know that I've matched you up with a tutor. I've handed over all your contact details and I'll leave it up to the two of you to arrange your sessions. I trust you not to let me down, Harley. You know how vital it is that you get those grades up."

My heart sinks at his words. A part of me had hoped he might forget and I could continue burying my head in the sand with my quickly declining math grades.

"I'll do my best, sir."

"Any issues, you know where I am."

"Great."

"I'll look forward to your next test results."

"Well, that makes one of us," I mutter to myself as I walk away and resume the journey toward my locker.

Pulling the door open, I poke my head inside and just about resist the need to scream out my frustration. My eyes land on the photos of Ruby, Poppy, and me that are pinned to the back and a smile curls at my lips.

I'm sifting through my books, pulling out the ones I need for the night when my cell buzzes in my back pocket.

Unknown: Congrats, tutor girl. Looks like you're stuck with me now! First session starts in an hour...

Another message comes through with an address.

I know Mr. Wilson said he was going to leave it up to us to organize but I kind of assumed it would happen in the library at least.

I tap my finger against the side of my cell as I try to decide what to reply with. I want to say that I'm not interested and hope that whoever's at the other end will be glad to get out of it.

Harley: Who is this?

Unknown: Your new tutor. Come meet me and find out...

Some movement at the other end of the hallway startles me and I find most of the football team, my brother and Kyle included, joking around as they emerge from the locker room where they must have just finished a conditioning session.

"Alright, sis?" Zayn calls when he spots me.

I nod at him but I don't return his delight at seeing me.

I'm still annoyed with him for how he's accepted Kyle back into his life, which in turn annoys me even more because he has every right to.

My skin tingles as Kyle runs his eyes down my body, his lips curled in disgust as he does so.

In a moment of defiance, I lift my hand and flip him off.

I'm not in the mood for his bullshit. Especially now that I have to spend my night doing fucking math with some nerd.

His eyes widen at my move before he shakes his head at me.

I roll my eyes in their direction as they make their way down the hallway toward the parking lot and then probably Ace's. Good thing that's not where I'm going.

I grab what I need, before following where they disappeared a few minutes ago.

I head home to freshen up, seeing as I had no plans to see anyone after school, I didn't bother showering after volleyball and whoever my tutor is will probably appreciate me doing that before gracing them with my sweaty presence.

Mom's home when I get there, but as usual she's locked in her office. We haven't spoken since yesterday afternoon. I think she's giving me time to cool off, but right now, I don't feel like forgiving her any time soon. Keeping that from me was wrong, even if she did believe she had until Monday for him to start at school.

I take a quick shower, blow out my hair and pull on a clean shirt and Rosewood High hoodie. Not really feeling like making an effort, I brush a little mascara on my lashes and rub some balm onto my lips.

Checking myself in the mirror, I give my hair one last brush through with my fingers and grab my bag. The red is starting to grow out, I really need to get my roots done but I can't help feeling that it's time for a change. Pink, maybe. I feel like I need to make a statement. Show that his appearance doesn't affect me one bit—which of course is a big fat lie because in reality I've spent every moment since I discovered his arrival looking over my shoulder.

I plug the random address into my GPS and follow the directions. I know the area but I have no idea which street it is.

The street is lined with cars when I drive down it. I spot the house but have to park a ways down and walk up to it. All the houses are slightly run-down bungalows but it's not a bad area.

The driveway is empty when I walk up to the porch and there's no sign of anyone being home.

I look around, worried that I've got the wrong house but the number is clear on the mailbox by the sidewalk so I continue forward, pulling my bag up higher on my shoulder nervously.

The steps creak, probably announcing my arrival the second I stand on them.

I pull the screen open and knock on the door.

Silence.

I knock again.

"Hello?" I call when there is still no answer.

Blowing out a frustrated breath that this has all been one big waste of my time, I'm about to turn around to leave when I sense someone behind me.

"Surprise, Kitten."

5

KYLE

I press the length of my body against her back and I can't fight the smile that curls at my lips as a shudder rips through her.

I couldn't believe my luck when Mr. Wilson passed me her details as my new tutee.

I didn't get a say in taking part in the tutoring program. Bea had already signed me up. It was one of the things—aside from football—that I enjoyed the most during my time at Harrow Creek. I'd been tutoring freshman throughout my junior year. The boy I'd been matched with was keen to learn and soaked up everything I said. It made me feel like I was useful and actually giving something back to the shitpit that was that school.

"K-Kyle?" she breathes as if she can't really believe this is happening right now.

"I was wondering when you'd build up the courage to talk to me. I guess fate took care of that for me, huh?" My nose brushes against the shell of her ear and she trembles once again.

"I'm not scared of you, Kyle."

"And that might be your biggest mistake yet, Kitten."

"Stop calling me that," she hisses.

"Why? You like it, remember. The way you purred that night."

"Stop it," she snaps. "Just stop it."

Stepping forward, I force her to move with me as I reach out and twist the handle.

With my hand on her waist and her back still to my front, I push her inside and close the door behind us.

Before she has a chance to think, I spin her around and slam her back against the wall. She gasps in shock, her eyes going wide and her lips parting.

"You've been avoiding me, Kitten." I rest my forearms against the wall on either side of her head, caging her in. "And I don't like it."

"C-can you blame me? You're not exactly welcoming."

Her eyes hold mine, trying to appear confident but I hear the slight quiver in her voice.

"And to think, I was looking forward to us... reconnecting."

"Whatever you want to do to me, Kyle. Just get it over with."

A humorless chuckle rumbles up my throat.

"What makes you think I want to do anything?"

She growls at me, the sound makes my cock threaten to go full mast. I fucking love her attempt at defiance. It's so sexy.

The house is in silence as we stare at each other, the only noise that can be heard is that of her increased breathing.

A smile pulls at one side of my mouth knowing that my proximity affects her.

The vibrating of a cell catches my attention, I know it's not mine as it's in my pocket.

Dropping one arm, I slip it behind her and run my palm down her back until I cup her ass, finding exactly what I wanted.

"Kyle, what are you—"

"I think I'll take this. You have previous history after all."
Pulling her cell from her pocket, I drop it into mine for safe
keeping. "No one is coming to your rescue this time, Kitten."
I drop my lips to her ear. "Even if you scream." She swallows
nervously, a quiet whimper passing her lips.

Pulling back, I look her dead in the eyes.

"I think you lied to me earlier."

She shakes her head.

Lifting my hand, I brush my knuckles down her cheek.
Her skin is warm and soft, exactly as I remember. Tucking
my fingers under her jaw, I tilt her head up.

"W-what are you doing?" she stutters as I study her.

She looks exactly the same. Her eyes are dark, mysterious
and immediately draw me in, her golden skin looks good
enough to eat and I know from the sweet scent coming from
her that she'll taste fucking divine too. Her lips are full,
begging to be kissed and when she sucks the bottom one into
her mouth and bites down on it, my urge to claim it as my
own almost gets the better of me.

"Remembering that night." My voice is deep as I think
back. Lust and anger colliding and sending me into a head
spin. "Remembering how you felt on my lap, how you
ground down on me." I lower my face to hers so my lips
brush the corner of her mouth. "How desperate you were for
me to touch you."

I trail my fingertips up her bare leg, her skin breaks out in
goose bumps and she shudders when I get to the hem of her
skirt.

"Or aren't I enough? Should I get Gray on the phone, see
if he wants to come join the party?" It's a low blow and I
know it hits exactly as I intended as her body stiffens
beneath me.

"Fuck you, Kyle. FUCK YOU," she screams, her arm
flying out like she's about to slap me but I'm quicker.

I pin her arm against the wall above her head.

My chest heaves as my anger swells.

"That's what you like though, isn't it? Two of us. Two of us touching you. Two of us making you lose your goddamn mind." My hand snakes up her body, squeezing her small breast through her hoodie as I go before wrapping my fingers around her throat. A move I remember Gray doing that night and how wild her eyes were.

"Get the hell off me," she growls.

"Kane should be home soon." Total lie, once again I have no fucking clue where he is. "Maybe he'd like a turn."

Her teeth grind as her eyes hold mine.

"Such a shame we never got to finish what we started that night, huh?"

Her eyes scan my face and a smile curls at her lips. "Did the boys in juvie finish you off? Bet they loved you. The nerd with the glasses who'll bend to their every whim. I bet the wolves fucking loved you, pretty boy," she spits.

I get right in her face, our noses touching, our breath mingling.

"You need to watch your fucking mouth," I warn.

"And you need to watch your fucking hands."

Before I've had a chance to even register her words, pain radiates out from my groin and I drop to my knees.

"You fucking bitch," I squeal, cupping my junk and my eyes water.

"Whoops," she says innocently, looking down on me with accomplishment in her eyes. "But look how easy you go down." She drops to her haunches in front of me and runs her eyes over my body. "Tell me, Ky. Just how many other boys got their chance with you inside, huh?"

"Jealous?" I ask, the pain finally starting to lessen so I can attempt to stand.

"Of them fucking you over?" She thinks for a minute. "I think I've already done that."

I straighten to full height, and at six-foot-two, that's a hell of a lot taller than her. We stand chest to chest with me staring down at her, rage barely contained behind my eyes as all the things I want to do to her play out like a movie in my head. Yet despite seeing all that, she doesn't back down. Not one little bit.

Stupid, girl. Stupid, stupid girl.

As we stand in silence waiting for who'll break first, an engine rumbles to a stop outside. I'd recognize it a mile away and a smile pulls at my lips.

"Ah, perfect timing, looks like our playmate has arrived."

Harley's throat flexes as she swallows nervously.

"You know Kane has always had a thing for Hunter girls. I'm sure he won't mind that you're the wrong one."

She takes a huge step back, her eyes wide in fear.

"Run, Kitten, and I'll tell Mr. Wilson you refused my support and that will be the easiest bit of what I'll do to you. You owe me, Kitten. So I suggest you do as you're told from here on out."

She looks back at the door when Kane's boots hit the porch.

"Let's get the party started then, shall we?"

We're still staring at each other when Kane pulls the front door open and steps inside.

"Ky—Harley?" I don't look up at him, my eyes are trained on her but I know if I did, I'd find his brows drawn together in concern. He specifically told me to stay away from her and yet here she is standing in the middle of our new little home.

I knew giving her this address was a risk. But there was no fucking way that we were having our first meeting in the library while surrounded by other kids.

Her need to be polite, finally wins out because she rips her gaze from me and turns toward Kane.

"Hey," she squeaks. "Good to see you again."

Kane's eyes shoot to me and narrow in suspicion.

"Is... everything alright here?"

"Yeah, everything is great. You wouldn't believe who I got paired up with to tutor. It's like fate or something."

"Or bad fucking karma," Harley mutters under her breath.

"Are you sure that's a good idea?" He takes a step closer, looking between the two of us.

"Of course. It's great to reconnect after all this time. Isn't that right, Kitten?" I run my hand down her spine until it lands on her ass and I squeeze hard.

"Yeah," she blurts as the pain hits her. "It's great. Making up for lost time."

"O-okay. Shouldn't you have books out or something."

"Thought we'd have a little catch up first, isn't that right, Har?"

"Sure."

"I'll just grab a drink and get out of your hair." Kane continues to look between the two of us but he must not see anything of great concern because as soon as he pulls a can of soda from the refrigerator he disappears down to his room.

I know there's no love lost between him and the two Hunter girls. After everything he's been through with Letty and then Harley getting me locked up, I'm surprised he's allowing her to stay in the house.

The second his bedroom door closes, I take a step toward the table.

"Get your shit out."

"W-what?" she asks, frozen on the spot I just left her in.

"Grab your bag and get your shit out. Where are we starting?"

An unamused laugh falls from her lips. "You're not serious, you don't actually want to do this?"

No, I really fucking don't, but like hell am I letting her know that.

"I need the extra credit for this if I'm ever going to graduate." Lie. "If you walk out right now and I have to tell Wilson that you refused my help, then you'll probably screw me over twice in as many years. So how about you do as you're fucking told and sit your pretty little ass down and get to work."

Her lips part to respond and she gazes at the door longingly but when she finally takes a step, it's toward me.

"Good little kitten."

"Fuck you, Kyle."

"Ah I do love having nice polite students, it makes it that much more of a pleasurable experience."

"Trust me, there is nothing pleasurable about this."

"Huh, maybe we need to add in some extracurricular activities then. I already know you're wet for me."

HARLEY

He pulls my bag toward him and drags out my textbooks as if those words didn't just fall from his lips. My mouth opens to respond but I soon close them again when I discover that I have no words.

My head is spinning, my brain is misfiring, and my body is still trembling from how close he was to me earlier.

I want to say his touch disgusted me. I want to say that the reason I didn't fight him off right away was shock, but it wasn't.

My face heats as I think about the sparks that shot around my body the second he laid a hand on me. Just like that night.

There's no doubt in my mind where that night would have gone if things didn't turn out the way they did. If I had any clue that my drink was being spiked, if I had any idea that someone else other than Kyle was getting ideas about where our night was going to go then I'd have run as fast and as far as I could.

"Did you know?" I blurt out, needing an answer to at least one of my questions from that night.

"Did I know what?" he asks, keeping his eyes on the book he's flicking through.

"Did you know he was spiking my drink?"

He pauses and sucks in a breath before dragging his light blue eyes up to mine. Only, they're not the color I was always used to, they're almost silver with his anger, his hatred of me.

"What do you think, Kitten?" he asks, throwing it back on me.

"If I knew the answer to that question then I wouldn't have fucking asked, would I?" I snap, getting beyond frustrated at this situation. I didn't want to meet anyone for a tutoring session as it was, I really, really didn't want this.

I look to the door once more, wondering if he'd actually allow me to escape should I try.

"Go on," he taunts, clearly able to read my mind. "Try it and see how far you get."

"I hate you," I seethe.

"Oh, Kitten. Trust me, how you feel about me has nothing on what I feel for you."

"So let me go, you don't have to look at me then."

"And what would be the fun in that?"

I study him as he scans the page he's selected before him. He's got his backward cap on like he has had every time I've seen him this week with his dirty blond hair poking out the sides, his jaw is covered in a light layer of scruff and his eyes are free from the glasses I teased him about earlier. It's been years since he wore them but I know how much he hated them as a kid.

There's a scar above his right eyebrow that I'm sure wasn't there before and his nose is slightly crooked. It might be my imagination, I'm not sure I've ever really spent any time looking at his nose before but I'm sure that's new. It makes me wonder what his life has actually been like the past year.

He shifts in his seat, telling me that he's aware of my

attention although he doesn't look up or do anything about it.

"So, algebra?" he says, making my stomach drop. As if being stuck here with him isn't bad enough, we have to do math too.

I watch as he slides a mask over his face and focuses on what we're supposed to be doing.

"So Mr. Wilson said to start here as it's one of your main weaknesses." My stomach twists at those words. I hate that people think I'm weak because I struggle to add up a few numbers.

"Great," I mutter, reaching for my notepad and a pen.

He slides his chair closer to me as he talks through a technique that I've never been shown before but as much as I try to focus, the heat of his arm burning into mine is too distracting and I find myself zoning out despite the fact this is making much more sense to me than it usually does.

"Harley?" he snaps a few minutes later, dragging me from my own head.

"Yeah."

"I asked you a question."

"Um..." My cheeks burn as his eyes narrow at me. "I... I agree."

"You agree." He chuckles, but there's no humor there, just irritation. "Unfortunately for you, it wasn't a yes or no answer."

"Um..." I hesitate again, my heart racing.

"T-ten?"

"Fucking hell, Harley," he snaps, pushing his chair out behind him and stalking to the other side of the room. "This isn't a fucking joke, Kitten."

"You think I don't know that?" I shout back, standing from the chair and turning to watch him pace. "All of this... it's a fucking mess."

"This... mess," he says, stopping and pinning me with a

look. "Is my life," he bellows. "Fucking hell, Harley." He drops his head into his hands and for a second, I actually feel sorry for him. I see the boy from the past, the vulnerable one who just wanted something better for his life. But then that image morphs with my hazy memories from that night and it vanishes almost as fast as it appeared.

"You need to get the hell out of my house." His voice is so low that I think I misheard him.

"W-what?"

"Get out. Just get the fuck out," he bellows before a door down the hallway opens and Kane steps toward me.

He's shirtless and my breathing falters when my eyes first land on him because... whoa, but when Kyle growls and I remember where I am and that I'm supposed to be leaving.

"With pleasure. This was a mistake anyway."

"Don't think that because you're about to walk away that this is over."

"It should be."

"Well, it's not," he warns as I stuff my books into my bag and head for the door.

"Wait," I say, spinning on the balls of my feet and staring right at him. "Cell?" I demand, holding my hand out. There's no way I'm leaving here without that.

He reaches into his pocket and pulls it out. He looks at the screen for a second before a smirk appears on his lips.

"Kyle," Kane warns, clearly sensing where his head is at.

I'm rooted to the spot as he marches toward me. He doesn't stop until his front crashes against mine and I stumble back until I hit the door.

"Kyle?" I breathe. It's hard to think with his heat burning into my skin and his angry eyes boring down into mine.

"Kyle," Kane growls again, but he completely ignores him, his focus solely on me.

"This. Isn't. Over," he says so low that only I can hear the warning.

"I-I'm s-sorry," I stutter, needing to say anything to get me away from him right now before I do something I'll regret. I've already got enough of those to keep me up at night.

A smile pulls at the corners of his lips but it's pure evil.

"It's a bit late for that now, don't you think, Kitten?" His hand slips around my body and he slides my cell into my back pocket where it was when he first found it.

He leans into my ear and my eyes close as his breath caresses my sensitive skin.

"I'll be in touch for our next session soon. I hope that one might be a little more..." I gasp as his hand slips under my hoodie and wraps around my ribs. "Satisfying."

Before I know what's happening, his burning touch is gone and he's opened the door at my back. With a squeal, I go stumbling back until I land on my ass.

"Whoops," Kyle says with a shrug, his eyes locked on my sprawled legs.

"Fucking hell, bro," Kane snaps, stepping forward to help me up.

I take his hand when he offers it to me and he pulls me up.

"T-thank you," I whisper when I'm on my feet again, but I'm unable to look into his eyes with him this close to me. Just his presence makes me nervous let alone being up close and personal to his bare chest.

"Just give him time. He'll come around."

I look around Kane to his little brother who's still fuming behind him. His chest heaves, his lips are pressed into a thin line, his jaw tics with frustration and his eyes are that dark grey once more.

His eyes widen a little in shock when he notices my attention but he soon schools his features so he's scowling once more.

"Yeah, we'll see." I turn away from both of them, hike my

bag over my shoulder and try to walk away with as much dignity as I can muster.

I'm halfway down their driveway when Kyle's deep voice makes me pause.

"Make sure you wear those little red panties next time, Kitten."

Lifting my hand, I flip him off over my shoulder and keep walking without looking back at him.

Asshole.

The second I'm in my car, I lock the doors, rest my head back and close my eyes.

My heart continues to race and my palms sweat as I replay our time inside his house.

I knew the first time we got close would be a disaster but I didn't think it would be quite like that.

"Fucking hell," I mutter to myself.

My phone buzzes in my pocket and I'm reminded that it was going off before Kyle stole it.

Lifting my ass from the seat, I pull it out and stare down at the screen. There's one message in our group chat but all the others are from Nathan.

A knot twists in my stomach knowing that Kyle saw he was messaging me. I feel ridiculous for even thinking about it. I have every right to have a boyfriend and for him to message me. Kyle has never been anything to me. Just because my inner pre-teen crushed on him for years and we had one night that could have turned into something before his life changed forever, it means nothing.

I open his messages.

Nathan: Have you had a good day? I've got so much homework to do tonight.

Nathan: I can't wait to see you this weekend.

Nathan: I hate dorms. The music is so loud I can barely think. What are you doing right now?

"Jesus."

I close his messages and open the group chat to find Ruby demanding we all get ready at her place Saturday afternoon for Justin's party.

My thumb hovers over the screen, trying to decide how I'm going to get out of going but I don't bother because I know there's nothing I can say that will achieve what I want. Especially if Nathan is going to be there.

I go back to my conversation with him.

Harley: Sorry... was doing homework with a friend. What's the plan for this weekend? You want to do something Saturday night?

He starts typing instantly but his reply is exactly what I didn't want.

Nathan: Me and you have plans Friday night. Saturday is Justin's party. It's for you guys so you gotta be there.

I groan. The party being for the squad is just an excuse for a party, not that anyone really needs one. No one will give a crap if I'm there or not.

Harley: I'd rather just spend time with you.

A little hope washes through me that he'll happily swerve the party at the promise of something happening.

Nathan: We'll have plenty of time just the two of us.

I roll my eyes. *I'm really not going to get out of this, am I?*

Throwing my cell into the console, I start my engine and pull away from the sidewalk, more than ready to get away from Kyle and the memories of what happened inside that house this afternoon.

If only it was that easy.

7

———

KYLE

"How the fuck is that staying away from her?" Kane barks, turning his murderous eyes on me.

Shaking my head at him, I spin around and head for my room.

"Don't turn your back on me," he booms, making me stop in the doorway. "I've done all of this for you. Fucking all of it. The least you can do is what you're told."

"Fuck off, Kane. What do you think I'm going to do to her?"

He closes the space between us. His shoulders tense and his fists curled in frustration.

"You're pissed at her, I get it. But you need to leave her alone."

"And why is that?" I ask, taunting him. "Because you don't want to have to see Letty ever again."

His lips twist and I know I'm touching a sore spot.

"This has nothing to do with her."

"Does it not? Why the hell would you care about what I did with Harley otherwise. She's nothing to you."

"No, she's not. None of them are." He's lying, I can see it in his eyes. "You're pissed at her. You want to hurt her for what she did to you, I get it. Hell, I want to as well. But you need to move on unless you want to end up back where you just came from."

I scoff. "You think I'm going to hurt her. Don't you fucking know me at all?"

Turning away from him, I pop the button on my jeans and drop them down my legs in favor of my sweats.

"All I know is that you want revenge, but let me tell you, little brother. It won't make you feel any better."

"Careful, bro. Or you'll get close to admitting what happened with her that night."

"This isn't about me," he bellows, his face turning beet red.

"It's always about you, Kane," I fume, shoving my feet into my sneakers and storming past him.

"No, Kyle. This right now, all of it is about you and making sure you have a future ahead of you. Why the fuck do you think I searched out Jada fucking Hunter to help me with this shit when I want nothing to do with them. It was for you, asshole."

"Oh so now you admit who you went to for help."

"I didn't think you'd have taken it too well to begin with. It was bad enough we were coming here."

"Whatever, bro."

I push through the front door and take off running.

I need something to expel the energy running around my body after having her beneath my hands.

I blink away the image of her dark eyes staring up at me like a scared little mouse.

"Fuck," I scream as I take the path between a couple of the houses and pick up speed. I need to do something that doesn't involve finding out where she lives and finishing what we started.

My fists clench as I remember the way she trembled as I ran my fingertips up her thighs, how I know my words to her at the table were true. If I were to go higher, I know I'd have found those little red lace panties soaking wet for me.

Desire floods my veins and my cock threatens to swell despite the speed I'm going.

I really need to get fucking laid.

I think of those girls I woke up with the other morning. There's no way anything happened with them. I'd have felt a little relief if it had, but as it is, I'm as pent up as I have been since getting locked up and having nothing but my hand to take the edge off.

That cheerleader from the diner pops into my head. She could sure come in useful, but even as I think about it as a possibility, I lose all interest.

I run until my muscles ache and my skin is covered in sweat. I have no idea where I end up and it's only by chance that I manage to find my way back to our street.

Unsurprisingly, Kane's car is gone as I slow to a walk up our driveway. Thankfully, though, he left the front door unlocked. The last thing I need is to spend the night on the porch because the fucker locked me out.

As I make my way through the house toward the bathroom, something on the dining table catches my eye.

I pick up the small baggie of weed and stare down at the note.

Chill out a bit, yeah?

Shaking my head, I leave it where it was and continue forward.

I stand under the warm spray and allow the water to wash the day off me but as I stand there, all I can think about is her. I knew inviting her over was a bad idea but it was the only place I could see our first meeting happening, away from prying eyes.

My cock throbs as I think about how soft her body was, as I remember the little whimper that rumbled up her throat as I touched her. Then I'm back at that party over a year ago as she danced straddled across my lap in her little dress. She was wearing red panties that night too.

My fingers wrap around my shaft as I remember hooking them to one side and running my fingers through her wetness.

"Fuck," I hiss, my other hand resting on the tiles before me as I work myself to release with images of her in my head. Her fucking banging body, her bronzed skin, her dark captivating eyes and her full lips.

"Fuck." My grunt fills the small bathroom as I come into the shower tray.

I tip my head toward the torrent of water but no sooner has my heartbeat returned to normal do I realize that my run and that release have done shit all for me.

Irritated with myself and my need for her, I turn the shower off and step out.

After drying off and dragging on some clean clothes, I grab the baggie of weed and head out to the swing seat on the porch in the hope of doing as Kane suggested and chilling the fuck out.

———

"My place tonight. Got the house to ourselves," Zayn announces after our conditioning session after school on Friday.

A smile pulls at my lips at his words. I might have only been here a few days but I am more than ready to discover where he—and Harley—live.

"Legend, you in?" he asks, walking over with a towel around his waist.

"Damn straight. I'm ready to see how you party over here."

"Tonight is a quiet one, the real party is tomorrow night.

Ain't that right, J?" he calls over to Justin, who is apparently hosting this weekend's official party.

"You got it, man. Parents are already gone but Nathan is kicking me out tonight so he can hang with your sister."

A groan rumbles up Zayn's throat at the mention of Harley but I'm sure it's nothing compared to the way my stomach twists at the mention of her being in a house alone with her boyfriend.

I want to ask about him, about them, but I swallow down my questions. I don't need Zayn looking too closely into things. As far as I know, he has no idea about what went down at that party, just that Harley called the cops and I ended up doing time because of it. I'm sure if he had any idea that I'd had my hands on his little sister then I wouldn't have been invited into his circle the second I appeared here.

"You'd better give him some fucking house rules. I ain't having some prep boy corrupting my little sister, J."

"Nah, Nathan's good people, bro. Plus, I've heard the plans for tonight. That fucker is so whipped by her it's not even funny."

"I don't want to know about my sister whipping anyone."

A few of the guys continue to tease Zayn and make a few suggestions about what Harley might be getting up to tonight but thankfully the second he pins one of them against the wall by their throat, everyone seems to stop. Thank fuck because I was two seconds away from doing something similar and I don't need anyone here looking too deep at my feelings for Zayn's little sister. Hell, even I don't want to put any thought into it. As far as I'm concerned, I want revenge and that is all.

Revenge.

Everyone begins to disappear once they're dressed but as Zayn makes a move to leave, he stops by where I'm shoving my damp, sweaty clothes into my duffel.

"Wanna head back with me now? We could order some pizza before the other fuckers turn up."

"Uh..."

"I've got weed and vodka."

"Sounds great, man." Not that I really needed a sweetener, I just didn't want to look too eager.

"You can follow me back."

The drive to Zayn's place is quick and I do a double-take when he pulls up into a driveway of a fucking massive house.

I knew that his mom had done well for herself but shit. This place is a million miles away from the shitty trailers we grew up in.

"Wow, this place is..." I say after parking behind him and stepping out, my eyes sweeping over the huge home before me.

"I know, right. Bit of a shock after the Creek."

"Fucking right."

"Come on, I'll give you the tour and we can get food."

I nod and follow him inside.

"Jesus," I mutter to myself as I walk into the huge hallway with an impressive staircase leading up to the second floor.

"Afternoon," Zayn sings as he turns left. Footsteps race toward us and when I look up I find his girl jumping into his arms.

"Zayn," another familiar voice—one that gives me tingles —warns. "What the fuck is he doing here?"

"He's just come over to hang before the boys get here. I didn't think you'd mind, you're going out with lover boy." Zayn steps aside as he says those final words and Harley's eyes find mine.

I nod at her in greeting.

"Special night planned, huh?" I ask, accepting a can of soda that Zayn grabs for me from the refrigerator.

She stares at me for a beat, her eyes narrowing in anger.

"I'm going to start getting ready."

Without another word, Harley hops down from the barstool and all but runs from the room.

"Well, that went well," I mutter, taking a seat on the stool she vacated.

"I'm just gonna..."

"Just leave her, Pops. She's going to have to get used to having him around."

Poppy's eyes find mine.

"At school, yeah, but you didn't need to bring him here and rub him in right under her nose."

"I just wanna hang out with my old friend. Is that so bad, baby?" He pulls her into his arms and nuzzles her neck.

"Do you two want to be left alone?" I ask, amusement filling my voice.

"Nope, I'm going to check on Harley. Just... be a little sensitive." Poppy turns her eyes on me and they narrow in warning.

"What? Was I anything but nice?" I ask defensively. In truth, I have no idea what Harley has told her friends about me. They're either as oblivious as Zayn as to what's gone down between us or they know everything.

The way Poppy is looking at me right now, I'd go with the latter. I guess I should expect it really. Chicks tell each other everything.

"I'll come down and find you in a bit." Poppy brushes her lips over Zayn's but pulls back before he can take what he really wants.

He watches her leave, practically drooling as she goes.

"Can't believe your mom allows you to live together," I mutter, wondering why he doesn't just follow her and take what he so clearly wants.

"It's complicated. If she didn't live here, I have no idea where she'd have ended up."

"Your mom likes helping lost kids, huh?"

"You have no idea. Shall we?" he asks, tipping his chin toward the door.

"Sure."

He makes his way through the house as if it's normal—which I guess it is—I, on the other hand, gawk at every room we pass. This place is huge and only makes me appreciate what Jada did that much more. People don't just get out of Harrow Creek, and if they're lucky enough to do so then they really don't find this level of success. It really proves that Jada Hunter is one of a kind.

This is the shit us Creek kids dream of but know in our minds it's totally out of reach. This makes me reconsider. A decent year at Rosewood High and hopefully a shot at a college somewhere and I could do something—do anything—more than the life I'd have been condemned to in the Creek.

"This is my den."

"And it's bigger than our entire house." I gaze around the room at the massive flat-screen TV that takes up almost an entire wall, the floor to ceiling windows that cover another along with two giant couches, a refrigerator and everything else a group of boys would need to entertain themselves for a while.

"You're welcome anytime, man. Mi casa es su casa."

"I'm not sure everyone under this roof would agree with that."

"Harley will get over herself. Just give her time."

I agree with him because there isn't much else to do but I'm pretty sure things are going to get better rather than worse.

I drop down onto one of the couches and prop my feet up on the coffee table.

"This is the life, man. You're a lucky motherfucker, you know that?"

"Yeah." He laughs. "Yeah, I do." He makes himself at

home on the other couch, then looks over at me. "So what's the plan then? Year at Rosewood then…"

"Let's see if I survive the year first." He chuckles.

"I know it's only been three days, but that place is like a playground compared to the zoo we're used to. You won't have any problems there. Plus, you're a shoo-in for the team, and you've started tutoring again, right?"

"Uh… y-yeah. Didn't think I told you about that," I mutter, knowing full well that I didn't because I didn't want to tell him that I'd been given Harley as a tutee.

"Nah, Ash mentioned it. You wanna go to college, right?"

"Yeah, I guess. I don't even know if it's possible right now. Kane put everything we have into the house to get me here. I have no idea what the future holds."

"It's whatever you make it, man. Start looking at colleges, see what they need for scholarships, they'd be stupid not to accept you."

"We'll see. One step at a time."

A knock sounds on the door and Ashton pokes his head inside.

"Alright?" He drops down beside me. "Ruby's gone up to help Harley," he explains.

"So basically this is where you two hang out while the girls do their hair and shit?" I ask, looking between them with a smirk.

"That's basically it."

"You know they're probably upstairs right now talking about you both, right?"

"Nah, they're talking about you. Harley fucking hates you, man."

8

———

HARLEY

"I really fucking hate him," I whine as Ruby slips into my room while I sit at my vanity unit curling my hair.

Poppy sighs. "Focus on tonight. You can't show up to a date with your boyfriend while angry with another boy. Especially if you won't tell us why."

My lips part to tell them about the tutoring session but no words come out.

"You're right. You're right. Just think about Nathan."

"Do you know what he's planning?"

"Nope, just that we've got the house to ourselves because Justin will be here and his little brother is elsewhere."

"Is tonight the night?" Ruby asks, wiggling her hips excitedly.

I'm pretty sure butterflies are supposed to make an appearance in my belly at those words, but they don't. I feel totally flat about tonight.

All I can think about is him and our time together in his house last night and how badly I want to hurt him. To show him that he can't play me like he's trying to, that I won't fall for it.

Damn him. He's been here three freaking days and he's driving me to the brink of insanity already.

"I don't know."

"You could sound at least a little excited or nervous... or anything, to be honest."

"I will be once I get there and see what he's planning. Right now there are too many ideas spinning around my head. I don't want to assume anything and then it not happen."

"How are you so levelheaded about this? I'd be a nervous wreck."

I pin Ruby with a look over my shoulder in the mirror.

"What?"

"N-nothing. What are you wearing?"

I look over to the dress that's hanging on the door to my closet.

"That's cute."

An awkward silence descends on us as I watch the two of them exchange a worried glance behind my back.

"Do you want to fill me in on your little silent conversation?" I snap, my irritation levels growing.

"We're just worried about you. Kyle's arrival has—"

"Has what?"

"Put you in a weird mood. We're just worried about how you're dealing with it."

"There's nothing to deal with. He's here. I'm ignoring him. End of."

"That's why when I walked in you were talking about him?" Ruby raises a brow.

"He's downstairs with Zayn," I tell Ruby.

"Oh."

"Everything is fine. It's just weird seeing him here. My life in Rosewood it's... it's different from the life I had when he was a part of it."

Poppy narrows her eyes at me. "Is there something you're

not telling us? He's Zayn's friend, I know you crushed on him but... is there more?"

My skin burns as they both stare at me.

My lips part to lie but I soon find no words come out.

"I freaking knew it."

"You can't tell Zayn, Pops. He'll kill me."

"Zayn doesn't have a leg to stand on, Har. He's banging your bestie so I think you should get a free pass. You've warned him that you're going to enough."

"This was before though," I mutter. "He can't know anything happened between us. It's in the past. Over."

"Which is why it's still affecting you?" Poppy helpfully points out.

"I was young. It was nothing more than that."

"But you've kissed him?"

"Enough," I bark, slamming my straightener down on the counter and standing from my stool. "It's all in the past. Yes, something happened but it was a mistake. It's over. There is nothing between us. He hates me, with good reason. What I need right now is to be as far away from him as possible and to not even be thinking about him as I get ready for a date with my boyfriend." I pin them both with a look and they back down quickly switching up the conversation to some gossip Poppy overheard in physics earlier.

I zone them out as I sit back down to do my makeup, trying like hell to focus on what tonight might hold instead of worrying about the boy downstairs.

"Okay, I'm ready." I hold my arms out at my sides once I've returned from the bathroom after shimmying my dress up my body and wait for the girls' verdict.

"Gorgeous, as always."

"Nathan's not going to know what's hit him," Ruby says. "Are you wearing a bra?" she asks when I spin away from where the two of them are sitting on my bed, showing them the open back.

"No. Is that the wrong thing to do? I don't want him to think—"

"It's perfect. He'll love it."

"Okay," I breathe, blowing out a breath and pulling the short hem down a little. Suddenly the nerves I thought I should have been feeling earlier assault me.

"Throw a jacket on and get out of here. Don't make him wait any longer," Poppy says, climbing from the bed, Ruby quickly following so they can go and find their boys.

Okay, let's do this.

The guys' voices filter up to us as we descend the stairs.

"Harley, baby, you're killing me," Justin announces, his hand over his heart as if he's in pain. "Remind me why I'm allowing him to have the night with you."

"Because if you so much as lay a finger on her, asshole, I'll gut you like a fucking fish," Zayn growls as he emerges from the kitchen, arms loaded with drinks and snacks.

Justin's eyes run the length of me, lingering on my legs longer than should be appropriate. My body heats at his interest despite the death glares he's receiving from my brother.

"Har, don't you think you should wear something a little more..."

"A little more what?" Poppy barks at her boyfriend, taking a step forward as if she's protecting me. "She looks beautiful."

"Hot," Justin scoffs before disappearing around the corner before he gets his ass beat.

Thankfully, Poppy manages to placate Zayn and the second she runs her hands up his chest, he forgets all about me.

"Go on, get the hell out while he's distracted," Ruby says with a laugh, pushing me forward.

"Are you sure this is okay?" I look down at myself, once again second-guessing my outfit choice.

"You look beyond stunning, Har. Nathan's going to love it."

"But you don't think it'll make him think..."

"Har, he's a teenage boy, he'd be thinking that if you turned up wearing a sack."

"I guess," I mutter, glancing back up at the stairs, suddenly wishing I could go and hide.

This time last week there would have been nothing I wanted more than to hang out one-on-one with Nathan. But now... now *he's* shown his face and sent my world into a tailspin I don't know what I want.

"He's a good one, Har. He won't do any more than you're happy with." She says it with so much confidence and internally I wince at myself.

I've always claimed to want a nice boy, one my dad would approve of, but I know that only stems from my past experience with the bad boys.

Without instruction, my head takes me back to Kyle's place and how it felt to be crushed between his body and the door. My heart rate increases. Given half the chance, he'd have taken exactly what he wanted. If Kane wasn't right there watching, I have no doubt it would have gone farther. The warning was right there in his eyes, his need evident in his demanding touch.

And you would have let it happen. I shake the little voice from my head but as I do, I turn back to say goodbye to Poppy and Ruby. They're standing at the bottom of the stairs where I left them but it's not them that capture my attention. That's the boy standing in the doorway to Zayn's den with the dangerous eyes.

My breath catches as our gazes lock before he rips his away in favor of my body. He's wearing his standard backward cap, a black hoodie with the sleeves pushed up to his elbows, and dark jeans with his hands stuffed in the pockets. From the tightness of the muscles in his forearms,

I'd say that his fists are clenched right now and it sends a bolt of excitement through me that I can cause a reaction out of him.

"Okay, well…" I say, holding his narrowed stare. "I guess I'll see you guys later. Don't do anything I wouldn't do."

"Shouldn't we be saying that to you?" Ruby chuckles.

With a smile in Kyle's direction, I turn back around and reach for the front door to make my escape and see what my night holds, only I don't get out of the house before Poppy opens her mouth and makes me wish the ground would swallow me up whole.

"You got condoms, right?"

"Fuck my life, I can't listen to this shit," Zayn grumbles and stalks off.

"I'll see you all later." The excitement that zipped through me only seconds ago vanishes as I close the door behind me and blow out a long breath.

Tonight's going to be fun, it's what you've wanted since you first met Nathan a few weeks ago.

I force my legs to carry me to my car and drop down, resting my head back and sucking in another calming breath.

After a moment, I pull myself together, start the engine and begin backing out of the driveway, only the second I look up, I lock eyes with *him* standing at one of the hallway windows.

Not needing to get lost in his hate stare, I rip my eyes away, pretending I didn't see him, put the car into drive and slam my foot down on the pedal to get away from him.

The faster that happens, the better. My life was perfectly fine before he decided to gate crash it with his pretty face and haunting eyes.

School was good—math aside—cheer was epic, and I had a nice boy, someone who wanted to treat me right and make me smile.

Why does all of that seem so pointless now?

Damn him.

I'm at Justin's house in record time and pulling up next to his Porsche.

Nerves make my hands tremble against the wheel. Shaking my head at myself, I pull down my visor and check my hair and makeup before swinging the door open and climbing out.

I'm putting too much thought into all of this. I'm just coming to hang out.

The front door is open before I get halfway across the driveway and Nathan's eyes track down my body, just like someone else's did not so long ago.

I banish thoughts of him from my head as I climb the couple of steps up to the front door.

"Harley, you look... wow."

A smile tugs at my lips and I slip my hand into the one he's holding out for me. Wrapping our joined hands around my back, he pulls me into his body and drops his lips to mine.

"Hey," I say almost shyly when he pulls back.

"Hey, I'm so glad you're here," he says, his eyes bouncing between mine.

"Me too," I whisper honestly. Now I'm here and I can put everything that was going on at my house behind me, I'm actually excited.

He smiles at me and I'm reminded of the night at Ethan's a few weeks ago when we first met. His dark hair is styled perfectly, his hazel eyes have that same sparkle and his jaw is so sharp and square it makes me want to trace it with my fingertip.

"Come in, you must be freezing."

He doesn't release me as he drags me in and swings the door closed behind us.

"I... uh... wasn't sure what to wear."

"You could wear anything and still look beautiful, Harley." His hand wraps around the back of my neck as heat plumes in my belly.

His lips brush mine once again before his tongue trails along my bottom one. Eagerly my lips part for him and he more than willingly ramps things up. His other hand drops to my waist, pressing us tightly together until I have no choice but to feel his length between us.

"Did you cook?" I ask when he finally lets me up for air.

"Kind of. I'm not really any good in the kitchen. Come on." He laces his fingers through mine and pulls me farther into the house after allowing me to take my heeled booties off and leave them with the others in the hallway.

As we make our way down the hall, it gets darker and a twinkle starts from the very far room which I already know is Justin's living room.

"Oh wow," I breathe when I step inside the room to find fairy lights strung up and a picnic already laid out on a rug in the middle of the room.

I glance over at him as he studies me shyly, waiting for my response.

"You did all this for me?"

He shrugs. "I just wanted tonight to be something you might remember."

I swoon, I can't help it. Nathan is like the perfect boyfriend. Everything I've wished for since moving to Rosewood.

"It's perfect. What's to eat?" I ask, stepping onto the blanket and lowering down beside the basket.

"Literally everything I could think of." He laughs, coming to sit on the other side and opening the lid, allowing me to see the insane amount of food inside.

"You know it's only the two of us, right?" I ask with a laugh just to confirm that he's not planning on feeding the entire team tonight.

"I know. I just wasn't sure what you liked. We've only eaten together a couple of times and both times were pizza so…"

"Fair enough." I help him lay it all out before us, a smile playing on my lips the entire time.

"I sure hope you're hungry," he says to me once the basket is finally empty.

"Yeah, I am. I was too nervous to eat lunch," I admit. Although I keep the fact that it wasn't entirely because of him to myself. This is a Kyle Legend free zone.

"Yeah?" he asks like I've just told him that tomorrow is Christmas or something.

"Yeah. This is nice having no one else around."

"At last, right? Any preference?" he asks, holding up the TV remote.

"Music?"

"Sure."

He clicks through a few channels before deciding on one and lies back so he's on his side and rests on his elbow, giving me a chance to really check him out.

He's wearing a navy Henley with the arms pushed up to the elbows and a dark, almost black, pair of jeans. It's not all that much different to *him,* the main difference being that the clothes that are wrapped around Nathan's body are branded with labels that I'm sure might impress his prep school friends but they do very little for me. They're just clothes. I couldn't give a crap about the name on them.

I stare at the sliver of skin that is exposed around his waist and bite down on my bottom lip at the sight of the red waistband of his boxers. Nathan is fit, that much is obvious but he's much leaner than *him.* I guess that's not hard really seeing as it looks like he's spent his entire year away inside the prison gym.

My stomach clenches at the thought of him being locked

up but I stuff it back down. I shouldn't be thinking about all of that right now.

I'm sitting here with an incredible guy who looks at me like I'm something special and my head is with someone else, someone I don't want it to be with.

"Are you okay? You seem a little distant." Concern fills his voice and I hate it. "I know we haven't talked much this week, I was just hoping it was because you were busy?" he suggests.

"Y-yeah, it was. I'm sorry, things have just been a bit crazy this week. I've fallen out with my mom, schools been hard work. I'm sorry, I really want to enjoy this with you."

He smiles at me, his concern thankfully dissipating.

"Just relax, yeah. You don't need to worry about any of that tonight."

I blow out a slow breath. "That sounds so good."

"Here," he says, offering me the bowl of chips that is closest to him. Reaching out, I take a couple and throw them into my mouth.

"So you've both got the house to yourself for the weekend? Don't they miss you at school?"

"Nah, no one will even notice. And it's not like my parents will care."

His expression doesn't falter but I see something flicker through his eyes. Pain.

"How come you don't want to go out of state for college?" I ask. He's already told me that he's been accepted to MKU but the way he talks about school and his parents, I wouldn't have thought he'd want to stick around.

"I don't know," he mumbles around a sausage roll. "It's home, I guess. Just feels right."

"Fair enough."

"You any closer to making any decisions?"

"Nah, not yet. I've got plenty of time," I say, although as

the words fall from my lips I can hear Mom's voice in my head nagging at me to make a decision about my future.

I understand her need to ensure the three of us are all well educated but I really don't need the pressure. Right now, I need to get those damn test results up before I even think about applications.

We chat away about nonsense while we pick at the food he's laid out.

"You sure you don't want one?" he asks, knocking the top off his second bottle of beer.

"No, thank you. I need to drive home."

"Do you?" he asks, looking at me from under his long dark lashes.

My stomach flutters in anticipation.

"I... uh... I don't know. But I want the option."

"Think you're going to need to run away from me?"

"Who knows. You might turn out to be a murderer yet," I joke.

He chuckles. "I could well be. Have you finished?" He nods down to the leftover food that neither of us has touched in a while.

"Yeah, I'm good. Thank you, it was delicious."

"It was just a picnic."

"Best picnic I've ever had," I say with a wink as I help him pack it all up.

"There's no need to sweeten me, babe. I'm already all yours."

I shake my head at him and follow him through to the kitchen to dispose of everything.

"Did you get anything for dessert?" I ask, spinning to watch him move effortlessly around the kitchen as he tidies up.

I bite down on the inside of my cheek as I watch his muscles pull across his shoulders as he works.

"Yeah, I got—" His words falter when he turns and finds

me staring at him. "Fuck," he breathes, lifting his hand and running his fingers through his hair as he stares back at me.

My skin heats as his eyes drop down my body, my nipples puckering against the fabric of my dress at his attention.

"What?" I ask, a shy smile pulling at my lips when he doesn't do or say anything for long seconds.

"You, you're just so... I don't even know."

"Thanks, I think. So dessert?"

"Oh, y-yeah." He clears his throat and turns toward the refrigerator but I don't miss him rearranging himself before he pulls the door open.

The knowledge that I affect a guy like Nathan makes me feel like a freaking queen.

Pushing from the counter I was leaning against, I walk up to him and wrap my arm around his waist as I peer inside.

"I got these," he says, pulling out a couple of chocolate mousse cups.

"Perfect. I just need something a little sweet."

I take one from him as he closes the door but I don't get a chance to walk away because he's faster and he spins us until my back is once again pressed against the counter, only this time, he steps right into me.

I part my legs, allowing one of his thighs to slide between as our hips meet. He stares down at me, his eyes searching mine.

"I can't get enough of you, Harley," he whispers, his hand landing on my waist and sliding up until it stops on my ribs, less than an inch from my breast which becomes heavy, desperate to feel his touch.

"I'm right here, Nathan."

"You make me lose my mind," he admits, his nose brushing against mine. "But I'm trying to do the right thing here."

I have no idea if he's been with other girls. From his looks and the fact he's one of Maddison Prep's star basketball players, I would be very surprised if he hadn't been with at least a few. He certainly seems to know the right moves and the right words to say to make me melt. But I appreciate that he's keeping things slow. I haven't told him that I'm a virgin but I think he knows. It's why he's holding back. Letting me take the lead.

"You say that like I'm a good little girl," I breathe, our lips so close that the heat of his burns into mine.

"Harley," he groans as if he's in pain as his length hardens between us.

If I were a different member of Rosewood's cheer squad then I'd probably already be on my knees for him. But I'm not, and nor do I want to be.

Our squad's reputation needs to change and once the seniors graduate, it's one of the things Ruby and I want to work on, should we both get voted to take charge that is.

"Kiss me."

His fingers tighten around my ribs a second before his lips take mine in a bruising kiss.

Unlike when I first arrived, there's no restraint on Nathan's part. His kiss is hard, wet and dirty and I soon find myself drowning in it—in him.

A groan rumbles up his throat as his tongue delves into my mouth and a rush of heat floods me.

"Harley, fuck," he grunts into our kiss.

Abandoning his dessert, his large palm wraps around the back of my thigh and he lifts my leg from the floor, wrapping it around his hip and opening me up to him.

I gasp, breaking our kiss, then his hardness presses against my sensitive core.

"Good, huh?" he asks smugly but he doesn't give me a chance to respond to how it feels because he dips his head, his lips latching onto my neck.

"Oh God," I whimper as he sucks on a sensitive spot

beneath my ear. An entire body shudder rips through me at the move.

"We should probably get out of the kitchen," he mumbles against my skin after a few minutes.

"Uh... y-yeah," I agree, although I have no idea if my legs will hold me up and allow me to walk anywhere right now.

He pulls back, his eyes scanning my face but the second mine land on his lips, I can't help but laugh.

Reaching out, I run my thumb along his full bottom lip and rub at my lipstick.

"It's not really your color," I admit, holding my thumb up for him to see the dark makeup.

"I don't care what color it is as long as it's come from you. Come on."

He takes a step back and thankfully, I don't collapse to the floor on my jelly legs. He takes both of the desserts that had been abandoned on the counter in one hand than mine in the other.

Part of me wonders if he's about to lead me upstairs, and a refusal is right on the tip of my tongue when we turn back to the living room.

I don't like my initial reaction to the prospect of us taking this further, especially after just being like putty in his hands.

Maybe tonight isn't the night.

I hate that he might be disappointed if I can't go through with it, but a big part of me knows that he'll understand.

I don't realize my steps falter as I look to the stairs.

"What—oh. Did you want to..." He trails off and I look past him into the room, not wanting to see any excitement in his eyes.

"No, here's good. We could... err... find a movie or something."

"Yeah," he agrees without missing a beat and continues leading me inside.

He throws a few extra cushions down on the floor and we retake our places on the blanket as he flicks through the movie channels to find something suitable.

He finally lands on some high school rom-com and places the remote down. It's not really my kind of movie but I don't complain. I have a feeling we're not really going to be watching it anyway.

I'm still trying to get comfortable as he pulls the top of my dessert off.

"Here," he says, holding out a spoonful of chocolate goodness.

"I can feed myself, you know," I say with a laugh.

"Humor me." He gives me one of his knee-weakening smiles, dimple and all and I cave.

I part my lips and allow him to slide the spoon past them before I close my mouth around it. The sweetness almost immediately explodes on my tongue and I can't help but close my eyes and groan. It's so freaking good, and exactly what I needed.

"Fuck, babe. You're killing me."

"It's so good."

"Yeah?" he asks, lowering the spoon back to the cup but instead of trying it, he leaves the cup where it is and scoots closer. "Let's see how good."

His hand cradles the back of my head and he lowers his lips to mine.

"Mmm... I didn't think you could taste any better."

The length of his body presses against me, one of his legs threading through mine as he continues to kiss me.

"Nathan," I moan when he once again attacks my neck, licking, sucking and nipping at the skin.

My entire body grows hot and it feels like my skin is suddenly too small.

"Yeah, babe? Tell me what you need."

"I... I..." I stutter because while my body knows exactly what it needs, my head isn't entirely on board.

His hand skims down my body. I gasp when his thumb catches my nipple but he doesn't stop, instead, he descends until his palm lands on my bare thigh.

"This dress, Harley. It's sinful."

I bite down on my bottom lip, wondering once again if wearing it was a mistake.

"Do you have any idea how sexy you look right now?" My chest heaves as I watch him take in every inch of my body. "The things I want to do to you," he murmurs, and my stomach twists. But my thoughts are cut off when his lips find mine once more and I lose myself in his kiss, in his burning touch.

His hand lifts until it's under the hem of my skirt.

Heat floods me a second before his thumb brushes the fabric covering me.

"Fuck, babe. You're soaked," he whispers in my ear.

My back arches as he presses against me a little harder.

"You want me to touch you, babe? You want me to make you come?" His voice is so deep and rough in my ear and my eyes close of my own accord.

My breathing is erratic, my heart out of control in my chest as his own rapid breaths caresses my neck and shoulder.

"Nathan," I moan again when his lips latch onto my neck and he sucks hard enough to leave a mark. "Oh God," I cry out when he slips my panties aside and runs his fingers through my folds.

His body vibrates with his growl of approval at how ready he finds me.

My eyes squeeze tight and my back arches once more as my body tries to absorb the sensations he's igniting within me.

It's not the first time someone's touched me like this but it's not— "No," I cry, suddenly sitting up.

It takes a second to register what's happening but the second I do, I drop my head into my hands.

"I'm sorry," I mutter, it's muffled against my palms so I have no idea if he can hear me or not.

My face burns and my eyes fill with tears that I've just rejected him like that. And the reason... no. I can't. I can't even think about it or I'll fall off the ledge I'm already precariously balancing on.

"I'm sorry," he says softly, wrapping his fingers around my wrist and trying to pull my hands from my face but I fight him. "It's my fault. I shouldn't have pushed you. I'm sorry."

Sucking in a calming breath, I wipe at my eyes before pulling my hands away.

"I think I should go."

"No, Harley. It's okay. You don't need to—"

"I do. I'm so sorry I ruined your night. All of this," I say, gesturing to what he's done for me. "All of this was perfect. I'm sorry."

I run before he has time to stand and I'm already in the hallway shoving my feet into my booties and pushing my arms into my jacket when he finally joins me.

"Please don't run. We can watch the movie. Just chill out."

His hands land on my upper arms to stop me and when I refuse to look him in the eyes, he ducks down so I have no choice.

"I'm sorry," I whisper again, my voice full of emotion.

"Harley, stop." One of his hands cups my cheek and he catches the tear that falls with his thumb. "It doesn't matter."

I rip my eyes from his, too embarrassed to look into them, but when I look down, I find his cock still tenting his jeans and I hate myself all over again.

What the hell is wrong with me? I've got the kindest, sweetest guy standing in front of me practically begging me to spend time with him yet when I close my eyes all I see is *him.*

It's been over a year since I was anywhere near him. I shouldn't even remember that night, let alone allow it to fill my mind when I should be enjoying my time with my boyfriend.

"It... it does to me. I'm sorry."

Pulling myself from his grip, I pull the front door open and race through it.

9

KYLE

It's nice feeling part of something again and as I look around at Zayn's friends, I wonder if this was where I was supposed to be all along.

There's music playing in the background and there are football replays on the TV but no one's paying any attention to them, they're either too drunk, high or have a girl in their lap. Okay, so that's just Zayn and Ashton whose girls are here. For some reason, they've banned any others from joining us tonight. Seems a little unfair if you ask me but there we go.

"You two wanna take it upstairs. I might have missed you, bro, but I don't want to see your cock," I slur at Zayn who's got Poppy grinding down on his lap beside me. "Unless you wanted me to join. I'm sure I could teach your girl a thing or two."

"Shut the fuck up, Legend, and keep your fucking hands to yourself," he growls although he never lifts his head from his girl's neck.

"Touchy," I mock. "I bet Ash isn't so possessive."

"I wouldn't put any money on that bet, man. You want to get your dick wet, just wait until the cheer squad are off their faces tomorrow night. You'll have them lining up to welcome you to Rosewood properly."

"Zayn," Poppy squeals. "You're a pig."

"You gonna try telling him that it's not true?" He stares at his girl with his brow raised.

Her lips are swollen from his kiss, her cheeks are red and her eyes are blown with lust. Reaching down, I rearrange my semi. Fuck, I want a girl looking like that on my lap.

"Err… no, he's right. They're a bunch of whores. Just be careful, yeah. We all know where they've been." She glances around the room before training her eyes back on her boy.

"Hey, I'm a one-woman man."

"Now you are," she points out.

"Damn fucking straight and I'm about to prove it. Excuse us." Zayn stands with Poppy still in his arms and after telling everyone in the room to fuck off out of his house, they disappear out the door.

"Pussy-whipped motherfucker," someone calls after him.

"Let's get the fuck out of here. The juniors are partying at Richstone's. Shall we?"

A round of agreement sounds out and after a few minutes, everyone starts to leave.

"Fury, Rubes, you coming?"

"She's fucking coming alright."

"Ashton." If Ruby was supposed to be chastising him then it fails massively when his name leaves her lips as a moan.

"Fuck, I need to get laid," Justin mutters before he follows the others from the room.

"Right, well, I'll leave you two to it."

"Appreciated, man," Ash says as he kisses down Ruby's chest. "Work out in the morning?"

"Sure. Message me when you don't have a chick attached to you."

He flips me off behind Ruby's back and I slip out of the room, closing the door behind me to give them some privacy.

I've got my hand on the front door, about to rip it open when I look over my shoulder at the stairs. A smirk pulls at my lips as an idea hits me.

Jada's out and the two couples left in this house are most definitely preoccupied, so...

Before I've finished processing the thought, I'm halfway up the stairs that I'm hoping will lead me to Harley's bedroom.

"Oh God, Zayn," Poppy cries out when I hit the top step.

I shake my head, wondering how Jada and Harley put up with that shit on probably a daily basis before I come to a stop at the door opposite where the noise is coming from and push it open.

I know it's hers almost immediately and not just because the walls are as red as her hair but it smells like her. Everything about the space is just like her.

Closing the door behind me, I step into the middle of the room, taking everything in.

I'm standing at a bookcase on the other side of the room, running my eyes over the insane number of framed photos she has when the door opens behind me.

I was so lost staring at snippets of her life that I didn't hear any movement outside the room.

Her sobs rip through the room and when I spin around, I find her with her back to the door and her face in her hands.

Okay, this was not what I was expecting.

I open my mouth to say something but soon realize I have no words.

I watch her for long seconds as she crumbles before me.

Part of me enjoys seeing her pain after the agony she sentenced me to this past year, but there is a softer part buried somewhere deep inside me that feels for her and wants to help. Sadly, when she does realize that she's got an audience, it's not that nice part of me that emerges.

I take a step forward and the floor beneath my feet creaks loud enough to be heard over her cries.

Her head lifts from her hands and her eyes go wide as a scream rips from her throat.

I'm on her in a heartbeat, my hand wrapped around her mouth so she doesn't alert Zayn.

Her tear-filled eyes stare into mine. Confusion, shock, and misery swim in them.

"Hey, Kitten. What a surprise to see you here." I smirk down at her as she claws at my forearm, desperately trying to remove my hand from her mouth.

"Get the hell out of my room, asshole," she seethes the second I release her.

I chuckle, stepping closer and forcing her to press herself back against the door.

"I think I might hang around for a bit if it's all the same to you. It looks like you might need some company, Kitten." Lifting my hand, I reach out to wipe at her tear tracks but she snaps her head to the side before I can touch her.

"What's wrong? Couldn't he get it up for you?"

"Fuck you, Kyle."

"Ah, was that the problem?" I lean in until my lips brush the shell of her ear. "That he wasn't me?"

She gasps but at no point does she try to argue, which I find interesting.

"Get the hell away from me and out of my house."

Her palms slam down on my chest and she pushes but her strength is no match for mine.

"It's almost cute that you think you can push me around."

"If you'd just leave me alone then I'd have no reason to touch you, let alone push you."

"And what would be the fun in that. I wouldn't want you to forget me."

"Trust me, that's impossible," she spits, staring up at me with her top lip curled in disgust.

"Why's that, Kitten? Am I in here?" I tap her temple with two of my fingers.

"Will you stop touching me?"

"No. No, I don't think I will. Do you know why?"

"If I let you tell me, will you do me a solid and get out of my fucking bedroom?"

I pretend to think about it. "No."

She rolls her eyes at me, and I reach out and take her chin in my hand.

"Ow," she complains, pulling at my arm in the hope it'll make me let go.

"What happened tonight, Kitten? What did that motherfucker do to have you back here before midnight in tears?"

"N-nothing."

"Oh really? You two had the entire house to yourselves for the night so I heard, so in my mind, you should probably be naked right about now."

I step into her body, my knee pushing between hers and my hips pinning her to the wall.

"J-Just because we had an e-empty house, it doesn't mean—"

"You're trying to tell me that he wanted to play scrabble, Kitten?" She tries turning her face away from me, but my grip tightens and I hold her in place ensuring she has nowhere else to look but into my eyes.

"So what happened?"

She purses her lips shut, refusing to talk to me, although whatever it is that sent her running is still playing on her mind because her eyes are still full of unshed tears.

Tension crackles between us as I silently plead with her to tell me so I know if I need to go and knock the stupid motherfucker out for making her cry while she begs me to let it go and leave her alone.

She might not have figured it out yet, but only one of us is winning this silent battle.

"Shall I tell you what I think, if you're not going to tell me what I need to know?"

Her eyes narrow at me but still, her lips remain sealed.

"Okay." I smirk at her. "I think Prep Boy isn't who you really want. I think you know that he can't give you what you need. You think he's who you should want. You think he'll look after you with his fancy fucking car and weighty trust fund.

"But he doesn't do it for you, does he?

"See, you can take the girl out of the trailer park, Harley, but you can never take the trailer park out of the girl."

Her breathing increases as I talk, her chest heaves and her nostrils flare with her need for air where she still refuses to part her lips.

"I think..." I continue. "He touches you like you're made of glass. Like you're something precious that he needs to treasure. Whereas—"

She gasps, "Kyle," as I rip her jacket from her arms and throw it to the floor behind me.

In seconds, I have both of her wrists pressed against the door above her head in one of my hands.

"Oh, so now you have something to say. Kinda proves my point, don't you think?"

"You have no idea what you're talking about."

A smug smile pulls at my lips. "Don't I? I know you, Harley Hunter. I know you better than you think I do, and I know exactly what you need. Want me to prove it to you?"

Her eyes hold mine, shining brightly with defiance, daring me to do exactly what I just said although she's terrified to actually demand it of me.

I crowd myself against her, loving the heat of her skin against my body. It's been too fucking long since I've felt anyone's body against mine and I fucking crave more.

Skin on skin.

My cock aches at the thought of having her bare beneath me to show her just how it should be done.

"You look so beautiful when you cry." My voice is softer than it was before and her eyes narrow in suspicion.

Leaning forward, I lick up her cheek. Her salty tears coat my tongue and the need that's growing within me almost explodes.

I've no doubt I could lift her against the door right now and take her. She might want to fight me. She might hate me. But there's no denying what her body wants. She wanted it that night and she wants it now despite her spending the evening with her prissy boyfriend.

"There's just one problem though." I cup her cheek tenderly and swipe a fresh tear with my thumb. Leaning in closer so our lips are almost touching, I tell her what I'm really thinking. "I wasn't the one who made you do it. *He* did."

She gasps as my hand wraps around her throat. Her lips parting and her eyes widening.

"Now tell me, Kitten. Why did that motherfucker make you cry on your big night?"

"Leave please," she begs but there's no strength behind her words. It's what she thinks she should be saying.

"Kitten, stop trying to be a good little girl, we both know you aren't. Tell me the truth."

"Fuck you."

"Trust me. I'm about thirty seconds from doing just that."

She swallows nervously under my grip, her pulse hammering against my fingertips.

"Oh, is that what you want? You want me to fuck you, Kitten?"

"No, I—"

"Wasn't he man enough for the job? Do we need to show him just how it's done?"

I drop my lips to her neck and bite down on the sensitive skin right above where my thumb is digging into her flesh.

"Kyle," she cries, her knee lifting as if she's going to take another shot at me.

Not this time, baby.

I thread my knee between her thighs once again and ensure it pushes against her pussy, knowing that she's not going to resist the urge to grind on me if she's as turned on as I think she is.

"Fuck, you taste too good to be so bad."

I drag my teeth down her collarbone, the heat of her skin damn near burning my lips.

"Did he do this to you, Kitten? Did he kiss every inch of this sinful body before he made you cry?"

"Kyle, you need—" she whimpers but her words are cut off when I make my way down to the neckline of her dress and the swell of her breast.

"Did he get here, Kitten? Did he find out that you weren't wearing anything beneath your dress?"

She shakes her head and it's damn near impossible to contain my smile.

"What a stupid motherfucker. Right there for the taking and he didn't unwrap you and take what was his."

I drag the front of her dress down and expose her breast. Small, perfect and begging for my lips.

"Oh God," she gasps as I suck her peak into my mouth and swirl my tongue around the hard bud.

"This what you needed, Kitten?"

"Fuck, you need to stop, Kyle. We shouldn't be—"

"Fuck what we should and shouldn't do, Harley. You fucking owe me, and I want to fucking punish you for it."

"W-what are you going to do?"

I don't answer her, mainly because I don't have one.

I've pictured a million and one ways I've wanted to hurt her for what she did to me that night. But now we're here, her scent filling my nose and her taste is on my tongue, all I want to do is take.

Take everything from that stupid motherfucker who wasn't man enough to make her his.

I work my way back up to her neck and drag my lips across her cheek until they're hovering right above her full lips.

My mouth waters to kiss her. To remember exactly what it was like to lose myself in her and forget the outside world and all the bullshit in our lives.

But I don't.

Instead, I find the bottom of her dress and lift it higher, not that it's covering much as it is.

"What about here, Kitten?"

I rub my fingertips along her lace-covered seam. She trembles in my hold, her throat working on overdrive as she swallows and her pulse races.

A whimper falls from her lips but I refuse to give her anymore until she answers me.

"Kitten?"

Her eyes hold mine, narrowing in anger and frustration.

"If you want more, you're going to need to answer my question."

"I hate you," she seethes.

"And yet you're so fucking wet for me. Are you lying to me, Kitten?"

"No. I really fucking hate you."

"Good," I snap, startling her. "Because I really fucking hate you too. Now tell me, did he touch you."

Something sparkles in her eyes and her lips twitch at the corners.

"Yes," she states proudly. "Yes, he had his fingers all over my pussy. That what you wanted to hear?"

Something explodes within me and I rip my hand from

her throat and slam it down on the door beside her head, startling her.

"Kyle, what the fuck?"

"This..." I say, cupping her with my entire hand, her juices coating my fingers even through the lace as her heat burns me. "This is mine. Do you understand that?"

"He's m-my boyfriend."

"Who sent you home tonight from your date crying. I really think you should reconsider, Kitten."

"F-for you?" she stutters.

A wicked chuckle falls from my lips. "No, Kitten. I already own you."

"Kyle," she squeals as I rip her panties aside and sink my fingers into her wetness.

"So fucking wet for me, Kitten. How long have you been thinking about this, about me touching you?"

Her lips part but as I push deeper into her heat, no words come out.

I press the length of my body against her as my finger continues to work her, stroking her walls as her muscles clamp down around me. Her hands wrap around my forearm, her nails digging in but at no point does she try to stop me or pull me away, just like I knew she wouldn't.

"Did he feel this good?" I groan in her ear, my cock rubbing against her hip desperate to get in on the action.

She shakes her head violently from side to side.

"Kyle," she gasps when I slide a second digit inside her. "Oh God."

I bend my fingers, searching out her sweet spot as her juices continue to drip down my hand.

"Did he make you come?" I whisper in her ear but this time she remains silent. "Answer me, or I stop. Did. He. Make. You. Come?"

She shakes her head, although a little less enthusiastically than before.

A smile tugs at one side of my lips. *Fucking prep school pussy.*

"Why, Kitten? Why couldn't he get you like this?" I pull back to watch her as she rides my hand.

The straps of her dress have fallen from her shoulders, lowering the neckline of her dress, and although her breasts are covered, it doesn't leave much to the imagination. Her chest heaves, exposing her nipples every time she sucks in a ragged breath.

Her teeth attack her bottom lip as she races toward the end, her entire face is flushed hot and her eyes are tightly closed.

"Look at me," I demand, hating that in her head she could be elsewhere right now. She could be imagining she's with *him.*

After a beat, her eyelids flicker open and her dark, lust-filled eyes find mine.

"Why didn't he make you come, Kitten?"

"B-because... shit," she gasps as I press my thumb to her clit. Her eyes shutter but they don't completely close.

"Because?"

"Oh God," she whimpers, her pussy clamping down on me as her orgasm begins to crest.

I immediately stop moving.

It takes her a few seconds to register what's happening but when she does, her expression hardens.

"You're a fucking asshole, Kyle."

"Never claimed to be anything else, Kitten. Now tell me what I need to know and I might give you what you need."

"You might?" she sasses.

"Well, I wouldn't be the first one to leave you hanging tonight it seems."

Her lips purse in anger.

"Now, Kitten, tell me why he couldn't get you off."

"Why do you care?"

"Because you came home crying. I want to know what he did to cause that so I know how badly I need to fuck him up."

"No," she cries. "No, don't touch him."

"Why not?" I growl, getting right in her face, our noses touching and our breaths mingling.

"B-because..." I stroke her G-spot encouragingly. "Because he wasn't you," she spits, her eyes going wide a beat later as she realizes what she just confessed.

A wide smile spreads across my face as my chest swells.

"Were you thinking about me, Kitten, while he was finger fucking you?"

Her lips press into a thin line, stopping herself from saying anything else she'll regret.

"Fuck, do you have any idea how hard that makes me?"

Reaching out, I peel her hand from the door and place it against my crotch.

"Kyle," she whimpers as her fingers flex around my length.

I work my jaw as I attempt to restrain myself.

"So, let me get this straight..." My fingers begin to move again. "While he was knuckles deep in your pussy, your eyes were closed and you were imagining that it was me. Fuck, Kitten."

"Kyle, Kyle, fuck," she whimpers as her lost orgasm returns.

Her body locks up and I lean into her ear as she rides out of the waves of pleasure I've allowed her to have.

"You're really going to regret admitting that to me, Kitten," I warn, my voice low and menacing.

The second her body goes limp, I remove all my contact and step away. If I don't put some space between us right now then I'm not going to be able to stop.

"Open," I demand, lifting my fingers to her lips.

She refuses and my anger ratchets up a few notches.

"I said open," I growl, my hand returning to her throat.

Her lips part in surprise and I push my fingers into her hot mouth.

She sucks my fingers, her tongue licking at my skin, tasting herself and my restraint snaps.

Pulling my fingers from her mouth, I slam my lips down on hers, needing to taste her. My tongue invades her mouth, searching for hers. I half expect her to push me away, to knee me in the nuts again but all she does is sag in my hold and kiss me back.

Reaching out, I wrap my hands around the backs of her thighs and lift her, dragging her away from the wall and carrying her deeper into her room.

The second my shins hit the edge of her bed, I release her, throwing her down in the middle and watching her bounce with her dress hitched up around her waist, showing me her tiny, soaked panties.

Lifting my hand, I run my thumb over my bottom lip, remembering just how hers felt.

"Next time," I warn. "I'm not going to walk away so easily." I spin on my heels and march to her door.

She's silent behind me aside from her heaving breaths.

"And, Harley?" I ask, keeping my eyes on the wood before me, knowing that if I look back all bets are going to be off. "Get rid of the Prep Boy before I break him."

10

HARLEY

I laid awake for hours last night, tossing and turning and trying to get the events of the evening out of my head.

I was so angry at myself as I walked away from Nathan. I felt so pathetic.

He's perfect. Literally everything about him is perfect yet when he touched me it was nothing like how it felt when *he* touched me.

Kyle's touch burns in a way I've only ever experienced with him. It might have been a little over a year since that night, but I still remember it as if it were yesterday.

I can vividly recall how every demanding touch affected me. I remember just how high my body soared when he whispered dirty things in my ear and pulled my panties aside.

Before that night, no one had ever touched me. I wasn't really expecting anyone to touch me that night either, but then I wasn't exactly planning on ending up in the state that I did.

Ripping my eyes open, I stare at my closed bedroom door, imagining how we looked last night with his hand beneath my skirt, his lips on my skin and his hand around my throat.

My hand flutters up to my neck to where his touch burned. The skin is tender, but it wasn't hard enough to leave a mark. He's not that stupid, although I'm not sure I'd have been able to stop him if he wanted to though.

His eyes, his words, his touch. All of it—as it always has—rendered me useless and as much as I might have wanted to fight him, I knew it was pointless the second he pressed his body against mine.

I blow out a slow breath as I regret every moment of last night.

I shouldn't have worn that dress. I shouldn't have let things get so far with Nathan—or, maybe I should have and fought harder to get Kyle out of my head—and I should have kicked Kyle out the second I found him in my bedroom.

My phone vibrating on my nightstand drags me from my depressing thoughts.

Reluctantly, I turn over and pull it closer.

My heart jumps into my throat at seeing Nathan's name staring back at me.

Couldn't he have just sent me a message?

I consider ignoring him. Kyle's parting words come back to me. But I don't want to dump Nathan. I really like him, and I want to see where things could go between us.

If only he hadn't shown his face, I might actually be able to focus on the right now.

Cursing myself for allowing my past to affect my present, I connect the call and put it to my ear.

"Hey." I wanted to sound excited but the reality is I just sound half asleep.

"Crap, did I wake you?"

"No, it's okay. I've been awake a while."

"I'm sorry about last night."

"There's nothing to apologize for. I'm the one who should be. I ruined your evening."

"Not possible. I spent it with you." I swoon at his words and smile to myself.

"What are you doing today?"

"I have no idea, but Justin seems to have a plan before tonight's party. Why, did you want to do something?"

"Not if you're busy. I'll see you later on."

"I can cancel," he offers.

"No, it's okay. I'll do something with the girls. I can't wait to see you later though. I want to make it up to you."

"Harley, I'm serious. It's fine. I just want to enjoy the night with you. I have no expectations. There's no rush."

My stomach twists as I picture how badly he wanted us to continue last night but then that image morphs into the memory of Kyle pressing my hand to his cock only an hour after I left Nathan.

Fuck, I'm such an awful person.

Nathan and I might not have put a label on our relationship, for all I know he could be sleeping with multiple Maddison Prep girls, although I very much doubt it. He doesn't seem like the type to do that.

I'm the only bad person here.

Guilt swamps me. I should take Kyle's advice and end things before it gets serious. But the selfish part of me doesn't want to. Things were good before *he* turned up. He shouldn't just get to show his face and send my life into a tailspin.

"O-okay. I'll see you later then, I guess."

"Yeah, I'll be waiting."

I end the call, questioning myself as to whether I did the right thing not.

As much as I might want to think Nathan and I could have a future, I fear that with Kyle around, we're doomed to fail no matter how much I attempt to put a wall up between us.

Like you did last night a little voice says in my head but I push it aside as I curl back up under my covers.

I don't even get a minute of peace before my cell starts ringing again.

Dragging it back out from under my pillow where I shoved it after I hung up on Nathan, I find Ruby's smiling face looking back at me.

"Morning."

"Are you okay?" she asks in a rush, making my heart skip a beat.

"Yeah, why?"

"Shit," she mutters to herself. "What happened last night?"

"Um... Nathan made us a romantic picnic in Justin's living room it was—"

"I don't mean that, I meant what happened after. I saw him, Har. I saw him coming down the stairs and when we left, your car was parked in the driveway. Do not tell me that he wasn't up there with you."

Now it's my turn to curse under my breath.

"How'd you know he wasn't with Zayn?"

"Because Zayn was balls deep in Poppy."

"Ew, thanks for that."

"What happened, Harley?"

"Okay, fine," I huff. "Things didn't end well with Nathan. I came home earlier than I expected and I found Kyle snooping in my room."

"And that's it? He was just snooping?"

"Yeah, I mean we... *talked* briefly." It's not a lie, there were a few words said between us.

"You talked?" she asks, not believing a word of it.

"Yeah, it was nothing," I say, trying to play it off as such so she stops digging. "So what's the plan for this afternoon, we still getting ready at your house?" I ask, hoping the subject change will distract her.

"Yeah, but I need to go to the mall, I've got nothing to wear."

"I really doubt that, Rubes."

"I want something new. I'll pick you up in an hour?"

"What time is it?" I pull my cell away from my ear to look at the same time Ruby says, "Just past eleven."

"Christ," I mutter. "Yeah okay, I'll be ready."

"Good, because I expect the full story about what happened last night, Harley Hunter."

"You did not just last name me," I gasp in mock horror.

"I did and I'll even pull out the middle one if you don't—"

"Yeah, yeah. I get it. No need to be so cruel."

"Good. Now get your ass in the shower, I'll be there soon."

"K, bye."

After a beat, I flip the covers back and head for the door, pausing on the way to the bathroom to call for Poppy who I can only assume is in my brother's bed still.

I knock. "Pops, you in there?"

It takes a couple of seconds and some rustling but eventually she answers. "Yeah, what's up?"

"I'm going to the mall with Rubes. You coming?"

"Can't, we're going to Maddison to see the kids. I'll be at hers later though to get ready."

"Okay, no worries. As you were."

Zayn's low chuckle fills the silence before Poppy squeals and I all but run for the bathroom before I hear any more.

Of all the boys in school, why did one of my best friends have to pick my brother to bump uglies with?

I shower, dress and I'm skipping down the stairs a couple of minutes before Ruby's due. Although the second I turn the corner and find Mom in the kitchen sipping on a mug of coffee and reading something on her iPad, I regret it.

"Hey, sweetie. Going somewhere nice?" she asks, taking in my outfit. It's nothing exciting, just jeans and a sweater but she seems to approve, not that I need it.

"Mall with Ruby," I reply coldly. She's tried to talk to me a couple of times about this whole Kyle thing but I'm not interested. As far as I'm concerned, she never should have agreed to help Kane.

"That will be nice. Are you getting something for the party tonight?"

"I don't know," I snap.

She lets out a long breath. "Harley, I know you're angry with me—"

"Angry? I'm more than angry, Mom. I'm angry at you for helping, but I do understand to a point. But the fact you didn't tell me..."

"I know and I was wrong. Everything's okay though, isn't it? He was here last night with Zayn from what I've heard, and he seems to be settling in okay."

"Yeah, sure. Everything's great." *If you consider him trying to ruin my life and get revenge for me sending him away in the first place then yeah, everything is just perfect.*

"He was always such a good boy, a great influence for Zayn. I'm glad they're reconnecting again."

"A good influence?" I can't keep the words in, disbelief drips from them as they pour from my lips.

Mom's eyes hold mine, waiting for me to say more, to explain myself but thankfully, the sound of Ruby's car pulling up outside is the perfect excuse I need to run.

"Ruby's here. I'll see you later."

I'm out of the door before she even has a chance to say goodbye.

"Perfect timing," I mutter, falling down into Ruby's passenger seat.

"Why, what's wrong?" She glances over, concern pulling her brows together.

"Ugh, just Mom trying to talk to me."

"You still ignoring her?"

"I'm not ignoring her, I'm just avoiding her."

"Okay, same difference. Just talk to her. Get it all out."

"I thought you'd probably figured out by now that I don't really want to talk about it."

"I know, but it might help. Your mom just wants to help."

"That's how I ended up in this mess in the first place," I mutter. If she didn't feel the need to try to bail every kid out then I wouldn't be living this nightmare.

"So go on, what happened?"

"You're really not going to let me get away with this, are you?"

"Not a chance in hell, Har. Tell all then I'll buy you one of those caramel latte macchiatos you like to make up for it."

"Nathan was really sweet. Everything he set up for last night was perfect," I confess. "But I screwed up." Ruby glances over but she doesn't say anything, she just lets me spew it all out until the events that led up to me leaving Justin's house early are out in the open.

"I think you're making a bigger deal out of it than necessary. He sounds like he understood."

"Yeah, and that makes me feel even more awful. He totally got it. All he wanted me to do was stay but I was mortified."

"The time just wasn't right."

"But how do you know when it is?" I ask, already knowing what her answer is going to be.

"No idea. You just know."

"What if he's not the one I should be giving it up to?" I whisper, not wanting to even say the words out loud for fear of them being true.

"Then you need to end it with him if that's what you really think."

"No, it's not what I think. It's just... I don't know. I like him, Rubes. I really like him. He's sweet, and kind and caring, and—"

"Not what you want," she finishes for me.

"No, he's exactly what I want," I argue.

"Okay, so he's not what you need."

My lips part to respond but I slam them shut again before I say something I could very well regret.

"So what happened after? You said he was snooping but I saw him coming down the stairs. He wasn't just up there snooping." She looks over and raises a brow at me in question.

"He may have finished what Nathan started," I admit quietly.

"Harley!" she squeals.

"I know, I know. I'm the worst person in the world." I slam my closed fists down on my thighs in frustration at myself. "He was just there and he was saying all these awful things and I just—"

"Couldn't' help yourself."

"Yeah, how'd you kn—Ash."

"Like I said before, the good ones aren't all they're made out to be. The bad ones however…"

"Man, this is a mess. I hate him, Ruby. Hate him."

"What happened, Harley? Like, what really happened that night?"

I shake my head, even after telling her everything that went down last night, I'm still not ready to go there.

"It was just a party that got out of control. I panicked and called the cops and he was the one that got caught."

"Why? What happened to everyone else?"

"They ran."

"So why didn't he?"

"B-because he was h-helping me." My voice cracks with emotion as I remember snippets from the end of that night.

"Okay so if he helped you then why do you hate him?"

"Because… because I do. I'm not going near him again though. Last night was a mistake of epic proportions."

"You know he's going to be there tonight, right?"

"Yeah, and so is my boyfriend, and I intend on making

things up to him."

"Har, you can't do it just because you think you owe him."

"I'm not," I argue. "I'm doing it because I want to."

"Just please... please don't do something that you're going to regret."

"I think it might already be a little late for that."

Ruby gives me one of her hard stares before letting out a long sigh and climbing from the car. I don't blame her, I don't really want to have the conversation either.

I follow her lead and meet her at the hood of her car.

"Retail therapy fixes everything. Come on, let's go find you something killer to wear tonight to knock everyone's socks off."

"I thought we were shopping for you," I argue.

"We're shopping for everyone. Hell, we can buy a dress for Poppy if we find one."

"Sounds good." I thread my arm through hers as we make our way to the mall. "Thanks for this."

"Hey, what are best friends for if not to force you to tell all your secrets and give you bad advice."

"You haven't given me bad advice," I insist.

"Maybe not. But after what Ash and I went through, I'm surprised you're listening to me."

"Rubes, that boy loves you something fierce. I'd kill for that."

"Well, lucky for you, you might not have to. The two boys who want you, on the other hand, that could get bloody."

"Nathan's not like that. I don't think he's a fighter."

"And the other one?"

"Umm..." I think back to our childhoods in the Creek, of the many fights I'd witness that involved Zayn, Kyle, and their other friends. "Yeah, he is."

"I hope Nathan knows he needs to watch his back because a boy from the Creek is about to wipe the smile off his preppy little face."

"Rubes, is that really necessary?" I mutter, not thrilled with the visual emerging in my head of the two of them going a round over me. "There will be no fighting."

"We'll see. Oh, look, that dress is perfect," she says, changing the subject so fast I almost get whiplash as she points at a little red dress in the window of one of my favorite stores. "You have to try it on. Nathan will come in his pants just looking at you."

I snort a laugh but allow her to thread her fingers through mine and drag me to the store when she sets about finding the dress along with an armful of others for both of us to try.

We find ourselves a dressing room big enough for the both of us and set about finding the perfect dresses for tonight.

"The red one first," she demands as I pull my jeans from my ankles.

"Fine." Unsnapping my bra, because I already know there's no chance in hell of wearing one with how low cut it is, I drop the fabric to the floor and pull the dress from the hanger.

"Okay, what do you—fucking hell, Ruby," I gasp, taking in the marks on her chest. "Jesus, was he trying to actually eat you or something?"

Her cheeks flush as a wide smile pulls at her lips.

"Pretty much. I'm pretty sure I've got carpet burn on my back from the carpet in Zayn's den too." She turns around and sure as shit, there are bright red marks across her shoulder blades.

"Jesus. Can you two actually keep your hands off each other?"

"Sure can." She gives me a sly wink before looking down at the dress wrapped around me. "You're buying that," she states before continuing to pull the dress up that's hanging around her waist.

11
____

KYLE

"What the fuck was that for?" I bark at Ashton as the sting from his hit eases. I rub at the side of my head, wondering what the hell I ever did to him.

"You fucking cockblocked me last night," he grumbles as we set off from my house on the running route I've found myself over the past few days.

The last two people I expected to find when I got to the bottom of the Hunter's stairs last night were a satisfied looking Ash and Ruby.

Clearly, they'd made use of the empty room I'd left them in. The sight of the two of them looking so happy did nothing for my mood as I got farther and farther away from Harley.

"'Evening," I mumbled, walking straight past them and out the front door. I knew if I hung around in that house a second longer than necessary then I would turn around and walk straight back up those stairs and finish the job I'd started.

Their shocked stares burned into me as I passed them. Ruby wanted to say something, that much was obvious when she tried to step forward, but Ash gripped her tighter and kept her into his side.

"I refused to let Ruby go up and see if Harley was alright and as punishment, she wouldn't put out."

"Wow, however did you cope," I deadpan.

"What happened?"

"What do you mean, what happened?"

"Well, you went up to see her, right? We know she was back, we saw her car."

"Yeah, I saw her." He glances over at me as we continue running side by side. "We just... hashed a few things out."

"Riiiight."

"What?"

"Oh nothing, we *saw* you, remember. Whatever it was you were hashing out... well..."

"What the fuck ever, man. Harley and I... we have unfinished business."

"Yeah well, I hope you finished her business better than she did yours."

"You're an asshole."

"Takes one to know one."

Picking up my speed, I leave him behind for a bit as he chuckles at me.

"So what's the deal with you two then?" he asks when he easily catches up with me.

I blow out of breath. "Some shit went down before I got carted off that night."

"She made the call, right?"

"Yeah," I sigh. "My crew, they... they took things too far, Harley got caught up in the crossfire and I paid the price."

I slow to a stop when the ocean emerges in the distance and together we walk down onto the sand and sit our asses down in one of the secluded dunes.

"Okay. So you're hating on her for calling the cops?"

"Yeah and..." I trail off, really not wanting to talk about this.

"And..."

"I don't know, man." I pull my legs up in front of me and rest my forearms across them as I look out at the sun sparkling on the ocean before us.

It's sure not Harrow Creek.

I shake my head as images of that place fill my mind. It's really like hell compared to here.

"You want her?" His question makes my heart lurch in my chest.

Yeah, I want her. I want to fucking hurt her. But I don't tell him that.

"She's Zayn's little sister, even if I did, she's off-limits."

He looks over at me, his amused eyes holding mine for a few seconds.

"I'm the wrong person to talk to about off-limits. I'm fucking my stepsister."

I shake my head at him. "How'd that come about anyway?" I ask, glad to have a way to turn this conversation away from me.

"Pretty much the same as you right now. I hated her, wanted to hurt her. Turns out... she's pretty fucking awesome."

"I never said—"

"You didn't need to. I see it, man."

"Right," I mutter, ripping my eyes from him and back out to the horizon.

"Just... just try not to do something you're going to regret. They can only forgive so much."

"I don't want her fucking forgiveness."

"I know, I'm just saying."

We fall into an easy silence as we watch the waves crash onto the beach. The sound of kids playing in the distance filters down to us, and I wonder what it might have been like to grow up here with a decent family.

I blow out a sigh and it seems that Ashton knows exactly what I'm thinking.

"It's a different life here, eh?"

"Yeah, you could say that."

We haven't really talked much about his past but I know enough to know that it's probably why we're drawn together. We know how hard life can be. We've seen the deprivation, the desperation, the sheer hopelessness. We've also experienced the loss.

"You been back yet?" he asks, I assume about the Creek.

"Nah. I have no interest in going back. My life there was over the second I was put in the back of that cop car."

"No other family?"

I shake my head, not that he's looking at me. "Parents died when we were young. Gran died while I was away. It's just me and Kane."

"That's shit."

"It is what it is. Things can only get better, right?"

"What about those you left behind. You got busted for possession, doesn't someone want their stash back?"

His question makes my blood run cold.

I know it's not even been a week yet, but even so, I'm amazed I haven't seen or heard from anyone. Gray never was one to let things go and I went down with my pockets full of his fucking blow.

"Yeah, I can't imagine he's forgotten." I could go to the Creek and find him, save me waiting but like fuck am I willingly walking back into the lion's den.

"Well, I've got your back, man. Should you need it."

I look over at him. "Thanks. I appreciate that."

"You're coming to this party tonight, right?"

"Hell yeah, I been locked up for a fucking year. Ain't no way I'm passing up that chance, man."

After a few more minutes, I push to stand, brushing the sand from my ass.

I nod at him. "Ready to head back?"

"Yep, let's go."

————

Kane is gone all day. I still have no fucking idea what he's doing, not that I have a chance to ask seeing as he's never here.

I spend the afternoon doing homework before jumping in the shower again and getting ready for this party.

Memories of some of our Creek parties fill my mind, and I wonder how different these parties here will be. I hope a lot, seeing as the last one I went to ended up with me being arrested.

I'm shoving my feet into my sneakers when a car horn sounds out. Grabbing my cell, I make my way out before locking up the house and jogging down to the road.

Zayn's car is idling at the sidewalk.

"'Evening," I mutter as I drop down into his empty passenger seat.

"Where's Poppy?"

"She's getting ready with the girls. They're going to meet us there later."

I nod, excitement erupting in my belly at the thought of seeing Harley again.

It might only have been a few days, but as Zayn drives us through Rosewood, I realize that I'm already starting to get used to the place.

At first, seeing the luxurious houses set back from the roads was weird. I was used to shitty trailers that were dumped on any bit of land anyone could occupy.

"It's weird, right?" Zayn asks, clearly seeing what's

capturing my attention. "It's like a different world. It's good though."

"Yeah, I'm starting to see that. I can understand why Kane thought this was a good idea."

"Anywhere would have been better than going back to the Creek."

"Too fucking true."

"You still go back to see your old man?"

"Sadly. Stupid fuck still refuses to leave."

"I guess there are people that like living like that."

"Yeah, fucking idiots."

"Any word from Gray?" he asks, and just like earlier the sound of his name gives me pause.

"No, you?"

"Nah, man. They all cut ties with me long before you went down."

Guilt swamps me because I was one of them. I cut ties the second Zayn left the Creek. Although it wasn't through choice.

"Listen... I'm so—"

"You don't need to do that, Ky. I get it."

"Yeah, well. It still sucks."

"I left. I knew I was starting over. I wasn't expecting to continue to fit in."

I blow out a breath. "I missed you, man."

"Aw, little Legend, you getting all soft on me."

"It's better than being hard for you," I deadpan.

"Save it for the fucking cheerleaders, man. Speaking of, you wanna know the best ones to play with?"

"You got it. I've been stuck with my hand for a fucking year. I need all the info, man."

He laughs beside me before starting on who I do and don't want to make a move on tonight. I make all the right noises in the right places to make him think I'm interested. But in truth, there's only one girl I'm searching out tonight and I don't give a fuck if she thinks she's there with her boyfriend. He needs to be taught a lesson as much as she does for allowing her to leave in tears last night. Fucking pussy.

There are cars already filling Justin's driveway when we pull up and Zayn parks his car.

"Right, let's get you used to partying Rosewood style."

"As long as it ends better than the last party I went to, I'm good."

Zayn claps me on the shoulder as we make our way to the front door.

There are people everywhere, most I don't recognize, but then I've only been at Rosewood High for three days, so I'm hardly surprised. I follow Zayn through to the kitchen where we find the majority of the senior year football team.

"Hunter, my man," Justin slurs, clearly having started the party earlier. "Legend." He lifts a bottle of beer toward me and I happily take it and knock the top off.

"Cheers, man," Zayn mutters, accepting his.

"This is Nathan, my cousin." He nods toward a preppy looking kid in a perfectly pressed white Henley. Exactly what I expected.

Zayn nods at him but I notice that the scowl never leaves his face as their eye contact holds.

After a few seconds, Nathan tips his drink to his lips somewhat nervously.

Yeah, I'd be scared too, motherfucker.

The beer soon turns into vodka and someone produces a baggie of weed that soon gets passed around once we've made ourselves comfortable in Justin's den.

I have no idea what it is with these kids and having their own dens. Kane and I didn't even have our own fucking bedrooms growing up. But as I bring the J to my lips and take a hit, I can't say I'm too fucking bothered right now.

"Fuck, that's good," I say to no one in particular.

"Ethan always gets the good shit," Zayn mutters from beside me.

I pass it over before pushing from the couch. "I'm going for a piss."

"Down the hall on the right," someone helpfully points out, clearly listening to our conversation.

I make my way out of the room, the vodka I've drank starts to make my head swim a little but I revel in the sensation of checking out of real life for a few hours. I fucking need it.

There are kids everywhere out here as I make my way down the hallway. Of course, there's a fucking line. Seeing a door for outside, I opt for that instead. I'm sure Justin won't give a shit if I water his flowers a little.

There are kids outside crowding around the pool, laughing and dancing as they enjoy themselves.

I slip into the darkness at the bottom of the yard and do my thing as kids splash about in the water behind me.

Once I've finished, I turn around and watch them from my hidden spot for a few minutes and wonder what it must be like to live a life where you have nothing to worry about.

Girls in bikinis flirt with the guys who are splashing about with them and others stand off to the side dancing and grinding together to the beat of the music.

My fingers twitch at my sides, desperate to have a girl moving against me like that.

I have no idea how long I stand there like some fucked-up peeping Tom, but eventually my need for another drink and another hit get the better of me.

I push through the bushes and slip back inside to locate the kitchen.

I fight my way through the crowd at the door and eventually get to the counter where the bottles of liquor were lined up earlier in the evening.

I help myself to a bottle before turning to rest back against the counter as I twist the top off.

I find Justin, Prep Boy, and a few others passing around hallucinogens.

I watch as a couple stick them straight into their mouths but Preppy and a few others hesitate.

"You want in?" Justin asks me when he notices that I'm watching.

"Nah, man. I'm good. You all have fun though." I turn to Nathan who's still holding his looking very much like the prep boy that he is. "Eat up, I hear they do wonders for your sex life," I quip. "You've got a girl, right?"

His lips pull into a smile. "Yeah, she's on her way."

My stomach clenches at his words.

"Better take that and show her a good time then," I say, hoping like fuck that I know what I'm doing.

"Come on then," he says, nodding toward Justin's hand.

"Fuck it. To a good night."

12

HARLEY

I hold my dress down as I step from Ruby's car in my attempt to not flash Ash or any of the kids that are loitering out the front of Justin's place.

"Come on, girl. I need another drink," Ruby shouts, already three sheets to the wind.

"I'm going to be carrying your ass home tonight, aren't I?" Ash mutters from behind us as Ruby and Poppy each take one of my arms and we walk toward the front door together.

"If you're lucky," she shoots over her shoulder. "You can totally take advantage of me."

I can't help but laugh when he complains because I know full well that she hasn't put out since seeing Kyle emerging from my room last night. And it's not for lack of trying on his part either as evidenced by the fact he walked straight into her bathroom while she was showering earlier. I didn't need to see her smug face to know she got hers while she left him hanging. He looked murderous after she kicked him out and forced him to return to his own room with blue balls.

He might act like a grumpy fucker, but secretly, I think he's enjoying the little game. I know that Ruby sure is.

"Hey, Ash," she says, stopping and turning to face him.

"Did I tell you that I'm not wearing any panties?" She pulls her dress up her thighs a little as if she's going to flash him and anyone else who might be looking in our direction—probably every guy in earshot thanks to that little announcement.

"Don't you fucking dare," he growls.

"You'll have to find out later then. Be a good boy and go and get us all a drink."

He rolls his eyes at her but as we walk into the house and head for Justin's den, he goes for the kitchen, probably more for a drink of his own than one for Ruby. I think he's going to need one.

"At fucking last," Zayn calls the second we walk into the room. He's up off the couch in a heartbeat and has Poppy in his arms. "Fuck, you look hot," he mutters quietly, although not quietly enough for me not to hear.

"Ugh, puh-lease."

"Fuck off, Har. Go find your prep boy."

"At least he's got some class," I mutter, stepping away from them and doing as he suggests.

"Are you sure about that?" he calls from behind me, but I pay him little mind.

"Thank you," I say to Ash when he appears with four Solo cups in hand.

"Don't get used to it."

"It's amazing what guys will do for some action," I say as he walks toward where Ruby is talking to some of the squad.

I make my way through the house looking for Nathan. I get the attention of more than a few guys as I go proving that Ruby was right about this dress. And if it weren't for the fact Nathan was here, or the fear that Kyle is too, I might be revelling in the attention. But I'm not, and I wonder if once again my dress choice was a massive mistake.

"Whoa, baby Hunter, has your brother seen you?" Justin

slurs, clearly off his face, the second I step into the kitchen. "You look smoking, baby girl."

"Shut up, J. And get your eyes off my tits."

He holds his hands up in defeat but his eyes never leave the low cut of my dress. Whatever.

Scanning the room, I finally find Nathan but my eyes almost bug out of my head not only when I take in the darkness in his but also who he's standing next to.

Of course fucking Kyle found him before me.

Nathan's smile lights up his face when he sees me, and just like every other guy, his eyes drop down my body, his mouth hanging open as he does.

"Hey," I say, sliding up to him and turning my back on Kyle. "You having fun?"

"Harley, fuck." I can barely make out the words, they're so slurred.

"How much have you had?" I ask with a laugh.

"Enough to tell you that you look fucking banging and to demand that you dance with me right fucking now."

He wraps his arms around my waist and pulls me into his body and without second thought, he slams his lips down on mine.

The taste of alcohol fills my mouth as his tongue plunges past my lips. I eagerly return his kiss, glad that there's no awkwardness after last night. His hands slide down from my waist until he's gripping my ass and pulling my body tight against his.

I feel him grow hard against my stomach as our kiss continues and heat surges through my body knowing that I'm turning him on right now. Well, I tell myself that it's that and not the stare that's burning into my back from the person I refused to acknowledge as I walked over here.

"Let's go dance," I whisper when he finally pulls back from my lips.

Reaching up, I rub at the lipstick on his face but it barely budges.

He wraps his arm around my waist and leads me from the room.

My skin is still tingling with Kyle's attention and just before we turn the corner, I look back over my shoulder, a smile playing on my lips.

My stomach flips at the murderous expression on his face but it doesn't stop me. Last night should never have happened, but that's on him, not me. He shouldn't have been in my room. He shouldn't have put his hands on me.

With the vodka from Ruby's warming my belly and flowing through my veins, it's easier to push it all to the back of my head and just enjoy myself. And seeing him there with the muscle in his neck pulsing and his hands curled into tight fists, I'm certainly enjoying myself.

Lifting my arm, I flip him off over my shoulder before I disappear from sight.

We move as one unit toward where the pounding bass is coming from and the second we're in what's usually Justin's parents' living room, we join the dancing crowd and Nathan pulls me into his arms.

It's a million miles from the little love shack that Nathan created for me last night and a thrill races through me that hopefully it won't end in the disastrous way either.

"I didn't think you were going to come," he slurs in my ear as he moves to the music although totally out of rhythm.

"Fashionably late," I whisper-shout back.

"And it was worth it. You look good enough to eat." He lifts his arm and encourages me to twirl for him.

The full skirt hemline of my dress flares out as I do and his eyes feast on my bare legs.

"I need you so fucking bad," he groans in my ear as he pulls me back into his body and grinds his length into my stomach.

Gone is the good boy who was concerned about my

feelings last night and in his place is the kind of guy that I'm more used to handling.

I look at him, his eyes are totally blown.

"What have you taken?" I ask him.

"I dunno, but I feel fucking good right now."

"Nathan, I do—" I don't get to continue because he takes advantage of my parted lips and slips his tongue between them once again.

His kiss is wet and dirty, and I can't help but drown in it.

The alcohol surges around me and I forget that we're in a room with tons of others and I kiss him as if we're once again alone.

I have no idea what song is playing, the only thing I can focus on is him and the way he makes me feel. I might not be burning quite as hot as I was against my bedroom door last night but it's hella close and I'll take it.

"I missed you last night," he groans in my ear after kissing across my jaw. "Tell me that you'll stay longer tonight."

Draining what's left of the drink Ash gave me however long ago, I drop the empty cup to a shelf beside us as I turn to look at Nathan once again.

His eyes are hooded with lust, his cock still solid between us but he kinda looks like he's fighting to stay awake right now.

"I'll stay as long as you want me to."

The smile that pulls at his lips melt me and when the song changes, I twist in his arms and push my ass into his crotch.

I regret the move the second I look to the doorway and find that we've got an audience.

I shake my head at Kyle as I drop down low and rub all the way back up Nathan's body.

Kyle's lips purse in anger and the Solo cup that was in his hand collapses under the force of his fist.

I smile at him as I lift my hands behind me once I'm at full height and thread my fingers through Nathan's hair, twisting my head to the side to find his more than eager lips.

His hands slip up my waist until his thumbs brush over my nipples.

I gasp at the sensation, my belly clenching in desire and heat flooding my core.

My eyes are closed as I absorb the sensations zapping through me but all my muscles freeze the second a body presses against my front and another pair of hands land on my waist.

"What the—" My words are cut off as I stare into a very familiar angry pair of eyes. "Get the fuck off me."

He rips his stare from me and looks to Nathan who's still moving against my back, seemingly oblivious to the sudden tension between me and Kyle.

"Good shit, right?" Kyle asks Nathan.

"Yeah, man. I feel fucking epic."

"Hell, yeah," Kyle agrees, but his words hold no sincerity. He's lying. His eyes might be dark, but that's only anger, whatever Nathan has taken, Kyle hasn't had the same.

"What the hell are you doing?" I ask when he rolls his hips against me, moving in time with the music, unlike the guy behind me who seems to be dancing to his own song. "What have you given him?"

"Me?" he asks innocently, as if my question offends him. "Justin was the one who brought drugs to the party. I learned my lesson the hard way, Kitten."

If Nathan has any cares about me being sandwiched between him and Kyle, then he shows no sign of it. His hips continue to move as his cock grinds against my ass and his fingers dig into my hips, holding me close.

"You need to back off," I warn Kyle.

"Kitten, don't be like that. We both know how much you like two guys at once."

"Fuck you, Kyle." I slam my hands down on his chest but if it hurts at all then he doesn't so much as flinch and it pisses me off.

"Come on now. We both know you're wetter now I'm touching you instead of that pussy."

"Never. And he's right there."

"Kitten, he's so high right now he has no fucking clue what's going on."

"I can't believe you. I—" My words are cut off as he leans over me, his hard chest against my face as he whispers something in Nathan's ear.

I breathe a sigh of relief when Kyle takes a step back.

His eyes hold mine for a few seconds before they run down my body. He sucks his bottom lip into his mouth, his teeth biting down on it. The sight shouldn't affect me as much as it does but I can't stop the heat that surges through my body.

He lifts his backward cap and smooths down his hair before replacing it once more.

He blows me a kiss before looking up at Nathan and nodding.

I don't move until Kyle has left the room and disappeared from my sight.

Spinning in Nathan's arms, I stare up at him, my eyes narrowed in curiosity.

"What the hell was that?"

"Just enjoying myself, babe. Let's go get a drink, eh?"

My need for a breather means that I agree. We find our way to the kitchen and he pours me a vodka before helping himself to the rest of the bottle. Justin walks up to him and Nathan turns away from me for a few seconds but I think nothing of it as I sip at my drink and watch a few girls bounce off each other as they attempt to find the front door.

I have no idea what time it is, but I know it's late. We didn't get here until well after the party had started, taking way too much time getting ready. The bottle of vodka Ruby had went down far too easily as we did our hair and makeup, and we ended up having way too much fun at our own little party for three.

"Let's go somewhere quieter," Nathan suggests, turning back to me and wrapping his hand around the back of my neck.

"Y-yeah, okay," I agree. I came here with the intention of getting him alone and making up for last night, but I wasn't expecting him to be quite so off his head and that we'd actually be able to hold a conversation that he might remember.

"Come on." He threads his fingers through mine and drags me down the hallway and then up the stairs.

"Nathan, I'm not sure—"

"Shhh," he slurs. "It's okay. No funny business. Just me and you."

His lips curl into a knee-weakening smile, the exact one that pulled me to him that first night at Ethan's house and I follow with my half-full cup in my other hand.

He leads me to a doorway at the far end of the hall and we both slip inside the guest bedroom which I assume he's claimed as his.

"Mmmm," he mumbles as he wraps his arms around me from behind and drops his lips to my neck. "This is better. Just the two of us."

The music from downstairs vibrates the floor beneath our feet but still, he pulls his cell from his pocket and syncs it to the speaker sitting on the side.

He twists the cap on the bottle in his hand and takes a huge swig, his eyes on me the entire time. They drop down my body, eating me up and I remember why I wanted to see him tonight.

"That dress, babe. It's insane."

"Thanks." I step toward him and run my hand up his

chest. "I'm really sorry about last night." I brush my lips against his and he immediately accepts my kiss.

His hand brushes down my back until he grips on to my ass. A move that I'm sure he never would have done last night without whatever influence he's under.

He walks us backward until he lowers down on the couch by the window and pulls me on top of him so I'm straddling his lap.

"I really like you, Harley," he admits, ripping his lips from mine and once again lifting the bottle to his and swallowing down a generous shot.

He offers it to me, and I take it from him. The neat vodka burns the second it hits my throat and I instantly regret it, although after a second when my stomach starts to warm, I change my mind.

"I like you too." I take another swig before handing it back and bending down to kiss his neck.

His hands slip up my thighs until he's cupping my bare ass and helping me to grind down on his crotch, the bottle of vodka abandoned on the couch.

"Fuck, babe. You keep doing that and I'm gonna come in my pants," he slurs happily.

"Can't have that, can we?" His eyes flash at my words and his lips curl in excitement as my fingers search out his waistband.

"Harley?"

"Sssh," I whisper, pressing two fingers to his lips, although I miss on my first attempt. "Let me make it up to you."

I pop the button on his jeans but before I get any farther, I hear the click of the door behind me.

I suck in a breath, knowing exactly who has just joined us. I don't need to turn to look, I can sense him. The tingles that run down my spine only exist when *he* looks at me.

"What are you doing?" I ask without even acknowledging

him.

"Coming to join the party, Kitten. I'm all for having a bit of fun, but there we're a few too many people downstairs, don't you think?"

"Y-you need to l-leave," I stutter when the heat of his chest hits my bare back.

"Don't be like that, Kitten." His fingers drift around my exposed throat and my eyes involuntarily flutter closed at this familiar touch.

"Kyle." His name is no more than a warning growl as he presses his front harder against me.

"As you were, Kitten." His fingers trail down my arm and my eyes fall closed at his touch.

Damn vodka.

"You need to leave," I repeat, knowing that this situation is going to lead to disaster. "You shouldn't be in here."

"Your boy here doesn't seem to have an issue."

Ripping my eyes open, I look at Nathan. My breath catches in my throat when I see his eyes are closed.

He's passed out.

Thankfully his chest is heaving, telling me that he's still alive.

"What has he taken?"

"Just some acid. He'll be fine once he's slept it off."

His thumb caresses my pulse point and I swallow down my need to give into him.

"Kyle," I force out, trying to sound as strong as possible. "You need to leave."

"Why? I don't think your boy is very interested in what you have to offer right now. Unless you've got a thing for sucking him off when he's passed out."

"I thought it was you that was into that," I snap.

"Kitten," he growls, lifting me from Nathan's lap and putting me back on my feet, although he doesn't spin me around. "If you really believe I did anything to you while you were out of it, then you're stupider than I thought. You have no reason to hate me, Kitten. Well… not yet anyway."

"W-what are you g-going to do?" I try to twist out of his arms but the one he has locked around my waist tightens.

"We're going to have some fun, Kitten."

"But Nathan—"

"Nathan needs to learn who you belong to. Because… allow me to let you in on a little secret," he whispers in my ear, making my entire body shudder as his breath caresses my neck.

I rest my head back against his shoulder and close my eyes, the room spins with the amount I've drank but I don't focus on that. Instead, I focus on his touch. It's too good not to.

"It's me," he breathes. "You belong to me."

"Fuck you, Kyle." I fight to get out of his grip and to my surprise, he lets me. But I soon realize my mistake because my back hits the wall beside the couch and his hand wraps around my throat, pinning me in place.

"Yeah, that's exactly what I was thinking."

His eyes drop down my body, locking on the two small red triangles that cover my breasts, and I glance over at Nathan.

He's not really intending on doing this with him in the room, is he?

I don't know why I ask that question. The answer is freaking obvious and staring me in the face.

"Yeah, Kitten. I am," he answers, making me wonder if that question slipped past my lips or not. "And if he happens to wake up, he's going to learn a very important lesson."

He lifts the hand that's not around my throat and he trails it along the fabric from my collarbone all the way down over the swell of my breast and down to where it meets the waistband a little above my belly button.

"This dress," he murmurs, almost as if he's talking to

himself. "It was a fucking brave move, Kitten. You walked in here tonight asking for trouble, didn't you?"

"No, I walked in intending on spending the night with my boyfriend who you've fucking drugged."

"Whoa, careful there, Kitten." His eyes find mine. "I didn't give your *boyfriend* anything. He took that shit of his own accord because he's a fucking idiot."

"No, he's not. He's just—"

"Not looking after you properly. I mean, if he was, then you wouldn't have been thinking about me a minute ago when you were grinding down on his lap."

"I wasn't—"

"Don't lie to me, Kitten." His grip on me tightens as my lips part on a gasp.

"I-I'm not."

"Suuure," he drawls. "Let's just pretend that he gets you wet, shall we? Just for the fun of it. We'll pretend that these are hard and begging to be sucked on because of him." He circles one of my nipples with his forefinger and it puckers harder for him. "And we both know your panties are ruined right now. Or are you going to try to lie about that too?"

"Kyle," I whimper as he continues teasing me.

"Beg me all you want. I'm not leaving this room until I've proved you wrong."

"Go on then," I say, holding my hands out to my sides. "Do your worst."

An evil yet hungry smirk curls at his lips.

He takes a step back, releasing my throat and allowing me to take a deep breath. My eyes dart to the door but I don't get to take a step.

"Don't even think about it."

Swallowing down my nerves, I look back to Kyle as he swipes up what's left of the bottle of vodka that Nathan abandoned.

He sits down on the edge of the bed as he twists the cap

and lifts the bottle to his lips.

I can't rip my eyes away as he swallows, his Adam's apple bobs and the muscles ripple.

Without putting the cap back on, he rests his elbows on his spread legs and hangs the bottle between, looking up at me expectantly through his lashes.

"W-what?"

"You owe me, Kitten."

My fingers twitch against the wall they're pressed against as what he means dawns on my alcohol-filled brain.

"Go fuck yourself, Kyle."

"See... that's the thing. I've been locked away on my own for a long time... *because of you.*"

My lips part to respond, to tell him that it's not my fault, but it is. I made that call, I am the one to blame.

"You were more than willing to help him out a few minutes ago." He flashes a look to Nathan before bringing his eyes back to me and raising a brow. "So," he says, lowering the bottle to the floor and resting back on his palms.

My heart is like a runaway train in my chest as I stand there staring at him.

His eyes hold mine impatiently as he sucks his bottom lip into his mouth. I mimic the move, my mouth watering for a taste of him.

The kiss he gave me last night... it wasn't enough.

My fingers curl against the wall as I run my eyes over his jaw, down the fitted black t-shirt he's wearing that shows off every line of muscle he's rocking beneath, to the little sliver of skin that's exposed before the black waistband of his boxers and then his dark jeans.

My eyes linger on the bulge at this crotch and tingles erupt in my belly that he's turned on by me. Just like I am him. Our hate is addictive, thrilling. Dangerous. But that doesn't mean I'm about to walk away, if anything it just spurs me on.

"Harley?" he asks, his deep voice rumbling through me, forcing my eyes back up to his face.

I study him for a moment. He's still so much like the sweet boy I remember from my past. But the changes from the past year are obvious to me. The edge, the vicious words and barbed touches. They're all new and I know they're my fault.

I might not know what happened to him while he was in juvie. And I might never know. But I do know that it changed him. *I* changed him and I can't help but wonder if I might have entirely broken that little boy who had so much potential despite the shithole we lived in.

"My patience will only last so long, Kitten."

With my eyes locked on his, I take a step forward. An accomplished smirk appears on his lips but the sight only makes my insides flutter with anticipation.

In a heartbeat, I'm standing between his legs, drawn to him like a moth to a flame.

He sits up, bringing his chest to my stomach and runs his palms up the back of my thighs until he finds my bare ass.

"I swear to God, if you're not wearing any—" He moves his hands higher and his words are cut off when he finds the waistband of my thong. "Did he touch you?" he growls.

I'm desperate to look away from his electric gaze, but I can't and my head stays bowed so I can keep the connection with him.

I shake my head so subtly I'm not sure he can see it.

"Kitten," he says softly. "Did that motherfucker touch you tonight?"

His little fingers run down the scrap of fabric between my ass until they're right over my entrance. A growl rumbles up his throat as he discovers that the fabric is soaked.

Leaning forward, although still keeping his eyes on mine, his lips part right above my left breast and he sucks the skin into his mouth.

"Kyle," I gasp as he sucks to the point of pain before sinking his teeth into me.

"M-i-n-e."

"You're fucking crazy," I squeal, looking down at the angry mark on my breast.

"Yeah, and whose fucking fault is that, eh Kitten?" Before I get a chance to answer, his fingers wrap around my panties and they're ripped from my body.

I gasp as the fabric is peeled away from me and the cool air of the room surrounds my heated flesh.

"I think you like me a little crazy though, eh?" Lifting his hand, this time up the front of my dress, he runs a finger through my folds, rubbing my wetness around my clit.

"Oh God." Reaching out to find something to hold on to, my hand lands on his hat. Not happy with that, I knock it off his head and thread my fingers through his hair and grip tight enough that I know it'll hurt.

His eyes flash up to mine, excitement shining in them. "Give me all the pain you can muster, Kitten. It'll only make me harder."

Without thinking, I pull my other hand back and slap it across his cheek. The hit is so hard his head snaps to the side despite the fact I'm holding his hair.

A growl rumbles up his throat. "You're going to fucking pay for that."

"I already thought I was. This is a punishment after all, right?"

Before I know what's happening, he pushed on my shoulders so hard that I find myself on my knees before him.

"I was going to take it easy on you," he says softly as if he's that sweet kid I once knew, but I can see the evil intent shining in his eyes. "But you fucked up. More than once."

"W-what are you—" The vodka flowing through my system makes my brain misfire as I stare up at him.

"You look right at home on your knees begging for forgiveness, you know that, Hunter?"

"Fuck you, Legend." I narrow my eyes at him, hoping it shows just how much I hate him right now despite the desire that's burning through me.

He fucking knows it too.

He reaches out and cups my cheek, the move is almost tender, and my eyes shutter at his contact.

"You ever sucked anyone's cock before, Kitten?"

I once again shake my head so subtly I have no idea if he sees or feels it.

"Good. You'll remember this." He slips his thumb into my mouth and I can't help but wrap my lips around it and suck. "Fuck."

His eyes close for a beat and I realize just how much power I have over him right now.

I could get up and walk away and leave him here alone with his tented pants and my passed out boyfriend, or I could do something I've imagined more than once and take even more control from him.

I smile up at him. My newfound power going to my head. I might be the one on my knees right now begging for forgiveness but the second we do this, I'm the one calling the shots and he damn well knows it.

Pulling his hand from me, he rests back on his palms once more, offering himself up to me.

"Go on then. I don't have all night."

I grind my teeth as I stare at him. My head spins with the vodka, the desire, the hate. I have no idea which is the strongest but I also know that I'm not about to walk away, like I know I should.

Something in the back of my mind begs me to look over at Nathan, but I can't. If I see him lying there behind me then it'll change everything. And right now, I don't want to change a fucking thing.

13

KYLE

I stare down at her, my heart slamming against my ribs and my cock aching and she tentatively reaches out and runs her hands up my thighs.

Her touch burns like I was expecting it to and my mouth waters for what's to come.

I wasn't going to make her do this. But then she fucking slapped me. My cheek still burns from the hit and I resist the need to lift my hand to soothe it.

Hesitantly, she fumbles with the button at my waist. I know I could help her out and have it open in a heartbeat, but watching her is too fucking good.

"You're killing me, Kitten," I growl, making her eyes fly up to mine.

They're so dark they threaten to pull me in and drown me in their depths. And I can't deny that it's exactly where I want to be right now. Lost. Lost to her and everything she can give me.

That night. That party. It was never supposed to end the way it did. It was supposed to end exactly like this. With me making her mine despite the consequences of what her brother, or the rest of Harrow Creek, might think. I'd wanted her for too long to pass up the opportunity.

But Gray fucked it up.

Harley thinks it's her fault, and she's partly right. And while she was the one who made the call, I can't place all the blame on her. If Gray hadn't got carried away, thinking he was fucking God, then none of the events that followed would have happened.

My fingers curl in the sheets beneath me as anger slams into me. He's the one who did this to us. Who turned me into this.

I know I might be avoiding him right now. But I know it's not going to last forever, and I will never forget what he did. How he hurt both of us. I couldn't give a shit about his lost blow. That's nothing to me. The girl on her knees before me though. My future. That's fucking everything.

My stomach flips when she finally manages to open the button and pull down the zipper.

Lifting my hips to help her out, she pulls my jeans down. Her eyes lock onto my cock despite the fact it's still covered by my boxers.

I know she's a virgin. I know the reasons she ran from that motherfucker last night and the thought of being the first one she touches like this, it makes my chest swell. No matter what happens from here on out, she'll never fucking forget this.

"Scared, Kitten? I won't bite, well, not while you're down there."

She sucks in a breath, her dark eyes locking on mine once more as her warm finger brushes the skin beneath my waistband before she tugs. I lift up and she lowers the fabric until I'm exposed.

"Kyle, I—" Reaching out to cup her face once more, I rub my thumb over her cheek tenderly.

"No talking, Kitten," I warn, sliding right to the edge of the bed.

"O-okay." Sliding my hand up, I thread it through her hair and force her to look down at me.

My cock jerks under her stare and a smile plays at my lips as she gasps.

She hesitates for a second and I half expect her to twist out of my hold and run for the door. I brace myself for it because I know that if I've read her wrong and she really doesn't want this then I'll let her go. I'm not *that* guy.

But when she does move, it's not away from me.

Her hands skim up my bare thighs, her eyes still locked on my cock. Her fingers graze my length and the simple touch is enough to shoot electric sparks through my entire body.

There's no way I'm going to fucking last.

I push down the thought because right now, I don't think Harley gives a shit, and I sure fucking don't.

"Kitten," I grit out, my need for her to take me in her delicate hand is all-consuming. "Oh fuck." I release her hair and fall back on my elbows as her burning fingers wrap around my length.

My head falls back as she starts to pump me slowly, my teeth grinding as I try to get control of myself.

"Fuuuuck," I groan when I look forward once more to find her studying me. My lips part to say something but I lose all sense of myself when she moves her face closer to me.

"This what you wanted, Ky?" Her lips right over my tip, her hot breath rushing over my heated skin.

My fingers thread into her hair once more and she tenses, thinking that I'm going to force her down. I'm sure that one day soon I will do just that, but right now isn't it.

She might hate me but I'm not a total cunt.

"Harley, don't just fucking tease me."

"Why?" she breathes. "You deserve it." Her eyes hold mine, challenge shining bright in them.

"And you deserve me to thru—fuck." Her tongue laps at my tip, collecting up the precum that's beaded at the slit, cutting off my warning.

She licks at me like I'm a fucking popsicle before sucking me into her hot little mouth.

"Holy fuck. Shit, Harley." My fingers tighten in her hair to the point I must be on the verge of pulling some out but I can't help it.

It's too fucking good.

I watch as she lowers her head, taking more of me until I hit the back of her throat and she pulls off before she gags.

Her tiny hand continues to grip the base of my cock, the pressure she uses is fucking perfect, yet I know she has no idea.

"Feel better now you've got your cock in my mouth?" she asks, tilting her head to the side and running her tongue along her bottom lip. "Feel powerful?"

My chest heaves as she stares at me, her hand still working me slowly.

"Powerful? You have no fucking idea, Kitten," I growl. I think we both know who holds all the fucking power right now.

The image of her walking out and leaving me like this hits me, and my grip on her tightens even more. She should walk out, I think we both know that would be the right thing to do right now, but we also both know that she's not going to.

I sit up and pull her up to me, slamming my lips down on hers. My tongue plunges into her mouth and after a second hers joins in.

A soft moan rumbles up her throat and I swallow it down like it's mine. I want all her moans of pleasure and pleas for me.

Our kiss is dirty, our teeth clash and our bites sting. It's exactly as it fucking should be.

I suck her bottom lip into my mouth and sink my teeth into her soft flesh until I'm sure I break the skin.

"Suck me, Kitten. I want to come in your wicked little mouth."

I push her back down between my legs and she takes me back in her mouth without missing a beat, almost like she missed me.

"Fuck, yeah," I moan as I watch her head bob.

I want it to last forever, but after an embarrassingly short amount of time, I know it's coming to an end.

"Kitten," I groan, wanting her to know what's coming. She stills, so I know she's heard me but she doesn't stop.

She takes me farther back than she has so far and I lose control.

"Fuck. Fuck. Harley," I chant as my cock jerks and I come down her throat. A groan rips from me and fills the room around us as my body goes limp and my muscles quiver from the intense release that I've needed for so fucking long.

I don't realize that I've collapsed on the bed until she speaks and she sounds far away. Too fucking far away.

"Where are you—"

"I've paid my debt now, Ky."

I sit up as she backs toward the door.

"You think that's it? You think you get to suck my cock and I'll forget everything?" I stand, pulling my pants up and shake my head. "That was just the beginning, Kitten." I close the space between us in a heartbeat. My hand wraps around her throat and my lips crash to hers.

"Kyle, what are you—" I squeeze her throat, forcing her to stop talking so I can continue kissing her.

Resting my other arm against the wall beside her head, I press the length of my body against hers, tucking my thigh between her legs so I can feel her heat.

I kiss her until my lungs burn.

"This is far from over, Kitten," I whisper in her ear. "Now, are you going to play nice and do as you're told or am I going to have to make you?"

Her chest heaves against me, her small fists twisting my shirt. I'm not sure if she's aware of it but she's holding me to her and it tells me everything I need to know.

"Depends on what it is."

I laugh, but there's no humor in it. As much as I love her defiance, I'm not sure I have it in me to deal with it right now. I know what I want, and my patience is already running thin.

"Get on the bed, Kitten." I drop my hand and squeeze her waist as I suck on the skin of her neck, once again ensuring I leave a mark. I want her to look in the mirror tomorrow and remember exactly who was here. "Now." I twist us around and push her in the direction of the bed in the center of the room.

She stumbles on her heels but she manages to catch herself.

"On your back," I demand and she scoots back until she's laid out in the center, although her head is up so she can follow me as I make my way across the room to her.

"Spread your legs, Kitten."

"Wha—"

"Don't argue. You had your chance to run. You didn't take it."

"I... I don't think—"

"Kitten," I warn, my voice a low rumble in my throat.

She blows out a shaky breath but slowly parts her ankles.

"Wider." I run my eyes over the inches of bare, bronze skin before me but what I really want is covered by the skirt of her dress. It's cute. She looks hot in it, but it's going to look even better on the floor.

"Lift your dress."

Time seems to slow down as I wait for her to follow instructions but it damn near stops when she does.

So fucking pretty.

"Kyle, what are you—Oh my God," she squeals as I dive on the bed, wrap my hands around her thighs and latch my mouth onto her clit.

Her taste coats my tongue and I want to fucking drown in it.

Her hands find my hair and she pulls, trying to drag me closer as I lick, suck, and nip at her clit with my teeth.

"Fuck, fuck, fuck, Kyle."

Hearing my name ring out through the room makes my chest swell.

Fucking yes, Har. Scream it fucking louder.

Her back arches off the bed and I suck hard on her, her nails scratch at my scalp and my cock once again strains at my pants.

Unwrapping one of my hands, I find her entrance and begin circling it with one digit.

"Oh shit," she screams as I push just the tip in. Her muscles ripple trying to drag me deeper but I refuse her, drawing this out as long as possible.

"You gonna come, Kitten," I growl against her clit, making sure she feels the vibrations from my voice.

"Ky, fuck."

"I could eat you all fucking night, Kitten."

"Kyle," she squeals as she falls over the edge. My scalp burns as she pulls my hair harder, her back arches and throws her head back. "Oh my God," she chants as her entire body convulses in the center of the bed.

I don't stop licking at her until she's come down from her high, then I sit up, wipe my mouth with the back of my hand and launch myself over her.

My lips find her neck as I kiss, suck and bite at her sweet

skin.

"Kyle," she cries, clawing at my back as I tease her.

"I'm going to fucking ruin you, Kitten," I promise before tucking my fingers under the straps of her dress and pulling the top half down to expose her tits.

I graze my teeth over her collarbone and work my way down, not wanting to leave an inch of her skin untouched by me.

Her dress ends up in a pile on the floor, followed soon after by her shoes before I go down on her again but I remain fully dressed.

With my hands wrapped around her tiny waist, I bring her to orgasm again with just my tongue speared inside her.

She fists the sheets beneath her as she rides it out, my name a plea on her lips.

"Fuck yeah, Kitten," I growl. "Who fucking owns you?"

"You do," she answers eagerly after so many orgasms at my hands—and mouth.

"Say it."

"You do, Kyle."

"I do what, Kitten?"

"You fucking own me, Kyle."

Lifting up from her pussy, I don't bother wiping my mouth, instead, my hand finds her throat and my lips slam down on hers. She moans as she tastes herself but she doesn't try to pull away, instead, she sucks my tongue into her mouth making me wish it was my cock again.

"I fucking own you, Kitten. You. Are. Mine."

"Yes, yes," she pants, her eyes barely open after the number of releases I've dragged out of her and the amount of vodka she's drank.

"And don't fucking forget it." I look to my left and find a pair of eyes trained on me, just like I knew they were. A smile curls at my lips before I dive for her once more just to nail the point home.

14

HARLEY

I roll over and the feeling of the covers tickling my skin where it usually wouldn't is my first sign that something isn't right. The second is the fucking marching band in my head. The third, that's my stomach turning over, but that's not to do with the vodka so much but with the speed of my memories from last night hit me.

I push up on my elbow, ready to run toward wherever the nearest bathroom might be but the second I open my eyes and find Nathan staring at me from the couch, I freeze.

"Fuck," I breathe.

"'Morning." He sits forward, resting his elbows on his knees, but he keeps his eyes on me.

I want the bed to swallow me whole as I pull the sheets tighter to my naked chest.

"H-how are you feeling?"

"Better than I should." His voice is cold in a way I've never heard before and it makes my stomach sink.

The silence stretches out uncomfortably between us but still, I can't find anything to say to him as shame burns through me.

"I saw you." His words make my breath catch. "I saw you... with him. I... I heard you... with him."

I swallow but my mouth is so fucking dry that I can't even do that.

"I-I'm sorry."

"Is that why you ran the other night? Because of him?"

"No, I—"

He pins me with a look. "Don't lie to me, Harley. It's too late for that. Did you run the other night because of him?"

"Y-yes. I'm sorry," I add in a rush like it might actually make any of this any better.

"Who is he?" Nathan asks, his brows furrowing as if just asking the question itself is painful.

"A boy from my past. He only arrived in town last week. I had no idea he was coming."

"He an ex?"

"N-no." I hesitate and hate myself for it. "I mean, something had happened before he went..." I trail off, for some reason not willing to share everything about Kyle with him. "But we were never together."

"I guess we weren't either."

I sit up in bed trying to keep myself covered as I move.

"Nathan, I'm so so—"

"Don't," he barks, pushing to stand. "You're right. We never said we were exclusive. I guess I just assumed—"

"I didn't mean to," I say in a rush.

"No, maybe you didn't. But you did it anyway. While I was passed out right there." He points to the couch and my entire face flames.

Of course I knew he was there, I was grinding down on his lap when Kyle walked in.

Fucking hell, Harley. You're nothing but the cheer slut everyone assumes you are.

"If you hadn't—"

"Don't turn this on me."

"I'm not, I'm just saying, that you'd taken... whatever, and you passed out on me. If you didn't, then—"

"Then what, all three of us could have had some fun? You know that was what he wanted, right?"

"No, I—"

"When he whispered in my ear when we were dancing. He was setting it up for the three of us..."

"And you agreed?" I ask, my eyes almost popping out of my head.

"I was wasted, Harley. I'd have agreed to anything last night."

"Fucking hell," I mutter as I drop my head into my hands. "I'm so sorry for dragging you into this mess."

"I just wish you'd have told me the truth. I like you, Harley, but I don't want to get in the middle of anything."

"It isn't anything," I argue.

He shakes his head as if it's the most ridiculous thing he's ever heard.

"It is though, isn't it? You wouldn't let me touch you because of him, and you let him do all that while I'm in the room without second thought."

"I was drunk."

"It doesn't matter, Harley. What you told him last night was true."

"W-what did I tell him?" I might be able to vividly picture a number of things that happened right here on this bed last night but I could have said literally anything to him during that time.

"That you're his. He's sure left enough evidence behind." He nods down to my chest and I lower the sheets a little.

"Jesus," I mutter, staring down at all the marks littering my skin.

"I'm just going to..." He trails off as he walks to the door.

"I'm sorry, Nathan. Really, sorry."

"It was fun while it lasted, Harley. Take care of yourself."

Pressure builds behind my eyes as I watch him slip from the room but I hold back my sobs until the door closes behind him and I know he's far enough away not to hear me.

I pull the covers over my head and cry for all the stupid mistakes I've made that involve Kyle freaking Legend over the past year. Last night being up there as the worst.

I have no idea how long I lie there crying to myself, but my eyes sting from my tears when there is a knock at the door.

"Harley, it's me. Can I come in?" Hearing Ruby's voice only makes me cry harder.

"Yeah," I call out, my voice cracking with emotion.

"Hey, Nathan said you were in here and that you might need a friend."

She walks over to the bed and sits on the edge, her face full of sympathy.

"What happened?"

"I fucked up. Big time."

"Too much vodka?" she asks, trying to make light of the situation.

"Way, way, way too much vodka."

"Oh sweetie. Come here." She pulls me into her arms and I cry on her shoulder.

"I really hurt him. He didn't deserve that."

She rubs my back in comfort. "He's okay, Har."

"Is… is Kyle still here?"

"I haven't seen him since early last night."

I wish my heart didn't sink like it does knowing that he snuck out after everything.

"You want to talk about it?"

"Yeah, but I really need to get dressed and get out of here."

"Okay, how about we go back to your house, you can change and then we go for breakfast?"

"Not at Ace's," I say in a rush. I don't want to see anyone.

"Okay, whatever you want."

She slides to the end of the bed and leans down.

"You need this?" she asks, handing my dress over.

"This," I say, snatching it from her. "Was a mistake."

"You can't blame the dress."

"I can and I will." I throw the fabric over my head and shimmy it down my body without flashing Ruby.

"Do I need to ask what happened to your panties?" she asks as I climb from the bed, clearly failing in my mission not to expose myself.

"Use your imagination," I mutter, walking to the other side of the room and opening a door that I really hope leads to an en suite. My entire body aches, but nowhere more so than the muscles in my inner thighs. What the hell did he do to me last night?

My cheeks burn as I remember watching him between my legs. I squeeze my thighs together as the memory of just how his tongue felt against me.

I knock my palm against my forehead, hoping that it knocks the thoughts straight out of my head.

The sight of Nathan's toiletries sitting around the sink does nothing for my regrets.

I make use of the toilet before finger brushing my teeth in the hope of freshening my mouth up and rejoining Ruby.

"Ready?"

"Any chance of sneaking me out of a back door?"

"We can try but I need to tell Ash that we're leaving."

"You do that. I'll meet you at your car."

"Okay. Here," she says, pulling her keys from her purse. "I won't be long."

"Thank you," I say sincerely.

"Always, Har." She kisses my cheek before disappearing out of the door and allowing me a few seconds to compose myself before attempting to sneak out and not get caught doing the walk of shame in last night's dress.

By some miracle, I actually make it out of the house unseen and I'm hiding in Ruby's car when she emerges from the front door—unlike me who snuck out the back—a few minutes after shutting myself inside.

"Ready to leave last night behind?" she asks me.

"So ready. Any chance I can leave my memories here too?"

"That bad?" she asks, glancing at me after starting the engine so she doesn't miss the blush that covers my face and down my neck which of course only highlights the many, many hickies I'm rocking. "Oh my God. How did I miss those upstairs?"

"Can we not?"

"Did he try to eat you?" she jokes, clearly remembering my words to her not so long ago.

"He did, a few times," I admit, much to her amusement.

"Harley Hunter, you naughty little slut."

"Like you can talk."

"Hey, I'm not denying anything." She chuckles. "Just tell me... was jailbait good?"

"Fucking hell, just drive. I need to shower and get out of this dress."

"You're right. You smell like sex."

"I'm pretty sure that's you."

"Nope, I showered."

"Great, so I guess I'm guilty then."

Ruby continues to laugh lightly at my expense as she backs out of Justin's driveway and heads for my house.

"I got out of Justin's unnoticed. I'm not going to have the same luck here, am I?" I ask, seeing both Mom and Zayn's cars sitting in the driveway.

"Only one way to find out." But instead of reaching for the door, Ruby throws herself between the seats and reaches for something. "Here, put this on. If Zayn sees you, he's gonna throw a fit."

"Thanks," I say, taking her hoodie and shoving my arms into it.

Once I've covered up as much as I can, I blow out a long, calming breath before pushing the door open and climbing out.

The house is in silence as we step in through the front door, but it only lasts so long because footsteps soon head our way.

"'Morning, girls. Good night?" Mom asks, looking between the two of us.

"Yeah," I lie. "Excuse me."

I take off for the stairs knowing that Mom's concerned eyes follow me.

After a couple of seconds, Ruby catches up with me.

"You should just speak to her, hear her out."

"I will, when I'm not hungover and drowning in regrets."

"Oh come on, it couldn't have been that bad."

"Not that bad?" I ask, turning on her the second we're in the safety of my bathroom. "The boy I hate went down on me, again and again, while my boyfriend was passed out on the couch. And the kicker... said boyfriend was apparently watching."

Ruby's chin drops.

"He watched?"

"I don't think he actually watched for entertainment, I think he came to and happened to find us doing... well, that." I walk over to my closet to pull out some clean clothes.

"Did you fuck him?" Her question stops me in my tracks.

"No. Well, I don't think so." I risk a glance over at her standing beside my bed with her hands on her hips.

"You don't think so?"

"I mean, I remember... *things*. But I don't remember that. Although I don't remember falling asleep or him sneaking out either, so..."

"You'd know if you did. You'd feel it."

"Well, that's reassuring, I guess."

"Go shower. We need pancakes before we talk about this anymore."

"I couldn't agree more. You okay while I shower?"

"Take your time."

I turn the shower on hotter than I usually have it, strip out of my dress and stand under the spray, wincing as the water stings my skin but I don't turn it down. I need it to help rid me of the memories and sensations of last night.

I scrub at every inch of my skin, trying to wash him from me, sadly it does little for what's in my head.

Once I'm done, I take off what's left of last night's makeup and pull on a pair of leggings and an oversized sweater that I can hide in. I refuse to look in the mirror at my reflection, I don't want to see the magnitude of my mistakes.

"Feel better?" Ruby asks the second I rejoin her back in my room.

"No."

She waits patiently while I blow dry my hair and apply a little makeup to make myself look less like death.

"Come on then, the syrup is calling."

"Where do you want to go?" Ruby asks as we make our way down the stairs.

"Anywhe— shit," I mutter under my breath when a very familiar voice filters up to me. "He's here."

"So? Hold your head up high and walk straight past him. Don't let him see he affects you."

"I wasn't intending to," I snap, making Ruby wince. "Sorry. He just drives me a little insane."

"I've noticed."

"Come on." I throw my hair over my shoulder and continue down, knowing that the second I look into the kitchen, I'm going to find him with Zayn.

"'Morning, sis. How's the head?" I look at Zayn, refusing

to meet his burning stare but my skin tingles as Kyle leisurely checks me out.

"Fine thanks, *bro.*" I narrow my eyes at him.

"Ruby." Zayn nods at her over my shoulder. "Going somewhere nice?"

"We're going for breakfast," Ruby says over my shoulder.

"Do we need a word about where you went with your boyfriend last night?" Zayn asks me.

"Oh yeah," I hiss. "Just like we need to talk about where you and Poppy often disappear to."

"Hey, I'll tell you anything you need to know about what we get up to."

I faux gag at his words.

"I'm pretty sure he broke up with you last night, didn't he, Harley?" Kyle asks so sweetly it makes me want to jam a kitchen knife through his eye socket.

"Oh?" Zayn asks, looking between the two of us.

"I'm not discussing this with you," I mutter, turning my back on my brother and marching toward the front door and storming through it.

I rip open Ruby's passenger door and drop down onto the seat before she's even left my house.

"He looked at you like he wanted to take you against the wall."

"I don't want to know. I didn't look at him for a reason. Can we please talk about something else? What did you do last night?"

Ruby lets out a sigh before starting the engine and heading to the other side of town to ensure we don't see anyone.

15

KYLE

I'm still smiling to myself as the door slams behind a pissed off Harley. Knowing exactly what her baggy sweater was covering and who put it all there makes something flutter inside me.

"She's a bitch when she's hungover," Zayn mutters, going back to making our coffees.

I shouldn't have accepted his invitation to come and hang out today, but the thought of being here and seeing how Harley was this morning was an offer I couldn't resist.

"Most girls are," I mutter, trying to swallow down my real reaction that her feistiness made me hard. Fuck, everything about Harley Hunter makes me hard.

"How'd you know things are done with her and Preppy?"

"Uh... I overheard some of the guys talking about it, apparently, he got totally wasted last night."

"Don't tell me he cheated on her," he growls, going all protective big brother on her ass.

"I don't know, man. Don't shoot the messenger."

"Come on, we got guys to shoot." He holds out a mug for me before we head for his room and he turns his Xbox on.

"Where's your girl?"

He laughs lightly. "In bed, sleeping off a killer night."

"Oh yeah. I thought you disappeared early." It's a total lie, I was so focused on Harley last night that I have no fucking clue what anyone else got up to.

"I'm not one to kiss and tell, man." He doesn't look away from the screen but I see the massive fucking grin on his face.

"I've been fucking celibate for a year, you can give me more than that," I joke.

"You telling me that you didn't dip it in one of the cheerleaders last night?" he asks, the tone of his voice rising with shock.

"Don't kiss and tell," I tease.

"Fuck off, who was it?"

"Nah, not telling, man. She sucked fucking good though."

"Krissy," he states as if he knows all the girls' skills personally. Which, I guess he might.

"My lips are sealed."

"Unlike hers," he jokes.

Relaxing back on his couch, I stretch my legs out in front of me, enjoying the normalness of this morning. Shooting the shit with Zayn, killing a few guys on the game he's set up. It's all so... normal.

Good thing he has no idea that the girl who had my cock in her mouth last night was his little sister.

Zayn and I were always tight, but I'm pretty sure him finding out what's really going on is probably the one thing that could shatter this. But even as I sit here enjoying myself, I know that I'm not going to be able to leave her alone. I guess I'll just have to deal with the consequences when the time comes.

It's almost two hours later when his sleepy girlfriend finally emerges and finds herself a seat on Zayn's lap.

She looks almost as exhausted as Harley did earlier,

although she makes no attempt to cover up the love bites running down her neck.

"'Morning, baby," Zayn purrs, slipping his hand into her hair and pulling her lips to his. She twists around on his lap, the shirt she's wearing—clearly his—rising to expose her thighs.

"So I guess I'll leave you two to it," I say, placing the controller on the coffee table and standing from the couch.

"Okay," Zayn mutters against her lips. "See you in school tomorrow, yeah?"

"Yeah. Later." I look back when I'm at the door after hearing no response but I soon discover why. "Fucking hell," I mutter to myself before slipping from Zayn's den and making my way to the front door.

I'm almost there when I get intercepted by Jada who's walking out of the kitchen with a mug in her hand.

"Kyle, it's so good to see you. How is everything going?" She smiles softly at me and it reminds me so much of Harley that I almost ignore her and continue the way I was going.

"Yeah, it's, uh... different."

"You can say that again," she says with a chuckle. "How's school? Are you settling in okay?"

"So far so good. Almost makes me glad I screwed everything up in juvie."

"Everything happens for a reason, Kyle. I was delighted when Kane reached out to me to ask for my help. I just knew that you both would do well here."

"Why did you do it? After... after everything." I have no idea how much she knows about that night, but something tells me Harley hasn't said much, so it can't look very good on me. I remember all too well the position we were in when the police stormed in.

"Because everyone deserves a second chance. If you'd have gone back to Harrow Creek, I think we both know how it would have gone." She raises a brow and my stomach drops at the thought.

Yeah, going back there would have been a bigger sentence than my time in juvie.

"It's great to see you reconnecting with Zayn, you were always such good friends, I hated the way you were forced apart."

"It's great to spend time together again."

"And... what about Harley? Have you had time to talk yet?"

"A little."

A humorless laugh falls from her lips. "She'll come around. I should have warned her sooner."

"Everything will be fine." I give her a reassuring smile which she can't help but return. "You don't need to worry about Harley."

She reaches out and squeezes my upper arm in the kind of motherly way I didn't realize I missed until her touch warms me from the inside out.

"If you need anything, you or Kane. I'm here. I can't imagine how hard things have been, for both of you."

"Thank you," I force out passed the lump in my throat. I learned long ago to push down my feelings, my grief from now not only losing our parents when we were just kids, but now our gran too. She was all we had back then and she took us in without a second though. But now she's gone too and it's just the two of us against the world. "I really appreciate everything you've done for us."

"Anytime, Kyle. We might have left the Creek behind but that doesn't mean we still don't look out for each other."

I nod at her as I take a step toward the door. Part of me wants to make all the excuses I can so that I can still be here when Harley gets back, but I know I need to leave. I know I need to give her some space. For now at least.

———

"Well, aren't you a sight for sore eyes," I say when Kane pushes through our front door, finding me sitting on the couch with a textbook on my lap.

"Fuck off. Good to see you're taking graduating seriously," he mutters, taking in the stack of books on the coffee table.

"Yeah well, I don't want it to take any longer than it's already going to. You out playing football?" I ask, spotting the mud covering his legs.

"Yeah," he says over his shoulder as he yanks the refrigerator open and pulls out a bottle of water.

"Was that before or after you got your ass kicked?" I ask, unable to miss the black eye and split lip he's sporting.

"How about you just get back to your schoolwork, eh?"

I push the book from my lap and stand, walking toward where he's leaning back against the counter and drinking his water.

"How about you stop talking to me like I'm a fucking kid and tell me what the fuck you're up to."

"Kyle," he breathes. "I'm not up to anything. I've been working. One of us has to keep this roof over our head."

"Nice, Kane. Real nice."

"What? That wasn't a jab, it's the truth. I'm not going to force you to get a job because I want you to settle in and sort out school before anything else."

I hold his eyes, looking for any hint that he's lying.

"Your birthday next weekend?"

"What about it?" I ask, not entirely happy with how he's diverted the conversation away from him.

"We're having a party."

"We really don't—"

"We do. It's not every year my little brother turns into a man." He rustles my hair as he passes me, heading to his room.

"Bit fucking late for that, don't you think?"

"Meh, we all grew up fast in the Creek, but still, it's an excuse for a party, and I need a fucking night off." He disappears into the bathroom before I get a chance to respond. I have a feeling though, that it doesn't matter what my opinion on it is, if Kane wants a party then we'll be having a party.

I grab myself a bottle of water and drop back down on the couch to carry on with my homework.

I grab my statistics book and pause with it on my lap. I need to arrange our next study session...

I spend the night at home working but the second Kane emerged from his room freshly showered and with clean clothes on, he fucked off leaving me to sort my own dinner.

I don't care about having to look after myself, it's not like I haven't done it before, but after being locked away and unable to see him for the best part of a year, it would actually be nice to spend a little time with him.

I'm lying on my bed long after midnight staring up at the ceiling wishing that I could fall asleep but totally unable to. I used to sleep great, until I suddenly had to constantly look over my shoulder. Then it was like I just stopped. I'd hoped that when I got out, I'd break the habit but it doesn't seem that I'm able to.

I must drift off at some point because when I open my eyes again the sky outside my open curtains is a burnt orange as the sun begins its climb for the day.

I drag on a pair of sweats and a shirt and take off. My muscles burn with my exhaustion but I don't allow it to slow me down. I push until I have nothing left to give. Exercise helped me survive up until this point, so I have no doubt it'll get me through my time in Rosewood.

By the time I get back to the house, my shirt is soaked with sweat and my muscles quiver with excessive use, but I feel better than I have in a while.

I shower, gather up my stuff and head for my car, ready to begin my first full week as a Rosewood High student.

There are kids everywhere when I pull into the lot. I find a space and just watch them.

I never used to give a shit about what other people did. Probably because I'd have ended up having my ass beat if I pried into other's business in the Creek but it's different here. No one is looking over their shoulder just waiting for their secrets to be exposed. Everyone is just living life. They don't need to worry about just trying to make the best of it. The majority here have everything they could possibly want handed to them on a platter. College is an option, they have a future that can be in or out of this place. The world is their oyster.

That's not how things were where we were brought up. College was something that happened to others. Or aspirations were restricted to which end of the trailer park we wanted to end up living on, and if we were able to work our way to a decent position with one of the gangs to allow us some sense of safety.

I blow out a breath. It all feels like it happened in another lifetime, but at the same time, I feel like I left that place only yesterday.

The bell rings out and all the kids that are hanging around start moving toward the building but I still can't find it in me to move. I try to convince myself that it's not because I haven't seen her. I'm pretty sure we don't have any classes together today and I'm already wondering how I'm going to get my hands on her.

My cell burns red-hot in my pants pocket and I pull it out, finding our previous conversation. A smile curls at my lips as I read back the short messages.

Opening up the keyboard I start to type.

Kyle: I feel like I've already taught you so much... Are you ready for another lesson?

It only takes two seconds for her to read the message and for the dots to start bouncing. I can't help but laugh when her response pops up because I expected it.

Kitten: Fuck off. WE ARE DONE.

Kyle: It amuses me that you think you get to call the shots here, Kitten. You might want to keep looking over your shoulder. I'm coming for you.

I add a little kiss emoji at the end to try to soften the blow and I smile, knowing just how her lips are going to press into a thin line as she sees it.

My cell vibrates once again and when I look down, I find a gif of someone flipping the bird staring back at me.

In response, I quickly shoot back someone blowing a kiss and shove my phone into my pocket before climbing from the car and walking toward the building before I end up too late. I don't need to give Principal Hartmann, Bea, my parole officer or Kane any reason to be on my ass.

My birthday is only days away. Bea will sign me off as an adult and I can finally take charge of my own life. The prospect should probably feel more freeing than it does in reality because until I turn my back on getting my diploma then I'm stuck here for the foreseeable future.

With the satisfaction of knowing I got to her, I walk into the building feeling a little lighter. Now all I need is to see it with my own eyes.

16

HARLEY

I don't want to do it, but I find myself doing exactly what he told me I should. I spend the entire morning looking over my shoulder trying to find him.

I know he's here. It's like I can sense his presence.

I also know that he's seen me because when I was standing in the hallway earlier with Ruby and Poppy, my skin tingled with awareness and my temperature soared, but as I looked around as desperately as I could, I couldn't find him.

"Hey, how are you doing?" Stella asks, coming to sit next to me on a bench I thankfully found empty after walking out of my last class in my need to avoid the cafeteria.

I blow out a breath. "Great," I mutter.

"Justin's party was banging, huh?"

I look over at her so fast that I swear my head almost snaps clean from my body.

"W-what?" she asks, her brows drawing together.

"N-nothing," I mutter, slumping down on the seat and remembering that just because I refuse to think about the events of that night, it doesn't mean that everyone else had one of the worst nights of their life. "I didn't see you there. Were you with the squad?"

"Yeah, Ruby invited me. It was fun. I saw you dancing with your boyfriend. He's cute."

"Ex-boyfriend."

"Oh?"

"It's okay. It wasn't meant to be." Or maybe it was and Kyle decided to steamroll the whole thing regardless. I push the thought down because as much as I might like to blame all of this on Kyle, I know that at least half of it is my fault. I didn't need to do any of that on Saturday night—hell, or Friday night—but I did, and now I need to pay the price. "You hook up with anyone?"

"I kissed some guy. I'd never seen him before, I don't think he goes here but he was decent," she says with a nod.

"Decent?" I chuckle.

"Yeah, I'm not sure he was entirely into it. He was kinda distracted, like he was looking for someone else."

"Trying to make someone jealous?"

"Maybe. I wasn't really complaining though. It's not like I was looking for anything serious."

"You still leaving?"

Her eyes widen in shock that I know.

"Shit, Ruby let it slip. Sorry, should I have—"

"It's fine. Honestly, I have no idea what's going on. I never do."

"Why do you move so much?"

"Dad's job. I hate it. I just get settled somewhere, make some friends and then I come home from school one afternoon to find the house being packed up and off we go again."

"That sucks."

"I mean, I've seen a lot, learned a lot. It has its benefits, I guess. But I just want a home and to graduate someplace I've stayed for longer than a few months, you know."

"It must be hard. Do you stay in touch with any of your friends from old schools?"

"To start with I tried, but everyone moves on, we grow up and it just fizzles. Dad is my only constant."

"Well, if it makes you feel any better, I really hope you get to stay here to graduate with us."

"Me too. I like it here."

"Yeah, it's not bad."

My stomach growls so loudly that Stella can't help but hear it.

"We should go and get you some food." She laughs.

I look over my shoulder at the building where the cafeteria sits knowing that he's probably in there finding his footing with the team and being dragged into my group. I bet even Ruby and Poppy are in there with Ash and Zayn making him feel welcome.

"Nah, it's okay. I don't—"

"Don't let him see that you're scared of him, Harley."

"What? I'm not scared. I'd just rather not have to look at him."

She raises a brow at me. "You're hiding," she states, pissing me off despite the fact it's blatantly the truth.

"I—"

"Come on. We'll stop in the bathroom, touch up your makeup, slap on some confidence, and walk into that motherfucking cafeteria like you own the place. Yeah?" She jumps up and I can't help but feel some of her excitement.

I don't want to be this girl. The weak one who hides from the boy who's making her life hell. I want to be strong. I want to hold my head up high. I'm Harley fucking Hunter after all.

"Hell yes."

I thread my arm through hers as we march toward the closest bathroom.

"Don't you have friends to be hanging out with instead of standing here being my personal cheerleader?"

Stella's face pales and for the thousandth time in the past

twenty-four hours, I want the ground to swallow me right up.

"Shit," I breathe, realization hitting me that the reason she's standing with me is that she doesn't have anyone else.

"It's okay, Harley. I learned long ago that it's easier to just not connect with anyone. It hurts less when I leave and get forgotten about soon after."

"I'm sure that's not—"

"Stop," she says, holding her hand up to cut me off. "I dealt with it a long time ago. It is what it is."

"Well, I appreciate this. I just want you to know that."

She smiles at me and my heart aches for her. She's been nothing but awesome since she joined the squad and was quickly picked for varsity alongside Ruby and me, but hearing her talk like this, it makes me realize why she's kept her distance like she has. "And from now on, no more running from friends. Okay?"

"As long as you don't run from him." She pins me with a look. "You want to hate him, hate him in the same room so he knows it."

"You got it, girl. Let's go."

I pull my tank down a little, readjusting my girls, not that there's much of them, and run my fingers through my hair once more before threading my arm through Stella's and making our way toward where I know he is.

The commotion from the cafeteria can be heard long before we get to the doors and the closer we get, the more butterflies seem to take flight in my belly.

"You've got this. Show him that you don't give a fuck."

"I don't."

"Exactly."

I walk in with my head up high and the second we're inside, we head straight for the tables where the team and squad are.

His stare burns into me the second we move toward

them, but I refuse to look his way, instead, I walk toward Ruby when she calls me.

"Where have you been hiding?"

I cringe at her words, knowing that it was exactly what I was doing.

"She was helping me with something," Stella pipes up to save me.

"Okay, cool. Come sit," she encourages both me and Stella, who easily fits in with our group despite the fact she's never really hung out with us before.

"Yo, baby Hunter. What happened to your prep boy? He dump your ass?" Rich shouts over. I roll my eyes at him before he shouts. "Ow," he complains as someone hits him.

"That's my cousin, you ass."

"Nah, he dumped her because she wouldn't put out."

My chin drops in shock as I turn to the owner of that comment.

"Excuse me?"

"You heard me." Kyle narrows his eyes on me, amusement dancing in them.

"Fuck you, Ky. You don't know what the fuck you're talking about."

Our eye contact holds, tension crackling between us and everyone falls silent around us waiting to see what's to come.

"I'm only going by what he said."

"Well, that's great. You believe what you like."

"It's true though, isn't it, virgin?"

"Wha—" I shake my head, not believing this is happening right now. "What's that even got to do with anything?"

"Just saying. He probably thought he'd get with a cheerleader and get his dick wet."

"You're a fucking prick, Kyle."

"So, prove us wrong."

"W-what?"

"Prove. Us. Wrong," he spits.

"What? You want me to fuck someone in the middle of the cafeteria to make you feel better about yourself? Fuck you, Kyle."

"Legend," Zayn warns, suddenly piping up. Apparently, even my fucking brother is enjoying the show. Ass.

"Pussy," Kyle breathes as I turn away from him.

"Fuck you."

I walk straight toward Rich who's totally engrossed in the drama unfolding before him, grip his chin in my hand as I straddle his lap and slam my lips down on his.

A loud gasp sounds out behind me, and I lift my spare hand to flip them all off.

His shock means he doesn't respond to me for a few seconds but the moment his brain catches up with his body, his fingers thread in my hair and he holds me tight.

Someone growls behind us and I can only assume it's Zayn. I've threatened to go after his friends more than once but other than Kyle. I've never touched one. Until today.

I grind down on him, feeling him harden beneath me before climbing off and dropping my hand to his crotch.

"You want to know why I haven't fucked any of you?" I look around at the team. "Much like your boy here." I rub him harder and he gasps. "Your cocks are all too small. Girls?" I ask looking to Ruby, Poppy, and Stella who are staring at me with a mix of pride and shock on their faces.

"Harley, wait—" Rich starts when I take a step back.

"Come after me and I'll fucking bite it off," I warn.

I lift my eyes to Kyle as I back away, a smirk playing on my lips as he shakes his head at me, anger darkening his eyes.

Right before I'm forced to turn around, I flip him off once again with both hands and then disappear around the corner.

"Girl, what the fuck was that?" Stella squeals excitedly. "I said go in there and show him you're not scared, not make Rich almost come in his pants."

I shrug like it's no biggie. In reality, my hands are trembling and my heart is racing faster than I'm sure it ever has before.

"Did you see his face? That was so his 'I'm about to come' face." Ruby laughs.

"Ugh, he's such a dog," Poppy complains. "They all are."

We all turn our eyes on her.

"What? Zayn used to be just as bad. I'm not excusing his behavior before we got together."

"Kyle looked like he was gonna pop a blood vessel. Did you see his eyes almost bug out of his head when you touched Rich's cock?" Ruby asks as we continue walking down the hallway with no destination in mind.

"Man, that felt good," I admit.

"You do realize that you're in serious trouble now, right?" Poppy says.

"How so?"

"Well, firstly, Zayn's going to lose his shit with Rich for kissing you back. Sec—"

"He was shit, in case you were wondering."

Ruby and Stella snigger as Poppy continues.

"Secondly, he's probably going to take Kyle down for the way he talked to you."

"And that's my problem because? Fucker deserves it."

"Thirdly, you're just asking for Kyle to come after you for that stunt."

"She's right. You might have just shown him that you're not scared, but you've upped the ante."

"Yeah well, he can fuck off. I'm not going anywhere near him again."

"Again," Poppy screeches, successfully spraying Ruby with a mouthful of water she was attempting to drink.

"You didn't tell her?" Ruby asks with a wince.

"No, you may not have realized it but I didn't want to talk about it."

"Whoops, my bad."

"What happened, Har?"

I look up at the shitty tiled ceiling of the hallway we've stopped in, trying to come up with the right words.

"He was right, nothing happened with Nathan..."

"Because..." Ruby encourages excitedly like she's about to explode.

"Because it happened with him."

"You fucked him?" Poppy shouts way too loudly for a school hallway.

"No, I didn't. He's right there too. I'm a virgin. But things... happened."

"But you hate him."

"Yeah well, I owed him one, so."

"You blew him to make up for the fact you sent him to juvie. Har, that's messed up."

I turn to Stella who's standing silently beside us probably being corrupted more by the second.

"I'm sorry. If you want to run now, I'll let you off the whole friends thing."

"No, no. Please continue. I'm enjoying this."

"Great. I'm glad someone is."

"Oh come on, Harley. It's not that bad. So what you sucked him off, I'm assuming you got yours too," she says, shocking the fuck out of me, I always thought she was such a good girl.

My face burns with the truth. "Um... I actually came out of it a hell of a lot better," I admit quietly making all three of them howl with laughter.

"So what happened to Nathan? That last time I saw you, you were grinding up against him," Poppy asks.

"Err..." I hesitate, mortified by the answer to that question.

"Tell her or I will."

"Ohhh... does this get even juicier?" Stella asks. "Where the hell was I when all this was going on?"

"Kissing a stranger?" I ask, hoping to take some of the heat off of me.

"Oooh... who were you kissing?" Ruby asks, momentarily forgetting that she was about to confess my mortifying secret.

"No idea. He was hot though. Rough." She wiggles her eyebrows in excitement.

"Har, you were saying..." Poppy prompts.

"Oh, um... Nathan was passed out on the couch," I whisper.

"In the same room?" she once again screeches.

"Yes."

Thankfully the bell rings putting an end to this mortifying conversation.

"What have you got last?" Ruby asks.

"Math," I groan. The last thing I need is Mr. Wilson breathing down my neck and asking about my tutoring sessions.

"I'm going that way. Walk with?" Stella asks, nodding in that direction.

"Sure."

"This isn't over," Poppy warns me.

"I didn't think I was going to be that lucky," I sass. "We'll talk later, yeah?"

"You can bet on it."

We all part ways and head to class.

"I think I might have got things wrong," Stella admits when we come to a stop outside my classroom. "I think being friends with you guys might just be worth it for the entertainment value."

"Trust me, girl. It's not usually this bad." I laugh, wondering if that's actually true when I think of the events of this year alone. Poppy and Zayn, Ruby and Ash. Yeah, maybe the boy drama really is becoming normal for us. And that can only mean one thing... we're turning into seniors.

"I'll believe it when I see it."

"You wanna hang out after school one day this week?"

"Yeah, I'd like that."

"I'll message you later."

She gives me a little wave as she twists away to go to her own class and a smile plays on my lips. Everything might be just a tad fucked-up right now but having Stella join our little threesome is a good thing. Not to mention that she's single and will give me back up against the two happy couples that mostly make me want to gag.

I'm still smiling when I walk into my classroom, although that soon falls when Mr. Wilson's concerned eyes land on me.

Great. Now what?

Class is... as hard as it always is.

I take all the notes, listen to everything he says, I even get some right answers, but no sooner have I figured it all out do I forget once again and it all goes tits up.

Tears burn the back of my eyes as I stare down at the page full of numbers. It shouldn't be this hard. I'm intelligent. I'm passing all my other classes, but math, argh.

I grip the pencil in my hand so hard I worry it's about to snap in two as Mr. Wilson brings the class to a close seconds before the bell rings.

"Harley, could you wait, please?" he asks as everyone else begins to make their way to the door.

I blow out a breath as dread settles in the pit of my stomach.

"What's up, sir?"

"Have you had your first tutoring session yet?"

I cast my mind back to going to Kyle's last week.

"Yeah."

"And, how was it?"

"It was… sir," I say, changing tactic. "I really don't think it's necessary."

"Harley," he warns. "The test we did last week." Hesitantly, I take it from him and at the sight of the big F at the top of the page, the tears that were already threatening fills my eyes.

"I'm so sorry," I whimper.

"Harley, you don't need to apologize, and please, don't get upset. We're going to make this better. I'm going to schedule some sessions at lunch and with Kyle's help, you'll get there. All of the rest of your grades are fantastic, Harley. We just need to figure out a way to help you understand the numbers."

"O-okay," I sniffle.

"It'll be okay, Harley. We'll get you there."

"T-thank you," I whisper, wiping at my eyes and turning away from him.

I hate this. I hate feeling like I'm failing at something when I'm trying so damn hard.

"Hey, what's wrong?" Ruby asks the second I emerge from the classroom.

"It's math. What's right?"

"Come here." She pulls me into her arms to comfort me. It's a move that's happening all too often at the moment.

"I'm okay," I say, squaring my shoulders and running my finger under my eyes to wipe away the tears and stray makeup.

Movement over her shoulder catches my attention, but I don't get a chance to look up and see what's going on because Ruby tucks her arm under mine and starts walking us down the hall.

"Chelsea wants to see us."

"Oh, why?"

"To talk about next year, I assume. I don't really know."

Arm in arm, we walk to the gym before slipping down the hidden hallway to Miss Kelly's office. To both our shock, our elusive cheer coach is actually sitting behind her desk.

"'Afternoon, girls," she says when we enter and join Chelsea who's sitting rubbing her bump as she talks to Miss Kelly. "Harley, is everything okay?" she asks when she must see the remaining tears in my eyes.

"Yeah. Everything's fine."

"Okay, well. Take a seat. We need to talk about the squad's future and I have a feeling you two will want to be involved."

We both eagerly take a seat and set about listening to her plans, which in itself is comical seeing as she's never here.

"I know you want to take charge, and I think you'll probably get it. We'll put votes out as soon as auditions are done but in the meantime, I need you both to ensure your grades are stellar and your behavior is impeccable." Miss Kelly turns her eyes on me and my stomach drops. Not only am I failing math but my behavior in the cafeteria earlier wasn't exactly exemplary.

"You've got it," Ruby agrees for us.

"Brilliant. I'll see you all here after school tomorrow and we'll get started on building next year's champion squad."

Ruby and I nod before following Chelsea out and in the direction of the locker room.

"Anyone would think she gives a shit about the squad the way she just went on," Chelsea complains once we're safely inside the empty room.

"It's a bit of a joke," Ruby agrees, dropping down to the bench where Chelsea has left some of her stuff.

"You two are going to have a lot to take on, you know that, right? She won't help like she promises."

"We know. We've got it."

"I'll be around, I'm taking a year off with this one, so if you need anything I'm all in, I'll help wherever I can. You two just need to focus on those grades." She turns to me. "I saw yours, Harley. Is math going to be an issue?"

"No, I'm working on it."

"Good. Like I said, I'm here for anything, but math isn't exactly my strong point. Shane's pretty good but—"

"I've got it under control."

"Good. I trust you, Harley. I trust both of you. I know my squad will be in good hands." She pulls her cell from her pocket and stares down at the screen. "I gotta go. I'll see you both tomorrow, yeah?"

"Sure thing," Ruby agrees. "I need to head out too. You okay?" she asks me.

"Yeah, I'm just going to use the bathroom then I'm heading home."

"Okay. Call me later, yeah?"

"Will do." I watch them both walk out before pushing from the wall I was leaning against and head for the bathroom.

I sit down and tip my head up to the ceiling. Today has been a fucking disaster.

Regret fills me with what I did at lunch. I wanted to prove a point, but I think I might have taken it a bit too far.

I drop my head into my hands as the image of that F on my math test taunts me. I've got to do something. I can't have my place on the squad in jeopardy because of a stupid grade.

"Argh," I scream into the empty space around me but it doesn't make me feel any better.

I wash my hands before reluctantly looking at myself in the mirror. Tears still fill my eyes as I think about my reality. If I don't fix that grade, Miss Kelly will boot me from the squad and I'll never get to stand beside Ruby as her assistant captain.

I suck in a shaky breath before drying my hands and walking back to the locker room to grab my purse and head home—to do some math homework.

I'm not looking where I'm going, I'm too lost in my own head but that soon ends when I walk straight into a solid yet warm wall of muscle.

"K-Kyle?"

"Kitten, fancy seeing you here."

17
———

KYLE

"Yeah weird, seeing as this is the girl's locker room and I'm assuming you watched my ass walk in here," she sasses, making my dick harden as I close the already limited space between us.

My fingers find her throat and I push her backward until she crashes up against the lockers.

"Trying to be cute isn't going to help you right now," I warn, my eyes boring into hers.

"I'm not being cute," she seethes. "Let go of me." She pulls at my forearm with all the strength she can muster but I don't budge.

"That stunt you pulled in the cafeteria... you think I'd let you get away with that?"

"I don't really give a fuck, Kyle." She squirms in my hold, desperate to get away, but she's achieving nothing.

"You fucking kissed him." I get right in her face. My nose pressed against hers and our heaving breathes mingle as I tighten my grip on her throat and wrap my other hand around her waist. "You fucking kissed him," I repeat, my anger exploding within me as I remember watching her tongue delve past his lips. How they're still attached to him right now is a fucking miracle.

"You started it."

"I was only telling the truth, Kitten."

"Yeah, and maybe I've been dying to kiss Rich for years."

A growl rumbles up my throat.

"You're a really shit liar, Kitten."

"I. Don't. Care."

I stare at her as her chest heaves, her body trembling under my touch. I drop my eyes from hers, to her lips and then down to her chest. She's wearing a tank and zip-up hoodie, it's not an overly sexy outfit but fuck if I don't want to rip it off her and lay her out on the bench.

My cock swells against her hip, there's no way she can't feel what her defiance is doing to me right now.

"Why were you crying?" I ask, my voice softer than before.

The tears might have gone, but I can see the redness around her eyes. Not to mention that I was waiting for her after her math class and saw her come out upset.

"Why? Do you want to shout about that around the cafeteria to shame me as well?"

"Nothing shameful about being a virgin, Kitten."

"I know. If I were that bothered I'd have given it up to Rich by now."

"Don't even think about it," I growl, getting so close to her our lips brush. My mouth waters knowing that I could take her right now if I wanted to. I have no doubt she'd comply despite her anger.

"Why were you crying?" I try again, lifting my hand from her waist and running my thumb along the underside of her breast.

"None of your business."

A humorless chuckle falls from my lips. "See, now that's

where you're wrong. Do you remember what you told me Saturday night?"

"No, I've blocked the entire event from my mind. No point remembering."

My brows rise as her words hit where they intended.

"Huh." I move forward, my lips against the shell of her ear. "So you don't remember screaming my name over and over as I made you come again, and again… and again."

"Nope."

"And you don't remember telling me that I fucking own you?" I drop my hand, cupping her pussy over the fabric of her jeans and she gasps.

"No. I was drunk and probably drugged knowing you."

"Careful, Kitten. Throwing accusations around isn't going to help."

"I have a right to be suspicious, you've got history."

"The only thing I handed you that night was neat vodka in a bottle that you willingly took." I pull back to look at her, hoping that she can see the truth in my eyes. "I'd never drug you, Harley. I'm not a fucking monster."

She laughs manically, throwing her head back and exposing her neck to me. Unable to resist, I lower my hand and suck her skin into my mouth.

"Kyle," she cries, her throat flexing beneath my lips.

She slaps at my shoulder trying to force me away but all I do is suck harder, leaving more evidence behind that I was here.

"Tell me, Kitten. Tell me why you were crying?"

"Fuck you." I'm still lost in the taste of her when she brings her knee up. I should be expecting it, she's got history after all.

I manage to move before she makes any real contact but the shock is enough for me to release her and she bolts to the other side of the locker room, her back to the door where she's about to escape from.

"You're playing a dangerous game, Kitten."

"Leave me the hell alone, Kyle. This little game you think we're playing... I never signed up for. I'm done. So fucking d-done." Her voice cracks on the final word and I stand back to my full height and take a step toward her. "No." She holds her hand up as her eyes fill with tears and her bottom lip trembles. "Just no. We're done."

I'm motionless as she flees from the room, leaving me alone with nothing but the scent of girl's perfume filling my nose.

"Fuck. FUCK," I bark, planting my fist into one of the red lockers beside me. The door buckles under my force but it doesn't make me feel any better.

"Fuuuuck," I groan, tipping my face to the ceiling and taking a slow breath.

I know that I should walk out before I'm caught but when my legs move, it's not toward the door, it's toward one of the benches. I drop my elbows to my knees and rest my head in my hands. I keep my eyes shut for a beat, trying to force myself to calm down. If I don't then the temptation to go and cause some damage—ideally to Rich's face—is going to be stronger than I can control.

When I finally drag my eyes open, I find a piece of paper by my feet. Swiping it up, I flip it over, and find that it's a report card. Harley's report card to be specific.

I scan my eyes down the subjects, taking in all the good grades, until I get to one.

Math.

Fail.

My shoulders drop. That's why she was crying.

Guilt twists my stomach that I should be helping her with this.

"Fuck," I mutter, pushing to stand and shoving the paper in my pocket.

I manage to exit the girl's locker room unseen and head for my car.

———

The second I pull to a stop on our street, I wish I'd stayed at school longer, or even better, went after Harley because the person who's leaning against the porch waiting for me is one I hoped I'd never have to see again.

Gray stands there with his boot propped up on the first step, his body clad entirely in black—much like mine—and his head bowed as he stares at his cell. From here I can see the ink adorning his fingers that never used to be there.

I was never scared of Gray although a lot of kids always were. He's the youngest of five brothers. Five brothers who taught him how to look after himself from a very young age.

He doesn't look up, but I'm not stupid enough to think that he doesn't know I'm here so after sucking in a breath, I climb from the car to find out what he's got in store for me.

I lost him a lot of money. I can't imagine he's here for a nice little catch-up chat. I'm just grateful he waited a week.

The second the car door slams behind me, he pockets his cell and looks up.

I notice instantly that the ink on his hands isn't the only new addition because he's also got something beside his eye.

"Gray," I say as I step up to him. He studies me silently for a few seconds, probably seeing if he can unnerve me, but he should know me better than that. We've been through too much, done too much shit together. A year away won't change any of that.

"Legend," he finally says with a nod of his head.

Walking past him, I take a seat on the swing sweat, rest my elbows on my knees and look up at him. There's no fucking way I'm inviting him inside. Not that he'd wait to be invited if he wanted to venture inside, I'm sure.

"What do you want, Gray?"

"Now there's a question," he mutters, almost to himself. "How was your... little break?" A smirk appears on his lips and my fists curl in my need to knock it off. It wouldn't be the first time we've fought, and it wouldn't be the first time I've won either.

"Fuck you."

"Legend, now, that's not nice."

"Not nice? You really want to talk about what's not fucking nice?" I ask, my anger getting the better of me as I push to stand once more. "Not nice is getting carted off with your fucking blow filling my pockets. Not nice is the search they did to make sure I wasn't hiding any more. Not nice, is being locked in a tiny fucking room for hours on end, not having anyone to talk to, only people who want to beat the shit out of you. Not fucking nice is not seeing the one woman who gave a fuck about me before she died and having to attend her funeral in fucking handcuffs, you motherfucker." Spittle flies onto his face at my outburst but he doesn't react.

"You know what's really not going to be nice?"

I step closer, my fists ready to break his fucking nose.

"What?" I spit.

"What's going to happen when you don't pay your debt."

"Fuck you, Gray. I owe you nothing. You'll have made that back ten times over by now."

"Not the point. You lost my gear. You. Owe. Me."

"I have nothing." I take a step back and throw my arms out. "I have fucking nothing, Gray. Everything is gone. What the fuck could you take from me?"

He thinks for a minute and something about the look on his face makes my blood run cold.

"Harley Hunter is looking good these days, huh?"

My teeth grind, my jaw popping despite the fact I don't want to react to this motherfucker.

"Come on, Legend. Don't pretend you haven't noticed."

He leans in. "Because I know you have. You've wanted her longer than you'll ever admit. That night... that night I was just helping you out. Giving you the little push you needed."

I have his hoodie in my fist and him pressed against the railing of the porch before I've even realized I've moved.

"You fucking drugged her, Gray. You're fucking sick."

"You didn't look so bothered when she was getting ready to bounce around on your dick."

"Fuck you," I seethe, slamming him back against the wood.

"You're just angry because I wanted to play too. She'd have fucking loved it, and you know it. You could have been deep inside her cunt while she chok—" My fist flies, his nose crunching under the force of my hit. Blood covers both of us as an evil smile curls at his lips.

"Yeah, just as I thought."

My entire body is pulled tight ready for him to fight back, but instead, he just walks backward toward the stairs, spitting out a mouthful of blood as he does.

"You might want to keep a close eye on her, Legend. I'd hate for her to become payment."

"Don't you dare fucking touch her," I warn, but it's too late, he's already inside his car.

I watch as he wipes his nose on his sleeve before starting his car and wheelspinning down the street.

"Motherfucker," I bellow after him before pulling my cell from my pocket and opening mine and Harley's conversation.

I want to warn her. I want to tell her that he's just threatened her. But if he's just playing me...

Gray doesn't play.

But would he be stupid enough to mess with Harley knowing that he'll be going up against not only me but Kane and Zayn as well?

"Fuck," I shout into the empty street beyond.

I pull my cap from my head and pull my hair back, pulling until it hurts.

"Fuck."

Pulling out my key, I unlock the front door and storm inside.

I pace back and forth through the living room with my cell still in my hand trying to figure out what I should do.

I think about her tear-filled eyes as she fled from the locker room earlier and then the report card that's stuffed in my pocket.

Without putting much thought into it, I storm to my bedroom, flip open the textbook to the page we were working on last and I send the page and exercise number to her.

18

HARLEY

I slam my bedroom door after running up the stairs faster than my legs wanted to carry me.

I don't want to see anyone. I just want to hide from him, from math, from life.

"I fucking hate you, Kyle Legend," I bark into my empty bedroom.

Tears burn my eyes once more as I think about everything today threw at me.

The memory of kissing Rich makes my stomach turn. Nothing about him attracts me, I've only ever threatened to do anything with him to piss off my brother. But now I've kissed him, touched his cock. Ew. My lips curl in disgust but not at him, at myself. It was a stupid thing to do. But that's what he does to me. He makes me fucking stupid and drives me freaking crazy.

His scent still fills my nose from where he was so close to me in the locker room. His hard, sculpted body was pressed right up against mine, his hard cock digging into my hip reminding me of just how he tasted on Saturday night, how he looked as he lost control, how it felt when he came down my throat.

My body grows hot at the memory and annoys me even more.

Irritated with myself for allowing him to affect me even after I've walked away from him, I push from my door, turn my speakers up high and fall down onto my bed.

I've got work to do and continuing to put it off isn't going to get me anywhere.

I pull my math textbook out and flip it open.

I stare at it for a few seconds not really seeing any of it as my brain tells me not to even bother trying. But I know I need to shut that down. If I want to be on the squad for my senior year, then I need to do this. Hell, if I want to graduate then I need to do this.

"Okay, I can do this," I tell myself, leaning over and reading through the exercise I should be working on.

I'm halfway through my homework when my cell buzzes. It's face down on the sheets and I know that I really should ignore it.

It'll just be Ruby or Poppy checking in, they can wait.

But no matter how much I tell myself that, not two seconds later do I find myself reaching out and turning it over.

I groan the second I see who it really is.

Asshole: Turn to page 154 and start with exercise 3a.

"What?" I breathe.

Harley: What the hell?

Asshole: Don't argue, Kitten. Tell me how to work it out. Show me how you work it out.

I stare down at the screen, tempted to just turn it off and banish him from my life for a few hours but then I remember how he explained things to me during our first tutoring session once we called a truce and I find myself typing.

I write the sum on the page, I tell him how I think it should work and then I give him my answer once I've done the equation.

It's wrong. Obviously. But then he starts explaining why and even though he's not here, it's like I can hear his voice in my head as he spells it out in a way that I've only ever experienced with him.

Asshole: Now do the next one. Just like that.

I eagerly follow his instructions and soon discover that my next answer is right.

A little thrill goes through me as he messages back to confirm what I already know.

Asshole: Now do the rest. You've got this, Kitten.

Butterflies erupt in my belly as I stare down at his little pet name for me that I usually hate.

He just helped me. Why?

I shake my head, immediately realizing that I'm not going to figure him out quite that easily.

I quickly go through the rest of the exercises on the page and send him a list of my answers which, to my utter amazement are all correct.

An accomplished smile curls up at my lips, maybe I can do this. Just one step at a time.

I stare at his last message trying to figure out what to send back. There are a million things I want to say to him, to ask him when he's not full of anger and out for revenge but even now, I refrain.

Harley: Thank you.

Asshole: What are tutors for? What's next?

Harley: English paper. You?

Asshole: Same.

We message back and forth for the next three hours. It's nice. Weird. But I can't deny that I get a little thrill every time my cell buzzes and I see his name staring back at me.

It's when he tells me that he's done for the night and that he's going to shower that I realize I might have a problem because I almost demand we switch to video call just so I can go with him.

In the end, I go with something a little less desperate.

Harley: Thank you. I'm going to do some more math before bed.

He reads it but he doesn't respond, and my heart drops a little as I realize that he wasn't getting as carried away with our interaction as I was.

I place my cell back down, and after getting myself a snack and drink I pull my math book back onto my lap and attempt some more.

I've got another test on Wednesday; I'm determined not to fail this one.

———

The second I walk into class the next morning, his eyes are on me from the back of the room. His face is impassive and totally unreadable. I have no clue if he's still angry like in the locker room or if our messages last night softened him at all.

Ruby's fingers twist with mine as we make our way to our seats. I haven't told her about what happened after she and

Chelsea left, and I certainly haven't told her about our impromptu tutoring session.

"Ignore him," she whispers, clearly seeing who's holding his attention.

My temperature burns red-hot as his eyes run over every inch of me as we get closer. Thankfully, our seats are far enough away that we can't talk because after everything that happened yesterday, I have no clue what to say to him, or even where to start.

Even long after turning my back on him to take my seat, I still feel his gaze on me. My skin prickles with awareness and tingles continue to race up and down my spine.

I can only hope that this is the only class we share today because he's already messing with my head.

I manage to escape him and it's not until I'm standing at my locker before heading to the cafeteria before lunch that I feel him.

Every muscle in my body screams at me to turn around and look at him, but I stand firm and instead remain staring at the back of my locker, hoping that he'll leave, or that I'm wrong and he's not there at all.

Sadly, that's not what happens.

My body startles when his large warm hand lands on my stomach and the length of him presses against my back. I only just manage to stifle the groan that threatens to rumble up my throat at his contact.

"Do I need to lock you up somewhere this lunch or are you going to be able to keep your hands to yourself, Kitten?"

I suck in a breath, unable to come up with a response as quickly as I'd like.

"What's wrong, cat got your tongue?"

His hand slips under the hem of my shirt, his touch scorching my already heated skin.

"I need to go, Rich is waiting for me," I lie, knowing it'll piss him off. "That was the best kiss I've had in quite a while."

"Harley," he growls in my ear, sending goose bumps racing across my skin. "I warned you about lying to me."

"Am I though?" I ask, fighting a smile. "Excuse me." Amazingly, when I twist out of his hold, he lets me go.

I slam my locker closed and march toward the cafeteria, my stomach growling for Taco Tuesday with every step I take.

I find Ruby, Poppy and Stella waiting for me at the entrance and together we join the queue.

"What the fuck is he playing at?" Poppy seethes, looking over my shoulder in the direction of our tables.

I don't have to turn around to know she's talking about Kyle. I can tell by the anger on their faces as they watch whatever is playing out.

My cell vibrates in my pocket. Despite knowing that nothing good can possibly come from it seeing as my girls are standing with me, not on their cells, I pull it out.

Asshole: Wanna see how it's really done? Turn around.

I fight it, I really fucking do. But when all three of them gasp, my body moves without instruction from my brain.

The second I look up, my eyes land on Kyle who's got Aria straddling his lap, his hands disappearing under her skirt and her lips on his neck while he stares right at me, a satisfied smirk playing on his lips.

"You just gonna let that happen?" Ruby asks me.

"Uh... yeah. Why wouldn't I?" I try really fucking hard not to allow the hurt I'm feeling come to transfer into my voice. But when her eyes soften in sympathy, I'm not sure I'm all that successful. "He's nothing to me. He can do whatever he wants."

"You really believe that?" Poppy asks.

"Yeah, I really do. He's just trying to get a reaction from

me and he's not going to get one. I don't care," I say, turning back to him and ensuring he can read my lips.

I take my tray from the rail once we've all paid and we make our way over. I try not to look as we get closer but it's impossible to ignore the fact that Aria is now sitting beside Kyle with her hand resting high on his thigh while she looks up at him like he just hung the moon.

"He's watching you," Stella whispers to me as we pass. I don't need her to tell me though, I feel it.

I ignore her, pull out a chair and sit down doing the best I can to pretend that I don't give a shit about what he's doing behind me.

The second we finish eating, Stella and I escape in favor of... well, anywhere other than the cafeteria, and leave everyone—including Kyle and his new cheer slut—behind.

"That was brutal."

"It was nothing," I mutter, trying to play it off like it didn't hurt.

"You don't need to do that, you know."

"Do what?" I force some lightness into my tone that I really don't feel as we allow a couple of girls to leave the bathroom before we enter.

"Pretend it doesn't bother you."

"It doesn't. He can do whatever he wants."

She stares at me for a beat before disappearing into one of the stalls while I pull my makeup bag out in the hope I can cover up the truth that I'm sure she can read all over my face.

By the time she emerges, I've got a whole new layer of confidence plastered on.

"Just so you know, my dad has a cupboard full of guns, and I'm a pretty good shot." The seriousness she says this with makes me burst out laughing.

"Oh my God, you're serious, aren't you?"

"Deadly. I'm sure we could hide the body and get away with it."

"I'll keep that in mind."

"Okay, well if not, he's also got some scary-ass friends that I'm sure would do me a favor if I asked sweetly enough."

"Who the hell is your dad, the fucking mafia?"

"Honestly, I have no idea. He's secretive as fuck but I do know that whatever he does do isn't totally above board. Please don't tell anyone I said that."

"Of course not. Your secret's safe with me." I wink, shoving my makeup bag into my purse and getting ready to head to class.

We go our separate ways once we emerge from the bathroom. Stella toward her Spanish class and me history.

"Hey, how it's going?" Carl asks, dropping down into his seat beside me. The two of us have occupied this desk at the very back of the classroom all year.

"It's good. You?"

"Not bad." Carl is on the baseball team so he's mostly oblivious to the gossip surrounding the football team. He's easy to talk to and he's not bad to look at either. He's also been in love with his girlfriend for as long as I can remember which makes him even easier to talk to. "So ready for this week to be over though."

"It's only Tuesday," I say, although the way my week is going, I'd be inclined to agree with him.

"Yeah well. Misty and I have the house to ourselves this weekend so..."

"Say no more." I wink. "I hope you've got plenty of romantic shit planned."

"I'm doing my best." He starts rattling off some of his ideas, most of which make me swoon. Although the second I realize they're all the kind of things that Nathan would have done, my stomach twists painfully.

I had the sweet guy right there making all the right moves and saying all the right things, and what did I do? I fucked it all up. Epically fucked it all up.

The volume of chatting filling the room suddenly lessens and assuming our teacher has just entered to start the class, the two of us turn toward the front, only, I don't get a chance to look that far because my eyes lock on a very angry pair staring down at Carl.

"Move," Kyle demands, his voice hard, leaving no room for discussion.

"Ignore him," I say, placing my hand on Carl's shoulder without thinking.

A growl rumbles up Kyle's throat the second I make contact with him.

"I said. Move."

"Kyle, stop being an asshole," I snap. "There's like a million other seats in here. Just go sit in one of those."

He tilts his head to the side for a beat as if he's considering my words before one word falls from his lips.

"No."

"Honestly, it's fine. I'll just..." Carl begins gathering up his stuff.

"No, it's not fine. This is where you sit."

"I know but..." he shoots Kyle a concerned look and it's then I realize that he's scared. Brilliant. Fucking brilliant.

Carl disappears to the other side of the class giving Kyle the space he clearly wanted, so he could drop down beside me.

"Hey, Kitten."

"Go fuck yourself. Or better yet, go fuck Aria, if you haven't already."

"Careful, Kitten. You sound a little jealous there."

I snort a laugh. "Careful, asshole. You sound even more arrogant than usual."

He chuckles at me, sliding his chair over so it's as close to mine as physically possible.

"What the hell do you—"

"Afternoon everyone. All ready to get started?" Mr.

Anderson says, effectively silencing the entire classroom as he slams the door closed behind me.

"Hmmm... I am more than ready to get started. What do you say, Kitten?" Kyle breathes in my ear, making me shudder as he sits back in his chair and rests his arms across the back of mine, his fingers brushing my shoulder blade.

"Get your hands off me," I snap, sitting forward and putting as much space between us as I can.

"What did I tell you about lying? I know you're more than ready," he whispers, his fingers ghosting down my spine until they run along the slivers of skin that's been revealed between my shirt and my jeans. "Are you wet for me, Kitten?"

I cut him a scathing look.

"I thought you wanted to graduate?"

An irritatingly stunning smile curls at his lips and something inside my tummy clenches.

His eyes drop from mine in favor of my lips. He sucks his bottom one into his mouth and all I can think about is doing the exact same thing to it.

Damn him.

I force myself to picture Aria on his lap barely an hour ago.

"Yeah, and I will. But right now, I've got more pressing issues."

His fingers move back up my spine and brush against my neck, almost massaging for a few seconds. My eyes shutter at just how good it feels before he wraps the fabric in his fist and uses it to pull me back against my seat, the neckline digging into my skin.

"Do you—" My words falter when I find his dark stare burning into mine.

He smiles once again, and I manage to snap myself out of whatever trance he had me under.

"Miss Hunter, Mr. Legend, are you following?"

We both turn toward the teacher, but his grip on my shirt

doesn't lessen. Thank God we're at the back so no one can see what he's doing.

My face flushes with embarrassment that we've been caught as I stutter out, "Y-yes, sir."

"Okay good, so you'll both know exactly what I just asked you all to discuss and you'll be able to explain your conclusion to the class?"

"O-of course." I smile sweetly at him. Never before in my life have I been this distracted in class.

I've always been the good student, the one who always hits deadlines and often does extra—math is the exception to the rule, I guess I figured that if I try hard enough elsewhere then no one will notice. Fail.

"Okay, brilliant. You all have twenty minutes in your pairs to discuss and come up with an argument."

Students' chatter begins to fill the room as they embark on the task at hand, I, however, am frozen staring at the board with the instructions on it as Kyle's stare burns into the side of my face.

He turns toward me a little, as if we're actually about to discuss something of importance and he leans closer. His scent fills my nose as his knee brushes against my thigh. It's a simple touch and one that shouldn't elicit such a strong reaction within me, but I can't help it.

"W-what are you d-doing?"

He slides the textbook on the desk between us, I can only assume it's open on the right page because I can't focus on it.

My chest heaves as I try to fight the sensations washing through my body at his nearness, at the tightness around my throat and the heat of him against my skin.

"What are you thinking about, Kitten?" he asks.

My spine remains rigid as image after image assaults my mind of him pushing me back against the wall and wrapping his hand around my throat.

My body burns up at the thoughts alone and I know it's evident on my face.

"We need to get to work," I force out and thankfully, his grip on my neck lessens until it's gone completely.

"Yeah, I guess we do," he murmurs.

I breathe a sigh of relief when his touch leaves me and he turns toward the book, pen in hand, ready to write notes whatever it is we're supposed to be discussing. But the second I move to do the same, his hot hand lands on my thigh under the table. It skims higher until his little finger flicks the seam at the juncture of my thighs.

"So I was thinking..." he starts as if he was actually fucking listening to what we're supposed to be doing. "What if the outcome of this meeting went the other way..." He pushes his fingers between my thighs and forces them apart.

"What the fuck?" I hiss about ready to snap his wrist to stop him but then he pushes harder against my core. "Oh God," I gasp, my body spiraling out of control at that one simple touch from him.

I know this shouldn't be happening. I shouldn't be allowing it. He just had Aria kissing him only moments ago in the cafeteria but fuck, I'm not sure I can stop.

19

KYLE

smile twitches at my lips as I discreetly glance over at her.

Her lids are lowered, her lips parted but her jaw clenches almost in frustration. She wants to stop me. She thinks that would be the right thing to do. But I also think she knows that she's not the one in control here. I am.

My fingers continue to move against her while I write a few notes because I already know that our teacher is going to be good on his word of making us give an explanation, and like fuck am I not going to have one.

I almost laugh when she relaxes back in her chair a little and widens her legs.

She's so fucking easy to play. But I know exactly why, because I feel it too the few times she's touched me.

Powerless.

Fucking powerless.

I continue working as her breathing begins to increase. I glance over once more but the table hides what I'm doing to her.

"Why didn't you wear a skirt this morning?" I ask as seriously as if I'm talking about the work.

Her lust-filled eyes turn on me and her hand wraps around my forearm, her nails digging into my skin.

"You're an asshole," she seethes.

"Yet you're still letting me touch you."

Her nails dig in harder until I'm convinced that she'll have drawn blood when she releases me, not that I give a fuck. The thought of having her mark on me only gets me harder.

"And you're going to let me make you come, aren't you, Kitten?"

"No," she snaps, a little too loudly.

"Harley, is everything okay?" our teacher asks.

"Um... yeah... I really need to go to the bathroom."

Oh, Kitten. Do you have any idea what you've just done?

"Be quick," he grumbles, already pissed off with us.

The second she's gone, I pull my cell from my pocket and send a message.

Not four minutes later is there a knock at our classroom door and a familiar head peers inside.

"I'm sorry, sir. I just need to borrow Kyle Legend for a few minutes as per Coach's orders."

"Fine," he groans, looking at me and nodding to the door, seemingly totally unaware that I've set the whole thing up.

Leaving my books on the desk, I push my chair out and walk to the door, closing it behind me.

"Cheers, man. I appreciate it."

"Gonna tell me why you needed to get out?" Ash asks, his brows pulling together. I knew the second he looked at my message that he'd understand. We're the same, Ash and I, we grew up the same and we have a similar way of thinking, which is why I'm even surprised he's asking this question.

"Why do you think, man?" I slap him on the shoulder as I walk away. "I owe you one," I call back as I head for the closest bathroom.

The room is silent as I push the door open and step

inside. Only one of the stalls is being used, and the second I rest my ass back against the basins, the flush is pressed.

My fingers curl around the counter as my heart beats steadily in my chest. If this isn't her, I could have an issue on my hands.

But something tells me it is. She wouldn't have run that far because she wouldn't have expected me to follow.

The lock on the door slides open and I wait for it to open.

The second it does, I know it's her. I recognize the dark purple nail polish that was sinking into my skin only minutes ago.

She doesn't notice me straight away, she's too busy staring at the floor.

Pushing from my resting place, I take a step toward her, totally unnoticed for two seconds. But my sneakers squeak on the floor and her head flies up, but I'm faster.

My hand wraps around her throat and I direct her back until she's against the wall.

"Surprise." I move forward until our noses are almost brushing.

"What the hell?"

"What? You really thought I'd let you run. I thought you knew me better than that, Kitten."

"W-we... we need to get back to class. Mr. Anderson will blow a fuse."

"Mr. Anderson doesn't give a shit or he wouldn't have let us both out," I growl, my lips brushing hers as my body presses her against the tiles at her back.

"Kyle," she warns as my hand lands on her waist and slips under her shirt.

"Kitten."

Our eyes hold, our breaths mingling and our chest heaving as we wait to see what the other is going to do.

Finally, her lips part, and as much as I might want to kiss

her, to dirty her up before she's forced to go back to class, I'm too intrigued as to what she's going to say to make use of her open mouth.

"I hate you," she seethes. "Why won't you just leave me alone?"

"Oh, Kitten." I laugh. "If only I could."

"What do you want from me? An apology? I'm sorry I called the cops and you got locked up," she says totally insincerely, throwing her arms out from her side.

"Oh yeah, because you totally meant that."

"You and Gray—" Just the mention of his name makes my blood run cold. "You were going to—"

"We were going to do what?" I ask, needing to know what she thinks happened that night.

"You were going to—"

"What the hell? Harley, are you okay?" a voice says from behind me and I freeze.

"Y-yeah. Kyle was just going back to class, weren't you?" She smiles at me but there's no kindness there, it's full of hate and bitterness.

"We're going to talk about this, Kitten," I growl, low enough so that our little one-woman audience can't hear me.

"Then maybe you should stop being a dick," she suggests.

"I'd love to, but you just bring it out in me." I flex my hips, ensuring my length presses into her hip.

"Get the fuck off me, asshole." Her palms slam down on my chest and I take pity on her and back away ensuring that she notices when I drop my hand to rearrange myself in my jeans. Her eyes zero in on my movement and then darken with lust.

I blow her a kiss before backing out of the room. At the last second, I glance at the girl who interrupted us. Her blue eyes narrow on me and she bares her teeth in anger.

"Down girl, you can get a turn as well if you like."

"Fuck off, pig," she barks, much to my amusement as the door closes behind me.

The hallway is empty as I make my way back to class and take a seat.

Mr. Anderson watches my every move, I can feel his attention on me, but at no point do I look up at him. Instead, I make use of the time I've got until she returns to write some notes.

After a few minutes, I start to think she's not going to come back, but when I glance at the floor, I find that in her haste to get away from me, she left her purse.

I smile to myself, sitting back just as the door opens and she steps inside the room, still looking totally flustered and uncomfortable.

"Is everything okay, Miss Hunter?"

"Yes, thank you, sir."

He nods at her as she pulls her chair as far away from me as she can and retakes her seat.

I look over at her, an amused smile playing on my lips.

"Don't," she snaps. "Don't say anything, don't do anything unless you want the end of this pen embedded in your dick."

"I love it when you talk dirty to me."

A growl rumbles up her throat as Mr. Anderson announces that we've got two minutes to bring our arguments to a close and be ready to present.

The hate covering her face morphs into one of panic as she realizes that we're going to have to give our opinion on this seeing as we've already been warned and she's not so much as thought about it.

"I hope you're ready." I turn away from her and look to the teacher who's got his eyes on the two of us.

Oh yeah, we're definitely going first.

"Right. Time is up. Miss Hunter, Mr Legend, why don't you start us off."

I smile at him. He's so fucking predictable.

"Go on, you can start," I encourage, nudging Harley's arm with my elbow.

"Harley..." Mr. Anderson says.

Hesitantly, she stands. Her chair scraping across the old tiled floor, ensuring that everyone in the room turns her way.

She stares at our teacher before looking down at me. Her eyes are wide as she clenches her fists at her sides.

"I... um..." Mr. Anderson's brows rise as his patience begins to vanish. "Err..." She looks down at me as if I'm going to help her but I just smile up at her as sweetly as I can manage. "So... what we thought was..."

Her eyes flick to the board behind Mr. Anderson as if she's even forgotten what we were supposed to be talking about—assuming she even knew in the first place.

"Miss Hunter?" he asks, crossing his arms over his chest as sniggers begin to rumble around the room as she awkwardly shifts on her feet.

I fight to keep my ass in the chair as she prays for the ground to swallow her up but I can't do it. She might think I'm an asshole, and I am, to a point.

I push my chair out behind me and stand beside her. She looks at me, probably waiting for me to make this whole situation worse but to her surprise, that's not what happens.

"What Harley is trying to say is that we thought if the decision went the opposite way that the Civil War would have started that much later, but that the intensity of the fighting would have been much more significant. Also that the death count would have well surpassed what happened in reality."

Even as I'm talking, I don't miss the huge sigh of relief she lets out that I just got us off the hook.

"Interesting point, Kyle." He continues to question me and I answer him as if we were discussing this subject the whole time.

He smiles at me before turning back to Harley. "Well, it

seems Mr. Legend has saved you from an afternoon in detention. You can both sit."

As our asses hit the chair, he begins to question another couple.

"How'd you do that?" Harley whispers. "How'd you know what to say?"

"I'm not just a pretty face, Kitten." I wink at her and she rolls her eyes.

The second the bell rings, she all but scoops her belongings into her purse and damn near runs from the door.

I hang back as students leave and Mr. Anderson wipes off the board and collects up the textbooks.

It's not until I stand and about to throw my bag over my shoulder when he speaks.

"I know things are done differently at Creek High but here, we don't tolerate our students trying to sabotage others."

I nod at him, not wanting to get into a discussion about Harley. "You got it, sir," I mutter as I walk through the door and join the mass of students heading toward the exits for the evening.

I head in the opposite direction of the majority as I go toward the locker rooms for a conditioning session.

Pulling out my cell, I can't resist sending her one more message.

Kyle: You're welcome!

Her response is instant, there are no words, just a hand emoji with its middle finger in the air.

I'm still smiling to myself when I walk into the locker room. The second I look up, I find a man standing in front of the team who I've only seen from a distance so far.

"Legend," Coach says to me as I come to a stop beside Ash. "I've heard good things about you from Coach West."

I nod at him, glad that something good might have come out of my few years at Creek High.

"With you, Fury, and a few of our JV team this year, we might just stand a chance of living up to this year's success. I'm going to be watching all of you over the next few weeks, Jake and the seniors too. I don't just want good players, I want decent fucking human beings on my team. So watch your backs, ladies," he says making eye contact with me, Ash, and the others who I know to be juniors. "If you play your cards right, you might just be able to call yourself a Rosewood Bear in the coming months."

Excited chatter vibrates through the group before Coach nods at Jake, who takes to the front of the crowd.

"Don't think it's going to be easy, you all have a reputation to keep. Get your asses changed and get out on the field, we want to see what you pussies are made of."

"How competitive was your old team?" Ash asks me once we've broken away from the crowd to change.

"Their biggest priorities were getting high and scoring pussy," I answer honestly. "We were never going to win fuck all unless you count collecting STDs."

Ash snorts a laugh as he rips his locker open and pulls his shirt over his head.

"What about yours?"

"Same. My old school was a fucking jungle. I'm buzzing to take this a little more seriously."

"You shooting for captain?" I ask, knowing that he held the position in his old team.

"Maybe," he says, but a small smile twitches at his lips. "We'll see. Why? You wanna be my assistant?"

I think for a minute. Kane was captain at Harrow Creek High. I wasn't there long enough to even get a chance. Do I want to follow in his footsteps and take the lead with Ash? "Hell fucking yeah I do."

"Damn right. This team is ours, man." I hold my fist out and he bumps it before turning back to drag on a pair of shorts.

20

HARLEY

nger swirls around me like a firestorm through our first cheer practice. Although we don't actually do much cheer because we spend most of the time listening to Chelsea and—shockingly—Miss Kelly explains what's going to happen next and the process of selecting our new varsity squad.

I find myself losing focus faster than ever thanks to *him* and his actions in history.

Did I want him touching me? I can tell myself that the answer is no until I'm blue in the face, but really, every time his fingers so much as graze my skin, I feel alive in a way I only ever have a few times in my life. And all of those times involve him—even if I thought I was going to die during one of them.

Ruby and Stella look at me with curious glances but I keep my lips firmly shut. They probably think I'm still stewing on the fact he let Aria kiss him at lunch. I guess I am a little. But so much has happened since then it's almost a distant memory. Almost.

"We heading to Ace's?" someone asks the second we're back in the locker room.

"Only if the team are going," Aria sings.

"Whore," Ruby mutters beside me. "We're going to Ace's."

"Uh... I'm not. I don't want to watch her grind her ass all over Kyle."

Both Ruby and Stella look at me with sympathy in their eyes. Stella more so after what she walked in on earlier.

She'd tried to get me to talk, but after all of that, I was in no mood. I'd attempted to convince her that it was fine and to drop it but I can already see that I'm on borrowed time.

"But—"

"No buts, Rubes. I'm not going. She can have at it." I keep my expression neutral while inside everything clenches in disgust at even the suggestion. "Come to mine, we'll order pizza."

They look at each other, the rest of the squad still discussing the team, before agreeing.

An hour later, Poppy has joined us, and we're hanging out on my bed with two giant pizzas between the four of us. We probably should be doing homework—I know I should be doing math—but it feels good to kick back after the day I've had.

"So how many high schools have you been to exactly?" Ruby asks Stella.

She sighs. "This is my fifth."

"Fifth?" the three of us echo.

"Two freshman year," she says, holding up her fingers to count. "One sophomore, and then another before I joined Rosewood."

"Jesus. And all across the country?"

"Yep, New York, Michigan, Colorado, Washington, here. And that's just high school. I've lost count of the number of schools before ninth grade."

"Fucking hell, it's amazing you know your own name after that," I say around a mouthful of pepperoni pizza.

"So where are you actually from?" Ruby asks.

"Well, I have no recollection of it, but apparently I was born in England. My dad moved us over here before I was one."

"What about your mom?"

She shrugs, a sad expression washing over her face. "Dead. I think that's why he moved. He couldn't be there without her."

"Shit."

"Meh," she says with another shrug, grabbing a slice of pizza. "It is what it is, gotta make the best of it, I guess."

"Well, I'm in awe of you," Poppy says sincerely.

"And you still have no idea where to next?"

"Nope. Just that it's coming. Dad's not said anymore but I can sense it. I know his tells. He's getting ready to move."

"We're going to miss you."

"Me too. I think Rosewood might be my favorite out of all my homes. I could see myself here."

"Shame you don't get a choice."

"Maybe I'll come back one day. Once I've finished college, I am finding myself a home and I'm staying put for a very long freaking time."

"Don't blame you."

Feeling sorry for Stella having to relive all her moves, I turn the conversation away from her and back toward cheer, much to Poppy's joy if her dramatic eye roll is anything to go by.

"You'd better get used to it," Stella tells her, clearly noticing her move. "If these two get captain and assistant, it's all they're going to talk about."

"It's fine," she says flippantly. "I can just go over the hall and bang the assistant's brother."

"Oh, you did not just say that." I launch a cushion at her head, both of us falling about laughing.

It feels good. So fucking good. But that all comes crashing down when my cell pings in my pocket.

My heart jumps into my throat. Without looking, I know who it is. I can sense it.

"You gonna get that?" Ruby asks when it goes off again a few minutes later.

"Um..." Reluctantly, I pull it from my back pocket and find exactly what I was expecting.

Asshole: Page 162 exercise 1a. Gimme the answers.

Clearly I don't cover up my feelings at seeing his words on my screen because as I'm still reading Ruby is asking who it is.

"Just my math tutor. Wants me to work."

"We can go," she offers.

"No, no. It's fine. He'll have to wait."

"Who is it?" Poppy asks. I knew the question was coming yet still, I don't have a decent response.

"Some nerd I swear I've never seen around school before."

"Is he any good?"

My head goes straight in the gutter and I'm right back in Justin's guest room with Kyle's head between my legs.

My cheeks heat as I stare down at his words on my cell.

"Ugh, yeah, he's all right."

It's probably about fifteen minutes later when another message comes through.

Asshole: Don't make me come over there.

The threat makes my heart skip a beat.

"Him again?" Poppy asks.

"Yeah," I say reluctantly.

"We should go. We know how important this is."

I don't get a chance to argue, not that I think they'd allow me to because they gather up the pizza boxes and the empty soda cans littering my bedroom and make their way to the door.

"We'll see you tomorrow," Ruby says as she and Stella slip out of my room.

"Call me if you need me. I'm just gonna do some homework," Poppy adds before following them out and leaving me alone with just the cell in my hand.

It pings again.

Asshole: You have five minutes to respond or shit's getting real, Kitten.

Rolling my eyes at him, I start typing.

Harley: I was busy, ASSHOLE. WHAT DO YOU WANT?

Asshole: I gave you my instructions, now… I want answers.

Harley: You're as demanding as my mother.

Asshole: Oh Kitten, I am so NOT like your mother…

My body flushes hot at what he could mean and my teeth sink into my bottom lip as those memories assault me once again.

Damn him.

Asshole: I'm waiting.

"Fuck's sake."

Leaning over the side of the bed, I grab my purse and pull out my textbook, my workbook and a pen.

Flipping the page open to the one he said, I groan at the sight of the exercise.

I go through the steps like he taught me last night and fire off my answers to him.

Asshole: First one is right. Others aren't. You need to go through the process again?

I fall back on my bed, tears filling my eyes faster than I can control.

I thought I had this. I thought I'd figured it out with his instructions last night.

Not wanting to admit defeat, I reply.

Harley: Let me try again.

I blow out a breath, turn to a clean page, and start over. Going through everything he told me last night. I get different answers this time but I have no idea if that's a good thing or not. They're probably still wrong.

I shoot him the new answers.

Asshole: Yes! Now, do the rest of that exercise.

I repeat the process again and again and every time he confirms that I've got it right.

I smile to myself as the latest 'well done' comes through, my confidence starting to grow. Maybe I can do this. Maybe I'm not destined to be a math idiot forever.

Asshole: Ready for more…

Jesus. Why do his messages about math send my head elsewhere?

Harley: Hit me.

Asshole: I'd rather not. I can think of something else I'd like to do though…

Harley: Focus. Unless you've already got Aria bouncing around on you right now.

Asshole: No, Kitten. I'm all yours.

An excited flutter rushes through me at his words.

"Focus, Harley. You hate him, remember," I remind myself as I look to the next exercise. I swallow my groan when I see it getting harder. My heart starts to race and the confidence I had started to build gets knocked down.

Kyle explains the next step of the process, and it sounds simple enough. I've already proved I can do the first part.

I set to work and quite quickly come up with some answers.

I send them to him full of hope that I've nailed it.

He reads my message immediately and starts typing. My heart pounds as I wait for his response. I've got a really good feeling about this, a part of me thinks that if I can nail this, then I can do all of it.

The dots bounce for ages and I start to wonder if he's writing an essay back.

My hope starts to wane when I realize that if they were right, he'd have already told me by now.

A lump forms in my throat and pressure builds behind my eyes.

Maybe I should just turn my cell off and avoid the inevitable. But just as I consider that option, it pings.

Asshole: I'm sorry, Kitten. But I think I know where you went wrong.

"FUCK," I scream into my room, throwing myself back on the bed in frustration. I really thought I had that.

Before he has a chance to say any more, I send him a message.

Harley: I can't do this. Sorry for wasting your time.

My thumb hovers over the off button but before I press it to put an end to all of this a call comes through.

A video call.

My hand trembles as I stare at his name.

I can't answer this. I've got tears running down my cheeks, makeup probably everywhere.

I can't answer—my finger swipes across the screen despite what my brain is telling me and the call connects.

"Kitten," he breathes when he gets his first look at me. "You were so close. Please don't cry."

A sob rips up my throat at the softness in his voice and more tears fall.

"I thought you wanted to make me cry," I mutter, trying to turn this away from me being a total failure.

His brows pinch as he stares at me, sympathy covering his features. He looks just like the boy I remember like this and it makes my heart ache.

I might not have intended the outcome of that night—he may have been involved, but he was far from the main player in trying to ruin my life that night—but still, the weight of what happened to him falls on my shoulders. The reason this is the first time I'm seeing the old Kyle, the fun loving, intelligent boy who had the world at his feet, is me.

"Not like this, Harley." The sincerity in his voice makes my breath catch.

We stare at each other in silence, only the sound of my shaky breathing filling my ears. No words are being said but I feel like a line is being drawn.

"I'm... I'm sorry, Ky."

He smiles at me, lifting his arm to run his fingers through what I now notice is damp hair. The second he drops his hand, his hair falls straight back over his brow and I smile, liking him without the ball cap that's constantly attached to his head.

His ice-blue eyes pierce mine and I swear I don't breathe as I wait for him to say something.

"Me too, Kitten. Me too."

"So..." he starts. "Did you want to try those again?"

His question damn near gives me whiplash. I was so lost in his eyes and my memories.

"Uh... not really." I laugh.

"Well, that's a real shame because I'm not hanging up until you've smashed it."

"You know I could just hang up on you, right?"

"Yeah, but you won't," he states confidently.

"Is that right?"

"Yep. Unless you want me there in person." He raises a brow and leans closer to the camera making me wonder if that is exactly what I do want.

"Never," I spit, hoping that it sounds like I mean it.

"You didn't seem so concerned that last time I was there."

"So math," I say, making him chuckle down the line. An easy smile curls at his lips and I have the urge to screenshot it because it's so beautiful and so at odds with the anger I've become used to since he appeared.

"Prop your cell up somewhere and let's do it."

I shift around, grabbing the holder that's on my nightstand and setting it up on the bed.

"Harley," he growls the second I place my cell in the holder and point it toward me. "What the hell are you wearing?"

I look down at myself and my cheeks heat. Shit.

"Um... we had practice. I've... um... not showered yet," I

admit with a wince. We hardly did any actual practice so I didn't bother changing after, just threw on a zip-up hoodie over my booty shorts and sports bra. Ruby and Stella were similar so I didn't think anything of it when I was with them.

Now though with his eyes drilling into my barely clad body, I'm regretting the fuck out of it.

"O-okay," he says, clearing his throat as I release the stand and wrap my hoodie around me to cover up. "Don't feel like you have to."

"This is a tutoring session, Kyle, not—" I slam my lips.

"Not what?" he asks, amusement dancing in his blue eyes.

"Not anything else. So this exercise, you said you thought you knew what I did wrong." I never thought I'd willingly be encouraging a conversation about math, but there we go.

I pull my workbook and pen onto my lap as Kyle starts talking through the process.

In only seconds, I can see the obvious mistake I'd made and I feel a little better about the whole thing.

"Okay, so do the next exercise. I'm just gonna grab a drink."

"Okay," I say without even looking at the screen as a thud sounds out where he must have put his cell down before his footsteps get farther away.

I make quick work of going through each exercise and by the time he comes back, I've got all the answers staring back at me.

"Done?" he asks, settling himself back against his headboard and staring at me through the screen.

"Yep." I hold up my workbook so he can see. He's silent as I assume he looks at the answers and the longer he doesn't say anything the more butterflies erupt in my belly.

I really don't want to have failed again.

"Smashed it," he finally says and I drop my workbook so I can see him.

"Really?" I ask, a wide smile splitting my face.

"Yeah. Let's do one more exercise and then we can celebrate."

"Celebrate?" I ask, unsure as to whether or not I like the sound of that.

"Yeah, you wanna have some fun with me, Kitten?" His voice is low and gravelly and it does weird things to my insides let alone what's going on between my thighs.

"Um... it's probably better that I don't. Fun with you doesn't always end up so... pleasurable," I breathe that one word and have to fight a laugh when his eyes widen in shock.

"Is that right? I seem to remember things being very pleasurable when we have fun."

"That's because your idea of fun is..." I hesitate, trying to come up with the right word. "More like torture."

"Torture?" He almost spits out the mouthful of soda he'd not yet swallowed. "Oh Kitten, I don't remember you complaining."

My body heats to uncomfortable temperatures as I remember just how willingly I got between his legs at Justin's.

Jesus, I was a damn slut that night.

Alcohol. It was the alcohol.

"With your hand around my throat, it makes it kinda hard to say anything."

He throws his head back and laughs. It was not the reaction I was expecting but the sound of his joy sure makes up for it.

"Harley?" he says, dragging his head forward and holding my eyes captive through the screen.

"Y-yeah?" The stuttered word comes out as no more than a whisper.

"Take your hoodie off."

"Um... I really don't think—"

"Harley," he growls and it sends shivers racing down my spine. "Be a good girl and do what you're told."

I hold his stare, my need to refuse is right on the tip of my tongue. But instead of parting my lips to do just that, I find myself shrugging out of my hoodie as he demanded.

Ripping his eyes from mine, he drops them down my torso. My sports bra is small. I've not got all that much that needs controlling so I can get away with cute little ones.

"Go on then. I want the rest of the answers."

"And what about you?" I tilt my head to the side and drop my eyes to the bottom of the screen but I can't see anything past his neck.

"Get the answers right and it might just be your lucky day, Kitten."

"Fucking hell," I mutter to myself, looking down at the workbook in my lap and snatching up my pen.

How the hell did I end up here?

"Nothing good happens to me when I'm around you," I say quietly, unsure if he'll hear it, not that it matters if it does.

"Is that right? I guess it's a good thing you're not actually near me right now then."

"Do you mind? I'm busy working."

"Sure, you carry on. I'll just enjoy the view."

His words make me look up and the second I do they collide with his sparkling blue-grey ones.

Shaking my head at him, I look back down and try to focus on what I should be doing.

He's silent as I work through each question but I can feel his stare despite the fact it's through a screen.

It's better this way. He might be infuriating but he's easier to manage when there's space between us. His presence is less suffocating.

"Done?" he asks when I straighten my back and drop my pen.

"Yep."

"And how confident are you?"

"Hmm... I don't know. I guess it depends on what I get in return."

He thinks for a beat. "I'll show you mine if you show me yours." He wiggles his brows and I bark a laugh at his craziness.

It's nice to laugh and joke like things between us are okay. I'm not stupid enough to think it's our reality though. The second I see him at school tomorrow, I know the scowl that seems to be constantly on his face will be back and he'll look at me like he wants to kill me. It seems to be our thing, like this right now is our little secret.

And I hate that I like it as much as I do.

"You're serious, aren't you?"

I haven't forgotten that while he had me totally naked on Saturday night that he barely showed me any skin and I'm damn near desperate to see those muscles that I've run my hands over, traced with my fingertips.

"I never joke about getting naked, Kitten."

"Fuck off, why don't you. That whole thing Saturday night was a game and you know it."

"Game? No. Revenge, Kitten. It's all about revenge."

"And what about this right now. How do I know you're not going to use this against me somehow? Shame me in front of the entire school for my extracurricular activities with my math tutor."

His eyes harden as he thinks about my words. "You think I'd allow any other fucker to see you like I see you?"

I shrug because I honestly have no idea. He clearly has a game plan here. This push and pull between us. This need for revenge mixed with the sweet guy I remember, he's playing me. There's no other excuse for it. "I have no idea, Ky. You tell me."

He sits up and lifts the screen, all I can see is his face and his captivating eyes.

"Never," he says slowly. "This thing between us. It's exactly that. Between us."

"That's why you had Aria grinding on your cock earlier, was it?" I know I shouldn't say the words, I know it's only going to piss him off and ruin the light banter we've had going but the words slip past my lips without permission.

"And why you kissed Rich and damn near made him come in his pants in the cafeteria."

"You're a prick. You started all this."

"If you count me coming on to you that night a year ago, me starting all this, then yeah, okay, guilty."

I swallow down the emotion that night threatens to drag up. "Y-you were going to—"

"Bullshit," he barks, making me jump. "You don't really believe any of that was to do with me, do you?"

I shrug, unable to talk through the lump clogging my throat.

"I just wanted you that night, Kitten. I'd wanted you for a fucking long time," he admits, but if the small gasp after is anything to go by then I don't think he was supposed to.

"Y-you wanted me before that night?" My brows draw together in confusion. "But you never—"

"How could I? Zayn would have fucking gutted me alive if I touched you."

"So what was different that night?"

He shrugs. "He wasn't there. You were, and my restraint snapped."

"Did you go after me knowing what he'd done? Did you know how the night was going to end?"

He chuckles and drops his head into his hand, scrubbing his fingers against his jaw.

When his eyes come back to mine, they're damn near silver.

"No, Kitten. If I'd have fucking knew I'd have got you out of there. I fucking wish I had."

I have no words as I stare at him after that confession. I knew deep down that Kyle had nothing to do with what happened that night. It's why I never said it was him, why he didn't end up in any more shit than he already was. Gray was the dealer, the one with the connections, we all knew that. Even if Kyle did slip me something, it would have come from Gray, without a doubt, but I really wanted to believe he didn't.

He might not have got me out of there fast enough, he might have got himself a little too drunk and allowed things to get out of hand, but he never left me and it's why he ended up where he did.

I blow out a long breath, knowing that I'm potentially about to get myself in a lot of shit. If he does what he just promised he wouldn't do and Zayn sees this. The thought is almost enough to stop me. Almost.

Crossing my arms in front of me, my fingers grip the bottom of my sports bra and I peel it up my body.

"Harley, what are you—shit." His voice is so fucking low that it makes heat explode between my legs.

"Your turn," I sass, trying to keep my embarrassment at bay and appear as confident with my body as I'd like.

21

KYLE

"**S**hit," I growl, my cell slipping from my grip the second I see her pull her top over her head revealing her breasts to me.

I was joking when I dared her. Well, I think I was.

"Your turn," I hear her say from where my cell's landed on the sheets.

I swipe it up and flip the camera around as I swing my legs from my bed. I aim the camera right at the mirrored closed door in front of me.

Her gasp of shock does nothing for the raging hard-on I've had since I first saw her through the screen.

I knew she was freaking out about failing at this and the second she told me she was done, I knew she wasn't. Not if I had anything to say about it.

I'd hit call before I'd registered the move but I'm so fucking glad I did. The moment I saw the tears on her cheeks, I knew I did the right thing.

Was she right, did I want to make her cry? Hell yeah, but I was hoping those tears would come while she had my cock in her mouth, not because she couldn't do a math equation.

I never wanted her to feel useless, I just wanted her to

understand what I went through because of what she did. Even though I know deep down that she was right to do it. I'm just pissed the wrong guy went down that night. Even more pissed he's still prowling about and threatening her.

"Holy shit, Kyle," she breathes as her eyes run down my body.

I'm only wearing a pair of boxer briefs, I have been this entire time, I just didn't let her see that.

"Yeah?" I say, cockily running my hand down over my abs, a pathetic attempt to hide the scar to avoid the inevitable questions about it.

A lot of shit might have gone down in juvie. I ended up in one too many fights, found myself being punished for them all too often. But the amount of time I had to work out isn't something I can regret when she looks at me like she is right now.

I was always too skinny. Too skinny for the kind of football I wanted to play like my big brother. I was fast though, so I was always picked for the team because of it. Bulking up was always my mission and juvie helped with that.

"You look... really fucking good."

"You're not looking so bad yourself."

She smiles shyly, making me want to get in my car right now and drive my ass to her house. My fingers clench around my cell as the temptation almost gets the better of me.

I drop my hand to my length that's tenting my boxers and she doesn't miss it.

"Touch yourself for me, Kitten."

"Um..." she hesitates.

"Too late to be shy now. You started this after all."

"Uh... no. I didn't start—"

"You took your top off first."

"Actually, it looks to me like you were half-naked first."

"Not my fault you didn't ask to see lower." I wink and she rolls her eyes at me.

"My head wasn't in the gutter like yours."

"Liar."

"What? I'm not—"

"You are. Your eye twitches when you lie to me."

"It does not."

"Want me to prove it?"

"How are you—"

"Want me to come over right now?"

"What? No," she shrieks, her eye twitching as she does.

"Right. So you don't want me to sneak into your bedroom, spread your thighs and eat you like I did Saturday night?" Her entire face flushes with embarrassment as her eye continues to twitch.

"No."

"Are you wet for me?"

"No." Twitch.

"Do you like math?"

"No, I fucking hate it." No twitch.

I laugh at her as she stares at me like I've lost my mind.

"See, I'm right."

"How does that prove anything?"

"Trust me, Kitten. It really does. Now, how about a little more proof."

"Depends on what it is."

"Lie back."

I flip my camera around and do the same, holding it as far away from me as possible so she can see all the way down to my waist.

Her eyes feast on me through the screen and I don't miss her gasp of shock when she finds the raised, rough skin of my scar.

"Not now." I growl, knowing that she's going to make a bigger deal out of it than necessary.

She stares at me for a beat, and I think she's about to ignore me and ask when she moves.

I watch her as she gets comfortable against her pillows. She's so fucking perfect. Her face is flawless, even with the smeared makeup around her eyes from where she was crying. Her long, slim neck makes my mouth water to sink my teeth in and her breasts. They might be on the smaller side, but fuck. They're round, full, the perfect fucking handful.

My fists clench, knowing that I can't fucking touch them right now.

This was a really fucking stupid idea.

"Now what?"

"Play with yourself, Kitten. Let me watch."

A surprised laugh falls from her lips at my request. "That is so not happening."

"Why? I am." I move my camera so she can see where my hand is still in my boxers, my fingers wrapped around my length.

"Kyle," she gasps, her voice full of lust.

"Don't be shy, Kitten. I've already tasted every inch of you."

"That doesn't—shit, Ky."

"Fucking love it when you say my name."

"You're serious right now, aren't you?"

I don't answer her with words, instead, I lift my hips and shove my boxers down.

"Holy fuck."

"That impressive?"

"Well, I've not exactly—" She slams her lips shut and a smile twitches at my lips.

"You've not exactly what, Kitten?"

"Do we really have to do this? Can't we go back to doing math?"

"You'd rather be doing math right now?"

Her eye twitches as she prepares her words.

"You'd rather do math than get yourself off while listening to my voice and knowing I'm gonna come for you."

"You're wicked."

"Too fucking right, Kitten. Be wicked with me."

She pauses for a second before her hand skims down her stomach and her fingers disappear into her shorts.

"I lied to you," she admits.

"I know, Kitten. You're fucking soaked for me right now, aren't you?"

Her eyes flutter closed and her full lips part as she touches herself. A little gasp of pleasure sounds out down the phone and I damn near come just hearing it.

"Yes," she breathes.

"Fuck. My dirty little kitten."

"Kyle, you've got a visitor," my brother's voice booms through the house. He's so loud that Harley's eyes fly open in panic.

"It's okay, he's not in the room," I say with a laugh, although I can't deny that my heart isn't beating hard enough to crack a rib.

"Did you forget your meeting with Bea?" he calls when he gets no response.

"Fuck. FUCK," I bark. "My fucking social worker is here."

Harley bursts out laughing. "Serves you right for trying to corrupt me," she mutters.

"Oh Kitten, I corrupted your ass on the weekend, and there's only more to come. I'll call you later, I need to deal with my boner before this bitch sees it."

She stifles a laugh before I reluctantly hang up.

"I'm coming."

I suck in a breath, willing my cock to stand down as I drag on some clothes—jeans, not sweats—and head out to meet Bea.

"Kyle, it's good to see you," she says sweetly from her position at the dining table.

"Uh, yeah, you too," I lie.

Kane studies me as I make my way over.

"You okay? Got a girl in there or something?"

"No," I snap, hating how fucking perceptive he is.

His eyes don't leave me as I pull a soda from the refrigerator and take a seat opposite Bea.

"I've heard good things from Principal Hartmann about you," she starts. "I knew that place would be a good fit for you."

"Do you need me?" Kane asks when she pauses.

"Nope, this is just an informal catch-up. You're eighteen in a few days and I can let you be free. You might be my shortest case ever."

"And easiest I hope," I mutter.

"Well, if you mean once you got here. The behind the scenes while you were in juvie wasn't quite so straight forward."

"Okay, well... I'm gonna..." Kane points over his shoulder before disappearing to his room.

"You're really lucky, you know," Bea says the second Kane's bedroom door shuts and he's out of earshot.

"I know."

"He'd have raised hell to get you here. He almost did."

I smile at her knowing the lengths Kane will go to to get what he wants.

"I'm not surprised. He's a force to be reckoned with."

"I know you don't need it, but he'll take good care of you."

"We look after each other. It's how it's always been."

"You're lucky to have each other," she says again. "Anyway, I just wanted to pop by, make sure everything was okay and to say happy birthday really."

"I really appreciate everything you've all done for me. I

know granting Kane guardianship, even for a few days, couldn't have been the easiest thing to do. He's not exactly—"

"A model citizen?" she offers.

"Yeah, something like that." I think of some of the shit he was involved in back in Harrow Creek and I can't help but wonder if he's still got a hand in all that. He's certainly up to something with all the hours he's out of the house.

Bea stays for a good twenty minutes chatting away. She talks about my future, about college options. I listen, but I don't really dwell on it. I'm not ready to be making those kinds of decisions yet. I'm barely used to being back in the real world, the future seems like a long way off right now. I've got more pressing things to worry about, like when Gray is going to reappear and where Kane goes almost every hour of the day.

"I know our time is almost up," Bea says as she stands in the doorway ready to leave. "But if you need anything, either of you, you've got my number."

"Thank you, but I think we've got this."

"I expect big things from you, Kyle."

"We'll see what the future holds."

I close the door behind her and head for my room. I fall down onto my bed, the entire thing creaking with my weight.

I close my eyes for a few seconds as I process all the things Bea said about the future and the next thing I know it's dark and there are voices coming from the kitchen.

"Fuck," I mutter, sitting up and rubbing the sleep from my eyes.

Standing from my bed, I pull my bedroom door open to see who's here, but I instantly regret it.

"Fucking hell, bro. You don't live here alone," I bark, finding him with a girl pressed up against the wall a few feet down from my door. He's got her skirt up around her waist, her ass on full display.

"Hey, sweetie." She winks at me after pulling her face from Kane's neck. "Who's this K, baby?"

Her voice is so sickly sweet it actually turns my stomach.

Kane reaches out and grips her chin in his hands.

"My kid brother. Eyes off."

"Aww, I'm sure we could have some fun."

"As tempting as that is, I'm gonna have to pass this time, thanks," I mutter, not able to think of anything worse than going anywhere fucking near her.

Kane's got weird fucking taste when it comes to women. I'm all for enjoying them but that fucker has zero standards.

Thankfully, before I close the bathroom door on them, he's pulled her from the wall and carries her down to his room.

Fucking dog.

I make myself some dinner to the sounds of my brother fucking his slut into next week before returning to my bedroom. But despite there being a bathroom between us and music playing, I can hear every single one of her moans and cries for God.

I stare at the ceiling trying to convince myself to stay put and when my phone buzzes beside me, I hope it's Harley to distract me but as I bring the screen in front of me, my blood runs cold.

Unknown: It's time to pay your debts.

Below the message is a photo and it's that image that terrifies me more than his words because it's a photo of Harley... in her house.

"Fuck." I sit up so fast my head spins. My heart races as I find her number and hit call.

It rings and rings but never connects.

"Fuck."

22

HARLEY

The second he hangs up, reality crashes over me like a bucket of ice-cold water.

Reaching out, I grab my hoodie and cover myself up.

What the hell was I thinking letting him talk me into that?

Although, he didn't really have to talk me into anything, did he? I went down that road quite willingly.

"Fuck, fuck." *You're an idiot, Harley Hunter.*

I slam my math book closed, irritated with myself at how crazy he makes me.

I wanted to kill him at school earlier when he continually acted like a total prick, but then on the phone, he was so sweet. He's the boy I remember and, gah, I can't help latching onto that and forgetting all the other bullshit surrounding us.

"Harley, dinner is in thirty," Mom calls up the stairs.

"Okay. I'll be there."

Mom and I still haven't talked properly but as each day passes the tension lessens. I know we need to sit down though. It's time I talked about that night, got it all out in the open and tried to move on. It's held me back for long enough. It's literally held Kyle back and it's time to put it behind us where it belongs.

He's got too bright a future for the anger he's harboring inside. If he wants revenge, I'll let him take what he needs so that we can both move on.

It's time.

I grab a change of clothes and head for the bathroom to shower before going down to find Mom. I have no idea if the others are here, but if they are, then we can talk after. Hell, I should probably just say what I need to say in front of them, they deserve the truth too, Zayn especially.

When I get down to the kitchen a little over thirty minutes later, I find Mom alone and three plates of lasagne at the counter.

"Hey sweetie, it's just me, you, and Poppy tonight," Mom says as I take a seat.

"Where's Zayn?"

"Out with the team, I think."

Poppy joins us a few minutes later and the three of us sit in an uncomfortable silence for a few minutes.

"Mom, can we talk?" I ask, the words eating at me from the inside out.

"Sure."

"Do you want me to leave?" Poppy offers.

"No." I look over and meet her eyes. "We're sisters now." I smile at her.

"Mom, I'm... I'm disappointed that you didn't tell me about Kyle—" She opens her mouth to argue, but I beat her to it. "But I understand. I know how seriously you take your job and I know how badly you want to help those who need it. I trust that you thought you had my best interests at heart. I also know that I never quite told the whole truth about that night."

Mom's eyes narrow at me. "Go on."

"Kyle did more that night than I let on at the time."

Her brows rise for me to continue.

"It was Gray who drugged me, of that I'm positive, but I don't think Kyle was aware for quite a while. Things went farther than I admitted."

"I know," she says softly.

"What do you mean *you know?*"

"I know what happened that night, sweetie."

"But... why didn't you say anything?"

"It's your story, Harley. I trusted that you would tell me when you were ready."

"Does Zayn know?" I ask, although I think the fact he's not broken Kyle's nose yet that the answer is no.

"It's your story," Mom repeats.

Silence settles over us once again, as my mind goes back to that night.

I really want to wish that Letty didn't make me go but the more I think about it, about the time I spent with Kyle before the drug I'd been slipped started to kick into action, the more I wonder if it was worth it. For me, anyway. None of that night was worth Kyle being sent to juvie though.

I blow out a slow breath.

"Everything will be okay, sweetie. Have you two talked about that night yet?"

Poppy helpfully scoffs beside me but tries to cover it up as a cough.

"No, we haven't done much talking." Mom raises an eyebrow in suspicion.

"Right, well... can I suggest that maybe you find some time to do that. And also, talk to your brother. If what happened that night is something, then he'll want to hear about it from you."

"Like he did with me when he decided to scr—get with my best friend."

"The past is in the past, Harley. We can't change it, all we can do is try to do better in the future and only you have the power to make the right decisions."

I nod at her, her words circling around in my head.

"If you need me, you know I'm always here for you. If you want to talk about that night, I'm all ears but I trust you, Harley, to make the right decision. I trust all of you to know the best things for you and your futures."

She places her empty plate in the sink and heads for the door.

"Have you heard from Letty recently?" she asks before disappearing.

"Um..." I think back to the last time I spoke to my sister. It's been weeks, at least. "No. Is everything okay?"

"I'm sure she's just busy with classes. If you hear from her, let her know I'm still alive, yeah?"

I chuckle. "Will do." She's almost gone when I call her back. "Mom?"

"Yeah, sweetie."

"Thank you."

"Always." She smiles at me before disappearing around the corner.

"So..." Poppy starts once we're alone. "What really did happen that night?"

A couple of hours later, I'm curled up in bed in the dark with the speaker beside me playing softly. There's a storm brewing outside and the rain is lashing against my window, the wind beginning to howl around the side of the house.

I love watching the rain and if I weren't so comfortable, I'd head down to the porch and curl up on the swing seat.

It's late, I should be asleep, but I can't switch off. My head is still stuck in that video call with Kyle. If he weren't called away, how far would that have gone?

I want to say that I'd have put a stop to it before it went too far, but it had already gone past that point.

I was topless on a video call with my hand in my...

Jesus, what was I thinking?

I roll onto my back, wondering if I should have messaged again after he hung up.

I kind of expected him to want us to pick up where we left off. He certainly looked like he was into it. Part of me is disappointed that he didn't. The other part knows it was right.

Finally, my body starts to get heavier and I begin to drift off, but that all comes to an abrupt end when the side of my mattress compresses and a warm hand covers my mouth.

I try to scream, my body lashing around, my arms trying to hit whoever the fuck it is but although I make contact, they don't fucking move.

Although in my panic I can make out the figure, with tears filling my eyes and the darkness surrounding us, I can't make out any features.

My heart pounds as if it's about to explode from my ribs as I continue trying to fight, although it's pointless.

Whoever it is might not have done anything—yet—but they could. Clearly they're stronger than me.

I try to scream again as the figure looms over me.

"Calm down, Kitten. It's just me."

Every inch of my body relaxes for a second as Kyle's voice washes through me.

Then the anger hits.

"What the fuck do you think you're doing?" I hiss at him.

I blink away the tears and he becomes clearer. He's right in front of me, his nose almost brushing mine and staring right into my eyes.

His intensity is overwhelming, and my mouth goes dry.

He doesn't move for long seconds, but when he does, he makes my world spin again.

His fingers grip my chin in a painful, vise-like grip as his lips crash down on mine.

I resist for longer than he's happy with.

"Kitten," he growls against my lips. His hand slips under my sheets and he pinches my nipple through my tank. I gasp, exactly as he was intending and plunges his tongue into my mouth.

I buck against his hold, but he fully climbs on the bed and presses his entire body against mine, keeping me still.

"Careful, Kitten. I'll start thinking you don't want me here," he murmurs into our kiss before continuing before I get a chance to respond.

Pinned to the bed with only my arms free and Kyle kissing me like he needs it to live, I do the only thing I can.

I kiss him back.

His tongue licks deep into my mouth, twisting with mine. His grip on my chin loosens as our kiss continues in favor of wrapping his fingers around my neck.

I swallow against his hold, loving how it makes me feel.

Lifting my hands, I knock his hat from his head, allowing it to tumble to the bed before threading my fingers into his hair.

"Fuck, Harley," he groans, kissing along my jaw until he bites down on my ear, making me squeal in shock and for heat to surge down between my thighs.

"W-what are you doing here, Ky?" I whisper, my back arching as he once again finds my breast beneath the sheets.

"Finishing what we started, Kitten. I'm so fucking hard for you," he growls in my ear, making every hair on my body stand on end.

"Oh God."

"Don't tell me that you weren't lying here thinking about earlier, about how badly you wished I was in the same room as you. Kissing you, touching you, giving you everything you needed."

"Kyle." I wanted it to come out as a warning but when his name leaves my lips it's nothing but a plea.

Lifting his weight from me, he throws the sheets from my body, leaving me covered in nothing but my tank and sleep shorts.

It might be almost too dark to see him, but I don't miss the way his gaze sweeps down my body. I feel it, feeling the heat of his stare as it connects with my skin.

He sits up higher before pulling his hoodie over his head and dropping it to the floor, when he comes back to me, the heat of his naked chest damn near burns me.

"Couldn't think of anything else," he admits, seconds before he latches onto the skin of my neck and sucks until it hurts.

My hand finds his shoulder and my nails dig in as he continues.

"Try to hurt me as much as you like, Kitten. It won't stop me," he warns, brushing his lips over my collarbone and pulling the fabric of my tank down so he has access to my breast.

"Oh God," I moan when his teeth sink into the sensitive flesh.

"Shhh," he warns. "I really don't want to deal with your brother right now."

I slam my hand over my mouth as he sucks on my nipple, circling his tongue around the tip before biting down, ensuring a bolt of pleasure shoots straight to my core.

"You like biting me." It's not a question I don't need to ask. That much is obvious.

"I want to hurt you, Kitten. I want to hurt you so fucking bad." His eyes find mine, the silver catching in the small amount of light in the room and a shiver runs through me.

He means it.

He should. I condemned him to a year of hell.

But I shouldn't want him to do it so badly.

"You ruined my life," he continues, moving to the other side. "You need to pay."

"Oh God." His touch, his words, they're like fuel on my already simmering fire.

He lifts up, takes my tank in both of his hands and the next thing I know, the sound of the fabric ripping hits my ears before it falls to my side. I sit up so fast my head spins.

"Oh my God, did you just—"

"You don't get to hide from me, Kitten. Not now, not ever."

"Fuck," I breathe as he begins his descent down my stomach, kissing and biting every bit of skin he can. Each bite sends shockwaves through my body and every kiss is like a salve for the skin.

It's really fucking addictive.

The second he's at my hips, his fingers wrap around the waistband of my shorts and he pulls them down my legs, leaving me bare for him.

"Are you wet for me, Harley?" he asks, pushing my thighs wide and blowing a stream of air across my heated skin.

"Yes."

"Good girl. You know how I hate it when you lie to me."

My chest heaves, my fingers curling in the sheet beneath me as I wait for him to do something, to touch me, anything but he's frozen.

I wish I could see him properly, read the expression on his face and take in every inch of his body. But he's cloaked in darkness, almost as if he's a figment of my imagination. But I know he's not. His touch burns too hot, his bites sting too much.

After long seconds, he finally moves but it's not in the direction I was hoping for.

Instead, he climbs off the bed, lifts his hands to his head and paces the room.

"What's wrong?" I ask, watching his movements in the shadows.

Part of me wants to reach for the light, but another part loves the darkness.

He comes to a stop at the window and stares out for the longest time, although I have no idea what he's trying to find. It's pitch black out there with the moon covered in a thick layer of rain clouds.

"Kyle, what's—"

At my words, he turns and drops his hands to his waistband, tugging at the fabric until it drops from his hips.

Oh God, this is happening.

Every muscle in my body clenches as he closes the space between us.

Without another word, he drops to his knees at the end of my bed, wraps his hands around my ankles and drags me to him, throwing my legs over his shoulders and sucking my clit into his mouth.

"Oh my—" I slam my lips shut, reaching for a pillow to cover my face with and he continues his delicious assault on my body.

My back arches, my hips lift, my heels dig into his back, my fingers tug at his hair but he never lets up. Not even for a second.

His attack is brutal. Each swipe of his tongue and graze of his teeth send me closer to an intense release that is almost in touching distance.

"Kyle, Kyle, Kyle," I chant as he slides a finger inside me, adding to the sensations that are already driving me crazy. "Oh my God, oh my God."

This is so much better than the last time—and I thought that was good.

"Come for me, Kitten," he growls against my clit and I'm powerless but to do as I'm told.

My body quakes as pleasure like I've never known crashes over me in wave after wave of delicious ecstasy.

He doesn't stop until I've come back down, and even then

he only moves as far as my inner thigh where he bites down so hard, I have no doubt he draws blood.

"Oh shit," I moan, the pain setting off aftershocks of pleasure.

I really fucking hope this isn't over yet because I already know that I need more.

23

KYLE

The taste of copper fills my mouth, but I don't stop. I need her to remember that I was here for a long time after I walk back out of her door.

Should I have come over here in the middle of the night and broken into her house? No, probably not. But I really don't give a shit.

Seeing that photo on my phone. Knowing that Gray is close to her. It fucked me up, and I needed to know that she was safe.

I want to say that my initial intentions were purely innocent. Make sure she's safe and leave. But I'm pretty sure I'd be lying.

After the way we were forced to end things earlier. This needed to happen.

I release my grip on her thigh and swipe my tongue over the bite mark as she shudders beneath me.

"Kyle?" Her voice is nervous and unsure, but it's deep and gravelly thanks to the orgasm she came down from only seconds ago, and I fucking love it.

Climbing up, I wrap her legs around my waist and fall

over her, taking her lips on mine and allowing her to taste herself on me.

I kiss her like I might die without it, and I realize that actually, I might. I've craved this for so fucking long. I've dreamed of this for so fucking long.

Everything about Harley Hunter, even when we were kids, spoke to me on another level. It wasn't just because Zayn was my best friend that I basically lived in their trailer as we were growing up. I had to be there. Then when she walked into that party a year ago looking like my every fantasy and her big brother nowhere to be seen, I knew it was my chance.

If only things happened differently.

I wonder where we'd be now.

My hand runs down her thigh until I grip onto her ass, rubbing my cock against her burning pussy.

"You're mine, Harley Hunter. You belong to me," I say against her cheek.

"Yes, Ky, yes."

Fuck.

My chest swells at her words as I reach down between us and take myself in hand so I can find her entrance.

I tease her with just the tip and she greedily tries to suck me deeper. She's so wet, so fucking hot, it takes every ounce of restraint I have not to just sink right into her.

"You want my cock, Kitten?" I ask her, half expecting her to freak out because I know she's a virgin.

But instead, when she rips her eyes open and locks her stare on mine the only word that falls from her lips is, "Yes."

My lips crash to hers as my free hand skates up her body until I find her throat. Her pulse thunders under my fingertips and her pussy gets wetter as she feels the pressure of my hold.

Kinky little kitten.

I pull back and look into her dark, addicting eyes. "You on birth control?"

She sucks her bottom lip into her mouth and nods.

"You remember I said I wanted to hurt you?"

She nods again.

"Get ready."

I thrust forward, filling her as much as I can in this position.

"Holy fucking—" My hand lifts from her throat to cover her mouth. This really isn't the position to be in when Zayn comes crashing through the door. I know I'm due a beating for this, and I'll take it, but not right now.

She stills beneath me and my teeth grind as I force myself to remain motionless inside her as she gets used to my invasion.

After long seconds, her eyelids finally flutter open and I drag my hand down from her mouth.

Something crackles between us as the only sound that can be heard is the faint music from her speaker and our heaving breaths.

"I'm okay," she finally whispers, reaching up and wrapping her hand around the back of my neck so she can pull me down to her lips.

My tongue plunges into her mouth as my hips move and her pussy ripples around my length in the most incredible way.

This... this right here is why I didn't fuck anyone else after getting out.

"Fuck, Harley."

"Make it feel good, Ky," she begs, clearly still in pain.

I drop my forehead to hers as I fight with my restraint.

I want to fuck her. I want to fuck her so hard that her eyes cross and I brand myself on her soul forevermore.

But I can't. Not yet anyway.

Next time.

I smile to myself as I realize that this is just the first of many times I'm going to get this.

She might think otherwise, but I already know who's going to win.

With my fingers back where they belong around her throat, I bring my lips to hers at the same time I flex my hips slowly.

Her kiss doesn't falter as I keep moving, so I take that as the sign that she's okay and lose myself in her.

"Kitten," I growl into her mouth. "You're so fucking tight."

She gasps as I push into her a little harder.

"Ky," she moans as I release her throat and drop my hand down her body to pinch her swollen clit. "Oh fuck."

"Good?"

"I... I think so." I chuckle against her neck.

"It's more than fucking good, Kitten."

I work her until her skin is damp with sweat and her legs are trembling around my hips.

"You gonna come on my cock, Kitten."

"I... I..."

"Let go," I demand in her ear before biting down on her and circling my hips in a way I've discovered makes her purr.

"Oh God, oh God, oh fuck." She slams her own hand over her mouth as her pussy clamps down around me. Her back arches as her entire body convulses beneath me.

Even in the darkness, it's fucking breathtaking.

"Fuck, you're sexy, Kitten." I thrust two more times before I lose control and my cock jerks violently inside of her. "Harley," I groan into her neck.

Still inside her, I grab her chin, forcing her to look at me before claiming her lips once again.

By the time I let her up for air, her eyes are almost closed with her exhaustion and my cock is hard and ready for another round. But I already know I can't act on it.

"So sleepy," she whispers, curling into my side as if she belongs there.

My heart pounds and she snuggles against my chest and I wrap my arm around her waist.

It feels... right.

Lifting my hand, I thread my fingers into her hair and pull her head back a little so I can press my lips to her head.

"Thank you," I whisper, knowing that she's already succumbed to sleep.

I hold her for the longest time. It would be so easy to fall asleep and then maybe take her again first thing in the morning. But that's not what this is and we both know it.

I have no idea how much time passes, but eventually I manage to convince myself that I need to move.

I slip from beneath her without waking her and stand before picking up the sheets from the floor ready to cover her up, only something hits my foot and when I look down to see what it is, it gives me a wicked idea that I can't ignore.

Draping the sheets over her feet, I gently wrap my hand around the back of her knee, exposing the bite mark I left on her thigh and set to work.

Only minutes later, I'm dressed and standing with my hand on her doorknob ready to leave.

My body begs me to stay, to get undressed and slide back under the sheets with her. But my head tells me to leave. She's going to regret this in the morning, I already know that, and I don't want to be here to witness it.

With one more look at her sleeping peacefully in the darkness, I slip out of her room and soon after her house.

It's a decision I regret the second I strip out of my clothes and slide into my own cold bed. I might have showered when I got in but I can still smell her, still feel her hot body pressed up against mine and hear the little noises she made when I was inside her.

My cock tents the sheets, taunting me and telling me that I should have stayed.

"Fuck," I hiss into the night as I turn over and attempt to get some sleep. I already know it's pointless. If it does come, it's going to be full of images of her laid out naked beneath me.

———

I know the house isn't empty like usual long before I pull my bedroom door open. Not only did I wake to the sound of that woman's irritating sex squeals, but the pair of them are now crashing around in the kitchen.

I hesitantly step from my bedroom and toward the kitchen. I might have been gone a year, but I can't imagine that Kane makes a regular thing of having breakfast with his hook-ups.

"'Morning, sweetie," she sings the second she sees me, her eyes running down my body as if she wants to eat me for breakfast.

"'Morning."

"Bro," Kane grunts when he turns from his place at the stove where he's cooking fucking bacon.

"You're cooking... for her?" I ask as if it's the most insane thing I've ever said.

"Yeah. Problem?"

"Nope. Please continue. I'll be gone in a few."

"There's plenty," he offers. I look from him and to the woman.

"Nah, you're all good. I've already had my fill." I nod my head toward his friend and Kane barks out a laugh.

"You know I like it when they scream." He winks before turning back to the bacon.

"I also know that you're a dog."

I don't bother hanging around or even picking up

something to eat, the second I've made use of the bathroom, I grab my school bag and get the hell out of the house.

I'm too early for school, so after parking, I head for the locker room and the gym that's beside it.

The hallways are silent as I walk through them and the locker room is empty, as is the gym.

Shoving my headphones in, I hit play on a running playlist I made the other night and get to work.

Eventually, a few others join me. Guys I recognize from our conditioning practices but no one stops to talk to me. Fine by me.

My shirt is damp and my hair is wet by the time I come to a stop and pull my cell from my pocket.

The second I see a message from her on the screen, a smile pulls at my lips and my heart skips a beat. But when I read what she's sent, I can't help but bark out a laugh.

"What's—whoa, dude. You do that?" Ash asks, coming to a stop behind me and staring at my cell over my shoulder.

"Gotta stake your claim, right?" I say, putting the screen to sleep before he sees any more.

"That who I think it is."

"I don't kiss and tell, man."

"Didn't look like you were kissing, bro. You a secret fucking vampire or what?"

I suck my bottom lip into my mouth as I remember the taste of her blood on my tongue last night.

I laugh. "Yeah, I might just be."

"You gonna shower before class? You stink."

"Fuck you." I laugh, walking through the gym and heading for the showers.

24

HARLEY

The muscles in my thighs pull as I roll over and everything down there feels really sore. My brows pull together for a second before everything hits me and my eyes fly open and I sit bolt upright, clutching the sheets to my bare chest.

Is he still here?

I look around not knowing what I really want the answer to that question to be, but as I find the other side of my bed empty and cold and no evidence of him even being here, disappointment floods me.

I wanted him to be here.

Fuck.

I drop my head into my hands. What the hell did I do last night? Why was he even here?

Did someone let him in? Does someone know he was here?

A million and one questions run around my head as my alarm starts blaring again.

"Alright, alright," I mutter, switching the thing off and climbing from my bed, my muscles protesting with every move.

I grab my robe and wrap it around me before going to the bathroom. I need to wash his scent off me and hopefully with it, the memories from my head because already I know that if I think about it too much then I'm going to want to do it again.

I should be regretting handing my V-card to a guy who can barely stand to look at me, but I'm not.

I push aside memories of vicious Kyle and focus on the sweet boy that I catch glimpses of when we're alone. When we're playing our little tutoring game and forgetting about our reality.

After brushing my teeth, I turn the shower on, drop my robe and step under the torrent of water.

It's not until I stand rubbing my sponge around my body that I realize anything is wrong.

I lift my leg and my eyes almost pop out of my head at what I find on my inner thigh.

I remember him biting me, I remember the pain as I stare at the mark as if it's happening right now, and damn, if it doesn't get me hot thinking about it. But fuck, I do not remember him doing anything else.

I run my finger over the black ink on my skin but it doesn't fucking move.

Owned by a Legend.

"You fucking..." I seethe, my teeth grinding as I stare at his handwriting.

I make quick work of finishing up my shower and after wrapping a towel around my body, I stand in front of the mirror, quickly wiping away the steam covering it. The second my eyes lock on my neck and chest, I gasp.

There is no fucking way I can cover all this up.

My hand lifts without instruction and I run my fingertips over each and every mark he left behind and I suddenly have the urge not to cover up any of them. Part of me really quite likes them.

Jesus, I'm fucked-up.

It takes me longer than usual to decide what to wear to school, my need to cover up almost every inch of my body makes it a challenge. It gets so late that Zayn ends up knocking on my door to ensure I'm alive and going to school.

"Yeah, I'm coming," I call back before he opens the door. The less he looks at me today the better.

I don't have time to think about what I need for cheer after school, so shove an outfit in my duffel bag and swing it over my shoulder in my need to not be late.

By the time I get downstairs, Zayn and Poppy have already left and I don't have time to eat anything, so I'm forced to grab a coffee in a travel mug and a cereal bar.

The hallway is packed as I make my way to my locker, keeping my head down as I go in fear that everyone will take one look at me and know exactly what I'm trying to hide.

I switch out my books and get what I need for my first class before taking off in that direction. Unfortunately, to get to English lit, I have to go by the team's lockers.

I suck in a steeling breath before I turn the corner. I spot them instantly, it's impossible not to with their god-like presence.

"Good to see you made it," Zayn shouts over when he spots me heading toward their group.

I lift my hand and flip him off.

"Watch out, lil' sis is touchy today. Rich, you should go cheer her up. We all know how much she likes your little cock," Ethan barks, laughing at his own terrible joke. But I don't bother to even look at him, I'm too busy trying not to look at the person standing beside Zayn with a smirk playing on his lips.

Fuck him.

My irritation levels grow knowing that he's getting to me by literally doing nothing other than breathing.

"You cold or something, sis?" Zayn asks, his gaze dropping to the scarf I have wrapped around my neck.

I don't need to look at Kyle to know his smirk has just got wider at my brother's comment.

"Yeah," I say slowly, nodding as I do. Then I rip my eyes from his and stare right into Kyle's ice-blue ones. "We need to talk."

Zayn's curious gaze flicks between the two of us as we stare at each other. My face burns every time he looks at me.

"Why? You wanna compare my cock size to Rich's?"

A round of jeers and dirty remarks sound out behind me.

"Fuck off, my little sister ain't going anywhere near this motherfucker's cock, ain't that right, bro?" he asks Kyle.

"Too fucking right." Kyle's eyes burn down the length of my body "Why would I go there when my brother brings home women every night."

"Oh hell yeah, bro," someone calls out, probably Rich and I fight the hurt that threatens to bubble up within me.

I want to say he's lying. He spent the night with me. But not the whole night.

You stupid, stupid, naïve bitch, Harley Hunter.

He told you he wanted to hurt you and you fucking let him.

"Great, well now we've got that cleared up." I put as much sass into my words as possible as I hold Kyle's eyes hoping like hell he can't see how fast I'm crumbling on the inside.

"I've got nothing to say to you," he spits as if last night didn't even fucking happen.

Asshole.

"Bro, I said don't touch her not insult her," Zayn mutters in an attempt to soften the blow. "I know you two got issues but shit."

"Whatever. It wasn't important anyway." I wave them both off and continue down toward my first class, my heart in my throat and tears burning my eyes the whole way.

Thankfully, the bell has not rung and when I push through into my classroom, I'm the only one in there.

I take my seat at the back of the room and suck in a shaky breath.

Last night didn't change anything and I hate that I'm being such a girl about it, thinking that he might have suddenly treated me differently today.

By the time others start filing in, I've somewhat got control of my emotions.

"'Morning," Ruby sings, dropping down in her seat next to mine. "How's it—what's wrong?" she asks the second she looks at my face.

Damn her.

"Nothing, everything is fine," I lie and the guilt of doing so to one of my best friends threatens to eat me whole. But I can't admit what happened last night, how stupid I was. I fell for every single word he said and it was all a lie.

Every touch, every kiss, every whispered word. All lies.

Pressure builds behind my eyes once again but thankfully, our teacher arrives and Ruby is forced to look away from me as he asks her a question.

Behind him, the door opens and the one person I don't want to have to even look at walks into the classroom.

He holds his head high as he makes his way to his seat. Right before he turns to sit down, he looks right at me. My entire body jolts at the look in his eyes but I'm too shocked and the contact is too brief to really decipher what he's trying to tell me.

I'm still staring at the back of his head when Ruby turns her attention back to me.

"Did something happen, you're shooting more hate at him than usual?"

"I don't want to talk about it," I seethe.

"I'll take that as a yes then," she says lightly. "You know

where I am." She places her hand on my forearm and squeezes in support as our teacher gets the lesson started.

My cell buzzes in my pocket, I know exactly who it is, I've been watching him type for the last few seconds. I knew it was coming but it doesn't stop my heart rate increasing to dangerous levels the second I feel it. Knowing that his words are sitting there waiting almost gets the better of me. Especially when he sends me another three that also all go unread.

But at no point does he attempt to turn to look at me. I know this because while our teacher talks, my eyes are stuck on him and my head is firmly still back in the events of last night.

I breathe a sigh of relief the second the bell rings out and everyone around me begins to pack up and move toward the door. That was my one and only class with him today. If I avoid the cafeteria at lunch then I shouldn't have to look at him again with any luck.

He disappears from the room before I'm even off my chair. Good to know he doesn't actually want to talk to me then.

"Are you sure you're okay?" Ruby asks as we finally make our way out and toward our next class that, thankfully, we share.

"Yeah, I'm good." My voice gives me away because it sounds broken even to my own ears.

"You wanna skip and go and get ice cream."

I laugh, it's either that or I'm going to cry. "I can't. If Mom found out..."

"What if she wouldn't?"

"I can't." I shake my head at her. I so badly want to say yes and throw caution to the wind, but I can't. I'm not that girl, I'm not that student. Plus, I've got math later and we all know that I need to be present for that class.

Second period is uneventful although I spent the entire

class with my head in the clouds while my heart continues to ache inside my chest.

I gave him too much last night. I gave him things that I can't get back and I'm starting to wonder if that's something I'm going to regret after not feeling that way in the slightest this morning.

I knew it wasn't going to be all hearts and flowers today. But the reality was so much worse than anything I could have imagined.

"What are you hiding?" Stella says the second I join her in our art class.

"Um…"

"Oh come on, you never wear scarves." She raises a brow knowingly.

"Do we really have to do this?"

"We certainly do, girl."

We both grab the paintings we started last time and take our seats as someone puts some music on and our teacher doesn't even bother to stand from her chair. Fine by me.

"Show me." She reaches for my scarf and I keep my hands at my sides, allowing her a peek at my neck.

"Whoa, girl. Someone had a fun night."

"You've no idea," I mutter, dropping my head into my hands.

"Tell me all."

So I do, much to her delight. I feel bad not confessing to Ruby earlier and instead trusting Stella with the events of the night before, but with her being outside of our circle, and more importantly, not close to Zayn, I feel a little safer talking about it.

"He just turned up in the middle of the night and…" She wiggles her eyebrows. "That's really fucking hot, Harley. Does he have any friends who might be up for doing the same thing but you know, at my house."

I make a show of gasping in shock. "Stella Doukas, are you a secret little slut?" I whisper.

She shrugs and tries to look innocent but seeing as she expressed her desire to have a bad boy sneak into her bedroom under the cloak of darkness, she fails massively.

"Don't judge," she says lightly. "I've met a lot of different... boys over the years."

"Okay, I think it might be time to turn the tables on this conversation. Tell me all..." I encourage, dropping my brush into the water pot between us and resting forward with my elbow on the table and my chin in my hand, ready for story time.

"Christ, where do I even start?"

"Well, this is getting better by the second," I joke, glad to be able to focus on someone else's bad choices for a while.

Stella and I end up staying in our art classroom over lunch, continuing our riveting conversation about her past conquests and slowly but surely working on our paintings. She slips out at one point to grab us both some lunch, totally understanding my need to remain hidden and when I get to math, I do so without seeing *him*.

I think I'm winning until Mr. Wilson's first words to the class are, "Surprise test."

I groan as I pull my pens out and wait for him to place the paper on my desk.

"You've got this, Harley," he says encouragingly as he passes.

I roll my eyes, knowing that there's no way that can possibly be true. But then I look down at the questions before me and I find equations exactly like Kyle and I were doing last night.

I tap my pen against my desk for a couple of seconds as I recall everything he told me while we were on video chat and I get to work, actually feeling confident about a math test for the first time in... well, ever.

"Okay, time is up," Mr. Wilson calls right as I'm finishing off the last question on the paper. "Grab a different color pen, let's self-grade them. Here are the answers..."

He projects the answers onto the screen and the second I realize the first one is exactly the same as what I've got written on my piece of paper, I can't fight my smile.

Holy shit, I did it.

I laugh to myself before covering my mouth with my hand before anyone notices my little freak out.

I go down the rest of the answers and those tears from this morning return but this time, it's with joy.

I did it. I fucking did it.

Noticing that something isn't right, Mr. Wilson walks over. "Is everything okay, Harley?"

I look up at him, my eyes full of unshed tears. I must look like I'm on the verge of a breakdown.

"I got them all right," I whisper, not able to believe it despite marking them myself.

"That's great, Harley. Well done." He smiles down at me and my chest damn near bursts with pride for myself.

He moves on to another student while I squeal internally at myself.

In a moment of madness, I reach for my cell and before I know what I'm doing, I'm staring down at the messages from Kyle that I've ignored all day.

"Shit," I mutter to myself, feeling stupid for my sudden need to tell him that I nailed this.

He won't care.

He got what he wanted.

He *hurt* me.

I let out a sigh as I stare at his words from earlier.

Asshole: I'm sorry.

Asshole: Talk to me.

Asshole: Kitten.

I can hear his growl of frustration in the last one and it makes goose bumps prick my skin.

When I start typing a second later, it's not to Kyle, but instead, Stella.

Harley: Wanna do something tonight after cheer?

She doesn't see the message straight away—as she shouldn't, she's in class as well after all—so I pocket my cell and try to force myself not to feel bad for ignoring his requests.

I spend the rest of class hanging on Mr. Wilson's every word as he explains what we're moving on to next, my confidence at an all-time high and ready to attack the next challenge sent my way.

Before I know it, class is over and I'm making my way down the packed hallway ready for cheer practice.

"Hey, sorry, I didn't reply. Miss Ash was on us all class," Stella says as we walk into the locker room together.

"No worries. You up for it?"

"Yes, I need to go home first though."

"Sure, I'm good with whatever."

"Do I get the feeling you might be avoiding going home?"

"Whatever might give you that impression?" I ask innocently.

"He was in my last class. He looked pissed."

"Good, he should. He's a dick."

"You mean you want his dick," she deadpans as we drop our bags to the bench and start getting changed.

The others join us, and after a few minutes, Ruby and Chelsea come marching through. I watch Ruby as she listens to whatever Chelsea says.

I smile at the two of them, I'm so damn proud of my girl. She's about to be an incredible captain.

"Harley Hunter," Stella gasps. "You did not tell me about that." Her eyes almost bug out of her head as she stares at my thigh.

Reaching out, I cover the bite mark and writing with my hand.

"Oh no, no-no." She knocks my hand out of the way and stares down at my skin. "He fucking branded you. That's so hot."

"He made me bleed, Stel. And then wrote all over me."

"You know why, don't you?"

"To piss me off?" I suggest.

"No, he's claiming you. That boy wants you, Har. He wants you bad."

"Oh yeah, and that's why he acted like he did this morning."

"Boys are douchebags, Har. They do all sorts of stupid shit in front of their friends—in front of the brother of the girl they're fucking."

"I'm not fucking him," I hiss quietly, trying to argue with her.

"Evidence would suggest otherwise." She nods down to my thigh and raises a brow knowingly.

"Let's just get changed, eh?"

Stella laughs at me as I pull a pair of shorts out of my bag and stare at them in horror. I thought I'd stuffed yoga pants in there this morning.

"Shit."

"Here, swap," Stella offers, taking my shorts and handing me her pants.

"Thank you."

"I'm sure I'll figure out a way to pay you back." She winks at me and I hurriedly step into the fabric to cover up the evidence from last night, hoping that the hoodie I opted for does the job on my top half.

———

"Wow, your house is gorgeous," I say, climbing out of my car after following Stella here after school.

"Thanks," she mutters, slamming the door of her Porsche and coming to join me.

I knew she was wealthy, you only need to look at her car, her clothes and the way she wears them to know that, but I wasn't quite expecting this, or for her to live quite so far out of town.

It's great though. Perfect, actually. Kyle will never find me here.

She leads us to a huge hallway. The walls are white, the floor tiles are white—probably some expensive marble or something —and all the fittings are matte black. It's really quite something.

"Okay wow. This is... wow."

"My dad has a thing about interior design."

"Well, he's certainly got an eye for it."

She leads me through to her kitchen which is similar to the hallway, the units are all white with black countertops, tiles and handles. Even the faucet is black.

"What did you say your dad did again?" I ask, looking around and taking it all in. There's a huge canvas at the other end of the dining room which is similarly just black and white but it looks like it's probably hella expensive.

She shrugs as she pulls open one of the doors to reveal a refrigerator enclosed behind it. "No idea. Soda?"

"Please." She passes one over before grabbing a bag of chips and tipping them into a bowl. "You've really no idea what he does?"

"Security of some sort, but that's about all I know."

"And you don't ask?" I ask, finding it odd how she can really have no idea.

"I used to. I gave up after a while when he wouldn't tell me anything. Apparently, it's better I don't know. Whatever." She throws a chip in her mouth and chews. "So what did you want to do? We've probably got the house to ourselves. There's a pool and jacuzzi, and sauna in the basement if you're down for it."

My chin drops, although I don't know why I'm surprised. Ethan's house is similar, although less modern. I guess I just didn't think there were any other houses around Rosewood that were this... big. But then after driving up the long-ass driveway that allows this place to be hidden in the trees, I shouldn't be surprised.

"Sure, if you've got a suit I can borrow."

"You got it. Shall we?" she asks, grabbing her soda and the bowl and heading for the door.

My cell starts buzzing almost the second I place it on the coffee table in Stella's bedroom—she has a full on living area at one end of her ginormous room. It's insane.

"Is that him?" she asks, glancing over at where it's flashing.

"Sure is."

"You gonna reply?"

"Nope." Picking it up, I go into the settings and turn the vibrate off because I have a feeling he's not going to stop at a few messages.

"He's gonna kill you for that."

"I'd like to see him try."

"Girl, he branded you on your first time. He's not going to have second thoughts about spanking your ass for ignoring him."

I can't deny that a flash of heat races through me at her words and the image they conjure up.

"O-oh, is that your plan?"

"What? No. I don't have a plan aside from showing him that he can't order me around and talk to me like shit and expect me to roll over and accept it. That's not who I am."

"Damn right, girl," she says, snapping her fingers and giving it all the attitude before she falls about in a fit of giggles. "Okay, this is for you." She hands me a tiny fire engine red swimsuit.

Bathroom is through there. She points toward a closed door and I take the scrap of fabric with me to change into.

Unlike the rest of the house, Stella's bedroom and bathroom is all cream and golds. It's stunning and much softer than the harsh black and white everywhere else.

In only a few minutes I'm attempting to make the swimsuit cover some of my marked skin but I soon decide that it's pointless even trying.

"Whoa, I think that might have been made for you," Stella says when I emerge. While I was gone, she changed into a silver suit that fits her like a second skin. "You want me to send him a photo, show him what he's missing."

"No," I say in a panic as she takes a step toward where my cell is.

She laughs at me as she picks up her soda.

"Let's go chill. I think you need it."

25

KYLE

I stare down at my cell, my teeth grinding.

Usually, I wouldn't give a shit if a girl doesn't text me back.

But Gray is on the prowl and the thought of him putting his hands on her makes me murderous.

Kyle: Where are you?

I know barking at her probably isn't going to get me the result I need. But I need to fucking know she's safe.

Twenty minutes later, I still have no response. She hasn't even fucking read it.

Throwing the book off my lap, I jump from the bed and shove my feet into my sneakers.

"Where are you going?" Kane asks as I storm past where he's curled up with the same woman—Alana—from yesterday. It's weird seeing him here, let alone seeing him with a woman.

"Out," I bark, ripping the door open and marching out into the rain.

I'm at the Hunter's in record time, but unlike last night,

the lights are on and I fear I'm not going to be so successful sneaking in. Her car isn't here, which should tell me everything I need to know, but I'm not risking finding out for sure.

I push the door open and poke my head inside. The hallway is empty but there's music playing from somewhere.

Darting toward the stairs, I run up two at a time and fly through her bedroom door.

I don't need to look up, I know she's not here. The lack of response to me barging in tells me everything.

I look around the room, finding it tidy as if she's not even been back here and my heart thunders.

If that motherfucker has her, I'm going to fucking kill him.

I blink back the images I have from that night of his hands on her body, my fists curling in anger.

Needing to get out of the house before I'm caught, I slip back out and head down the stairs.

"Kyle, are you looking for Zayn?" Jada asks, scaring the shit out of me as I turn the corner.

My hand lifts to cover my pounding heart as my head spins a little.

"Uh... yeah?" I don't mean for it to come out as a question, and from the way Jada's brow lifts I fear she didn't miss it.

Nervously, I look behind me at the stairs. Does she know I just came from Harley's room?

"He's down in his den." She steps aside, allowing me to walk down toward the room.

"Um... I guess I should have tried there first, huh?"

She studies me, but she doesn't say anything as I step past her toward the den.

I don't want to go down there. But he might know where she is...

"Hey, man. How's it going?" Zayn asks the second I push inside the room.

I find the other seniors hanging out on the couches, amazingly without any girls on their laps for once.

"Yeah, good. Alright?" I ask them all, tipping my chin up in greeting.

"You joining us or what?" Zayn asks when I hover in the doorway. "I'm sure Jake wants to talk to you about next year," he says, looking toward his captain.

"Uh... actually, have you seen Harley?"

"Harley?" he asks, his eyes widening for a beat.

"Yeah." An excuse for why I might want to talk to her sits on the edge of my tongue, but I hold it in and wait to see what his response is going to be.

"No, not since this morning. She's probably with Ruby and Poppy. Everything all right?" he asks, his eyes narrowing on mine.

"Of course."

"Great, now come hang with us." He nods to an empty seat and other than turning my back and walking out on them, I don't really feel like I have much of a choice.

Their previous conversation continues around me as I take a seat and open the soda Zayn throws at me.

"So, the Harriers," Jake starts, leaning forward and resting his elbows on his knees. "Your old team doesn't exactly have a good rep. You any good?" he asks, although from what he's said previously, he's well aware of my skills.

I might have kept up with his conditioning sessions but he's yet to see me play any actual football. And I'm fully aware of my old team's rep.

"Yeah," I state confidently. "I am."

"Well." He rests back once more. "I hope you're as sure of your skills as you are your confidence."

"You don't need to worry about me."

"I'm about to leave my team in someone else's hands. I'm fucking worried."

"You'll forget all about it the second you join your college team."

Silence ripples around the room at my words and I fear I might have said something I shouldn't.

"Yeah, I'm sure you're right," he finally says after clearing his voice.

"Legend, come get some more drinks with me," Zayn barks as he stands and collects up a few empties.

"Sure."

I can tell by the set of his shoulders as he moves in front of me that he's about to grill me about Harley.

"What's going on?" he asks the second we're in the kitchen and out of earshot of everyone else.

"Nothing," I lie. "I just had a question about our English lit assignment. Didn't know who else to ask."

"Bullshit, Ky. Wanna try telling me the truth?"

My stomach knots. I can hardly tell him that Gray is threatening to do something to her to get to me. The hot-headed motherfucker will get straight in his car and drive to Harrow Creek to find him. He'll probably end up getting himself fucking killed.

"That is the truth. Jeez, can you lay off the big brother thing?" I try to make it sound like a joke but I'm pretty sure I fail.

"You didn't even want to look at her this morning, now you want her help. If I find out you're lying to me, I'll fucking take you out, Ky."

I put my hands up in surrender.

"I'm just going to use your bathroom."

I back out of the room with him watching my every move. The second I'm out of sight, I pull my cell out and find Ash's number.

He answers the moment I close the bathroom door behind me.

"Hey, how's it going?"

"Is Harley with Ruby?" I whisper-shout, ignoring any niceties.

"Um... no. Ruby is with me, why?"

"Can you ask her if she knows where Harley is?"

"S-sure." There's some rustling before he does as I ask. "No, she doesn't know."

"Call her," I demand.

"What the fuck is going on?" Ash asks.

"Put me on speaker." There's movement as he does as I ask. "Ruby, please can you call Harley and find out where she is?" There's a hardness to my voice which has the desired effect.

"Okay, calling now. Is everything okay?" she asks in a much softer tone than Ash did, although I can hear the concern in it.

"Yeah, probably."

"It just keeps ringing. I'll message her and let you know when I find out."

I blow out a long breath. "That's great, thank you."

"You gonna tell us what the big drama is now?"

"She just ran off, wanted to make sure she's okay."

"What did you do to her?" Ruby growls down the line.

"N-nothing." We all know it's a lie, but I say the word anyway. I've no idea if Harley has confessed to her girls about what happened last night. The fact Ruby isn't ripping me a new one right now for it makes me think she might not have. She certainly wanted to cover up the evidence if the scarf was anything to go by this morning.

"Riiight. Well, if you decide you wanna tell us the truth, we're at home. But we'll tell you if we hear anything," Ruby says softly, but I don't miss the edge of anger in her voice.

Understandable, I've hurt her girl. I'm sure it won't be the last time either.

We hang up and I'm forced to rejoin Zayn to carry the cans back through to the den and spend my night talking football while I wait for my cell to ring.

It's almost three hours later when that finally happens.

I excuse myself from the room and slip out into the hall.

"Yes."

"It's nice to hear from you too," Ash deadpans.

"Do you know where she is?"

"Yes, she's staying at Stella's tonight."

The breath I didn't know I was holding comes rushing out of me.

"Okay, thanks, I appreciate it, man."

"You gonna tell me what all of this is about yet?"

"It's nothing. I... I was just worried."

"Okay well... I'll see you tomorrow then."

The second I return from that phone call, I make my excuses and get out of the Hunter's house.

———

My place is empty once again when I get back and I breathe a sigh of relief that I'm not going to have to put up with Kane and Alana going at it all night.

I grab myself a soda from the refrigerator and fall down onto my bed.

I've got a ton of homework to do but I can't focus on any of it. Instead, I stare at the ceiling, wondering what she's doing and praying that she's safe.

Right before I decide to actually get into bed and attempt to get some sleep, my cell pings. My heart skips a beat thinking that it might be her, but deep down, I know it's not.

Unknown: Our girl looks good in red.

My hand trembles as I stare at his words. His threat.

If he so much as touches a fucking hair on her head, I'll...

My thoughts trail off as I consider if I'm already in too deep in this.

I tell myself that it's just because I don't want her hurt because of me. I might blame her, want to hurt her for what she did to me. But I want to be the one to do it.

Plus, I wouldn't wish that motherfucker on anyone.

I close down his message, not wanting to give him any clue that he's getting to me. It's bad enough he'll know that I've read it.

I silence my cell and throw it to the other side of the bed in frustration and close my eyes, not that I think sleep will come anytime soon. Especially not when he's out there watching her.

Our girl looks good in red.

He just means her hair... right?

———

The sun was almost up by the time I actually fell asleep last night, but as I lay there thinking about a million and one things that Gray could do to Harley, I refused to allow myself to look at my cell.

If I found another photo of him watching her and I had no clue where she was I knew I'd freak out. I decided it was better not to know and trust that she was safe with Stella.

When my alarm goes off, my body refuses to wake up, it's so heavy with sleep, but I know I have no choice.

The second I open my eyes, I reach for my cell, my restraint long vanished.

My stomach clenches when I find a message from another unknown number. But when I look closer, I see that it's a different number.

Intrigued, I swipe the screen and open it up.

Unknown: You're welcome!

My chin drops as I scroll up and enlarge the image I've been sent.

"Holy shit." My cock swells as I stare at the image of Harley in the smallest red swimsuit I think I've ever…

Red.

Fuck. She's wearing red.

Without thinking, I hit call on the number.

"Good morning," a familiar voice sings. "Did you like your little gift?"

"Where is she?" I ask, totally ignoring her question.

"Um… in the shower. Don't tell me you want me to sneak in and get another? She's going to kill me when she realizes I sent that, let alone—"

"No. I just want to know she's safe."

"Of course she's safe, she's with me. Why wouldn't she be?"

"No reason. Don't tell her I called or say anything about this."

"Trust me, I—"

I hang up before she can finish that sentence and blow out a relieved breath.

She's safe… for now.

"Fuck."

I need to figure out what I'm going to do and how I'm going to get Gray off her back.

I'd like to say that I could find a load of money and that it'll make him go away, but something tells me that wouldn't be enough. He wants my blood, not my dollar bills.

I shove my hair from my brow, tugging on the strands until it burns with pain. Pain that I deserve for all of this bullshit. For putting her in danger.

I'm in the parking lot long before the rest of the school

once again. I have no idea what class Harley has first, so I figure I'll just sit here until her car appears.

Only, it never does and I have no clue what Stella drives.

The bell rings out and I'm forced to either get out or skip.

I go with the former and climb from the car in favor of my statistics class.

I see no sign of her, and by the time lunch rolls around, I'm damn near losing my mind.

I've messaged her over and over again but still, she refuses to read them.

My lips twist as I think about getting my hands on her and showing her just how infuriating her defiance is.

"Kyle, did you hear that?" Miss Harper asks pointedly.

"Um... yes."

"Good, so you'll know exactly what the homework task entails then."

"Of course. Don't sweat it." I give her my best smile and after blushing a little she turns away to terrorize someone else.

The bell sounds out and we all jump into action ready to go and find out what the cafeteria is offering up today, only when I get out into the hallway, something—or someone—else catches my attention.

There's a flash of red ahead that can only belong to Harley Hunter as she tries to make her escape.

While everyone else moves toward the cafeteria, I head for her.

She keeps her head down as she moves as fast as her legs will carry her. It's cute that she thinks she can outrun me. She should know by now that I'll always get her in the end.

I catch up with her right in front of a classroom door. A classroom that I pray to fucking God is empty.

I wrap one hand around her mouth and the other around her waist as I lift her from the floor and the pair of us crash through the door and into the classroom, which, thankfully, is deserted. Not only is it deserted but the blinds are all shut and it's dark. Bingo.

Twisting her around, I press her up against the wall but keep my hand over my mouth.

I lean in close to her, so close that our noses brush.

"Nice try, Hunter."

Her jaw flexes as she prepares to say something but my hand tightens around her mouth, stopping her.

"I've messaged you. I've called you," I seethe. "You fucking ignored me."

Her nostrils flare with her need to argue with me.

"That's rude. Don't you think?"

She doesn't react so I make her nod, much to her annoyance if her narrowed eyes are anything to go by.

"Now the question is... what should I do about it? How should I punish you for thinking you could ignore me?"

Her jaw flexes again but I don't let up.

Reaching around her, I pull her bag from her shoulder and throw it across the room before reaching into the back pocket of her denim skirt, knowing that her cell is going to be there.

Her entire body jolts when I make contact with her, and I have to fight the smile that threatens to curl at my lips.

"Oh look," I say, waking it up and showing her the screen that is full of notifications of messages from me. "It works. Next time I try to contact you, you reply. You got that?"

Finally, I drop my hand from her mouth, finding her lips pursed in anger.

"Fuck you, Kyle. Fuck. You."

Grasping her chin in my fingers, I press the length of my body against hers.

"I hate you."

"Oh, I know. Feels fucking great, doesn't it?"

I drop my hand to her throat and my sudden movement

makes her gasp, exactly what I was hoping for as I force my tongue into her mouth and tease hers.

Her hands lift to my chest and she tries, unsuccessfully, to push me away.

She resists kissing me to the point she bites my tongue but the second I turn the tables on her, suck her bottom lip into my mouth and sink my teeth into it, her body starts to relax. Her nails, that she was trying to claw my skin off with, suddenly vanish in favor of fisting my shirt in her small hands so she can cling onto me.

"See," I whisper into her mouth. "You can do as you're told."

"Fuck. You."

"Yeah, Kitten. I was thinking the same."

Dropping my hands to her thighs, I push her skirt up around her waist and lift her so she has no choice but to wrap her legs around my waist.

I grind into her forcing a moan to rip from her lips as my length aligns perfectly with her core.

"You feel that, Kitten?" She nods. "You fucking do that to me."

"Kyle," she cries as I reach around her, slip her panties aside and run my finger through her folds.

"So fucking wet, Kitten."

"Oh God," she gasps as I push one digit inside her.

"You want to get fucked right here in this classroom?" I drop my lips to her ear. "Where anyone could walk in and see that I fucking own you?"

I continue working her, knowing that she's long past the point of refusing anything I say to her. Her juices run down my fingers as she thinks about my words.

"You like belonging to me, don't you, Kitten?"

"No," she argues. I don't need to look at her to know her eye is twitching as she says it.

"Well, your pussy seems to disagree with you."

26

HARLEY

"Oh fuck, Kyle," I cry as he spears his fingers inside me before pulling them out and leaving me feeling bereft without him.

I shouldn't be doing this.

We *really* shouldn't be doing this.

I told myself that when I saw him next, I would rip him a new one and walk away from him for being such an arrogant, demanding prick. But then he put his hands on me and I forgot everything but how it feels when he touches me.

He drops me lower, with one hand gripping my ass while the other lifts the hem of his shirt.

"Go on then," he encourages, nodding down to his waistband.

"Ky, you're not serious?" I ask. He can't really be suggesting that we do this... here.

"I'm deadly fucking serious, Kitten."

I stare into his sparkling silver eyes, the blue vanished with his hunger. His abs jump when my knuckles brush them as I undo his button and help push his pants down over his hips.

One second he has his length in his hand and the next

I've been lifted higher against the wall at my back and I feel him pressing against my entrance.

I brace myself for his invasion, knowing that it's probably going to hurt like last time, although I hope not quite as bad.

"Relax, Kitten. It's just me," he says softly, his palm cupping my cheek and his thumb gently caressing my skin. It's totally at odds with his attitude only moments ago. I guess being on the verge of sex does that to a guy.

I take a deep breath and slide my fingers into his hair, knocking his backward cap to the floor in the process.

His lips find mine at the same time he drops me down onto him.

It burns, but it's nowhere near as bad as I remember.

A groan rumbles up from the back of Kyle's throat, the sound is so damn sexy and mixed with the knowledge that I'm the one who caused it helps me to forget the bite of pain as he pulls out.

"Okay?" he asks through gritted teeth, and I can't help but swoon.

He likes to make out he's all vicious and demanding, but once you peel back that hard outer shell, he's just the sweet boy I remember. The one who would always share his chocolate with me when my own brother would scoff, leaving me with nothing.

"Yeah." My fingers twist in his hair and I drag his lips to mine as he begins to fuck me.

It's rougher than last time, my shoulder blades smarting against the rough wall behind me, but feeling him moving inside me, hearing the quiet groans of pleasure that rumbled up his throat, is fucking everything.

"Oh God, Kyle," I moan, tipping my head back as I begin to get closer. His lips attack my neck, sucking and biting, the pain only adding to the pleasure shooting around my body.

"Come, Kitten. Let me hear you scream my name."

"Oh shit."

He slips his hand between us and pinches my clit, that extra sensation is exactly what I need to send me flying over the edge.

Seconds later, he drops his head into the crook of my neck before his cock jerks violently inside me.

His hot breath fans across my collarbones and sends goose bumps racing across my skin.

"Come to mine after school. We'll do your next tutoring session."

"You want me to come to yours to do math?" I ask incredulously.

"That, and other things."

"I should say no," I tell him honestly.

"Yeah, you probably should. Hell, you can if you want, but you're still going to find yourself in my bedroom after school with your clothes on my floor."

"Jesus, Ky."

"Go on," he encourages. "Tell me no. Tell me you don't want that."

"I... um..." His hand wraps around my throat once again and I have to fight not to sigh with contentment. It's fucked-up, but I've never felt safer than when I'm in his hands like this.

His eyes widen and his brows rise as he waits.

"I passed a math test yesterday," I blurt out, no longer able to contain my smile.

"Okay, wow. That wasn't what I was expecting but... well done."

"I... I couldn't have done it without you," I admit. "Mr. Wilson put the questions in front of me and it was like I could hear you telling me how to do it."

"Yeah?" he asks, his own smile beginning to emerge.

"Yeah, so... thank you."

Suddenly the silence around us is broken by the sound of

a group of kids walking past the classroom door and it's like a bucket of ice water is thrown over both of us.

Kyle lowers me to the floor before pulling his pants up and reaching for his cap.

"We should go and get food," I say, aware that I've still not answered him about after school. Part of me doesn't want to, just to see what he's going to do.

We walk toward the cafeteria together side by side. No words are said, but I guess that's an improvement on most of the time we've spent together while under this roof so I'll take it. He waits for me when I take a detour to the bathroom to clean up and gives me a killer smile which makes desire curl in my belly when I emerge.

We grab a tray each and get some lunch before dropping down on opposite sides of the team's table.

"You found her at last then?" Zayn asks Kyle, which immediately piques my interest.

"You were looking for me?" I ask, hoping to make him sweat under my brother's scrutiny. Mean? Maybe. But I don't give a shit. He's sure done worse to me.

"What?" I hiss at Ruby when she elbows me to get my attention.

My eyes meet hers but she doesn't say anything, instead, she flicks a look to my neck before covering her own with her hand.

My brows pinch together in confusion. But then the image of Kyle sucking on my neck only minutes ago in that classroom hit me and I immediately copy her move, covering my neck.

I twist away from Zayn a little more before lifting my wrap to my mouth.

"Yeah," he finally says. "I needed to know something about that English lit paper we were given."

"Oh yeah, what was that?"

A knowing smirk plays on his lips. He knows exactly what I'm doing.

"It's fine. I found someone else to ask. I... uh... can't remember her name, but that really hot blonde that sits at the front of class. She was more than willing to help."

I smile at him, hoping to hell that my true feelings aren't written all over my face as I say, "Oh, yeah. I bet she did," and roll my eyes so hard they actually hurt.

I swear everyone sitting at the table holds their breath as they wait for him to say something in response.

"Yeah, she had a real tight—ow," he complains, reaching under the table to rub at whatever that was, from the smirk on Ruby's face I'm assuming it was her shoe. "I was going to say understanding of what we had to do."

"Course you were." I roll my eyes and turn to Ruby, severing our connection. For now at least.

Sitting so far away from him for the rest of lunch but feeling his stare burning into me makes the time drag. It's no different as I sit in chemistry watching Ruby and Ash flirt in front of me knowing that I've got history with him next period.

I know he's going to bug me about going to his place after school, and although I already know that it's going to happen, I've come to terms with the fact I'm not going to be able to refuse, he doesn't need to know that.

He's already in his seat waiting for me when I finally make it to the other side of the school to our history class.

"I thought you were skipping on me," he whispers as Mr. Anderson starts the class.

"I considered it."

"Oh yeah?"

"Yeah. I like playing hide and seek." I flip my book open ready to get started, refusing to look at him despite the fact I know he's staring at me.

His hand skims down my back before his fingers tuck

under the waistband of my skirt, the heat of his skin burning mine.

He leans over, his breath tickling down my neck.

"You seem to forget that I always win."

"Who said that wasn't my intention?"

His growl makes my entire body tingle.

"Oh, Kitten, we're going to have such fun tonight."

"I've got cheer practice." My argument is weak, I know that, but it's all I have.

"And I've got a conditioning session. It's like fate."

"Yeah, if you believe in that shit."

"You don't?" he asks, shocking me so much I actually turn to look at him.

"You do?"

"Maybe. We'll just have to wait and see if fate lands you in my lap later."

"Fucking hell," I mutter, trying not to show how much I like the banter between us when we're not trying to kill each other.

"So... tonight, my bed, you in?"

"You're going to need to make it sound a little more tempting than that."

"Hmmm... okay." He shifts his chair a little closer, so he can whisper in my ear and his hand slips around to grip onto my hip. "My bed, me naked, you coming... again, and again... and again."

Holy shit.

My thighs clench as he growls out those words so roughly all my hairs stand on end.

"I'll think about it."

He chuckles, sitting back in his seat before we get caught and end up in detention together instead of his bed.

———

"You have got some explaining to do. The scarf yesterday and then that fresh one at lunch," Ruby says, helpfully pointing out the love bite in question, just in case Stella or any other member of the squad who care to be listening to us as they get ready for practice.

"Do we really have to do this now?"

"Just tell me it was him?" Ruby raises a knowing brow. She really doesn't need me to tell her the answer, she already knows.

"Yes. It was him."

"Oh my God," she squeals and starts clapping like a baby seal. "This is so exciting. He was freaking out when he couldn't find you yesterday."

"What? Why?" I ask, my brow furrowing.

"No idea, he wouldn't say."

"Come on, ladies. Get moving," Chelsea barks when she walks in and sees us standing around gossiping.

Ruby winks at me before turning around to get changed telling me that this is only the beginning of this discussion.

Thankfully, since we were runner-up at nationals a few weeks ago, Chelsea has let up on practice and we're spending our time perfecting new routines and moves. We've still got a few weeks until tryouts and welcoming new members to our squad so mostly we're just enjoying ourselves.

"Ace's?" Ruby asks hopefully once we're back in the locker room getting showered and dressed.

"I... err... can't. I've got a tutoring session."

"Oh right, is that what we're calling it these days?" she says, smothering a laugh.

"Well, no, actually Kyle *is* my tutor."

"Okay, when did this happen?"

"Last week, I just didn't confess."

"Harley Hunter, have you been keeping secrets from me?"

Guilt covers my face and my temperature picks up as she stares at me.

"A little," I whisper, lifting my hand and holding my thumb and forefinger just a little apart.

She places her hand on her hip and tries her best to look angry but she only lasts a few seconds before she bursts out laughing.

"You gonna spill all before you leave to meet him?"

"Nope," I say with a smile. "But know this... I'm probably making a huge mistake."

"Well," she says, deep in thought. "At least you're going into it with your eyes open."

"Yeah, although I have a feeling I'm still about to run face-first into a brick wall."

"You might not. Look at me and Ash. I'm sure there are plenty that would say we were making a huge mistake."

"I think your parents probably still are," I deadpan.

"Oh shush yourself." She laughs. "Seriously though, you know where I am, yeah? My ears are open."

"Thank you. Good news though, I passed a math test."

Ruby's face lights up, much like I'm sure mine did when I realized that I'd nailed it.

"OMG! That's awesome. See, maybe all of this might just work out. Crazier things have happened."

"Yeah, we'll see."

"Rubes, can I borrow you?" Chelsea shouts, successfully ending our conversation.

"Coming, boss."

"Call me, yes?" Ruby's eyes widen with her demand.

"If I can."

"On second thought, don't. Just enjoy him and give me all the details later." She winks before skipping over to Chelsea.

Knowing that Kyle is with the team right now means I'm in no rush to be ready. We finished early tonight so I know I'm going to have to wait for him.

"You coming to get your car, or are you going straight to his?"

"Straight there. Is it okay if I pick up my car tomorrow maybe?"

"Of course."

"Thank you. I wasn't really expecting to be going to his."

"Really?" she asks with a laugh.

"I hoped I'd be able to put up more of a fight."

"Girl, sometimes, it's just not worth it. Reap the reward for putting up with his ass."

"You're nuts," I say, dragging my skirt on.

"Only way to be." I shake my head at her craziness. Who am I to judge on how she gets by after being forced to move so much. "Have you found out why he was so freaked out about not knowing where you were yesterday?"

"Other than him being an asshole and a control freak?" I ask.

"Yeah, other than that."

"Nah. He was just being... Kyle." I shrug, not thinking anymore into it.

"Okay. Ready to head out?" Most of the girls have already left, thanks to my slow ass, but Stella hung back with me. For someone who claims to not make friends, she's a pretty good one.

"Yep, let's go."

A couple of the guys from the team walk ahead of us down the hallway and I can't help looking over my shoulder to see if Kyle is about to sneak up on me any minute. But he never does.

The second we're in the lot though, I know he's still here because his car is one of the only ones left.

"You want me to wait with you," Stella offers.

"No, you take off. I'm sure he won't be long."

"Sure?"

"Yes, go."

"See you tomorrow."

I wave her off and watch as she walks to her car. I do the same but toward Kyle's Volkswagen.

I find myself a seat on the hood and pull out my cell.

I'm scrolling through Instagram when some movement in the trees to my right catches my eye. I half expect Kyle to jump out and scare me half to death. But as I keep scanning the tree line, I don't see anything or anyone.

Feeling ridiculous, it was probably just a cat or something, I focus back on the post I was reading and forget the world around me exists.

The other few cars that were out here are long gone, leaving me alone with Kyle's car and what I'm assuming is Ash's bike.

I might not be looking up when the pair of them exit the building, but I don't need to be. I feel it.

My skin prickles with awareness and my stomach flutters in anticipation.

Lifting my eyes from my cell, I find him staring right at me as he walks this way. Ashton is talking to him, but I've got a feeling that Kyle isn't hearing a word of it.

When they get to Ash's bike, he slaps Kyle on the shoulder and says something. Kyle nods but his footsteps don't falter as he continues to close the space between us.

"Hmm... you on the hood of my car. This is a nice surprise."

"I do aim to please, Mr. Legend."

A growl rumbles low in his throat as he parts my knees and steps between them, sliding my ass down the hood to get us closer.

"Fuck, Kitten. What am I going to do with you?"

27

KYLE

"Holy shit," I gasp the second I push the door open and Ash and I step out toward the parking lot.

"Wha—oooooh? Something you need to tell me, man?"

"Something with her waiting for me like that doesn't already give away?"

"You're a lucky motherfucker."

"Err... have you seen your girl?"

"Yes, and I'd prefer it if you didn't *see* my girl."

"Oh fuck off. She's hot and you love it."

"Yeah, man. I fucking do. Now you gonna go over there and rock her fucking world, or what?"

"We've got a tutoring session."

I don't look over at him, my eyes are glued on Harley but I know he throws his head back laughing.

"Sure you have. Why do I get the feeling that the only thing you're studying tonight is her body?"

"Because she needs to not fail math."

"Damn bro, you're serious, aren't you?" he asks as if I might just have sprouted a new head.

I can't keep a straight face and bark out a laugh. "Partly. We'll do the math when we're having a rest."

"Fuck yeah, man." He slaps my shoulder and turns to his bike. "Have a good night. Don't do anything I wouldn't do."

"Which is fucking nothing, so I'm safe."

"Bro, that hurts."

"Fucking truth though, ain't it?"

"Meh." He mutters something under his breath as I walk away, but with Harley waiting for me like she is, I really don't care about whatever it is.

The second I'm in front of her, I force her knees apart and slide her down the hood until her legs wrap around my hips.

"Zayn's already left," she whispers as I stare down into her dark eyes.

"Don't care."

One of my hands slides into her hair and my fingers twist in the length as I pull her head back and capture her lips with mine.

Fuck, she's too addictive.

My cock hardens against her as I plunge my tongue into her mouth.

I shouldn't do this here out in the open. It might be empty but there are always eyes in a school just waiting to spread the next bit of gossip, but I can't stop myself.

I kiss her until we're both breathless and my need to rip her panties aside and take her right here is almost too much to ignore.

Dragging my lips from her, I trail them across her jaw and down her neck, sucking on the same bit of skin I did earlier, brightening my mark.

"You smell like strawberries," I whisper against her throat.

It flexes as she swallows. "M-my shower gel."

I pull back and look at her. Her eyes are hooded with lust, her cheeks bright and her lips swollen from my kiss.

"Wanna see my bedroom?" I ask with a smile.

"I'm not that kind of girl," she quips. Resting back on her palms and running her eyes down the length of me until she finds the bulge in my pants. She sucks her bottom lip into her mouth and bites down.

"I've got news for you, Harley Hunter. You are that girl and you're about to do some wicked things to prove me right."

Her lips part once again but she doesn't say anything.

"Get in the car before I fuck you right here."

I've barely finished the words and she's scrambling from the hood and racing toward the passenger door.

"Is the prospect that bad?"

"You want anyone watching?"

"As long as I'm the one inside you, I don't give a fuck, Kitten."

Her chin drops like she's about to argue, but she must change her mind because in the end all she does is rip the door open and drop into the seat.

I stare at her for a beat, appreciating just how good she looks in my car.

"Ready?" I ask once I've joined her.

"Honestly? No, I don't think I am."

I laugh at her as I start the car.

"Well, I hate to break it to you, but it's too late to back out now." I press the button to lock the doors, showing her just how serious I am.

"Pretty sure this is classed as kidnapping right now."

"Nah, Kitten. You're going to enjoy yourself way too much for it to be that." I smirk, starting the engine and pulling out of the space.

———

"This is... um... bare," Harley says as she walks into my room ahead of me. Thankfully, the place is empty but I don't have any intention of hanging out in the living room in case Kane comes back. He might be okay with flaunting his conquests but like fuck are his eyes getting on Harley.

"Yeah, well not all of us become the princess in the castle," I mutter, kicking the door closed behind me and stepping right into her.

Now I've had her again, I'm fucking addicted.

A year of only looking at guys and I need to be buried deep inside her again more than I need my next breath.

Sweeping her hair to the side, I press my lips to the skin where her neck meets her shoulder and smile when a shudder runs through her.

"That's not what I meant. I'm not judging."

"Sure you're not," I breathe, making my way up her smooth neck.

But she tenses in my hold, and I know she's about to pull away from me.

"I'm not," she snaps, her hands going to her waist as her hip pops. "I don't give a shit where you live, Ky. We grew up in shithole, damp and cold trailers. This is like a fucking castle compared to that.

"So what, I live in a big house. It doesn't change who I am. I'm the girl from Harrow Creek. I'll always be the girl from Harrow Creek, just like you'll always be the boy—shit," she gasps as my body crashes against hers and we both stumble until her back hits the wall.

My lips find hers as I wrap her legs around my waist.

"You're wrong," I whisper, my heart pounding so hard in my chest I worry it's about to come out. "You're not just a girl from the Creek. You're my fucking girl from the Creek."

I stare into wide eyes as my words settle around us both.

"Fuck, I need you now."

With one hand on her ass to hold her up, the other

threads into her hair and I carry her to my bed, my mouth attached to her the whole time, too afraid to pull away again in case some other scary shit falls from my lips.

Her back hits the mattress and I wrap my hands around the bottom of her hoodie, pulling the fabric up her body, releasing her lips for the briefest moment as it passes between us.

The second I drop it to the floor, I slip my hand around her back to release her bra and peel that away from her body as well, my hands moving so I can squeeze them both.

A moan rips up her throat as I do it.

"Fuck, Harley. You're so fucking sexy."

"Ky," she moans as I kiss and suck on the skin of her neck before grazing my teeth over her collarbones before making my way to her breasts so I can pull her nipples into my mouth.

"Good, Kitten?" I growl when her back arches from the bed. I kiss across to the other side and give it the same treatment.

"Kyle," she moans again. "I need—"

"I know what you need. Trust me?"

I look up at her and my eyes lock with hers. Something crackles between us but it gives me no clue as to what kind of answer to expect.

"D-do I trust you?" she asks between heaving breaths.

"Yeah, Kitten. Do you trust me?"

She searches my eyes as if she's going to find the answer she needs within them as she tries to find the word she needs.

I wait with my lips hovering right over her breast, my breath teasing her and keeping her nipple pert for me.

"Y-yes," she whispers finally.

"Yeah?" I confirm, a smile twitching at my lips.

"I shouldn't. But I do."

"Right answer, Kitten."

Instead of going back to her breast, I kiss down her stomach, undo the button on her waistband and pull her skirt and panties down her legs until she's bare before me.

"So beautiful."

She lifts her arms as if she's going to attempt to hide from me, but the second our eyes lock, she must read my warning because she drops them back to the bed.

"Why am I naked and you're fully dressed?" She lifts a brow as her eyes drop to my clothed body.

"Good question. What are you going to do about it?" I stare at her, daring her to move and she does, in the blink of an eye.

Her hands fist the bottom of my hoodie, pulling it up my body and revealing my bare torso beneath. Her fingers tickle down my skin, tracing my abs before finding the scar on my side. My muscles tense as she brushes the raised mark.

"H-how you'd get this?"

"Juvie initiation. It was nothing."

Guilt flashes through her eyes, her lips pressing into a thin line as she stares at it.

"You got hurt?"

"Kitten," I whisper, reaching out and cupping her chin, tilting her face up so she has no choice but to look at me. "That place was like a jungle. You've got to do what you've got to do, to survive."

"Ky, I'm so, so—"

"No," I bark. "We're not doing this now."

Her eyes fill with tears at my harsh tone but she quickly blinks them away.

"Now, you were about to do something," I remind her, rolling my hips to get her attention.

She reaches out and fumbles with my fly and shoves the fabric down my hips, allowing my cock to spring free.

"Fuck, Kitten," I bark as the sensation of her hand wrapping around me stops me in my tracks.

"Good?" she asks, much like I did earlier.

"Like you wouldn't believe." I quickly toe my sneakers off before kicking my pants from my legs.

"Kitten," I growl, my hand finding the back of her head as she sucks me deep into her mouth.

She takes me all the way back until I feel the back of her throat at the tip.

"Oh shit." My grip on her hair tightens as pleasure shoots through me.

She works me like a fucking pro, her hot wet mouth better than I could have ever imagined. Tears leak from her eyes as she fights her need to gag until I come down her throat.

"How are you so fucking perfect?" I ask, pushing her back on the bed and crawling over her, wiping the tears from her cheeks once she's settled.

She wipes her mouth with the back of her hand and smiles shyly up at me.

"I think we both know I'm far from that."

"Don't think about it," I demand, not wanting to give the past a second thought right now.

We've got a lot to talk about. The most pressing is the truth about Gray's threats that I'm keeping from her. But right now, I just want to enjoy this because I have no doubt that all too soon something will fuck it up.

"But we—" I cut her off with my kiss. I'm not interested in talking right now, that can come later, much, much later.

———

"I'd probably be able to concentrate on this better if you let me get dressed," Harley complains from her spot on my bed. She's got her math book on her thighs and that is it. Just as she should be. "And I'm cold."

"I can warm you up, Kitten."

She pins me with a look.

"We are doing this." She nods toward the book on her lap. "Nothing, and I mean nothing, else is happening until I've nailed this."

"I'd rather nail you."

"You already have. Twice," she reminds me.

"Yeah, well. I'm not doing it right now," I sulk.

Her eyes narrow as she thinks and my stomach clenches. I'm not going to like what she's about to say.

"Spit it out, Kitten," I encourage when she remains silent.

"I thought you hated me," she blurts before her eyes go wide as if she didn't actually mean to say the words.

"Yeah, well... turns out I like fucking you more than I do hating you."

"So you still hate me, fucking me softens the blow?"

She asks the question so seriously that I can't help but laugh.

"Yeah, Kitten. Something like that."

"Do that again?"

"Do what again?" My brows pinch at her request, unaware that I just did anything.

"Laugh again."

"Make me."

She throws the book to the other end of the bed and launches herself at me, her red nails going to my sides before she starts tickling.

I laugh, not because she demanded I do so but because I can't not.

This right now. This is fucking everything.

28

HARLEY

"You're not running this time, Hunter," Ruby says as she, Poppy and Stella approach me in the cafeteria the next morning, "We already know that you didn't sleep in your own bed last night." She looks at Poppy, ratting her out for snitching on me. "And we know you didn't stay at Stella's like you lead your mother to believe." She looks at Stella.

I shake my head at the three of them. "Looks like you've got me all figured out," I concede. Not that I really had a leg to stand on.

With most of the team elsewhere and the squad having their usual bitch fest at our normal table, we find another just the four of us so we can thankfully have this conversation in private.

"So..." Ruby starts, looking entirely too excited by what I might have to say. "Are you like... together now?"

"What? No. I'm pretty sure he still hates me."

"But you spent the night with him." Her words force me back to last night when he basically told me that I wasn't leaving before physically pinning me to his bed to stop it from happening. I'm also reminded of how I woke up multiple times in the night, and this morning to him asleep at my back with his arm thrown protectively over my waist.

It felt nice. No. It was better than nice. It felt incredible.

But I'm not stupid. I know this is nothing more than him taking what he thinks I owe him. And right when I allow myself to believe it could be more, he's going to force me to watch him turn his back on me, on this, and smile as I drown.

I push the depressing thought away because it's not going to happen. I'm not going to fall for him and he's not going to break my heart.

It's not going to happen.

"He doesn't have to like her to fuck her, I thought you of all people would know that," Poppy says, pinning Ruby with a knowing look.

"I know but—"

"There is no but there, just like there is no *us*. He's helping me out with my math and taking what he thinks he's owed after that night."

"Yeah and about that. When are you going to tell us what happened *that* night?"

"Um…" I glance at Poppy, aware that she already knows and grateful she's not told Ruby. "Fine," I huff, really not wanting to go back there but knowing my time is running out. "I went to a party that Letty dragged me along to. She'd not been back to Harrow Creek for ages seeing as she was at college, and she wanted to see some old friends.

"I didn't want to go. She'd had some… issues, shall we say, with Kane, Kyle's older brother, and I had a feeling he'd be there despite her protests that he wouldn't. Well, not an hour into the party and they both turned up.

"Kyle was already drunk and he made a beeline for me. Zayn wasn't there, so I guess he thought he had something of a free pass. I wasn't complaining. I'd crushed on him since forever."

"Rightly so," Stella adds with a nod, making me look up at her. "What? He's hot."

"Yeah, whatever. We were drinking, one thing led to another and..."

"And..." Ruby encourages.

"We kissed and stuff."

"And stuff."

"Yeah, touched a bit. Nothing crazy. Anyway, the rest of his crew were there, Kane and Letty had vanished, Christ knows where and I was enjoying life. But after a while, things started getting a little hazy. I knew I was drunk, but I hadn't had that much, you know.

"But then Kyle's friend Gray joined us, and I mean like... *joined us.*

"Kyle seemed up for it. He was wasted, mind you. So I played along. I felt safe with Kyle so I wasn't too concerned. I knew Gray was different... dangerous, but then most guys from the Creek are, it wasn't anything new to me.

"But things started to escalate, his touches more insistent, the things he whispered in my ear sent a shiver down my spine and I realized what he had done.

"I barely remember the call. Hell, until the cops turned up I didn't even really know if the call had connected or if they cared. I certainly wasn't going to lift my cell to my ear for him to see. I just knew that I needed to get out of that situation before something really bad happened because one look in Gray's eyes and I knew it was coming.

"He drugged me for a reason. He wasn't stopping."

"Jesus," Ruby mutters. She's leaning forward with her elbows on the table and her chin resting on her knuckles, totally invested in my story.

"So what happened next?" Stella asks, her jaw ticcing like she wants to go and physically hurt someone—Gray—for this. I'm not going to tell her so, but since seeing her house and hearing her previous threats, I'm kinda scared she actually has it in her to do it too.

"Things got really hazy. I remember leaning into Kyle, telling him to help me, and then I blacked out.

"I vaguely remember the commotion of the place emptying, I assume the second they discovered the cops had arrived. Then I remember an officer talking to me. Kyle was there. I remember that he was holding my hand and it made me feel safe.

"But the next time I came back to, he was gone, and I was in the hospital."

"Had he hurt you?" Poppy asks.

"No. And there was no evidence that Gray actually did anything. I knew it was him who did it, and as much as I wanted to believe Kyle wasn't involved, I couldn't be sure. They were best friends. It would have made sense for him to know."

"Did he?" Stella all but growls.

"I don't think so. He stayed while all the others ran despite the fact his pockets were full of Gray's gear."

"But he was drunk," she argues.

"Not drunk enough to sit beside me and hold my hand. Something tells me he sobered up pretty fast when reality came crashing down."

"So..." Poppy starts, looking totally confused. "If he was the one who helped you, why do you hate him."

I chuckle to myself. "I blamed him for allowing it to happen, and until he turned up here and acted the way he has, I convinced myself that he was a part of the plan."

"But you don't know?"

I shake my head. "No, I know he wasn't in on it."

"Has he said so?" Ruby asks.

"No, but he doesn't need to."

"Christ, okay. So this Gray guy..." Stella discretely cracks her knuckles under the table like she's gunning for a fight, which is hilarious because she's the small blonde girl who looks about as scary as a teddy bear.

I shrug. "Dead I hope."

Ruby gasps in shock.

"What? He'd have raped me that night, I have no doubt. He doesn't deserve to breathe the same air as us."

"True."

"So he's gone?" Stella asks with a scowl on her face.

"I mean, I guess. I haven't heard from him or seen him since that night so..."

"Okay," she says, deep in thought.

"What? What are you thinking?" I ask her.

"You said Kyle was arrested because of Gray's drugs. I assume they got seized."

"Yeah, I guess."

"Gray's going to want payment for the lost revenue."

"Uh... um... who are you?"

She laughs. "I've probably just seen too many movies," she argues, but I don't buy it.

"So you think he'll come for Kyle?" Ruby asks the words that I'm afraid to.

"I have no idea, but surely you've all seen the movies."

Silence settles over our table for a few seconds as my stomach knots uncomfortably. I don't want to be anywhere near him ever again, and I certainly don't want him anywhere near Kyle. He's already got him in enough shit.

"You going to his birthday party tonight?" Ruby suddenly asks.

"Whose?"

"Kyle's." She rolls her eyes like it should be totally obvious.

"It's his birthday?" I ask, horrified that I didn't already know this. I woke up in his bed this morning and I didn't know.

"Yeah, his brother is throwing him a party at their house. We're all going, right?"

"Uh…" Why didn't he tell me? Hell, why didn't he invite me?

"We're going," Stella states, putting an end to whatever I was going to say. That and the fact the bell rings.

"We'll all get ready at Harley's," Poppy announces, still unable to claim our house as her own.

"I've got some stuff to do after school," Stella says. "But I'll be there."

We clear away our trays and all head in different directions for our classes.

Ruby excuses herself to meet Ash and I make my way alone, crossing to a different building to our English lit class.

I'm almost there when a storage closet door opens beside me and someone wraps their hand around my arm and drags me inside.

"What the hell are you doing?" I hiss as Kyle crowds me against the wall. There's a dirty bulb hanging overhead that gives out just enough light to see each other. His hand skims up my body before it finds its home around my throat.

My heart thunders in my chest but I must admit that I'm starting to get used to him 'abducting' me when I least expect it. Hell, I'm starting to enjoy it.

"I needed something."

"Oh yeah. That's a coincidence because I need something too."

"Yeah?" he growls, pressing me harder into the wall. "Ow, what was that for?" he asks, rubbing the side of his head where I gently hit it.

"It's your fucking birthday. Why didn't you tell me?"

He shrugs. "Not important."

"Ky, you're eighteen. It's really important," I argue.

He shakes his head at me, a soft smile playing on his lips.

"I got to wake up and sink inside you, what could be more important than that?" he murmurs.

"Oh, I don't know, how about... tell me about your party?" I pin him with a look.

"How'd you... Ruby." He correctly guesses.

"Yeah, so am I not invited then, or what?"

"I don't know what Kane's got planned and I didn't want..." He trails off.

"How about you let me decide that?"

"I'm assuming he's invited the Creek group and..."

"Still you thought it was okay to decide for me?"

The truth is, I don't really have any intention of hanging out with his Creek buddies. After *that* night, I turned my back on that place, aside from visiting my dad.

He smiles at me and damn him because it makes my insides melt.

"Kitten," he breathes, making my insides quiver. "Would you like to come to my party?"

"I think I might be busy tonight, thanks for the invite though," I deadpan and he throws his head back and laughs.

His gaze is so intense when it comes back to mine that it makes my heart skip a beat, I swear.

"W-we should get to class."

"Yeah, in a minute."

His lips find mine and his hand slips under my shirt so he can wrap his hand around my waist, skin on skin.

The second his tongue slips into my mouth, I sag in his hold, grateful that he'll hold me up.

"I really want to fuck you," he admits after kissing across my jaw, his lips brushing my ears.

"B-but English," I force out, making him laugh.

"I know, Kitten. Is there anything I can do to make you skip with me?"

A million and one things that he could say to make me

agree run through my mind, but I don't say any of them because I know I can't allow it to happen.

"Nope."

"Everyone else thinks you're such a good girl, don't they?"

"Ky," I warn, his deep voice and desire-filled words making my refusal to stay locked in here for our entire class harder and harder to stick to.

English lit was hell after I finally managed to slip out from Kyle and escape the storage closet.

I can't deny that I'd have been more than happy to stay in there for the entire time, but I can't risk missing class, and I certainly can't risk the chance of Mom finding out. She might let us get away with a lot when it comes to parties and drinking but school is another matter entirely.

She's not stupid, she knows from experience the kind of upbringing we had in the Creek, and she knows the things we got up to way before we were old enough to be doing them. Hell, she is a Creek girl. But she also got out, and education is the only way to make that happen. And she wants better for us. I totally understand that.

Kyle's touch barely leaves my body throughout the entire class while he sits there trying to prove that what I did was wrong.

My skin tingles with awareness, my panties still damp from his kiss.

I know I probably made the wrong decision but it's too late to go back on it now.

"Come home with me now," he growls in my ear as he stands a little too close to me besides my locker as the rest of the students make a beeline for the exit to start their weekend plans. "We can start the party early."

"You've got a conditioning session," I say, poking him in the chest a little harder than necessary. "And I promised the girls that I'd get ready with them."

"What are you wearing?"

"I have no idea," I say honestly because I haven't even thought about it.

"Wrong answer, Kitten."

"Okay." I pause trying to come up with the right answer. "Something sexy?"

"Bingo."

"I'm assuming Zayn is coming?"

"Fuuuck. I'm just going to have to tell him that I'm banging his hot as fuck sister," he says with a shrug and my heart rate picks up a few notches.

"And get your ass kicked on your birthday?"

"Ow," I complain when he reaches out and twists my nipple through my shirt. "I can take your brother, Kitten."

"Riiight. Sure."

He stares at me with his brow furrowed.

"Okay fine. But not tonight. You're supposed to be enjoying yourself."

"Exactly, which means I need a free pass to your pussy."

"Jesus, were you always this insufferable?"

"Yep, you just never noticed."

"Not sure how because I spent a lot of time looking," I mutter but instantly regret it when an intrigued smile lights up his face.

"Oh really? Tell me more."

"I'd love to," I say, looking over my shoulder and finding the perfect excuse why I can't. "But I think your new team has come to collect you." I nod in their direction and he turns to find Jake, Ethan, Mason and Zayn heading this way.

"More issues with your homework, Legend?" Zayn asks suspiciously, his eyes flicking between the two of us.

"Yeah," Kyle mutters. "Something like that."

"Right well, as fun as this has been. We've got somewhere to be," Jake pipes up. "And just because it's your birthday, don't think that means I'm going to go easy on you. You've got a reputation to uphold, Legend," he warns.

I narrow my eyes at Kyle.

Was I the only one who didn't know it was his birthday?

"Let's go then. Seems I need to remind you of just how good I am."

"Arrogant much?" I mutter, feeling Kyle's eyes on me as I stare into my locker to get my books.

"You know you love it." I don't need to look over my shoulder to know he's got a shit-eating grin on his face.

"Let's go, asshole," Zayn mutters. "Before you make her want to claw your eyes out more than she already does."

A smile twitches at my lips at the hope in that statement. My brother isn't stupid, he knows something is going on here. I'm just hoping he's happy enough to live in denial about it a while longer. I'm not ready for the shitshow that would ensue when he finds out the truth.

Hopefully by the time that happens, Kyle will have had his fun and we can all return to our normal lives where he hates me and can barely look at me, and I can go on pretending that I want to screw any other member of the team just to piss off my brother.

My stomach twists painfully, reminding me that my head and my heart are already at war with this situation.

29

———

KYLE

"Whoa, cover your tiny cocks boys, there's a lady in da house," Ethan barks as we're all getting dressed after Jake's brutal session.

Glancing up after buttoning up my jeans, I find Stella walking through the boy's locker room as if it's normal. Her eyes flick around all the guys in the room, a small smile playing on her face.

"Afternoon boys. It's so good to *see* you," she jokes.

Once she's happy she's got her fill, her eyes land on me.

"Me and you need to talk," she states matter-of-factly.

"Err... we do?"

"We do," she confirms. "Get your shit together."

"Looks like Legend's getting a birthday treat," someone shouts behind me.

"Woohoo, get in there, boy," someone else jeers.

I flip them off over my shoulder because despite how this looks, I already know that isn't why Stella is here.

"He should be so lucky," she sasses, throwing her white-blonde hair over her shoulder and batting her eyelashes.

After another second, her eyes find me again.

"I'll be outside. Don't make me wait too long." With that

said, she spins on her heel and marches back out as fast as she marched in.

"What the fuck was that?" Zayn asks as Ash's curious eyes drill into the side of my head.

"Fuck knows, but I think I'm about to find out."

"Need company?" Ash asks. "There's something kinda scary about her."

"I'm pretty sure I can handle her."

"Wish I could fucking handle her," someone shouts.

I shake my head, laughing to myself. I might be in a better part of the country now, but the banter in the boy's locker room never changes.

"I'll see you later, yeah?" I say to Ash and Zayn.

"You got it, man," Zayn agrees. "Gonna party like we trailer park trash," he jokes.

I haven't invited the rest of the team, although I have my suspicions that they might just turn up anyway.

I'm assuming that Kane has invited some of our old crew and I'm not entirely sure how I feel about my past and my present colliding. Not to mention that the Harriers are loose rivals of the Bears. I say loose because the Bears would smash the Harriers even in their sleep so they're not exactly a threat to the Bears' success.

After shoving everything into my duffel, I throw it over my shoulder and head out to find out what Stella wants.

"Alright?" I nod at her as I approach.

"I guess that all depends on what you've got to tell me."

"Um..."

"Your car?"

"Uh... sure."

She pushes from the wall she was resting back against and marches toward the exit, leaving me to follow her.

The guys were right in the locker room. She's got a banging body, but she's not doing it for me. The girl I suspect she's come to talk to me about, on the other hand, is very much doing it for me right now.

I shove down the little voice in my head that tries to tell me that it's not just about the revenge it started out as because I'm not ready to deal with any of that.

I'm just going to get my fill of her. Get her out of my system and hope that I can then move on with my life.

She's been in my head since that night, and not for all the right reasons, it's time to purge her back out.

I press the unlock button for my car and Stella wastes no time in dropping down into the passenger seat, after throwing my bags in the trunk, I join her.

"So to what do I owe this pleasure?"

"Gray," she says, and my blood runs cold as her blue eyes hold mine.

"W-what about him?"

"Harley told us what happened that night. She said the drugs you got busted with were his."

"Right..."

"He's why you were freaking out about not knowing where Harley was the other night, wasn't he?"

My chin drops but I don't find the words to confirm her suspicions.

"Yeah, I thought so. So, what's the plan? What are you going to do about this motherfucker?"

My lips part like a fucking fish as my head spins.

"Who are you?" Is the question that finally falls from my lips when I manage to form some words.

"A girl who's worried about her friend. You're worried, which means she should be worried, but from what I see, she's no fucking idea he's even a threat. Why is that?"

"I don't want to worry her."

"Okay, I get that. I do. But she needs to know. If you think he's as big a threat as you seem to, then don't you think she deserves the heads up so she can keep an eye out, keep herself safe?"

"And if he's bluffing? Then I'll scare her for nothing."

"Is he bluffing?"

I blow out a long breath, twisting back into my seat and resting my head back.

"I don't know," I admit quietly.

Just saying the words makes me feel physically sick. The thought of him catching up with her and forcing her to pay my debt.

My stomach turns over.

"What are you doing about it?" Her stare burns into the side of my face while I keep my eyes focused on the license plate of the car in front of us.

"Umm..."

She groans in frustration. "Umm isn't an answer, Kyle. Not if she's in danger, which I'm assuming she is."

"I don't know what to do, okay?" I bark in frustration. "I don't want to scare her. I don't want her to think I've put her in danger. I don't want him anywhere near her."

"Huh," she says, sitting back and staring out the windshield.

"Huh, what?" I ask, more curious about the one small noise than anything else she's said during this strange conversation.

"You really like her, don't you." It's not a question. She's stating a fact and it makes my heart race and my palms sweat.

"N-no," I stutter.

"Right. So you're really going to sit there and tell me that all of this is just to get back at her for what happened? If you really wanted me to believe that you truly just want revenge then you wouldn't be so concerned about this. You wouldn't care what he might have in store for her."

My lips part to respond but I soon realize that I have no words.

The silence in the car is almost deafening as blood rushes past my ears so fast it makes my head spin.

I was quickly becoming aware that Harley was wriggling her way in deeper than I wanted her to, but it was easy to lock down when it was just my own crazy thoughts.

But being so obvious that others are noticing my feelings. That shit is scary.

"I can't let him get to her, Stella. I can't. What he was going to do that night, it..." A shudder rips through me at the thought. "It can't happen."

"I agree. But what I need to know is what you're doing about it. I'll help with whatever you need but I—Oh, don't give me that look, I'm more capable than you think."

"Are you about to tell me that you're a black belt in some martial art I've never heard or something?"

"Or something." She laughs. "Look." She turns to me. "Whatever you need to make this go away, just tell me. I've got... contacts who can help." I narrow my eyes at her, getting more and more confused as the conversation progresses. "Is he coming tonight?"

"I fucking hope not."

"If he is, point me in his direction."

She turns away and reaches out for the handle.

"Oh and Kyle?"

"Yeah?" I ask, wondering what on earth she might have to add.

"Tell her how you really feel."

Before I get a chance to respond, she's out of the car and the door slams closed behind her.

"Wow," I breathe, resting my head back and closing my eyes.

The rumble of an engine vibrates through me and when I

open my eyes, I find Stella flying past me in a matte black Porsche 911.

———

"I didn't think you were going to come back," Kane mutters from his spot in the kitchen where he's arranging bottles of alcohol.

"I took the long route home," I say, swiping one of the bottles of beer and knocking the top off.

Truth is, I just drove. I didn't have any destination in mind. I just needed to clear my head and the best way to do that is to turn my music up, drop the windows down and floor the gas. Before I knew it, I was on the other side of town on roads I've never driven before.

"You all ready for tonight?"

"It's just a party." *I've been to plenty.*

"Maybe but it's not every day that it's your eighteenth."

"Why are you making such a big deal out of this?"

"Because, lil' bro, we've had a shitty twelve months and it's time to put it all behind us and look toward the future. You're a man now and you're here. All the fighting I did to get you here paid off and now we can do as we wish without social workers breathing down our necks. It's time to live, bro. It's time to enjoy ourselves. Here," he says, bringing his little speech to an end and passing over a small wrapped box.

"You didn't have to do this."

"I did," he insists. "Go on then, open it."

I eagerly rip at the paper. I kinda assumed I wouldn't be opening anything this year, so it's quite a nice surprise.

"Holy shit," I gasp when I see the logo on the leather box in my hand. "Tell me this is fake."

"Just open it."

I do, and I find the most stunning timepiece staring back at me. "Kane. Tell me this is fake."

"Bro, I'm not going to fob you off with a fake Rolex. Is it still the one you wanted?"

A lump climbs up my throat as I remember pointing out as a kid and telling him that one day I'd own one. That I'd get out of the Creek and make something of my life.

"How'd you—I don't deserve—"

"Stop, Kyle. The words you're looking for are thank you." He lifts his brows and I take a step forward until I crash against him. We share a brief brotherly hug before I pull back and stare down at the watch once more.

"I can't believe this. Thank you so much."

"Should help you pull tonight, don't you think?" he asks as I pluck the watch from its box and stare down at it in disbelief.

"Turn it over," he instructs, clearly forgetting that I ignored his last question.

Owned by a Legend.

I can't help it, I burst out laughing.

"What's so funny?"

"Nothing, it's nothing. Seriously, bro, this is everything. I can't believe—"

"Things are looking up for us from here on out. I've got a good feeling."

"I really fucking hope you're right."

"Well, let's be honest, we don't have much left to lose."

"I guess you're right." But as I say the words, the fear I was feeling while talking to Stella not so long ago about Gray reappears.

Suddenly, I feel like I might have more to lose than ever before knowing that he's intending on going after Harley.

I think of Stella's demand to know what my plan was. I wish I had one.

"Here, take this and go and get yourself sorted. They'll be here soon." Kane passes me over a ready rolled J. "It's the good stuff," he adds with a wink.

"Who is they?" I ask, needing to know if Gray's been invited.

"Just some of our old crew, the decent ones," he tags on. "And those you've invited from school. It's not going to be anything too crazy." He smiles at me but unfortunately, I don't believe a word that falls from his lips. Anytime he's had a 'small' party, it's basically turned into an insane night of lost inhibitions and debauchery.

"Yeah, we'll see," I mutter as I turn my back on him and take my joint, my beer and new watch to my room.

Sitting on the edge of my bed, I stare down at my gift, a smile curling at my lips.

I can't believe he did this.

Thoughts run through my mind about how he could afford it, but I shove them down. He clearly doesn't want me to know what he's up to or he'd have told me by now. I guess, I just have to trust him.

I set it down, drain my beer and head for the bathroom.

30

HARLEY

"Ah-ha, finally," I call out, already feeling the buzz of the vodka that Ruby brought with her when Stella finally joins us in my room to get ready for tonight's party.

"Sorry, I've got this though." She holds up a bottle of Grey Goose and I make a beeline for her. "You look like you might have had enough," she says, watching as I sway a little on my feet.

"Pizza's on its way, it'll soak it up. Plus, I'm going to a party potentially full of Creek kids. I need it."

"Fair enough." She hands over the bottle and watches as I twist the top off and swallow a shot.

I'm not lying. The thought of walking into a party with some of the same people as that night scares the shit out of me. I probably should lay off the alcohol and go in with a clear head, but I'm too nervous for that. Plus, I'll have my girls by my side and I trust them to ensure the night doesn't end up anything like *that* night.

A knock on the door sounds out and Stella twists around to open it.

"Delivery," Zayn mutters, handing over a stack of pizza boxes.

"Thanks, bro."

"Lay off the vodka, Har. I actually want to enjoy tonight, not have to drag your sorry ass home early."

"Oooh touchy," I sing, rolling my eyes at his big brother act.

Stella swings the door shut on him and I howl with laughter at the look on his face right as it slams.

"Food, give me food," Poppy calls, hopping from the bed and taking the top box from Stella.

She wobbles and sways a little too.

"I know I'm late but how much have you three had?"

"Enough to get us in the mood," Ruby says. "Now come join us. We eat then we get ready. We need to make sure Harley looks kick-ass for her boy."

My stomach twists painfully at her words.

"He's not my boy. And, my brother is going to be there so nothing is going to happen."

"Just tell him," Poppy encourages "It won't be that bad. He's already suspicious."

"Have you said anything?" I pin her with a look, hoping like fuck she's not broken girl code and spilled all my secrets to my brother aka her boyfriend.

"What? No, I wouldn't. But he's not an idiot and he's seen the looks between you."

"Shit," I mutter. "I don't want them fighting over nothing."

"It wouldn't be nothing, it would be over you," Ruby points out.

"Same thing. I don't want it to happen. Especially when this thing between us isn't really a thing,"

"Isn't it though?" Stella helpfully adds, joining us on my bed and flipping open the last pizza box.

"No, it's not. He might already be bored of me and hook up with some other girl tonight."

Pain slices through my chest at the thought, but it damn near cracks open forcing the words out of my mouth.

"And you'd be okay with that?" Ruby asks.

"Of course," I lie. "I know what this is between us. I went in with my eyes open. Hell, I might even pull tonight."

The three of them stare at me like I've suddenly sprouted an extra head.

"What?" I bark, stuffing a slice of pizza into my mouth.

"He invited you. He wants you there."

"I didn't exactly give him a lot of choice," I mumble around a mouthful of meat feast.

"Trust me, he wants you there." My eyes narrow on Stella wondering how she sounds so confident about that comment.

"That's it," I declare. "Boy talk is banned from here on out."

"What the hell are we going to talk about then?" Ruby mutters.

"Umm..." I jump up and pull open my closet. "Which dress should I wear?"

The street Kyle lives on is lined with cars when we pull up almost three hours later.

The party is in full swing and we are very fashionably late.

I am also suitably drunk and almost prepared for whatever we might be about to walk into. Or at least I tell myself that.

The reality could prove very different.

Music booms from the house as we walk past Kyle's car

and join the crowd of people loitering, drinking and smoking on the porch.

There are faces I recognize from the Creek, and more than one nod in my direction as we make our way to the front door.

"We're no longer in Kansas," Poppy mutters behind me as we pass a couple practically going at it against the side of the house.

Ethan and the guys throw some wild parties, but without even stepping foot inside this house, it already feels different. Darker. More dangerous.

A shiver runs down my spine as I remember my last Creek party and one face in particular.

He won't be here, I tell myself.

I might be acting naïve but I'm happy with believing that Kyle has severed ties with Gray after that night. But I know the reality of the situation is probably very different. I'd just rather shove my head in the sand right now than consider the alternatives.

I push the door open to find the space full of people.

Bodies grind and gyrate to the heavy bass, the air is thick with smoke, the scent of nicotine, weed and whatever else might be getting inhaled is so strong that it burns my lungs.

We push through the crowd and immediately my eyes land on Kyle who's sitting on the sofa, only he's not alone.

"What the fuck?" Stella barks loud enough to be heard over the music as she comes to stand beside me and stares in the same direction. "Has he got a fucking death wish?"

I'm completely frozen as I stand there watching some brunette girl in Kyle's lap. She's got her lips attached to his neck while he downs a bottle of beer.

My fists curl as pain swirls around my heart.

It shouldn't hurt. I shouldn't care.

But I do. And I fucking hate myself for it.

Tears burn the back of my eyes as I watch his hand leisurely run up and down her back.

Bile rushes up my throat and for a few seconds, I wonder if I'm actually about to cover their living room floor with tonight's vodka and pizza.

Ruby and Poppy appear in front of me, Solo cups in their hands.

"What's—oh fuck," Ruby gasps when she follows our line of sight. "That motherfucking—"

"Leave it," I growl, reaching out to grab her arm when it looks like she's about to go marching over there.

"But he's—"

"More than welcome to her. Give me that." I snatch the drink from her hand and down it in one. Needing the extra alcohol in my system if I'm going to deal with this.

My heart tells me to leave, to stop it from getting battered any more than it already is. But my alcohol-laced brain tells me to stay put and play him at his own game.

Ash, Zayn, and a few of the other guys appear, joining our circle before Poppy and Ruby are dragged off to dance with their boys.

Neither Rich or Justin hide the fact they're checking both Stella and me out as they drop their eyes down our scantily clad bodies.

"Dance?" I ask Rich, whose face lights up like a freaking Christmas tree. Any sensible guy would tell me where to go after what happened in the cafeteria earlier in the week. But Rich is no sensible guy and he only thinks with his cock, especially after a few drinks and a J or two.

"What the hell are you doing?" Stella hisses in my ear.

"Enjoying the party. I suggest you get in the spirit of it too. Justin is a good dancer." I nod to him as Stella shakes her head at me. "You're playing with fire, girl."

"I just so happen to like getting burned," I shout back,

stepping into Rich's body and running my free hand up his chest and wrapping it around the back of his neck.

When I look up into his blown, bloodshot eyes, I realize just how out of it he is.

"You look sexy as hell, Har," he groans in my ear as both his hands drop to my ass, pulling me so tight against his body that I have no choice but to feel his hard length pressing against my stomach.

I feel nothing. Absolutely nothing about the fact I've turned him on.

There are no tingles. No excitement. No desire for more.

All I really want to do is crawl back home, curl up in bed, and forget tonight even exists.

But I can't do that.

I'm here now and I refuse to show that motherfucker that he affects me in any way.

I knew this was coming.

Now I just have to deal with it.

Tipping my cup to my lips, I find it's empty.

Fuck. I need more alcohol for this.

I lose track of time, but Stella helpfully supplies me with two more drinks after refusing to accept any from anyone who isn't one of my girls.

Rich's hands get more and more adventurous and desperate as the songs change and as the alcohol continues to lower my inhibitions, I probably encourage him a little too much but I can't help hoping that at some point, Kyle will see me and have something to say about this.

The reality though is probably that he's already seen me and doesn't give a shit. He seemed more than entertained by the brunette.

Everything is... almost bearable until I hear a voice that sends a violent shudder down my spine. It's a voice I could happily live the rest of my life never hearing again.

"Baby Hunter, long time no see."

My eyes lock on Rich's in the hope he can read the fear within them, but soon realize that he's too far gone to even know his own name right now, let alone that I need him to help me.

A warm, hard body presses against my back and I fight the need to ram my elbow into his ribs.

I need to see how he wants to play this before I allow him to see that I'm scared of him.

His fingers brush against my neck and I jolt at the contact as he brushes my hair from my it.

"I missed you, girl," he breathes as bile burns up my throat and pressure builds behind my eyes. I've never hated anyone as intensely as I do him.

For the things he did—or intended to do—to me that night.

How he's ruined Kyle's life by letting him take the fall.

For the way he walks around Harrow Creek like he owns the place when all he is is a jumped-up, asshat who's hungry for money, power and respect. He might somewhat have achieved the first two, but the final one he'll never gain.

"What do you want, Gray? I'm busy." I press myself closer to Rich in the hope of creating some space between me and the devil himself, but he just moves forward with me.

"You," he growls in my ear. Every single muscle in my body locks up at the warning laced through that one word.

His hand drops down my body and once again the vodka churning in my stomach threatens to make a reappearance.

"Well, you're too late. I'm dancing with Rich."

"I'm more than happy to share, Princess. I thought you already knew this."

"Harley, is everything—You." Stella pins Gray with a look. "What are you doing here?"

My chin drops.

"You know this asshole?" I ask her, picking my chin up off the floor.

"Yeah, I met him at Justin's party. He was the guy I told you about."

"Oh no. No, no, no." I shake my head.

Gray was at Justin's. He was kissing Stella.

Why?

That one word spins around my head as my hands tremble against Rich's waist.

Why is he anywhere near me, let alone trying to insert himself into my life?

The next few seconds happen so fast, I almost start to wonder if I'm imagining them. One second, my front is plastered against Rich, and the next I'm spinning around to face Gray.

I squeeze my eyes closed, not wanting to look into his evil pits of darkness, but the second his hand wraps around my throat and squeezes tight enough to stop my airflow, they pop open.

"We have unfinished business, Harley Hunter." He lifts me with only that hand, my feet leaving the floor as he scowls at me.

"No." I try to scream but with his tight grip, I can't breathe let alone make a sound.

Everything around me blurs, the music seems to get louder and he backs me somewhere, toward the door maybe, I have no idea.

Then, in the blink of an eye, everything changes once again.

His fingers release my throat with no warning and I crash to the ground, landing hard on my ass, pain shooting up my spine.

"What the—" I breathe, my hand coming up to my sore throat as my vision clears.

Girls scream and guys call for more, overtake the pounding music as I take in the scene before me.

"Kyle, no," I scream, trying to scramble to my feet as Gray lands a punch in Kyle's face.

It doesn't matter that Gray is already covered in blood, the sight of his fists connecting with Kyle's cheek will be more permanently imprinted in my brain.

I race forward in an attempt to stop them before Kyle ends up hurt, but a pair of strong arms wrap around my waist and I'm hauled back against a solid chest.

"He can handle himself," Ash breathes in my ear.

Thankfully, he's right and after taking that one hit, Kyle starts to get the better of Gray. He's got an even bigger advantage when my brother throws himself into the mix.

I might never have confessed the whole truth to him about that night, but deep down, he knows. He always had. I'd be stupid to think that the Creek rumor mill about that night hadn't got to him even if I never wanted to talk about it.

Despite the fact it's now two on one, Gray doesn't back down and before long Zayn is also bleeding, both his lip and eyebrow split.

"No," I cry once again when Gray's knee lands in my brother's stomach, forcing him to the ground so he can use his boot instead.

I thrash against Ash's tight hold, my need to go and help them the only thing I can think about despite the fact I'd probably be the one killed if I ran in the middle of the carnage right now.

Zayn gets to his feet once Gray turns his attention on Kyle and he manages to wrap his arms around Gray's torso, pinning his arms to his sides to allow Kyle a free shot.

The fury that Kyle unleashes scares the shit out of me as his fists rain down on Gray's bloodied face again and again.

It's not until he starts screaming at him that I realize someone has turned the music off.

"I'm going to fucking kill you, motherfucker," he bellows

as kids start moving to allow someone else to run into the center of the circle that's formed in the Legend's living area so they can watch the fight.

The second Kane steps in, a silence ripples through the crowd.

"Ky," is the only thing he says, and it's enough because Kyle lowers his fist and takes a step back, although his eyes remain trained on a barely standing Gray. If it weren't for Zayn, he'd be on his ass now.

Kyle takes another step back as Kane takes one forward so he's almost nose to nose with Gray.

"You're a stupid motherfucker for coming here. Now get the fuck. Out. Of. My. House." He pulls his arm back and punches him so hard that Gray's body goes limp in Zayn's arms. But he's done holding him up and he allows him to drop to the floor.

"Someone get that cunt out of here," Kane orders to no one in particular, but three guys instantly come running through the crowd to follow orders.

Poppy steps up to Zayn and spits a few choice words at him before the two of them disappear into the crowd while everyone else must decide the entertainment is over because they turn back to continue with their evening.

Kyle spins on his heels and his eyes immediately find mine.

They're so dark and his jaw is clenched painfully tight as something zaps between us.

Ash's arms loosen around my middle but I don't move.

"Everyone out of my fucking house," Kane booms, and kids immediately begin to move around me.

But neither Kyle or I so much as blink as we remain in our stare-off.

He's got blood trickling down his cheek from a cut on his eyebrow, his right eye is swelling and he's got a split lip.

He looks a mess, yet I can't look away from the devastation.

The commotion around us begins to lessen. But still, we remain immobile.

"Poppy has taken Zayn home," Ruby whispers in my ear. "Ash can take us. Are you coming?"

"I... um..."

Apparently, Ruby's whisper wasn't quiet enough because Kyle answers for me.

"No. She's not going anywhere," Kyle barks, speaking for the first time in what feels like forever. His rough, deep voice vibrates through me and affects me more than anything Rich did to me earlier.

Damn him.

"I really don't think—"

"I don't give a fuck what you think,"

"Don't talk to her like that," I snap, my own anger getting the better of me.

Kyle's eyes continue to hold mine, he's not even given Ruby the decency of a glance to apologize for his tone.

"It's okay, Rubes. You go. Kyle and I need to talk." I cringe as I hear my slurred voice. I wish I sounded stronger and more in control right now.

"Are you sure?" she whispers, quieter this time so only I can hear.

"Yeah, it's fine. Kane is here to stop me from killing him," I say loud enough for whoever is left in the house to hear me.

A smile twitches at Kyle's lips but I refuse to acknowledge it or to return it.

I'm too fucking mad. Although right now, I'm finding it hard to put my anger and thoughts into any sensible order and I have no idea what I'm more pissed off with.

"Okay," Ruby breathes. She hesitates by my side for a few seconds but she soon disappears.

"Call me if you need anything," Ash tells Kyle before they disappear from the house, leaving me alone with just the two Legend brothers.

Most might be intimidated. They're more than a force to be reckoned with. But I know them better than to cower down to them.

"Kane," Kyle growls.

"What? I want to see her attempt to follow through on her threat," he quips.

"Kane," he repeats, his voice low and haunting.

"Fine. Ruin my party and all my fun why don't you," he mutters, swiping a couple of beers from the side before crashing through the front door and slamming it behind him.

"And then there were two," Kyle muses.

"Don't try to be cute. What the hell was that?" I ask, my arm flying out and sweeping around the room behind me. I have no idea what specific part of tonight's clusterfuck I'm referring too, I don't even really care where he starts, I just need some fucking explanations.

"I didn't know he was coming."

"I should fucking hope not. Kyle, that fuck ruined your life, he almost rap..." I trail off, not wanting to say the words, it makes it feel too real and I prefer to live in ignorant bliss as much as I can. "You should have warned me. I wouldn't have come."

He takes a step forward and the scent of alcohol and weed that surrounds him like a fog fills my nose.

"Don't," I warn, holding my hand up between us. I can't let him get close to me. And I certainly can't allow him to touch me. Even when I'm sober I do shit I shouldn't when that happens.

"You should have told me," I repeat.

"But I wanted you here."

"Why? So he could do that to me? Ohhh," I say, an idea

hitting me so hard it makes my head spin. "Did you want a repeat too? I know I fucked up that night, but have you been lying all this time? You were in on it and you did want to see it through. To fuck me at the same time he did."

"No," he states, stepping closer. "Never. You're fucking mine, Harley. Not that cunt's or anyone else's."

"Right," I say, a manic laugh falling from my lips. "I'm so *yours* that you had some other chick grinding down on your cock when I arrived earlier. Miss me, did you?"

"You know I fucking did. But I didn't want her."

"It certainly fucking looked like it as you touched her. As you let her touch you. Kiss you."

"Jealous, Kitten? Did you want to be the one grinding down on my cock?"

"Fuck you," I seethe, taking my own step toward him, my fists curling at my sides ready to land my own punch on his annoyingly pretty face.

"I wanted to show him that you didn't mean anything to me. I wanted him to back the fuck off," he growls, making my brows pinch.

"Why? Why do you need that?"

"B-because... fuck," he barks, lifting his hands to his hair and tugging. When I first saw him tonight he was wearing his standard ball cap but that vanished sometime during the fight, probably at a similar time to when his shirt got ripped at the neck.

"What? What aren't you telling me, Kyle?"

"Nothing."

"Bull. Shit," I snap. "Tell me, Kyle. Tell me whatever the fuck is going on. I deserve to know."

"Do you? You're nothing but a fucking snitch. All of this is your fault. All of it."

"Really?" I ask incredulously. "You really believe that? Because while I might blame myself for what happened to you, I think we both know whose fault this whole thing is, and it's neither of us. It's that fucking cunt. Why was he at your birthday party, Kyle?"

His chest heaves, his nostrils flare as he stares at me, fighting with whatever words are on the tip of his tongue.

"Fuck."

His chest collides with mine before I've even realized he's moved. I crash back against the wall but my head doesn't slam into it like I was expecting because at the last minute he cradles the back of my skull with his hand.

His lips crash to mine in a bruising kiss that I have no chance of backing away from.

My hands slam against his chest, but my efforts are futile. He's too strong. And, if I'm being honest with myself, I don't want him to stop.

I want him to claim me. Prove to me with actions that whatever that was with that brunette earlier was nothing.

I want him to show me that he means what he says. That I'm his.

My fingers twist in his shirt, holding him against me as his tongue devours my mouth as if he's going to die without my kiss. The taste of copper fills my mouth from his split lip but it only spurs me on and I suck hard on his tongue making him groan and his hips roll against me.

"Kyle," I pant when he finally pulls back. "Tell me…" I force out between heaving breaths. "Tell me the truth," I demand.

"Damn it, Harley." He slams his hand against the wall beside me.

"What? I have a right to know. Who was the girl? Why was Gray here?"

"I… fuck." He pulls away from me and backs away until he's at the other side of the room.

"Fine. Fuck you, Kyle. You can't tell me the truth then we're done here."

His eyes widen in shock but I don't give a crap. I refuse to allow him to lie to me.

"I'm leaving."

"You can't," he says in a rush, racing toward me but I'm faster and at the door in a flash.

"Watch me." I push through the door, slamming the screen against the side of the house with my force.

"What the hell?" Kane is up off the swing seat and walking toward me before I get to the stairs.

"She thinks she's leaving," Kyle spits at his brother.

"I don't fucking think anything, asshole. I *am* leaving."

Flipping him the bird, I race down the steps on wobbly legs.

"Wait," Kane calls out. "Let me take you."

"What?" Kyle barks. "She's not fucking leaving."

Kane pins his brother with a hard stare. "She's not staying."

Kane throws his car keys at me. "Get in my car, Harley."

The second they're in my hand, I take off. Needing to be away from Kyle as quickly as possible. The more he begs, the more he pisses me off, but I can't deny that my restraint is slipping.

Even when I hate him, I want him.

Asshole.

"You've been drinking, you can't drive her home."

"Get in the house, Kyle, before I fucking make you."

"I'd like to see you fucking try."

Slamming the passenger door behind me, I watch through the driver's window as the two brothers stare at each other.

I brace myself, waiting to see who's going to throw the first punch. It wouldn't be the first time the two of them had got into it. But before that happens, Kyle spins on his heels, slams the front door so hard I can only imagine that the entire house rattles, and disappears from my sight.

"I'm sorry," Kane says cooly as he drops into the driver's side.

"You don't have to drive me. I can walk," I offer. I know the last thing Kane Legend wants to be doing tonight is play taxi for me.

"No."

He starts the engine and backs out of the driveway. Neither of us saying anything else.

A million and one questions spin around my head as the silence stretches on. I want to ask about Kyle, about Gray, about tonight and so many other things about his life, but more than anything, I want to ask about Letty, but even with the amount of vodka flowing through my veins, I'm not that stupid. So I keep my lips zipped as he flies through the streets of Rosewood until he pulls up in front of my house.

Everyone else is home and the only light in the house is that of Zayn's bedroom where Poppy is probably tending to his wounds, among other things.

I'm almost sick in my mouth at the thought.

"Are you going to be okay?" I give him a double-take when I hear the concern in his voice. It's so at odds with the anger and tension that's usually rolling off him in waves.

"I'll be nowhere near you two, I'm sure I'll be fine."

Kane doesn't respond, although I do feel his stare burning into the side of my face.

I bite back the questions that are once again on the tip of my tongue and push open the door.

"Thank you," I say before slamming it on him and making my way to the house.

The front door is unlocked. Zayn probably left it that way knowing I'd be following soon after them.

I grab myself some pills and a glass of water from the kitchen, knowing that this is going to hurt like hell in the morning, and I make my way up to my room.

I kick my shoes off the second I'm inside before letting

my dress slide down my body and discard it on the floor as I continue to my bed. I find a tank that I pull over my head to sleep in before curling up under the covers and willing the alcohol to drag me under.

But as I lie there, I can only picture one thing.

Kyle with that brunette grinding on his lap.

I know all of this is just a game of revenge to him. This is what he wants, me hurting and regretting what I did to him.

It shouldn't hurt this much. But I know I don't have the power to stop it.

Because I've already fallen. And he's already shattering my heart.

31

HARLEY

Eventually, I fall asleep with the events of the night playing out in my mind. Kyle's demands that I stay along with the state of him, make me wonder if I did the right thing.

Should I have stayed and cleaned him up? He was fighting for me after all.

My sleep is fitful and broken but I know it's just my mind that's stopping me from fully drifting off.

That is until I come too once again and the scuff of someone's shoe on my carpet hits my ears.

My eyes fly open, my heart in my throat that he's come after me. I should have known better than to assume he'd let me walk away like that.

Part of me is excited that he's broken in to get to me again, although I know I should still be mad at him. But I also know that the second he touches me, all bets are going to be off because I can only fight for so long when his touch burns me from the inside like it always does.

The side of the bed dips and I prepare to look into his blue depths and to submit to whatever he's come over here to take from me.

But when a hand wraps around my mouth and a pair of eyes pierce mine, they're not blue and I realize my mistake. His other hand wraps around my hip, pinning me to the bed and stopping me from bucking to get him off me.

This isn't Kyle coming to prove how good it is when we come together.

A scream rips up my throat but with his giant hand covering half of my face, no noise leaves me.

My heart thrashes against my ribs as my panic begins to get the better of me.

Why is he here? Why is Gray in my bedroom?

My eyes are wide as he closes the space between us, his nose bumping against mine.

His face is swollen and still covered in blood and I can't help hoping that it's as painful as it looks.

"You're a stupid fucking bitch, Harley."

I try to shake my head but it barely moves under his painful grip.

"He's not going to protect you this time," he breathes in my ear, sending goose bumps racing across my skin. Unable to hide my reaction to him being so close, my body trembles against his hold. "You are all mine. All. Night. The fun we're going to have, Princess."

"Fuck you," I growl against his hand. There's no way he could have deciphered the words, but I'm sure he could have a good guess at what I want to say to him. His fingers bite into my jaw in punishment anyway.

As if I weigh nothing more than a feather, he lifts me from the bed and holds me tight to his body, my back to his front.

I fight him. My elbows flying, trying to make contact with his already bruised and broken ribs.

"We can do this the hard way, Harley, or the really fucking hard way."

A moan of frustration rips up my throat as I continue to

try to fight him, but I'm no match for his size and strength, and by the time my muscles begin to grow weary, he's already carried me down the stairs and out the front door.

There's a black SUV parked at the sidewalk. He marches us right up to it and pops the trunk.

"No, No. Noooo," I scream behind his hand as he slams me against the car, pinning me there with his weight and reaches for a reel of tape before pulling a length off.

"You need to learn your place, Princess," he growls, momentarily releasing his hand and replacing it with the tape.

My scream pierces the air for less than a second before I'm muted once more.

My eyes narrow at him as he turns me to look at him, trying to show him just how much I despise him with just one look.

You won't get away with this, motherfucker.

He might be right. Kyle might not fight for me. But Zayn will. And the second he discovers I'm not in my bed where I should be, he'll raise hell to get me back.

He leans in closer and I twist my face away, not wanting to look at him for a second longer.

His fingers grip my chin and he drags me back to him.

My teeth grind with my need to hurt him but with his hips pressing me into the car and only my arms free, I doubt I'm going to achieve much. I lift one, in a brief moment of confidence but he sees it coming a mile off and his hand captures my wrist, bringing it around to my back.

"Don't even think about it," he seethes, his eyes bouncing between mine before they drop to my chest. "I almost couldn't ask for more," He lifts his free hand and pinches my nipple between his thumb and forefinger until it burns in pain. I don't so much as flinch as bile churns in my stomach at having his disgusting hands on me.

"We're going to have so much fun," he promises again,

making me want to turn my head and puke on the ground. He leans in so his vile breath races over my face.

He flips me around, pressing me so hard against the back of the SUV that it cuts into my stomach. Both of my arms are wrenched behind my back before he wraps rope around my wrists, binding them together.

"Get in."

I make no attempt to move which makes the vein in his temple pulsate with irritation, but I figure the longer I can remain standing out on the street with tape over my mouth the more chance I have of this being over soon.

Sadly, that's not how it happens because, after a second, he lifts me from my feet once more and throws me into the trunk like I'm no more than a piece of trash.

My shoulder smarts as it hits the floor first, quickly followed by my head. Lights flash behind my eyes from the force, a beat before all the lights go out.

"Motherfucker," I scream against the tape as the engine rumbles to life beneath me.

My eyes burn, tears threatening but I have no idea how long I'm going to be in here for and I have no intention of him seeing my tears.

I close my eyes, trying to keep them at bay and think of Kyle.

He'll notice I'm missing and find me, won't he?

———

I have no idea how much time passes, I drift in and out of sleep—or consciousness, I'm not really sure—but finally, the car comes to a stop and only a few seconds later the trunk opens.

He looms over me, a dark figure in front of the early morning sky. It should be the sign of a new day, of exciting unknowns, but I don't think I've ever been less excited and more terrified in my life.

"It's playtime, Princess."

He reaches in, wraps his fingers around my upper arm so tight, I have no doubt it'll leave bruises and hauls me out. My bare feet land on the sharp gravel and I wince in pain.

Gray slams the trunk closed before dragging me toward a dark, ominous-looking building.

I want to cry with every step I take, it's like walking on shards of glass and by the time he pulls me to the door and onto a concrete floor, I almost sigh with relief.

The door is unlocked and he pulls me right inside.

The first thing I notice is the smell. It's rancid. I wouldn't be surprised to find some kind of animal decaying in a corner.

My stomach turns over and I retch as he walks me further into the dark and damp space.

There are bottles littered everywhere, along with dirty needles and other drug paraphernalia. Clearly, it's not just an abandoned warehouse then.

The Creek kids used to party in old buildings almost every weekend, or whenever they found a new location. I wonder if this is one of those places. Maybe that smell is some party-goer who took things a little too far and was left in the darkness.

A violent shudder runs through me as he brings me to a stop by a giant hook-like thing that's in the ground.

"Welcome to your new home. I made it nice and comfortable for you."

I stare at the thin sheet covering the cold concrete on the other side of the hook and any fight I had in me seems to vanish.

I'm not getting out of this. And if he's right and Kyle doesn't care then there's a chance no one will find me, at least, not until it's too late.

He tugs harshly on the rope hanging from my wrists and I stumble to the floor, the rough ground scraping my knees as I scramble forward to save being dragged.

I don't need to look over my shoulder to know that he's attaching me to the hook.

"Perfect," he mutters, taking a step back to appreciate his handiwork.

He drops down on his haunches and stares me straight in the eyes. His are almost black with his anger and hatred.

"I've waited a long time for this, Princess."

In a surprise move, he reaches out and rips the tape from my mouth. It stings like a motherfucker, almost like he's just taken a few layers of skin with it and my teeth grind, stopping me from screaming out.

"Fuck you," I spit.

"All in good time."

"You're a fucking monster. Kyle should have killed you when he had the chance."

He laughs as if the idea of Kyle being able to is actually amusing to him.

His face turns serious once more before he pushes to stand and begins pacing back and forth in front of me.

"He's really got you fucking brainwashed, hasn't he? That cunt isn't capable of anything. He couldn't even keep my fucking gear safe."

"So this is about money?" I ask, the pieces starting to fit together.

Everything Kyle had on him that night would have been seized. Gray wants payback. But why me?

"I can get you money if that's what you want," I offer, although it's a total bluff. I'm not giving this fuck anything.

He laughs once more, a manic smile curling at his lips, splitting the cuts once more and allowing a trickle of blood to run down his chin.

"I don't want fucking money, Hunter, but Kyle owes me and it's time he learns that I'm serious."

"He doesn't care about me. You've already said so yourself that he's not going to rescue me, so what's the point in this?"

"Maybe I'm wrong. Or maybe I'm not and I just get to spend the next few days teaching you a lesson for my own amusement."

"You're sick. He's going to find me and he's going to fucking kill you." I put as much conviction into my words as possible, but deep down, I fear he might be right.

Kyle wanted revenge. He might not be the one dishing it out right now, but was this always where it was meant to end?

He studies me for a few more seconds before he disappears into the shadows.

The sun might be starting to rise outside but in the middle of this massive space, it's hardly noticeable from the cracks of light coming from the boarded-up windows around the edge of the building.

He crashes about a little before reappearing but the sight of him with a bottle of water in his hand makes my entire body tremble.

"No," I cry, assuming what's been dissolved into that liquid.

"I'm sorry, Princess, but I think you'll find that you don't get a say anymore."

He drops down before me and grips my chin between his fingers. My skin is already tender from the last time he held me this way and he knows it, digging his fingers in even deeper.

"Drink."

I press my lips together with as much pressure as I can muster and his eyes flash with anger.

I know I shouldn't provoke him, but there's no way in hell I'll voluntarily drink anything he gives me.

"Stupid fucking bitch. I don't even know why he wanted to fuck you that night. You're nothing special."

"You seemed up for it. I remember how hard your cock was as you rubbed it against my ass."

I don't see his arm move until it's too late. The sound of skin on skin rings out in the silent space around us a moment before the sting burns my cheek.

"Now. Fucking. Drink."

Still, I keep my lips closed when he tips the bottle to my mouth, sloshing the water down my chin and over my thin tank.

"You look like a cheap fucking whore."

"Then it's a good thing I don't give a shit about what you think, isn't it?"

He makes use of my open mouth and shoves his thumb inside allowing him to keep my lips parted so he can pour the water inside.

I push out as much as I can, but there's too much not to swallow any. I just have to hope it's not enough to affect me.

"Get some sleep, whore. The fun will commence in a few hours." With those words, he spins on his heels and disappears into the shadows.

Once he's gone, I succumb to the tears although I refuse to make a noise.

I sit there with tears cascading down my cheeks, my body trembling from the cold and praying that I'm not about to pass out, allowing him to do whatever sick and twisted shit I'm sure he's thought up.

32

KYLE

"What the fuck was that?" I bellow at Kane when he crashes back into the house after taking Harley home. "I thought you were supposed to be on my fucking side." My palms slam against his chest but he doesn't so much as take a step back.

"I'm always on your fucking side, Ky," he growls, his voice dangerously low.

"Then why did you take her? And fucking drunk."

"Not that I have to answer to you, but I'm not fucking drunk. I've had two fucking beers because I knew the second that cunt showed his face that someone would need to be in-fucking-control."

"Why didn't you just throw him out to start with?" I seethe.

"Because he clearly had the balls to show up after—"

"After?" I prompt, desperate to know if something has gone down between the two of them since I went away.

"Nothing. He shouldn't have fucking been here. But seeing as he thought it was a good idea, I wanted to see what his game was."

"And how did that work out for you?"

"Meh," he says, shrugging his shoulders.

"He had his hands on her, Kane. He shouldn't be anywhere near her, let alone touching her. He's already threaten—"

"He's spoken to you?"

I swallow nervously. I hadn't meant to admit that. I don't want to drag Kane into this mess more than he already is. He's done enough for me.

"Yeah. He threatened Harley."

"And you didn't think to tell me this?" he booms.

"What would you have done? You can't risk killing him and ending up inside as well."

His teeth grind as he thinks of all the ways he probably wants to end Gray for that stunt a year ago.

He lifts his hands to his hair and takes a few steps back from me, cooling off a little.

"You know, I told you to stay away from her for a reason," he almost whispers.

"Yeah well, I couldn't. Fucking sue me."

"She's it for you, huh?"

My lips part to agree but I catch the words at the last minute.

"She's fun for right now."

"Kyle," he breathes. "Lie to yourself all you want, hell, lie to her. But me? Nah, bro. You never fucking lie to me, you got that?"

We stare at each other in a silent standoff.

"We can't let him get to her. He wants me to pay and he wants to hit where it'll hurt the most."

"No fucking shit. It's one of the reasons I told you to stay away. I fucking knew you'd fall for her all over again."

"I never... I haven't..." He pins me with a knowing look. "Those Hunter girls are like fucking kryptonite, right?" I say, spinning the tables on him.

"Don't," he snaps. "Don't fucking bring me into this. It's got nothing to do with me."

"You moved us here. If you thought this was going to happen why not move us across the country."

"Because... because I couldn't."

I narrow my eyes at his cryptic answer but I don't try to dig for anymore. I know my brother and I know that I'm not getting any of his secrets out of him tonight.

"Why take her? Why take her if you know I need her?"

"Because," he sighs, his shoulders dropping and the fight leaving him. "It was the right thing to do. She doesn't need to witness you in this mood."

"Trust me, it would be fucking better right now if she was here."

"Why? Because you'd have used her to make you feel better? Don't forget, lil' bro, I saw you with Zoe on your lap earlier. You didn't seem to care so much about Harley's feelings while her lips were attached to your neck."

"That was for his benefit," I shout, throwing my hands up in despair. "I didn't want him to see how much I wanted her."

A smile twitches at his lips as I confess my feelings but he doesn't say anything. "I thought if he saw me with someone else, he'd think I don't give a shit about her and move on."

"You're a fucking idiot, Ky. The second you've slept off your hangover, you need to go over there and have this out with her. Tell her the fucking truth. Let her deal with all this alongside you, not keep her in the shadows. The Hunter girls, they're not weak and you'll only offend them if you treat them as such."

"Said by an expert," I quip.

His jaw pops with frustration and a little thrill goes through me that I'm not the only one who gets weak at the knees at just the mention of a Hunter girl.

"This isn't about me."

"Not right now, but we sure need to find the time to talk about you."

"Nothing to talk about."

"Sure."

He takes a step toward me, but if he thinks I'm going to be threatened by his stance then he's got another thing coming.

"Get your ass to bed and sleep tonight off. First thing, get your ass to the Hunter's and talk to her."

"So much for wanting me to stay away from her."

"Sometimes you just have to embrace it instead of fighting."

I narrow my eyes at him.

"That what you're doing?"

"Go to fucking bed. You can tidy up this mess after you've groveled your way out of the shit."

Before I get to say anything else, he marches down the hallway and disappears into his bedroom.

The house is fucking trashed, but I'm too angry, drunk, high, and horny to care right now. Turning my back on it, I follow orders and fall headfirst into my bed.

Before I succumb to my exhaustion, I find her contact in my cell and call her number.

It rings and rings.

I shouldn't be surprised, she's probably either long asleep or ignoring me. Or maybe both.

———

I wake when my cell starts vibrating in my hand, apparently, I fell asleep still clutching it.

"Harley?" I ask, pressing it to my ear without looking at the screen. My entire face aches as I speak reminding me of the night before.

"Stella," the voice says. "But speaking of, I'm assuming from your greeting that she's not with you?"

I push so I'm sitting against the headboard, my head spinning from last night's alcohol.

"N-no, she's not here. Kane took her home after things got a bit—Why, what's wrong?" I ask, realizing that she probably doesn't care about all this right now.

"We had plans to meet for breakfast but she didn't show up and her cell just keeps ringing."

"Probably still sleeping or stabbing a little voodoo doll of me."

"You fucked up last night," she confirms, not that I needed to hear it. "I'll head to hers then, if she's not with you."

"I'll be there after I've showered. I've got some groveling to do."

"Bring food, it might sweeten the apology."

"You're serious, aren't you?"

"Sure am. The way to a woman's heart, big cock, plenty of O's and good food."

"Thanks for that," I force out through the shock. "Message me when you find her."

"Will do. Later."

She hangs up before I get a chance to say goodbye. I laugh as I pull my cell from my ear. Whoever is lucky enough to snag her is in for a wild ride.

Tipping my face to the ceiling, I give myself two minutes before pushing from the bed and heading for the shower to wash last night off me.

One look in the mirror and I'm reminded of everything I'd rather forget from last night. I—we—might have won the showdown but I'm still sporting the evidence that it happened, I'm sure Zayn is too.

My eye is a pleasant shade of purple and barely opens and the split in my lip has opened up once again thanks to my conversation with Stella.

I reach up to wipe away a droplet of blood and wince.

Motherfucker.

He shouldn't have even been here, let alone had his hands on my girl.

My girl.

Hell yeah. I think Kane might just be right and it's time to lay all my cards on the table.

I shower, dress, grab an energy drink from the refrigerator and leave the chaos that is our house behind. As far as I know, Kane is still in his bedroom. Although knowing what he's been like since I've been back, I wouldn't put it past him to have snuck out already.

I'm at Harley's in record time, the journey is a total blur, my focus solely on what I need to say to her. The truths I need to confess.

I push my car door open after pulling up on the driveway and as I step out, Stella comes running down the steps from the house, quickly followed by Zayn.

"What's wrong?" I ask, the stricken looks on their faces making my stomach drop.

"She's not here," Stella says. Her voice is cool and calm but her eyes give away how she really feels.

"But she was. I heard her come home," Zayn adds. "No one has seen her. She's not with anyone we know."

"Fuck," I breathe, lifting my hand to my hair, irritated when I find my cap.

"H-he wouldn't. Would he?" Zayn asks, mirroring my concerns.

"I really fucking hope not."

My cell buzzes in my pocket and I reach to pull it out.

The unknown number that stares back at me makes my stomach drop into my feet.

"What is it?" Stella asks, obviously seeing my reaction.

"I-I don't know."

She comes to stand beside me and watches as I open the message.

"Holy fuck," I bark as Stella gasps beside me. "Fucking cunt."

"Wha—" Zayn grabs my cell from my hand, his eyes going wide as he stares down at the photo of his sister.

His sister, bound, gagged, barely clothed, and passed out.

———

"Kane," I bellow, running through the house with Zayn hot on my heels. I don't bother knocking, I crash straight through his bedroom door. Thankfully, he's still passed out in bed, although he sits up fucking fast as we fly into his room. "He's got her. Gray fucking has her."

"W-what?" he asks, groggily sitting up and pushing hair from his eyes.

"Gray has Harley," I say much more calmly than I feel. "You need to get up now."

It takes two seconds for the words to register in his head before he barks 'fuck,' throws the sheets back and stands.

"Where are they?"

"No idea, but he sent this."

I pass my cell over and he studies it for long, silent seconds.

"I know where this is."

"How?" I ask in utter disbelief. "How could you possibly know that?"

Okay so, I didn't study every inch of the image, my eyes were mostly trained on Harley, but I didn't see anything that would give her location away.

"I just do. Meet me at my car," he demands, pulling a pair of sweats from the floor and tugging them on as we leave.

"But..."

"Do you really want to get into this right now?" He pins me with a look that brings me to my senses.

"No. Hurry," I call over my shoulder as I rush from the

house, pushing Zayn along in front of me.

I swipe Kane's car keys from the side and we let ourselves in. Me in the front and Zayn in the back.

Every muscle in my body is pulled tight as I focus on that image that's burned into my retinas.

She looks so weak, so broken, so vulnerable.

If that motherfucker touches her and tries to take—a violent shiver races down my entire body, a mix of anger and devastation that I let this happen.

"Fucking hurry up," I mutter under my breath to no one.

"I hope you know that once we've got her out of this, I'm going to fucking kill you," Zayn quietly seethes from the back.

My lips part to tell him to fuck off, but swallow the words, because he's right.

"As you should."

"You're fucking her, aren't you?"

"Yeah, bro."

"If you've treated her like a piece of shit, I swear to God I'll—"

I twist around in my seat to look at him, my eyes narrowed in curiosity.

"Fucking asshole," he mutters, the fight leaving his voice as Kane drops down into the driver's seat and revs the engine.

"Ready to put this bitch down once and for all?"

"Less talking, bro."

I don't need to be looking at him to know he just rolled his eyes at me.

He flies down our street and turns toward Harrow Creek.

The entire journey to our hometown is silent and tense.

I'm still baffled as to how Kane knows where she is from just a dark picture but I'm not about to question it. I just need to hope that he's right because if we turn up there and she's not, I'm not sure what I'm going to fucking do.

I shift in my seat, rubbing my palms down my thighs in

my need to do something.

"Chill. I need you on point."

"On point for what?"

"Getting your girl back."

A low growl rumbles from the back of the car but we both ignore it. I knew Zayn would be fucking livid when he discovered that I've gone after his little sister. But right now, I don't give a fuck about his opinion. We just need to get her. We can fight it out later.

I mumble some kind of agreement as I clench my fists over and over, watching the cracks in my knuckles opening up and remembering just how good it felt to hit that fucker last night.

Thanks to Kane's more than reckless driving, we're at the Creek in record time and rolling toward an abandoned warehouse that I've never been to before on the other side of the town from where we grew up.

I know Gray has Harrow Creek High and the surrounding trailer parks under his control but I had no idea his reach stretched this far. Clearly things have changed in my year away.

I don't have a chance to put too much thought into it, not that I really care if he's currently hanging out on someone else's turf, it just means there's more chance of him dying tonight.

"Bingo," Kane says as he turns a corner and finds Gray's car parked half in the bushes. If he's attempting to hide it then he's doing a shit job.

"Okay, so what's the plan?" Zayn asks.

"We go in there and take his fucking head off," I announce.

"Oh, and how are you going to do that, bro? You packing?"

"Well, no but—"

"Fucking hell. I've got this, follow me, and don't do

anything unless I tell you to."

He's out of the car before either of us get to agree, and we hurry to catch up with him as he begins to stride toward the warehouse.

The place is silent, only distant birdsong and the movement of the trees overhead dancing in the wind.

Kane comes to a door and peers inside as Zayn and I share a look. He might be furious at me, but his concern for his sister shines brighter in his eyes.

"We'll get her," I assure him. He nods but I know my words aren't all that helpful. We're all aware of what Gray is capable of, so we know how risky this really is.

One second Kane is standing right there, and the next he's gone, disappeared in the darkness inside the building.

"Fuck," I breathe, racing after him.

The place is dark and it smells like death, which doesn't help the dread that is sitting heavy in my stomach.

A single light illuminates a spot on the floor as I come up behind Kane and the second I step aside to get a look at the scene before us, my blood runs cold.

"Get the fuck off her," I bark before I've even realized I've spoken.

Kane growls in frustration that I've just alerted him to our presence but it's soon drowned out by the blood racing past my ears.

That motherfucker is on top of my girl.

My fists clench as I move my leg to race forward.

Kane throws his arm out, stopping me.

"Wait," he demands and I immediately follow orders, assuming he knows more than I do.

And he's right because, after a beat, he stands, moving behind her, and dragging her limp body from the floor, the knife in his spare hand glinting in the spotlight trained on Harley.

My eyes drop to her and my entire chest burns in pain.

Her entire body and the few clothes covering her are dirty, her skin covered in cuts and grazes.

She just about manages to lift her head and her eyes lock with mine.

"Kyle," she mouths but she's too weak to make an actual noise.

"Don't fucking move," Kane growls once more as Gray presses his knife against her throat.

"Move and I'll kill her right now," he warns as Harley whimpers.

"Fucking shoot him," I whisper-shout to my brother, knowing he didn't walk into this unarmed like I did.

"Not risking it, not yet. He'll move quicker."

"Fuck."

Time seems to stand still as we all remain motionless staring at each other.

That is until three footsteps sound out behind us. Something whips past my ear and Gray cries out, stumbling back and releasing Harley.

I race forward without even thinking, needing to catch her before she hits the hard floor while Gray groans in pain.

"I've got you," I say softly. "I've got you. It's okay."

I pull her fragile body onto my lap and hold her tight as she trembles and sobs in my arms.

"Kyle," she whimpers, pain splinters my chest at the brokenness of her voice.

I hold her tighter, hoping she can take some strength from me as more footsteps sound out.

"Holy shit, Stella," I gasp. My chin damn near hitting the floor when she emerges from the shadows, a pistol hanging by her side with a silencer attached to the end.

She looks around the scene before her eyes drop to Harley in my arms.

Her lips part to say something but someone else beats her to it.

"Good shot, baby," an older man says as he wraps his arm around her shoulder and kisses the top of her hair.

As I stare at the two of them, a few more guys come rushing in and go straight to Gray, hauling him from the floor, ignoring his screams of pain, and they drag him from the warehouse.

"What the fuck is going on here?" Kane barks, looking between Stella, the man I can only assume is her father, and Harley and me.

"How did you know where we were?"

"I followed him last night after you kicked him out. His guys brought him back to Harrow Creek and left him in his trailer. I put a tracker on his car."

"You put a... right, of course you did," I mutter.

"Then when you unceremoniously abandoned me in the Hunter's driveway earlier, I took matters into my own hands. And aren't you fucking glad I did."

"But... how'd you... who are you?" Kane stutters, much to Stella and her dad's amusement.

"No one you need to worry about, son," the man says.

I focus on him. He's wearing a sharp black suit, shirt and tie. His hair is almost as dark with just a few flecks of grey at the sides. But his face is a stone mask. It actually sends a shiver of fear down my spine. Whoever he is, you don't want to be on the wrong side of him, I know that for a fact.

"I'm going to deal with that cunt. You good?" he asks Stella.

"Yeah, we've got this."

He nods once, squeezes her shoulder, and walks away.

We're all silent as he disappears into the darkness and no one speaks until his footsteps have vanished and a car speeds off in the distance.

"Okay, what the fuck just happened?" Zayn asks.

"I saved her ass from that sick fuck. Now let's get the fuck out of this shithole, yeah?"

33

HARLEY

I thrash about, trying to get his hands off me. His fingers are like tiny knives against my skin, and I wish he'd just carved it all off so I didn't have to feel it.

I lost all sense of time only moments after being abandoned in that dark space with no idea when he was going to reappear again.

I wanted to stay awake, stay alert, but it was impossible to fight the darkness that clawed at me.

I drifted in and out of reality, each time I woke, more terrified than the last.

"No," I cry when I wake again and he's there, looming over me with a deadly expression covering his face.

"It's time to play, whore."

"NOOOO," I scream.

"Kitten, it's okay. It's just me," a familiar voice says in my ear.

I continue for a few more seconds until my drug-fuzzed brain registers who it is.

"Kyle?" I cry, my entire body relaxing in his hold. I try to curl up in a ball on his lap to stop the cold assaulting my bones.

"Here, wrap this around her," another familiar voice says.

"Z-Zayn?"

"It's okay, sis," he says gently as a warm, soft fabric wraps around my arms.

Kyle's arms hold me tighter and I succumb to the exhaustion trying to claim my body.

I'm safe now. I can let go.

The next thing I know, I'm being lifted out of the car, still in Kyle's arms. While I'm here, I know that no one can hurt me and I don't so much as bother opening my eyes.

I know we're in our house the second we walk through the front door, the familiar scent of Mom's favorite candles almost makes me sigh with relief.

"Mom," I say in a rush. She can't see me like this.

"It's okay, she's not here, Har," Zayn says as Kyle begins carrying me up the stairs.

"I'll go run a bath," Stella says, her small footsteps pounding ahead of us.

I don't open my eyes even as Kyle walks us into my bedroom. I don't want to look at my bed.

This is a place I should feel safe, but knowing he got to me so easily makes me feel the opposite.

What if he comes back?

What if this isn't over?

"It is, Harley," Stella says softly, making me realize I must have said those thoughts out loud. "My dad has him. He won't come after you again."

At hearing her words, I rip my eyes open, my gaze landing on her. Her eyes soften as she crouches down on her haunches beside where I'm on Kyle's lap on the edge of my bed.

"But—"

"You don't need to worry. He's not coming back for you," she says again, her eyes pleading with me to believe her.

"O-okay," I breathe, needing to trust her.

"I've run you a bath, Harley. Would you like me to—"

"No, Kyle can." A growl rumbles at the other side of the room and when I look over, I find Zayn standing in my doorway, a murderous expression on his face and a concerned looking Poppy in his arms. His lips are pressed into a thin line and there's a vein I'm sure I've never seen before pulsating at his temple.

"It's okay, Z."

"No, it's not, Har. It's really fucking not," he fumes before turning his back and marching away. His angry footsteps pound down the stairs leaving Poppy behind.

"He'll be okay. Just worry about you," she says, walking over, sitting down beside us and taking my hand. "Let Kyle look after you, I'll sort Zayn out."

"T-thank you."

"No need to thank me, Har." She leans forward and presses a kiss to my forehead. "It's what sisters do."

A sob rumbles up my throat at her words.

"Yeah."

She squeezes my hand a little. "I'll go find him. He's probably taking it out on the treehouse."

"Biding his time until he can get to my face."

"Yeah," Poppy mutters. "You might want to watch your back."

"I'll take whatever is coming to me. I deserve it." Kyle shrugs as Poppy leaves.

"Where's Kane?" I ask, noticing his absence for the first time.

"Don't know. He took off the second he dropped us off."

"Har, would you like me to stay?" Stella asks after a few minutes of silence.

"Umm..." I hesitate.

"It's okay. I can just go and hang out downstairs for a bit. Ruby and Ash are coming over."

"O-okay. Thank you, Stella. I don't even—"

"Shush," she soothes. "All in a day's work, girl."

"I don't even—"

"It's okay. We'll talk later, yeah?"

She brushes a lock of my hair from my face before standing and walking out of the room, leaving the two of us alone for the first time.

"I'm so fucking sorry, Har."

A sob erupts and this time I can't contain my tears. I curl into his chest and cry wishing the tears would wash away the memories of this night from my head permanently.

"Let's get you cleaned up then you can sleep," he whispers, standing with me still in his arms and walking toward the bathroom.

The scent of my favorite bubbles fill the air and I sigh, needing to sink into that hot water and wash the dirt away.

"I'm going to put you down, okay?" I nod and Kyle drops my feet to the ground.

My legs feel weak and unstable but I manage to stand with the support of the basin as he peels my ruined tank up my torso and drags my panties down my legs.

I watch as his eyes track over all the cuts and scrapes. None are serious but they still look bad enough.

"Did he—" Kyle cuts himself off. "I'm sorry. Don't answer that." His blue eyes search out mine and I gasp when I find them full of unshed tears.

He stands, his chest brushing against my bare nipples causing a spark of lust to shoot down my body. It's a welcome feeling after the hopelessness the last few hours have brought.

I was sure the only thing I'd feel would be the slow painful death that Gray granted me.

His hands cup my cheeks, his thumbs brushing away the silent tears that continue to track down my cheeks.

"Fuck, Harley. I thought—"

"Shush, not now, okay. I just need... I just need you to hold me."

"O-okay." his voice cracks on that one word and a tear finally drops from his eyes.

My heart shatters at the sight of it.

My poor broken boy.

"I'm okay," I say, wrapping my hand around the back of his neck, reaching up and pressing my brow to his. "I'm okay. You saved me."

"Fuck, Kitten. You never should have—" I press two fingers to his lips, cutting off his words.

"Off," I demand, dropping my hand once more and tugging at his shirt.

"Are you sure?" I stare at him for a second and lift my brow. "O-okay."

He sweeps me off my feet and carries me to the tub. The second the hot water engulfs my skin, I groan in relief.

"Good?" he asks, the first hint of the humor I love so much about him in that one word.

"Like you wouldn't believe."

He lowers me right down, the water and bubbles swallowing my broken and battered body.

Gray might not have had me captive all that long but he certainly left his mark.

I wrap my arms around my knees and rest my chin on top as I watch Kyle strip down.

His body is in a similar state to mine after his fight last night. His face is a mess and he's got bruises forming on his ribs. He's still the most beautiful man I've ever seen though. His muscles ripple as he moves, giving me a nice show to make me forget reality for a few seconds.

"Scoot forward, Kitten."

I do as I'm told and in seconds, he sinks down behind me and is pulling me back into his arms.

His lips come to the top of my head and his lips press down as he holds me tight.

"I can't lose you, Har. I fucking can't."

His words echo around my head for the longest time. I want to return the sentiment, but my head is too messed up to talk about something as serious as that right now. I haven't forgotten the events of last night or the girl.

But right now, I need him. I need to be in his arms and soak up his strength. I'll worry about the rest and where we go from here later.

He slides us back, his legs trapping my body in and his arms wrapped around my chest, holding so tightly it's actually hard to breathe, not that I'm going to tell him that.

Eventually, he reaches for my sponge, pours a ton of shower gel onto it and begins lathering it onto my skin.

It feels incredible as he washes away all the dirt of my unforgettable few hours.

I groan, leaning back into him harder and feel his length press into my lower back.

My fingers dig into his thighs as he continues his trail around my body, setting my skin on fire with his gentle touch.

"Ky," I moan as he brushes across my breasts.

"Don't tempt me, Kitten."

"Make me forget, Ky."

"Kitten," he growls, clearly not happy with my request. "You've just been through hell."

"Right? So take me to heaven."

"Fucking hell, Har."

He places the sponge on the side of the tub and ghosts his fingers down my stomach, parting my folds and finding my clit.

"Oh God," I moan as his fingers drop lower to my entrance while his thumb circles my clit.

"Enjoy it, Kitten. It's all you're getting until you're healed," he warns, although his cock poking me in the back says otherwise.

If I weren't so exhausted, I might take it as a challenge to see how quickly I could break him.

His other hand comes up to my breast, pinching and pulling at my nipple, adding to the pleasure that's assaulting my body.

"Come for me, Kitten. Show me how good my fingers feel inside your pussy."

"Kyle, fuck. Kyle," I cry as I crash over the edge. Everything slips away as my pleasure engulfs the fear and the hopelessness that consumed me last night.

He continues working me until my body stops pulsating around his fingers before he pulls them out of me and rests his palm possessively over my stomach as my chest heaves and my heart rate begins to return to normal.

The silence returns along with my memories and I shiver against him.

"The water's getting cold, we should get out."

I swallow down my disappointment. I'm not ready for this to end yet.

"Will you... will you wash my hair?" I ask almost nervously.

"Anything for you, Kitten."

I sink down lower, allowing him to wet my hair before he begins massaging my scalp with shampoo.

It feels incredible and I almost demand he continues when he encourages my head back so he can wash the bubbles away.

"Come on, time to get out."

I sit forward, allowing him to climb out of the tub first and watch his ass as he walks to the towel rack.

Even with the towel wrapped around his waist, his erection is obvious.

He notices what's holding my attention as he steps up to

me, slips his hands under my arms and lifts me so I'm standing.

"Let me look after you, Kitten."

He leans forward and brushes his lips against mine in the sweetest kiss I think I've ever received, and just when I'm ready for him to deepen it, he pulls away, lifts me out, and wraps me in a warm towel.

After once again sweeping me off my feet, he carries me to my bedroom and sets about getting me dried and dressed for bed before encouraging me to crawl under the sheets.

"Don't leave me," I demand in a panic, reaching out to grab his hand, when he moves toward the door.

"I'm just taking the towels back and getting my clothes."

"O-okay," I whisper, feeling silly but still not wanting him to leave me alone.

"There's food and drink if you need it." He nods to my nightstand and I find a little picnic waiting for me. I have no idea who did it while we were in the bath but I've never been more grateful to see a glass of water.

"I probably should have thought about that sooner, huh?"

"You've been everything, Ky," I tell him honestly.

"I'll be back," he promises, and less than two minutes later he is crawling into bed with me, pulling me into his arms and encouraging me to sleep.

Seconds later, I do exactly as I'm told and allow sleep to claim me.

34

KYLE

Slipping from beneath a sleeping Harley, I sit on the edge of the bed and watch her for a few seconds, ensuring that she's not going to wake with my movement. My eyes flick over the bruises and cuts on her face and my fists curl in my need to find wherever that fucker has been taken to and put an end to him for good. A bullet in the shoulder isn't good enough.

Happy that she's in a deep enough sleep, I drag on my clothes and slip from the room.

"How is she?" Stella and Poppy ask simultaneously as I step into the Hunter's kitchen.

"Sleeping. Thanks for the food."

"It was the least we could do," Poppy says softly, sympathy for her friend oozing from her eyes.

"That was pretty badass of you," I say, pinning Stella with a look.

"It was nothing." She shrugs.

"When did you learn to shoot like that?"

"My dad had me at target practice when I could barely lift a gun. He's big on self-defense."

"Who exactly is your dad?"

"I don't have all the answers, but I do know that his men will make sure Gray regrets ever even breathing the same air as Harley, let alone putting his hands on her."

"They'll kill him?" I ask, needing to know that he's going to be wiped off the planet.

"They won't be that kind."

My eyes narrow on her but she just shakes her head, telling me that's all I'm going to get out of her.

I don't believe her denial for a second. She knows exactly what her father does. There's no way she'd have access to guns and trackers as easily as she does if she didn't.

"Is Zayn around?"

"You got a death wish?" Poppy asks, forcing out a laugh.

"I don't know, from what I've heard, he got off pretty lightly from your brother so he can't go too hard on me."

"Yeah, you keep telling yourself that," she mutters. "He's out in the garden."

"Okay, wish me luck."

"Here, take a coffee as a peace offering," Poppy says, jumping up and making him a mug.

"Do I get one?"

"Sure thing."

With two mugs of strong black coffee in hand, I make my way toward the back of the house.

I know where he is before I see him, the smoke floating up from the other side of the lounger a dead giveaway, the bitter scent of the weed another.

"Here," I say, placing the mugs on the table between his lounger and an empty one.

He doesn't say anything but I notice his entire body lock up tight at the sound of my voice.

When I glance over at him, I find his hard eyes trained on me, that same muscle in his temple pulsating to the point I'm worried he might be about to have a coronary.

I blink and he's no longer resting back with his joint

between his lips but instead, he's right in my face, his nose brushing mine and my shirt twisted in his fist.

His breath coats my face as his angry, dark eyes hold mine.

"Go on," I say, holding my hands out at my sides. "Hit me. Do whatever you think will make this better."

"She was supposed to be off-limits, man," he seethes, his grip on my shirt tightening.

"I know, and trust me, I held back for a long time."

"That night. She was with you, wasn't she?" he asks, but I know he already knows the answer. "Did you fuck her?"

"N-no. We just kissed." He growls in warning, but I keep going, it's time this was all out in the open. "I wanted to though, and I thought it was our time at last. I'd watched her, wanted her from a distance for a long time. But there she was, and you weren't and... she was as interested as I was. I just fucking wish I took her away sooner. If I'd have dragged her out of there that night then..."

He nods. "I fucking hate him."

"You and me both. If it weren't for Har calling the cops, I dread to think what would have happened that night."

"Fuck," he barks, releasing me and rubbing his hands over his short-cropped hair, his face twisted as if he's in physical pain.

"I really want to fucking hurt you," he admits, turning his back on me.

"You've got a free pass. I deserve it."

He looks over his shoulder, his eyes hold mine. The knowledge of what could have happened to Harley that night, along with what almost did happen last night darkens them even more than usual and before I know what's happening, his fist isn't flying toward my face but he's pulled me into a hug, his curled fists slamming down on my back.

"You'd better fucking look after her. If you so much as hurt—"

"I won't," I say, my voice full of a confidence in myself that I don't feel.

I think he knows it too because a laugh vibrates in his chest.

"What fucking bullshit," he says with a laugh as he pulls back from me. "We're both Harrow Creek boys, it's in our fucking DNA."

"I don't know," I say, dropping down to the lounger beside the one he's now in again. "You seem to be doing a pretty good job with Poppy."

He laughs. "You've met her brother, right? My life wouldn't be worth living."

"Know that feeling," I joke.

"There's still time for me to take you out for this, you know?"

"Yeah, and I'm sure one day you will."

He falls silent for a few seconds. "Who was the chick last night?"

"Fuck knows. It was a stupid way to make Gray think I didn't want Har. He saw the move a mile away."

"I hope you know you're fucking up before you've even started."

"I know. I should have told her the truth about him. I thought I was protecting her. It was naïve of me to think she needed that."

"Fucking right. Harley doesn't need protection from anything. Aside from Poppy, she's the strongest girl I know. Don't patronize her by making her think you underestimate her strength."

I nod at him, accepting the joint when he offers it to me.

"How's she doing?"

"Sleeping."

"Did he…" He trails off, not wanting to say the words that I equally don't want to hear.

"No, I don't think so. But I truly believe he would have if we didn't get there when we did."

He nods, and it makes my stomach drop into my feet, knowing that he agrees with me. It's no surprise. We know he's a monster. I just hate that he was part of our lives—our friend—for as long as he was.

Silence descends leaving us sitting there with just the sound of the birdsong overheard filling our ears.

There's so much more we both want to say, but neither of us vocalizes any of it. It's too painful.

"I'm going to cancel going away this week. She needs me here," he confesses, staring off into the distance.

"I think we both know that she'll hate you for doing that."

"I don't really give a shit what she thinks. She was just kidnapped and nearly fucking... again. I'm not leaving her for a week to be at some senior team booze fest."

Jake's girlfriend, Amalie, has rented a huge house for their winter break, and almost the entire varsity team are heading there with their girlfriends to celebrate the season.

"She won't want you babying her. Just go, Z."

"So you can stay here and look after her."

"No, that's not my reason." Although I can't deny that it sounds like a fantastic idea.

"You should go, you've already been invited along with Ash and Ruby so you can talk tactics with Jake all week."

"I'm not gate crashing your thing."

"You're going to be a big part of the team we leave behind, you have every right to be there."

"To get me away from Harley?" I ask, finally twisting in my lounger to look at him.

"No, I..." He blows out a long breath and turns to meet my stare. "Do you... do you love her?"

My heart tumbles in my chest as his eyes hold mine, drilling me for an answer.

"I... um... I think it might be a bit soon for that," I

mumble, trying to get out of answering for real. I wanted to have this conversation with Harley first, not her older brother.

"Bullshit. You just told me you've wanted her for a long time. You know exactly how you feel about her." His brows rise and he sips at his coffee while he waits for me to find my balls.

"Fine. Yeah, yeah, I do. Happy now?"

"Nowhere fucking near, man. Now you need to go and tell her." His voice leaves no room for argument and after a beat, I push from the lounger intending to do just that.

The kitchen is quiet as I drop off my mug and as I climb the stairs, I realize why.

"Hey," I say, slipping into Harley's room where all the chatter is coming from. "How are you feeling?" I ask, zeroing in on Harley who's sitting up against her headboard with the covers pulled up to her neck.

The second her eyes find mine, I know something is wrong.

My heart beats a little fast as our connection holds, but I already know what's coming before she opens her mouth. I sense it.

"I need you to leave," she says coldly, her features hard and unwavering as if she actually believes the words.

Pain coils around my chest as I think about the words I intended to say to her when I got up here.

"Can we just talk, please? Alone."

"No. I'm done, and you need to leave."

"But—" At my argument, there's movement off the end of the bed and Stella comes to stand in front of me.

"She's in shock. Just give her some time."

"But I—"

"I know, Kyle. I know," she soothes. "But she just needs a little space to get her head around everything."

She holds my eyes, silently begging me to do as Harley

wishes and not to make this any harder and my heart shatters in my chest.

"Fine," I bark, gritting my teeth and turning away from all of them before I make the mistake of showing them just how much this fucking hurts.

35

HARLEY

Watching Kyle turn his back on me and walk away like I just asked is the most painful thing I've ever experienced.

Part of me hoped that he'd fight. That he'd tell me that I was wrong and force me to change my mind. But he didn't.

He just turned and walked away, ripping my heart out and taking it with him for shits and giggles.

"Oh my God," I sob the second I know he can't hear me.

Stella and Poppy are there immediately, wrapping their arms around me and holding me tight. A few seconds later, my bedroom door opens. I panic at first, thinking that he's come back and about to witness my meltdown until I see Ruby running full pelt toward my bed and joining the huddle.

I cry until my eyes burn and I feel like I have no more tears to shed.

My body is weak and exhausted, and all I want to do is crawl under my covers and hide away from the world.

When I finally pull back, three sets of sympathetic eyes search mine.

"Are you sure that was the right thing to do?" Poppy

whispers, probably expecting me to lash out at her question. I might if I had the energy.

"He lied to me. If he'd had just told me the truth instead of playing these stupid fucking games then none of this would have happened."

"He was trying to protect you," Ruby unhelpfully adds.

"Yeah, and how did that work out for him?" I mutter, gesturing to my face. "I'm done. I'm so fucking done with him, with all of it. He never should have moved here."

Another tear drops on to my cheek as I imagine him not coming back into my life but I can't allow that to consume me. Everything has gone wrong since he walked into Rosewood.

I just want my old life back. Not this one where I feel like I can barely breathe with the searing pain in my heart.

"You need to eat," Stella says, always the levelheaded one. "What do you fancy and we'll order it."

"Thank you," I mouth to her. I have no idea if Poppy and Ruby know all the details about what happened in that warehouse only a few hours ago. But I have a feeling I might owe my life to that girl. And I sure as hell know I've got a million and one questions for her about how all of that went down.

Stella squeezes my hand in acceptance.

The three of them barely leave me all weekend, they must have come up with some kind of schedule while I was sleeping because they seem to come and go like a well-oiled machine ensuring that I'm never alone.

We order all the bad food we can get our hands on and watch sickly sweet rom-coms back to back, if it weren't for the reality of the situation, it would be a pretty sweet weekend. But as it is, it's probably one of the worst of my life.

Zayn pops in regularly to check on me and he intercepts Mom when she reappears after her business trip to save me having to relive everything to her all over again.

When she finally makes her way into my room, the girls all leave for the first time since they arrived and Mom pulls me into her arms.

"I wish you'd called," she whispers in my ear, her voice cracking with emotion.

"I'm okay. Zayn and the girls have looked after me."

"I know but—"

"It's okay, Mom."

She blows out a long breath.

"I'm so sorry, Harley. This is all my fault. I never should have offered to help Kane. I brought this on all of us."

I shake my head. "No, Mom. This isn't on you."

"But—" I pull back from her embrace and pin her with a look that stops whatever she was about to say. "Okay," she concedes, clearly seeing that I don't want to get into this right now. "I'm taking the night off, what would you like to do?"

———

Poppy and Zayn are sitting on my bed with me when Ruby appears the next morning, a sullen look on her face. I know both she and Poppy feel guilty about going away for the week while I'm here still recovering, but I point blank refused to allow them to miss the time away. They both deserve the break, and I'll be fine here with Mom and Stella.

Mostly I'm just glad I didn't have to go to school this morning and face the rest of our class looking like this.

"We really don't have to go."

"Stop please, I'm begging you. Just go and enjoy yourselves."

"You should come," Zayn suggests. But just like every other time he's suggested it, I turn him down. "Come on, he's not even going to be there."

"Don't whine, bro. It doesn't suit you."

It takes ten minutes, but I finally convince them all that

I'm going to be fine. I've got Mom and Stella to keep me company, but mostly, I plan on locking myself in my bedroom doing homework and hiding from the real world.

I stand at my bedroom window and watch the four of them load up Zayn's car before disappearing for their trip.

My heart aches. Of course I want to be there. But I know that I'm in no mood to be around people, and I know that the second the team takes one look at me, they're going to get all annoyingly protective and want to seek revenge on my behalf. And while I appreciate their support, it's really not necessary.

"Hey girl, your mom said to come straight up," Stella says over an hour later, her arms full of books. When I told her to get my homework, she happily agreed.

"Sure, come in, make yourself at home." She dumps the books on my desk and drops a couple of bags to the floor.

"Staying all week?" I comment.

"If you need me."

"Won't your dad want you at home?"

She shakes her head. "He's out of town all week."

"And you've come here? Shouldn't we be at yours with the pool and jacuzzi?"

"We can if you want," she says sadly, making me wonder if she doesn't actually want to be there herself.

"I'm easy. We just don't have the kind of luxuries you do."

"Maybe not, but this place feels like a home." I open my mouth to respond but I find I have no words, and I can hardly argue. For as incredible as her home is, I know exactly what she means.

She gets herself set up with a couple of textbooks on the other side of the bed to get started, but I have other ideas.

"Are you ready to start talking yet?" I ask her, addressing the elephant in the room.

"I... um..."

"You don't have to tell me anything you're not happy sharing, Stel."

"Everything I've told you is true. But it's just the tip of the iceberg. Dad works with some very bad people."

"Like gangs?" I ask.

"Yeah, that kind of thing. He—I—pretty much have access to anything we could want or need at any hour of the day. But sadly, that means I don't get him all that often. He's always away, probably scouting out our next location, I don't know," she mutters with a shrug.

"That sucks." Mom works a lot but at least she's in the house doing so most of the time. "It must be lonely."

"Yeah, then add in being scared to make friends because I know I'll just leave them in a few months. It really sucks."

"We should do something fun this week," I suggest.

"I thought you wanted to do homework."

"Yeah, but it sounds a little too depressing after everything, don't you think?"

"Yes, leave it to me."

She pulls her cell from her purse and starts tapping away.

"I just need to go and speak to your mom," Stella says, hopping up and running from my room before I have a chance to ask what the hell is going on.

Only ten minutes pass before she comes flouncing back in.

"Okay all sorted," she sings, hopping back up on my bed like nothing just happened.

"Uh... care to explain?"

"Nope. It's a surprise."

"Hmph. I don't see how that is fair." I cross my arms over my chest and pout.

"It'll be worth it, I promise."

"I hope you're right."

"Don't you trust me?"

"The girl who's pretty hot with a gun? Can I say anything other than yes right now?"

She barks out a laugh and pulls her textbook back onto her lap. "Get as much done as you can, after today, homework is banned."

"Now that sounds like a plan I can get on board with."

With music playing in the background, we spend the day working, stopping for drinks and snacks every couple of hours. Mom pops in to check on us a few times and delivers more food. All things considered, it's a good day. I mean, I'm not in a mansion in the mountains with my friends, but I'm happy. Kind of.

"Ugh, I hate this," I complain, throwing my pen across the room in frustration.

"Can I help?" Stella asks, looking at the book on my lap and pulling a face when she spots my math equations.

I sigh. "It's okay. It just drives me crazy." I refrain from pointing out that for some fucked-up reason, the only person I want to help me with my math is Kyle, but after sending him away yesterday, I'm pretty sure I've put an end to all of that.

"Missing your tutor?" she asks, a smile twitching at her lips that she's found a way to make me talk about him without mentioning his name again. She got shot down earlier when she tried.

"No," I spit out way too quickly for it to actually be true.

"It's okay, you know. You can miss him."

"Well, I don't. He lied to me and because of it I found myself in that monster's clutches. He can rot in hell for all I care." She stares at me, her eyes softening as my voice cracks and I blink back the tears that threaten to fall.

"Harley, I really think—"

"No," I say, putting my hand up and cutting off whatever it is she feels the need to say. "I don't want to hear it. We are done. Not that we were ever anything more than a bad decision in the first place."

"You don't really believe that, do you?"

"Yeah, actually, I do. I never should have gone anywhere near him, let alone allow him into my bed. What was I even thinking? It was all a game of revenge for him. He doesn't care about me, he never did."

"Harley," she breathes. "Have you seen the way he looks at you? That boy more than cares about you, and I think he always has."

"No, no," I say, shaking my head, refusing to allow her words into my brain otherwise they'll just fester and cause me to start doubting myself.

"Okay," she concedes before placing her own homework to the side and insisting on helping me with mine. She's a good teacher, although not quite as skillful as Kyle, but I'll take all the help I can get right now.

It's almost midnight when she finally gets up to leave.

"You could just stay the night," I offer.

"I need to go home to pack anyway, so I may as well go now."

"Pack? I thought you were hanging around Rosewood all week?" I ask, trying not to sound too disappointed because the thought of being alone terrifies me. I know she's promised that her dad has taken care of Gray, and I believe her, but that's not going to stop me looking over my shoulder for a while expecting him to reappear.

"I know, but I've made other plans."

"Oh... okay. Anything fun?"

"I guess we'll find out tomorrow," she says with a smirk.

"We?"

"Yep, pack a bag, girl. We're heading out of town for a few days."

"Oh my God, are you serious?" I ask, the prospect of leaving this place behind is almost too much to wish for.

"Yep. Just me, you, and a whole lot of nothing else. Pretty sure there's no cell service or anything so we'll get complete peace."

"That sounds incredible."

"I'm glad you agree. I'll be back at eight in the morning. Make sure you're ready."

I nod eagerly. "Anything I need to pack?"

"Your bikini."

"Done." I squeal. "I'm so excited. Thank you."

"You're more than welcome. I need this almost as much as you do."

36

______

KYLE

"Get in the fucking car, Ky."

"No." I stand my ground on the porch of mine and Kane's house while I have a stare-off with Ashton and Zayn.

"Stop being such a pussy, man." Ash shoulder barges me, storming into the house and soon after my bedroom.

"What the fuck?" I bark. By the time I get to him, he's already stuffing items of clothing into my duffel bag.

"You're coming. You need to get out of town and get her out of your head for a few days."

"She's not in my—" He turns and pins me with a look. "You're a pain in my ass, Fury."

"Yeah, yeah. You'll be thanking me when you sink your ass into the hot tub I've seen pictures of."

"Yeah, well, I'm sure you'll be sinking into more than just your tub this weekend."

A smug smirk covers his face and I can't help but roll my eyes.

"Sorry, man. This is exactly why you should come."

"So I can watch all you cozy couples getting it on? Oh yeah, sounds like a winning plan," I sulk.

"Not everyone will be coupled up," he argues. "You need to relax, man. Come on, agree already. I'm not really in the mood for abduction."

My face drops at his words.

"Shit, no. I didn't mean... fuck."

"It's fine. Forget it."

Knowing I have no chance of winning this argument with both Ash and Zayn on the opposing team, I take over my own packing and in less than five minutes, I'm throwing my duffel over my shoulders and striding from the room, much to Ash's delight.

"Don't make me regret this," I mutter to Zayn, who irritatingly just smiles at me in accomplishment.

"Would I?" he asks innocently.

I stare at him for a beat, registering the tension that's still evident in his features. He still wants to hurt me for going after Harley. I get it. I kinda wanna hurt myself for it too, hence why I was more than happy to be alone this week and drown in my own misery while hoping she might reach out but knowing she won't.

He blinks, breaking our silent conversation, and I throw my bag into his trunk before pulling open the back door and sitting my ass down before I change my mind.

"Alright?" I ask Ruby who's patiently waited this whole time in the middle seat. "Poppy." I nod at Zayn's girl when I find her eyes on me in the mirror.

Both girls stare at me, tension oozing from them.

"I'm sor—" My apology is cut off when the doors open once more and both Ash and Zayn climb in. "Where exactly are we going?" I ask once we're heading out of Rosewood, the atmosphere in the car getting heavier by the second.

It's obvious that it was the guy's idea for me to tag along because clearly the girls are still firmly on Harley's side and would happily throw me out of the moving car at any moment.

"The mountains."

"That's fucking hours away."

"Yup. Get comfortable, man." Zayn's eyes find mine for a beat before he focuses back on the road.

Great.

Zayn and Poppy take charge of the music while the couple beside me whisper fuck knows what to each other. All I do know is that Ash's hand has been getting higher and higher up Ruby's skirt the longer we've been sitting here.

"Ash," Ruby gasps, her hand wrapping around his wrist to stop him. "Kyle's right there."

"Kyle's also not deaf," I mutter, shifting over so there's as much space between Ruby and me as possible.

"Jealous, man?"

"Fuck off," I grumble, wondering why I let them force me into this.

Thankfully, he takes a hint and doesn't say any more, unfortunately, that's only because he's otherwise engaged with his tongue down Ruby's throat. The sound of their lip-smacking is louder than the music thumping through the speakers.

His hand pushes higher and she squirms.

"Just climb on his lap and let him fuck you. It'll put us all out of our misery quicker," I snap when a moan rips up Ruby's throat.

"No sex in my car," Zayn snaps. "The only girl who gets fucked in here is Poppy."

"Fucking hell," I mutter, twisting away from the horny couple beside me and allowing them to continue doing their thing. It's not like they're going to stop anytime soon.

I stare at the passing scenery and the low groans continue, my cock hard as I imagine being here right now with Harley like that.

Shifting in my seat, I pull my cell from the pocket and pull up our conversation.

It's not the first time since she sent me away that I've caved and sent her a message. I scroll up through my unread apologies.

I blow out a breath, my chest deflating in disappointment.

I'm not disappointed with her. She's acting as she should. Cutting me out of her life as she should. I'm disappointed in myself for thinking that the best way to handle Gray was to keep his threats a secret.

I don't know what else to say to her to prove how much I regret it. To tell her how I really feel and how much this is ripping me apart.

I hate that we're driving farther away from her, that my all-consuming need to drive to her house and demand she speaks to me is going to be impossible.

I guess that was Zayn's intention. Take me with them and keep me away from her.

Can't say I blame him. If I had a little sister, I'd want her away from me too.

We stop a couple of times and each time I race from the car like my ass is on fire in my need to get away from the happy couples and tense atmosphere for a few minutes.

My cell vibrates in my pocket as I walk out of the men's restroom. My heart jumps into my throat thinking that it could be Harley, even though I know it's not.

Disappointment still floods me when I look at the screen, although I can't deny that the person's name staring back at me is the next best thing right now.

"How is she?"

"She's okay. Sad."

Pain grips my chest at her words. Hurting Harley was the last thing I wanted in all of this.

"I've messaged her."

"She's refusing to check her cell." I'm not surprised by this, seeing as all the messages have gone unread.

"Can you try to get her to read them?"

"I can't make any promises, Ky."

"I know."

"Ky, I—" she says, but quickly cuts herself off.

"Yes, what is it?"

"It's... it's nothing. Forget it."

"No, Stella. Whatever it is, yes. Whatever I can do to make this better, I'm all ears."

"Did Zayn and Ash convince you to go with them?" she asks, her subject change giving me whiplash.

"Yeah, we're currently..." I look around at the gas station we've stopped at. "Fuck knows where."

She chuckles.

"Try to enjoy yourself, yeah. I've got your girl. You don't need to worry about her."

"No shit, she's got Little Miss Rambo as her personal protection."

"You're just scared I could beat your ass."

"Uh... yeah, that's it," I mutter, but I fear she could be right.

"Anyway... I'll call you if anything changes—"

"What's likely to change? She is okay, right? The drugs he slipped her are they—"

"Yes, Kyle. She's fine. She admitted that she didn't have much. They'll be out of her system by now, and yes, he's being dealt with, I promise you."

"Okay."

"Please, just try to enjoy yourself."

"Unlikely."

"Well, try. Speak soon."

She hangs up on me before I get to say goodbye and I pull my cell from my ear and stare at it in disbelief.

"Everything okay?" Ruby asks, finally unattached from Ash's side.

"Yeah. How much do you know about Stella?"

"Her name," she deadpans.

"I think she's got an interesting story."

"You think?" Ruby asks sarcastically, looking over at me and raising a brow. "I doubt we'll ever find out. She'll be gone before we get a chance to dig too deep."

"She's leaving?"

"I think so. Much like everything else, I don't really know. Come on, the guys are waiting."

"Oh goodie, back to the front row seat of my very own porno," I mutter, trailing behind her.

"We're not that bad."

"I guess I deserve the torture after everything."

"For hurting my girl? You sure fucking do." She pins me with a look that tells me she's still not all that happy about me being here.

I shoot her the best smile I can muster before we climb into the back of the car for the final leg of our long-ass journey. This place had better be fucking worth it.

It's almost three hours later—thanks to Zayn taking a wrong turn—when we finally pull up to a massive cabin.

It looks like something off a postcard. And it's by far the most expensive place I've ever stepped foot inside, let alone stayed.

"This is beautiful," Poppy breathes as the car comes to a stop.

"Makes the drive almost worth it," I mutter.

"Oh, it was very worth it."

"Says the one who spent most of the time with his finger inside his girl's—"

"O-okay," Zayn interrupts, killing the engine and swinging his door open.

As I follow his lead, the front door to the place opens, and Jake, Mason, and Ethan spill out, all dressed in board shorts and already looking three sheets to the wind.

"About time motherfuckers," Ethan barks.

"Blame the driver," Ruby shouts as she helps Ash to pull the bags out of the trunk.

"Not my fucking fault," Zayn sulks.

"We all told you to turn left."

"I didn't see the turnoff." He drags his and Poppy's bags from the gravel driveway, throws them over his shoulder, and stalks toward the cabin.

"I should probably go cheer him up."

"I'm sure it won't take much," Ash calls suggestively.

"Point me in the direction of an empty bedroom, I need some peace," I say to Amalie when she emerges.

"Follow me," she says with a chuckle.

"Rubes, you wanna see your room too?"

"Damn right we do."

"Fucking sex addict," I mutter, loud enough for him to hear.

"Aw, little Legend is jealous."

"Leave him alone," Amalie snaps, pinning him with a warning look.

It's easy to think that Amalie could be vulnerable and weak with her tall, slim body and soft English accent but I dare anyone to cross the woman who's tamed Jake Thorn. There can't be anything weak about her. I might not know Jake all that well but I know enough to know it must take one hell of a strong woman to keep him in line.

"Jake," she calls, spinning on her heels and walking backward toward the front door. "You coming to show the guys their rooms?"

"Uh... I was gonna..." She raises a brow at him. "Again?" he asks, the delight is clear in his tone. "Coming."

I chuckle at the pair of them as he sweeps her off her feet and jogs with her up the stairs.

"Legend," he says, pointing to another set of stairs. Right at the top, the final door on your left.

"Ruby, you and Fury are there," he says, pointing to a

door on this floor. Thank fuck. "If you need anything, ask the others, we're going to be busy for a while." They disappear through another door before Amalie's squeal pierces the air.

Great, just what I feared. A house full of loved up, sexed-up couples. This week shouldn't be frustrating at all.

Following instruction, I find a small room with a twin bed at the top floor of the house. The bed is tucked into the eaves and I have to damn near bend in half to get into it without taking my head off, but at least it's quiet.

I kick my sneakers off and crawl onto it, desperate for a few hours of peace before I go and find the others.

———

"Tell me you snuck in a few single chicks," Rich calls to me when I walk through the living area later that night with a beer in hand.

"Sorry, I was stuck with Ash fingering Ruby the whole way here."

The guys snort a laugh while Ash's face lights up in delight.

"Yeah, what of it? Don't tell me you weren't getting hard listening to my girl get off."

"Nothing about what you do gets me hard, Fury." I flip him the bird before falling down on one of the massive worn leather couches and tipping my bottle to my lips.

"This fucking blows," Rich says, leaning forward and resting his elbows on his knees. "Whose idea was it not to invite the rest of the fucking squad."

"Mine," Chelsea announces as she waddles into the room with her hand on her round belly. "This vacation isn't a fucking orgy." She flicks a deadly look between Justin and Rich. "We're here to enjoy ourselves to chill out."

"We could enjoy ourselves just fine with Aria and Marissa here."

"You're a dog."

"Says the pregnant cheer captain."

Shane shifts to the edge of the couch he's sitting on, ready to jump to his girl's defense but it seems it's not necessary. I guess Chelsea doesn't have the rep she does for nothing.

"At least I'm getting some."

"Oh burn," Ethan booms.

Despite Justin and Rich's almost constant moaning about the lack of girls, we have a pretty good night.

The place is stocked with everything all of us could need for the week, and as much as I hate to admit it, I think Zayn and Ash might have had a point about getting out of Rosewood and clearing my head.

We spend our days working out in the state-of-the-art gym in the basement and hanging with the girls around the pool. Even the guys stop moaning eventually, finally getting bored of their own voices.

Ash and I sit down with Jake to talk through next year, it seems that Jake has Ash pinned for next year's captain and he talks to me as if I'm going to be in a position to be worried about this shit. But I learned long ago not to count my chickens before they've hatched, so I'll just take each day as it comes and roll with the punches.

Hanging out with these guys, it's easy to forget where I've come from or what I've been through but the reality is that I have a record and a parole officer keeping an eye on everything I do. My life is a world away from the privilege most of these guys know.

I get daily updates from Stella to let me know that Harley is okay. But with every day that passes my hope of being able to salvage anything between us lessens as she still refuses to even read my messages.

My feelings about it must be obvious because even Poppy and Ruby start being nice to me by day three at the cabin. I know I look like a miserable motherfucker but the fact they're taking pity on me after what I did tells me it could be worse than I thought.

"You really like her, don't you?" Ruby asks when we find ourselves alone in the living area.

I scrub my hand over my face, sweep my fingers through my hair before placing my cap back on my head. "Is it that obvious?"

"Just a bit. You miss her." This time, it's not a question. There's no point.

"Yeah. I'm kinda used to it though. I've always been on the periphery when it comes to her. I stayed at arm's length because of Zayn and then... well..." I trail off because I know they know the truth about everything. "I stupidly thought that night was my chance. If I'd have known how badly it would have fucked everything up, I might have thought differently about it."

"You weren't to know."

"I guess not. But still, I'll blame myself for the rest of my life for what went down that night. I should have known what he'd done. I should have got her out of there before it got out of hand."

She reaches over and squeezes my forearm.

"It wasn't your fault. Just give her some time. Something tells me that she'll come around."

"Really?" I ask, sounding a little too hopeful.

"Ky," she sighs. "I'm sure I don't need to tell you that my best friend can be as stubborn as an ox when she wants to be. Just bide your time. The perfect moment to tell her how you really feel will present itself. And, it might even be sooner than you think." As she says the words, I watch guilt pass over her face.

"What are you hiding?" I ask, not wanting to beat around the bush when it comes to Harley.

"N-nothing," she stutters, looking anywhere but in my eyes.

"Is she coming here?" My heart rate picks up at the thought of seeing her walk through the door to join her friends.

"No. Forget I said anything." Before I get a chance to start begging her for information, she's up and out of the room.

Pulling my cell from my pocket, I shoot Stella a message to check in before shoving it back in my pants. I've stopped messaging Harley. Each one goes unread so I've decided that until she allows me to talk to her face to face then I'm going to hold back on everything else I want to say to her.

We're all sitting in the living room later that night shooting the shit, but while everyone else seems to be relaxed and enjoying themselves, I'm wound up like a fucking spring.

I can't help thinking that everyone knows something I don't. Not only does Ruby keep shooting me weird looks, but Ash, Zayn, Poppy, and even Amalie and the other girls are doing the same, not to mention that when someone goes to the kitchen to grab drinks, no fucker gets one for me.

I'm starting to think that either they've decided I'm not welcome anymore or there's something going on that I'm not privy to.

I'm just about to get up to get my own fucking beer when the front door crashes open.

A couple of sets of eyes turn to me before everyone looks to the door.

My heart is in my throat as I wait for whoever it is to emerge.

Heels click on the polished wooden floor and my need to get up and go and find out the truth for myself damn near gets the better of me.

I'm on the edge of my seat with my heart pounding in my chest when a shadow falls over the doorway and then a familiar body appears.

The breath I didn't know I was holding rushes out of me as I lock eyes with a blue pair I wasn't expecting.

"Stella? Is she here?" I ask, not caring what everyone around me will think about my desperation for my girl.

"Fuck yeah, get your ass over here, baby girl," Rich shouts, holding his arms out and making grabby gestures with his hands.

Stella rips her eyes from mine and pins him with a look that he really should be scared of.

"I'd probably snap your tiny cock in half, *bro*," she sasses as everyone in the room except me and Rich fall about laughing.

"It's not actually small. Chels, tell them," he whines.

A ripple of tension flows through the room as Shane curls his fists at his sides, but all Chelsea does is throw her head back and laughs harder for a few seconds.

"You're asking the wrong girl to come to your defense, tiny." She winks, holding her forefinger and thumb a couple of centimeters apart. "You need advice on which one of the singles will show you a good time, you come and see me, girl." She smiles at Stella before planting her lips on Shane to try to placate him. It clearly works because not two seconds later does he relax under her kiss and his unclenched hands slip under her tank.

Shaking my head at the two of them, I turn back to Stella.

"Shall we?" she asks, her eyes trained on mine for a beat before she turns and disappears from sight.

I look at Ruby, needing to know if this was what she was talking about earlier but all she does is smile sweetly as I walk through the room.

Stella's leaning back against the counter with a bottle of water in her hand, making herself at home, when I find her a few seconds later in the kitchen.

"What the fuck is going on?"

HARLEY

I wake from probably the best night's sleep I've ever had. I have no idea what time it is but the bedroom is still totally dark and the cabin is in blissful silence.

It's safe to say that I freaked the fuck out when she started heading toward the mountains.

But as promised, we didn't head to where the team was.

Although I'd tried to avoid my cell, or more so the messages that are sitting on it from Kyle, I'd caved to my need to look at Instagram, although I regretted it the second I did because I discovered that while I turned down the invitation to join them in their giant cabin, that Kyle hadn't because while I was miserable and missing him more than I'd ever admit, he was there enjoying himself. He was smiling in every single picture I found of him and it made my heart hurt worse with every one I saw.

I want him to be happy, of course I do. But I'm not sure I want him to find that happiness with my group of friends when I've been left behind.

I blow out a slow breath.

I have no idea where the location of their cabin is, I've

refrained from looking up how close we might be to each other right now. I don't need that kind of temptation.

Reaching for my cell, I wake it up and check the time.

It's past lunch. Jesus.

The two days we've had here have been beyond perfect.

I have no idea how she managed it, but the kitchen was fully stocked with all the food and drink we could possibly need and the log fire in the living area was already burning when we arrived.

This place really is a slice of heaven with its huge couches, massive wraparound porch complete with day bed, and hot tub overlooking the forest below.

When I get downstairs, I find that despite the silence, Stella is already awake and reading her Kindle in front of the fire with a mug of coffee.

"Morning, sleepyhead," she says when I drop down onto the couch opposite her. "How are you feeling?"

"So much better." The wounds from my ordeal are still there and will be for a few days yet, but they're healing and my body is aching less with every day that passes. Even my head is beginning to feel a little more stable thanks to Stella.

"Good, I'm glad." She smiles softly at me, and I'm once again reminded of how grateful I am that she gave me a chance when she usually runs away from making friends.

"It's this place. It's like it has magical healing powers."

"Yeah?" she asks, a hopeful look appearing in her gorgeous blue eyes.

"How couldn't it? You've seen it." I gesture around the cozy interior.

"Yeah, I never want to leave."

"You and me both. You want another coffee?"

"Please."

I take her mug before walking through to the kitchen and making us both a fresh one.

"What's the plan for the day?" I ask when I rejoin her. I

don't know why I ask, we agreed on the journey here that we were going to do absolutely nothing, and that was more than fine by me.

"I need to pop out, we've almost run out of logs." She flicks a look to the fire.

When we first arrived, the alcove beside it was full of wood, but it's all almost gone.

"I thought you said there was enough for our entire stay," I enquire. She had organized everything so well that it surprises me that we've just run out.

"There's more outside, but it's damp. The welcome pack gives an address for a place for dry stuff. Thought I'd go check it out."

"Okay. I can come."

"Nope. You are staying put."

I open my mouth to argue, but Stella pins me with one of her looks and my lips slam shut instantly.

"You can cook. There are ingredients in the fridge for lasagna."

"Okay, I can do that," I concede, although I'm not happy about it.

It's hours later when Stella finally makes a move to leave the cabin. She insisted on showering and applying a full face of makeup before stepping foot out the front door. I started to wonder if she was sneaking out on a hot date not just heading for wood.

"I'll leave the front door unlocked," she says when she comes to a stop in the living room.

"Okay. Once I've finished dinner, I might jump into the hot tub."

"I won't be too long."

Only minutes later she's gone and the cabin becomes even quieter.

I grab my AirPods from the table, press play on my favorite playlist, and I make a start on the lasagna.

I wiggle my hips in time with the music and sing my heart out, feeling lighter than I have in a long time.

Once the lasagna is assembled and just needs a blast in the oven, I clean up the kitchen, still rolling my hips in time with the music before heading to my room to change into my bikini to hit the tub.

I wasn't as organized as Stella—partly due to not knowing where we were going—so I don't have my Kindle, but I found a healthy supply of smutty romance books on the bookcase in the dining room, so I grab the one I'm halfway through along with my cell and I make my way down toward the porch to watch the sun go down behind the trees.

I glance at the clock on the wall as I pass the kitchen and notice just how much time has passed since Stella left.

Concern washes through me, and I check my cell to see if she's tried to call.

Finding nothing, I hit call on her number.

"Hey," she answers immediately. "I'll be back soon. I got lost and then started chatting to the guy at the wood place."

"Stell, have you snagged yourself a mountain man?" I tease.

"I haven't been gone *that* long."

"Long enough," I mutter jokingly. "Seriously, if he's that hot, stay longer. I'm good here."

"I appreciate that, but seriously, I'll be there soon. Dinner done?"

"Yep, just waiting for its diners. I'm just about to hit the tub."

"So get off the phone, and go and enjoy."

"Okay, okay, I'm going. See you soon."

I'm just about to hang up when she stops me. "Har?"

"Yeah?"

"Uh... nothing. I'll see you soon."

My brows pull together as I repeat our short conversation in my head. Something doesn't feel right about this.

Telling myself that I'm just reading into everything too much, I pull the refrigerator open and grab myself a soda.

I'm almost at the door when I notice that the fire has almost gone out.

Placing everything down on the side, I head over to put a couple more logs on.

I'm still poking at the embers, trying to get it to take when car tires crunch against the gravel out the front of the cabin.

"Come on, you fucker," I moan at the fire.

It's been mostly Stella's job since we got here and she makes keeping it going look so easy, but I'm thinking that might just be another of her hidden skills because it's clearly not that simple.

The front door opens and footsteps head my way, although I'm too distracted to realize they don't sound the same as the ones that left a few hours ago.

"How do you keep this fucking thing alight? I swear it hates me."

When she doesn't answer, I push from the floor and turn around to see what's the issue.

I gasp in shock when I don't find Stella looking back at me but the one person I've been fighting to get out of my head.

"What are you doing here?" I snap, my fingers curling into fists at my sides. But I can't deny the heat that floods my body as I stare at him. As always, his cap is sitting on his head, his angular face still showing signs of the fight, but it's his eyes that capture me. They are their usual light blue but there are shadows lingering behind them, regret maybe, and he looks like he hasn't slept since I turned him away.

Shaking my head, I push all those thoughts away. No good can come from thinking of that night.

His lips part to respond but no words come out.

"Stella set me up, didn't she?" I seethe, disbelief flowing through me. I fucking trusted her.

"Yeah, but don't be mad at her. She's trying to help."

"Where is she?" I ask, forcing my concern for my friend to the forefront.

"She's at the cabin with the guys. We've swapped."

I rush to the window and look out at the driveway, finding Stella's Porsche parked exactly where it was earlier.

"She's... you've... fuck."

He watches me warily as I pace the short length of the living room.

"Kyle, I—"

"No," he says, stepping up to me and forcing me to stop marching.

I try to move away but he reaches out and wraps his hands around my upper arms.

"I need you to hear me out."

"No, I don't need to do anything. I told you, we're done. You shouldn't be here. You should go back to the cabin. I don't want you here."

"You're lying," he states, stepping closer until the heat of his body seeps through the robe that's loosely tied around my middle.

"I told you, Kitten, I always know when you're lying." A smirk pulls at his lips.

"Not this time."

He stares at me, tension crackling between us. My body is desperate to lean into his heat, his touch. But I fight it.

He chuckles and all it does is kick my irritation levels up a notch.

I swallow, allowing myself a second or two to gather my thoughts. With him so close and his scent filling my nose, it makes it hard to form a thought, let alone conjure up an argument.

He releases my arm before I get to say a word, and for the briefest moment, I wonder if he's going to concede.

I should know better.

"Your eye twitches," he says softly, pressing one fingertip to the side of my eye.

I flinch at his burning touch and move to take a step back, but his fingers tighten on my arm, keeping me in place.

His finger trails down my cheek until it traces over my bottom lip. I want to pull away, but with the way his eyes are fixated on me, I can't find the strength to do it.

"I've missed you so fucking much," he whispers.

"It's been a couple of days," I sass, forcing myself to ignore the fact that I feel exactly the same about the situation.

A growl rips from his mouth at my words. His hand releases my arm but it's only for a beat because he's not letting me go.

His fingers wrap around my throat and I'm forced backward.

"Ky," I gasp, my back hitting the wall. He steps right into me as the intensity in his eyes makes a violent shudder roll down my spine.

"An hour was too fucking long, Har."

His chest heaves, his minty breath fanning over my face as our eyes hold in a battle of wills.

He wants me to submit, to admit my feelings, and risk putting my heart on the line for him.

But am I strong enough to do that after everything?

My pulse thunders under his light grip, and he feels it because his thumb starts caressing the spot I know where it's pounding against my skin.

"I'm so fucking sorry, Kitten. I thought I was doing the right thing by not telling you. I thought I was protecting you."

"You thought wrong," I growl, my memories of what his lies led to hitting me full force once again.

My stomach turns over as I remember the putrid stench

from that warehouse, Gray's vile touch, his murderous promises, and dark intent.

"You left me unarmed and allowed him to get to me."

Guilt darkens his eyes, pain leaking from them.

I feel it, I feel it as if it's my own.

But is that enough?

"You lied to me, Kyle."

"I know, and I'm sorry. I thought I could keep him away from you. I thought if I tried to show him that I didn't want you—" I think of that brunette girl wiggling around on his lap. My chest splinters as I picture his hands on her body. "I thought it was safer that way."

"Why was he even there? Did you invite him?"

"Fuck knows. I never wanted to look at him again after that night." He swallows and my eyes drop to his throat as the muscles pull and his Adam's apple bobs. My mouth waters, wanting to taste his skin, to keep the roughness of his jaw against my lips.

Damn him.

"I only ever wanted to protect you, Har." He steps closer, crushing my body against the wall in the most delicious way. "I only ever wanted you."

"Ky, I—" I try to argue but he presses two fingers to my lips to stop me.

He stares at me with so much emotion swimming in his eyes, it's all I can do to remember to take a breath.

"Shhh... I'm talking," he whispers, brushing his nose against mine and sending my body into overdrive. His hand drops and he wraps it possessively around my ribs. "I'm sorry, Har. For everything. For not taking you away that night, for being so drunk I let it go on too long. For the way I treated you when I came back. I spent a year locked away and you were the only thing I could think about. I wanted you, I hated you. I was a fucking mess.

"Then I saw you again, and fuck. You fucking slayed me,

Kitten.

"You were everything I didn't want to remember but was desperate for.

"I'm sorry for keeping shit from you when I should have trusted you. I'm sorry I didn't protect you in the way I should, and I'm sorry I hurt you, I'm even more sorry he got the chance to. But mostly, I'm sorry for not telling you this earlier." His hand releases my throat in favor of my cheek. "I..." He hesitates, his eyes filling with tears. "I love you, Harley."

"Kyle," I breathe, a frown marring my brow.

"Shush," he soothes. "I don't expect you to say anything. I just... I needed you to know."

His watery eyes plead with me to give him a chance, to say that I'll try.

But my head and heart are at war.

My heart feels like it's about to explode, like it no longer fits inside my chest after watching him rip himself open for me. But my head... my head wants to protect me from even more pain.

"I want to make it up to you, Kitten. Let me prove to you how I feel, how serious I am."

"But—"

"Trust me, Har, I know all the buts. I know all the reasons you should say no and turn me away. But I'm begging you, please, don't. I suffered through a year without you, it's our time now."

My lips part but I find that I can't dig up an answer as my body continues its silent battle.

"I love you, Kitten. I love you so fucking much." He drops his palm, slipping his hand inside my robe and pressing it over my heart. "I know you feel something too."

There's no way he can't feel how hard my heart is beating under his hand and my cheeks bloom knowing that he knows how hard I'm fighting for sanity right now.

"W-what will you do if I say no?" I ask, forcing the words out past the giant ball of emotions clogging my throat.

Pain slices through his eyes, but I stay strong.

"Then I turn around and walk back out the way I came in and send Stella back."

"Just like that?"

"I want to be what you need, Har. And if that's not me, then I'll just have to deal with that."

He presses his forearm against the wall behind me, caging me in. Although I know I'm free to run if I so wish.

"A-and… what if I say yes?"

Heat flashes through his eyes for a beat before he schools his features and leans in so close that our lips brush.

Liquid lust floods my body sending heat straight to my already simmering core.

"Then I'd never let you go ever again."

I sag against the wall, the conviction in his words making my knees weak.

"Okay," I whisper so quietly I'm not even sure I said the word, but the second the corner of his lip twitches up into the beginning of a smile.

"Harley," he warns as if he's worried that I'm playing him.

"I…" I bite down on my bottom lip, still battling with the argument raging but ultimately knowing that my heart is going to win out.

How can it not when he's basically bleeding out in front of me right now?

"Yes," I breathe. "Yes, Ky. I want—" My words are cut off as his lips slam down on mine and his tongue plunges into my mouth.

His kiss is all-consuming, and he steals all the breath from my lungs as he devours me.

His hands slide up to my cheeks so he can angle my head just so and deepen our kiss.

My toes curl in desire and my heart tumbles as I finally

allow it to take full control of the situation.

I let my walls down and fall hard and fast as he consumes me, claims me.

His fingers thread into my hair and he tugs my head up, ripping my lips from his so he can kiss across my jaw and down my neck.

"Ky, I..." I pant, trying to get control of my breathing to be able to say the words. "I... I think I love you too."

He pauses with his lips pressed against my throat and I panic.

Was I not supposed to say that?

But then I feel his lips move and I know he's smiling.

"Look at me," I demand, knowing that I can't miss this moment.

He hesitates for a second, but the wait is worth it when he finally moves and looks into my eyes.

Tears swim in his silvery-blue depths and he has the goofiest smile on his face.

I can't help but bark out a laugh at how ridiculously happy he looks. It's an incredible sight and my chest swells knowing how much he needs this kind of happiness in his life after everything he's been through.

"I can't offer you much, Har. I come complete with a parole officer and a record, but fuck, I promise to always put you first and do my best to make you the happiest woman on the planet."

"Oh Ky, I don't need anything aside from you. We can build the rest of it together."

"Fuck," he barks, slamming his lips to mine once more. "I need you so fucking bad, Kitten."

"The feeling is certainly mutual."

His fingers make quick work of the tie around my waist and in seconds, my robe is pooling at my feet.

"Holy shit," he gasps when he takes in my gold bikini. "Stella *is* straight, right?" he asks, his voice deadly serious.

I throw my head back and laugh. "You're an idiot."

"Apparently so." His face twists with regrets.

"Hey, don't do that," I say, reaching for his rough cheeks and pulling him closer once again.

"We've got so much to talk about, I've got so much more to apologize for."

"That may be true, but I'm not really in the mood for talking and rehashing all that shit right now."

His eyes light up as he steps into my body once more. His clothes tickling against my bare skin and the roughness of his tented jeans scratching at my stomach.

"What did you have in mind, Kitten?" he asks, his head dipped so our lips are only a breath apart.

"I... I was heading for the hot tub. Join me?"

"Fuck yeah."

My fingers grip the bottom of his shirt and I pull it up his body. He assists when I get it stuck on his head.

Trailing my fingers over his chest, I linger on a bruised patch of skin on his ribs. "This still hurt?"

"No," he says, I suspect he's lying as he reaches for my thighs and lifts me up the wall, his lips pressing into a thin line as if in pain. My legs automatically wrap around his waist, my core lining up with his hard length, figuring that he wouldn't do it if it were too much.

"Ky," I moan, flexing my hips against him.

"Fuck."

His lips find mine as he rips me from the wall and carries me across the room.

The right side of my body heats as he lowers me down and when I look over, I find my fire roaring away as my back lands on the rug before it.

"Your fire looks perfect to me, Kitten," he says, staring down at me as if I'm the most precious thing in the world.

"I missed you," I admit, needing him to know that everything he's felt since I sent him away wasn't one-sided.

"Why'd you do it?" he asks, rubbing his hands up and down my thighs, his thumbs getting dangerously close to my damp bikini bottoms.

"B-because you hurt me."

"Fuck, I wish I hadn't."

"Me too. Can you promise me something?"

"Anything." The honesty shining in his eyes tells me that he means it.

"Never lie to me again—"

"Ne—" I reach up and press my fingers to his lips, cutting off his words.

"I'm not finished." He nods and I continue. "Never lie to me again and never think that I can't handle the truth. I'm a Harrow Creek girl, I can handle anything."

"I know, Har. You're so fucking strong. I'm so sorry."

"Show me."

His hands drop to either side of my head, his fingers digging into the shaggy rug beneath me as he drops his lips to mine and rolls his hips in a way that makes me moan.

"Fuck, Har. You're so fucking sexy," he growls against my lips. "I'm never going to get enough of you."

"I hope not."

My nails scratch down his back until I find the waistband on his jeans and slip my fingers beneath them and his boxers, gripping onto his ass and pulling him tighter against me.

He kisses me as if I'm the air he needs to breathe, and I know without a doubt that I made the right choice. My heart couldn't cope with watching him walk away from me again.

"Kyle," I gasp when he pulls the small triangle of fabric away and pinches my nipple. My back arches off the rug with my need for more.

Ripping his lips from mine, he trails wet sloppy kisses down my neck and chest until he reveals my other breast and sucks the hard peak into his hot mouth.

"Oh God," I moan as his tongue laves at me.

"Missed you. Missed you so much," he mumbles against my skin as he descends my stomach, pulling at the ties at my hips.

The fabric falls away and his hands press on the inside of my thighs as he lowers himself to his stomach. He moves his face forward but he doesn't stop where I want him to. Instead, he latches on to the soft skin of my thigh and sucks until I swear the skin is about to break, rebranding me as his.

"So fucking perfect," he whispers, his fingertip tracing his mark, his hot breath sends a shiver of desire racing across my skin.

"Kyle," I moan, reaching for him.

I knock his cap off his head and thread my fingers in his long locks, pulling him toward where I need him.

"Horny, Kitten?"

"Kyle, yes," I cry, hoping it'll encourage him to stop teasing me. "Please."

"My pleasure."

He leans forward and sucks hard on my clit.

"Oh my God," I squeal, thrashing around on the rug.

He releases me after a second and his tongue sets to work making me lose my goddamn mind.

"Yes, yes," I cry as my release begins to crest.

One of his fingers circles my entrance, my muscles contracting, desperate to pull him deep inside me.

I pull at his hair harder, trying to tell him what I need without finding the words.

My head spins, my body flies, and my chest heaves as I climb higher and higher.

Finally, he pushes two fingers deep inside me and bends them in the perfect way that makes me detonate.

"Kyle," I scream as my body shatters into a million pieces.

Wave after wave of red-hot pleasure courses through my

body, leaving me heaving for breath and my limbs heavy with exhaustion.

He doesn't pull back until he's squeezed the last ounce of ecstasy out of me.

Sitting up, his lips pull into an accomplished smirk as his chin glistens with the evidence of my release.

Every muscle south of my waist clenches with the sight, to the point that I almost push him back down to do it all over again.

Clearly able to read my mind, he chuckles and wipes the back of his hand across his face before he stands.

I panic for a second that he's about to walk away, but then his hands drop to his waistband and he pops the button, pushing both his jeans and his boxers down his thighs.

"Oh God," I whimper as his hard length springs free.

He smiles down at me as he kicks the fabric from his legs and drops his hand to his length, stroking a few times as he trails his eyes leisurely down my body.

His gaze scorches every place it touches until I'm squirming with desire once more.

"Ky," I warn, hoping it'll break him out of his trance.

Hearing my voice, he drops to his knees between my parted thighs before rubbing the head of his cock through my folds, coating himself in my wetness.

Our eyes hold as silent promises pass back and forth between us.

"I love you," he mouths, dropping lower and pushing the tip inside me.

My body tenses at the invasion, but the second his hand skims up my body and comes to stop in its home around my throat, I relax.

Taking his weight on his elbow beside my head, he pushes the whole way in, and his tongue parts my lips, teasing mine with the same gentleness.

"Kyle," I moan, pleasure rippling through me as tears

burn my eyes.

"I'm so sorry. I'm so sorry," he says between kisses as he loves me.

"Ky." I pull his head up so he can look into my eyes. "It's okay. I understand. What's done is done."

He stares at me for a beat, his body stills.

"I..." he starts, but soon shakes his head before dropping his lips back to mine for a life-changing kiss.

I cling on to him, clawing at his back as he ups his speed. Wrapping his hand around my thigh, he presses it against my chest, allowing him to take me deeper and hit the perfect spot with every thrust.

"You feel so incredible," he murmurs when he's forced to break our kiss to drag in a few deep breaths. "So fucking tight."

"Kyle, I'm gonna—"

"I know, Kitten. I can feel it." He drops his fingers between our bodies and pinches my clit. "Let go, baby. Come all over my cock."

"Ky," I cry as I do exactly as I'm told thanks to another sharp pinch and strong thrust.

My body snaps and my pussy sucks him in deeper a second before he throws his head back and roars out his release.

The muscles in his neck, chest, and stomach ripple and pull, the sight sends aftershocks shooting around my body.

Dropping my leg, I slam my hands down on his chest. He's not expecting it and as I hoped, he falls back on his ass, allowing me to crawl onto his lap.

"Hey, Kitten." He smirks, his eyes sparkling in delight as he comes down from his high.

"Hey."

"I think I need to do that again," he admits, but it's not necessary, I can already feel him growing hard against me.

"Want to take this to the hot tub?" I ask as his hands trail up my back to undo my bikini top so it falls from my body.

"Hmm... I can't think of anything I want more." He balls up the scrap of fabric and throws it across the room.

"Okay but I'm going to need that." My eyes follow the movement of my top.

"Like fuck you are."

He stands with me in his arms as if I weigh nothing, and he carries me toward the door he entered through.

"We can't go in na—"

"Says who, Kitten?"

"The welcome pack," I admit, my cheeks heating at my rule-following.

"Fuck the welcome pack, you're not wearing clothes again until we're forced to leave this place."

His hands squeeze my ass until the bite of pain mixes with my desire and my core floods with heat.

"Fuck, I can feel that."

"Yeah, then you'd better do something about it."

Before I've realized he's released me, I'm on my feet, the top half of my body bent over the hot tub.

His hand lands on my bare ass cheek with a loud slap and I squeal in shock, my heat zeroing in on my pussy.

"My girl loves it a bit rough, huh?"

His hand skims up my spine, threading into my hair and pulling my head up, forcing my back to arch.

"Ready?"

"Hell yeaaaaah," I scream as he slams into me with each thrust. "Oh shit."

Gone is the gentle lover from beside the fire and in his place is the hot-headed, bad boy that I know so well.

"Kyle," I scream into the silent forest as he pounds into me so hard that my feet start to leave the floor.

His grip on my hair tightens, the pain so fucking addicting as he pushes me closer and closer to another release.

"Give it to me, Kitten. Give me everything."

"Kyle," I cry, my body quaking with the strength of my release.

"Who do you belong to, Kitten?" he asks between powerful thrusts as he chases his own orgasm.

"You, Kyle. Only ever you."

"Fuck yes," he booms as his cock jerks violently inside me.

He falls forward, his hot chest pressed against my sweat covered back.

Wrapping one hand around my neck and the other around my waist, he holds me tightly to him.

"Never fucking forget it," he whispers in my ear. "I'll go to the ends of the earth to find you, Kitten."

I nod, too overwhelmed by him and my intense release to respond.

"I love you. I love you so fucking much."

Standing, he pulls me up with him and drops his hand down my stomach until he finds my swollen folds.

I want to tell him no more, but he bypasses my clit and drops straight to my entrance, dipping his finger into the evidence of our multiple releases that I can feel beginning to run down my thighs.

"Me and you, Kitten. Me and you."

His lips find the side of my neck and he presses them there for the longest time as the fresh early evening air cools our heated skin.

"Ready to relax?" he whispers in my ear when I shiver in his arms.

"I should probably go clean up first."

"Be quick."

He swats me on the ass as I walk away, my skin tingling with his attention until I disappear into the cabin and all but run to the bathroom so I can get back to him quicker.

KYLE

I can't stop the smile that splits my face as I watch her slip into the cabin.

I knew going along with Stella's crazy plan was a risk and I told myself over and over on the drive here that being sent away again was the most likely outcome to this little stunt. But even with repeating that in my head, I couldn't stop my hopes from rising.

Stella thought she was ready to talk, to clear the air and consider the future. I had to trust she was right.

The moment Harley's shocked and angry eyes locked on mine, my heart dropped and I knew that Stella was wrong.

Fuck knows how I managed to change her mind, but I'll be forever grateful for whatever it was.

Unable to wipe the smile off my face, I flip the lid on the hot tub and climb in, allowing the hot water to soothe my muscles.

I rest back, looking out over the sea of trees before me, and rest my head back, wondering how I've managed to land myself here.

You're a lucky motherfucker, a little voice says in my head as I hear footsteps heading my way.

Looking to the side, I find my girl, still fully naked and with two bottles of beer in both hands.

"I've died and gone to heaven," I say, my eyes feasting on her bronzed, beautiful skin.

"This place is pretty insane."

"I'm not talking about the place, Kitten. You could be walking to me like that in my old trailer and I'd still be in paradise."

A shy smile curls at her lips.

"Too late for that, Kitten. I've already had you twice tonight, and I can tell you now that there's more yet to come."

"Oh yeah?" Fire burns bright in her dark eyes as she steps up to the tub and drops her gaze to my body. It's hidden by the water but I'm sure she sees enough to know I'm hard again.

Reaching for myself, I wrap my fingers around my length and start jerking off.

Her teeth sink into her bottom lips as she watches my movement.

"You're insatiable."

"I've been waiting for you for a long time, Harley."

"It's been a few days," she mutters, placing the beers in the drink holders and climbs in with me.

"Harley," I say with a smile, dragging her over by her hips and planting her on my lap. "I've wanted you for as long as I can remember. You were the first girl I ever really saw. No one else has ever compared to you."

"Ky," she breathes, snuggling into my side as I wrap my arms around her and hold her tight.

"It's always been you, Kitten."

She falls silent in my arms, probably remembering all the things I've done to prove the words I just said aren't true. But none of my actions were not because I didn't want her.

"I always thought you deserved better," I whisper, answering her unspoken questions. "I always knew that you'd get out of the Creek one day and make a better life for yourself. I knew that if anything happened between us, that I'd always hold you back. And of course there was always the little issue of Zayn digging me an early grave if I even looked at you a little too long."

She tenses against me as I mention her brother.

"It's okay, Har. He knows everything."

"And you're still breathing?"

"He's screwing one of your best friends. He didn't really have a leg to stand on."

"It's true but I didn't think he'd let that stand in his way."

"I talked him around to it. I have a way with words."

"It seems you do because when I first found you here earlier, I wanted to stab you with a blunt knife and look at me now."

She wiggles on my lap and I groan in frustration.

I twist her in my arms so she straddles my lap and I can look into her eyes. "I meant every word I said to you, you know that, right?"

"I do…"

"But?" I prompt when she loses herself in her thoughts once again.

"You still hurt me, Kyle. Just because I've accepted your apology, it doesn't mean I've forgotten."

"I know, Kitten," I say, reaching up and cupping her cheek. She leans into my touch and it's all I need to know that there really is a future for us from here on out. "I don't expect you to forget just like that, but I can't tell you enough how much I appreciate you giving me a chance."

She nods at me, sucking her bottom lip into her mouth.

"Spit it out, Har. No more secrets, remember."

"That's just it," she says almost nervously. "Is there anything else I need to know?"

"No, the only thing I was hiding was Gr—" Her hand

lands over my mouth and she shakes her head. "Okay," I agree, not saying his name out loud.

"You're not... you're not... involved with anything from the Creek, are you?" she asks hesitantly.

"No, Kitten. The other night was the first time I'd been back there. I have no intention of ever doing so again either."

She nods, accepting my answer.

"What about Kane?"

Unease zips through me at the mention of my brother. We've yet to have a decent conversation about how he knew where she was so fast because he's barely been at the house since. I already had my suspicions about what he's doing and it only made them worse.

I know who he was involved with before I went away, and I'm terrified that he's only got in deeper since being gone and losing Gran.

"I... I don't know. He won't tell me fuck all but honestly... I'm scared."

"Shit," she mutters. "He needs to leave all that bullshit behind."

"I couldn't agree more. But you know as well as I do that it's easier said than done if what we're both thinking is true."

"We need to help. We need to do something. We need—"

"Har," I say, cutting off her words. "I agree, of course I do. But we can't get involved. Kane will do whatever he wants, no matter what we think or do about it. And interfering will only make whatever he's doing more dangerous. We need to leave him to it and trust that he knows what he's doing.

"He's a good person beneath it all. We've got to believe that will win in the end."

We both fall silent, only the sounds of our breathing and the jets beneath us filling my ears.

"Does Letty know we're in Rosewood?" I ask, needing to break the silence and the concern that's coming off her in waves. Not that I think my question will alleviate any of that.

"Not that I know of. I haven't spoken to her in weeks, and I know Mom hasn't either. I'm worried about her," she admits.

"I'm sure she's fine. She's off at college enjoying herself. Isn't forgetting home and your family what you're supposed to do?"

She shrugs and falls forward into my chest.

"Everything will be fine, Har. I promise." Granted, it's a pretty lofty promise to make, but with her by my side, I'm pretty confident I can keep it. And ultimately, our siblings' lives have nothing to do with us really. It won't be long and we'll be heading off to college and embarking on the beginning of the rest of our lives. We're better off focusing on that than things we have zero control over.

———

The rest of our stay at the cabin was more than I ever could have wished for.

We spent hours talking about our childhoods, opening up about how we felt about each other and we've discussed what happens from here on out.

I'm not stupid, I know I'm still in the doghouse and have a lot of things to make up for, but I fully intend on doing so.

After we got out of the hot tub that first night, I stayed. Harley called Stella and ripped her a new one for her stunt. I could barely hold it together as she faked being angry with her friend. Credit where credit's due, she's a better actress than I ever gave her credit for, even I almost believed she was still angry.

When she finally came clean, she could barely stand she was laughing so hard. Seeing the pure delight on her face as she roared with laughter made my entire year. I pulled her into my arms and held her tight as tears of joy streamed down her face.

By the time we both climb into Stella's Porsche to drive back to Rosewood, I'm happier than I ever remember being.

"This is one sweet ride," I say, flooring the accelerator and throwing us both back into our seats with the force. "Makes this whole trip worth it," I deadpan.

"Keep going it'll be the last ride you get," she sasses, sliding her hand up my thigh until she's cupping my semi. She traces the outline through my sweats ensuring it's at full mast in seconds.

"Kitten," I growl. "We've got a long-ass drive, and unless you intend on following through, then I suggest you stop."

"I'd rather not have to grovel to Stella because you crashed her baby," she says, pulling her hand away from me.

I snatch it up before she drops it back in her own lap and I place it back on my thigh.

"I didn't say stop touching me." I glance over at her and give her one of my killer smiles that I already know will make her squirm in her seat.

"I'm not ready to go home," she admits, changing the subject.

"What do you think your mom is going to say?"

She shrugs. "It's all her fault. She can't really say anything."

"You need to give her a break. If it weren't for her then this might not have happened," I say threading my fingers through hers and lifting her hand to my lips, kissing her knuckles.

"I'm not mad she did it, I'm mad she didn't tell me."

"I know, but like you said, it's time to focus on the future now."

"You're right," she breathes.

We spend the journey back talking about our futures, what colleges we might want to go to and the things we want from life. It's incredible.

Not long ago, I didn't think I had any kind of future ahead

of me, certainly not a chance at a decent college. But thanks to Jada, Kane, and the amazing girl beside me. I might just get everything I ever wanted.

We go straight to the Hunter's house when we finally get back later that night. We walk inside with our hands locked together and wide smiles on our faces. Zayn's already back, his car was outside but I don't let it bother me.

We dump our bags in the hallway and make our way down to the den where they're waiting for us.

Harley pushes the door open and every set of eyes in the room turns toward us.

I pull Harley into my arms and drop my lips to hers, bending her backward as if we're in an old movie and making a show of claiming her as mine.

Whoops and hollers sound out around the room but they're soon drowned out when I pull her back up and she slips her tongue into my mouth, deepening the kiss.

I'm powerless to resist her and meet her move for move, holding her flush against my body. That is until something soft hits my head.

"Alright. Just because I said you could, it doesn't mean you get to rub it in my face, fucker," Zayn grumps.

"What? Like you don't do it to me with Poppy." Harley pins her brother with a death stare after ripping her lips from mine.

"Okay children, calm down," Stella says, taking control of the situation. She pushes from the couch she was sitting on, walks over and takes Harley off me, wrapping her up in a hug.

"Thank you," Harley whispers in her ear.

"I got your back, girl. Plus, I had fun with the guys."

"Hell yeah, she did. Justin and Rich didn't know what hit them," Ash announces, making Harley's eyes almost pop out of her head.

"Tell me you didn't," she begs her friend.

"It was just a bit of fun. You're right about his cock though." She holds her fingers up, mimicking the size much like Chelsea did as everyone falls over laughing.

"Come and sit down," Ruby encourages, forcing Ash to shift over on their couch.

"You want sodas?" Poppy asks, walking over to the small refrigerator in here.

"Please," we say in unison as I drop down onto the couch and pull her onto my lap.

The guys eagerly catch us both up on all the gossip we missed while in our private slice of heaven and the nine of us laugh and enjoy ourselves.

Back in the Creek, I hung out with a group of guys, all of whom I called friends, but it wasn't until I was locked away that I realized how little we really meant to each other. They never bothered reaching out to me or visiting, and I never invited them.

But this, this feels different. These people surrounding me make me feel like I belong for the first time in my life. They prove to me that things can be better and that I don't just have to be the guy from the Creek who ended up in juvie. Yes, that might always be a part of who I am, but it's only a small part.

I smile to myself as I sit back and enjoy the easy banter between the other three couples and Stella, who's more than capable of holding her own by herself.

Eventually, someone suggests ordering pizza and without planning it, we all spend the entire evening hanging out in Zayn's den. But as fun as it is, I'm already craving alone time with my girl. I've been spoiled this week, it's going to take a bit of time to get used to sharing her again.

"Wanna get out of here?" I whisper in her ear while the others are distracted.

"Sure. We're gonna head out," she announces to the room without even asking me what I had in mind.

She hops up from my lap and I take her hand when she offers it.

We walk down the hallway and when we get to the stairs, she moves as if we're going to head up.

"Not yet," I whisper in her ear, pushing her toward the front door.

"Where are we going?" she asks as we walk from her driveway.

"Wait and see."

It's not an overly long walk, although more time has passed than I was expecting by the time we step down onto the sand.

"You wanted to come to the beach?" she asks, her brows knitting together.

"Yeah, I thought it might be romantic."

"You don't need to make gestures to try to convince me of anything, Ky," she says, looking up at me.

"I know, and this isn't a gesture. I just thought it would be nice. Plus, I was getting annoyed with sharing you."

"Aaand there's the truth," she jokes.

"What can I say, I'm a selfish guy." I shrug like it's nothing and she laughs at me.

"You're right, this is nice."

We walk hand in hand along the damp sand in silence, lost in our own thoughts. A lot has changed for both of us in a very short amount of time, but I wouldn't have it any other way.

Even with the pain and heartache, we've ended up exactly where we should be.

When we're between two dunes and hidden from the few other locals out on an evening walk, I pull her to a stop and twist her into my body.

"Hey," she says, looking up at me with her eyes full of love and happiness.

"Hey, Kitten."

"What is it?" she asks, clearly sensing that I want to say something important.

"I just want you to know that I'd go through all of that again time and time again if it meant it ended with having you in my arms."

A goofy smile curls at her lips.

"You're the only thing I ever really wanted and the one thing I knew I couldn't have. I don't know what I did to get this chance with you, but I promise you that I'm never going to ruin it or take it for granted."

"Hey," she says, running her thumb across my bottom lip. "You don't need to—"

"I do, Har. Everything we talked about at the cabin, I meant it. I want everything with you, Harley Hunter. I always have."

"Kyle," she swoons.

"I love you, Kitten."

"I love you too."

I drop my lips to her and hold her tight as I kiss her as if it's our first and last rolled into one.

"How's it feel?" I ask when I finally let her up for air, both our chests heaving and desire darkening our eyes.

"How's what feel?"

"To be owned by a Legend?"

EPILOGUE

Harley
Three months later...

"Are you disappointed that you're not up there like you should have been?" I ask Kyle as we sit in the bleachers at school waiting for the graduation ceremony to start.

I'm sandwiched between him and Ruby. I have no clue how she and Ash managed to score tickets for today, but they're here supporting our graduating friends.

A wave of sadness washes over me that so many of the people who have been a part of our everyday lives for so long are going to be heading off to college soon and leaving us behind to endure another year at Rosewood High.

"Nah. If I were graduating now, it would have been from Creek High, and no one wants their diploma from there. It's better this way," he says, smiling down at me and squeezing my hand.

I know he's telling the truth, but still a part of me wonders how much he hates having to do another year.

"Plus," he adds. "I could never begrudge spending more time with you even if it means more high school."

Tingles race through me as I think about what our senior year is going to entail, and I can't fight my smile.

As expected, both Ruby and Ash have been promoted to captains of the cheer squad and the football team, with Kyle and I as their assistants.

Our new senior team might not quite match up to the ones who are down there with their caps and gowns on, but with a few more months of hard work, Ash and Kyle are confident that they'll see some success this year and do Jake and the boys proud.

Ruby and I are equally as positive when it comes to our new squad.

We were both blown away by the standard of the girls who turned up to tryouts a few weeks ago, even Chelsea was stunned.

And despite the fact we're now missing one of our key players, I'm pretty confident that nationals could be in our future once more.

I really fucking hope so because I'll give anything to see Rubes lift that trophy. Hell knows she's worked hard enough for it.

Pulling my cell from my pocket, I quickly snap a picture of all the graduates sitting in the rows in front of the stage and send it to Stella.

Only a couple of weeks after our break in the mountains, she showed up at school bearing the news we were all dreading.

She was leaving.

And she wasn't just hopping across the country this time, she was leaving the country and heading to England like she feared she might be.

"How's she doing?" Kyle asks, noticing who I'm messaging.

"She's good. Bored. She's not starting at her new school until September and she's beginning to lose her mind I think."

"Can't she come back for the summer?"

I open my mouth to reply, but think better of it and shoot her another message making the suggestion, but I don't get to wait to see her response because Principal Hartmann takes to the stage to begin the ceremony.

He talks through this year's graduating class's successes. He reminisces on the team's incredible season before discussing other teams and other events that deserve celebrating until he gets to our impressive second chance at nationals the other month.

When he starts inviting the students up to get their diplomas and to individually congratulate them, I begin to get emotional.

Because he can read me like a book, Kyle turns to me and places a kiss on my cheek.

"I fucking love you," he whispers in my ear.

"This is ridiculous," I mutter, wiping my eyes with the back of my hand as I watch my brother take to the stage. I glance over at Poppy who's sitting beside Mom and notice that I'm not the only one in tears.

She notices my attention and looks over, giving me a sad smile.

I know that Zayn is only going to MKU—after a very long discussion with Mom about his change of plans—and it's not far away, but the two of them have become very used to being in each other's pockets every minute of the day. It's going to be another huge adjustment for Pops. But I've got every confidence that she can handle it. Even if it means she takes over my place as the gooseberry of the group. I have a feeling that Zayn will be home any chance he gets, or he'll be sneaking her into his dorm at every possible opportunity. He tried to convince Mom to get him an apartment, but she drew the line at that, although I can't help thinking that she's just holding off until Poppy joins him in a year's time—because we all know that's what she's going to do.

"What are you thinking about?" Kyle whispers in my ear.

"The future."

"Ah, and what does that look like?"

I shrug. We've both said we want to go to college, but we haven't talked much more about it since our drive back from the mountains. It's something we really need to sit down and discuss as senior year rolls around. I have no huge desire to go anywhere specific, Letty and Zayn—not that he's following his, since he found love—were the ones with the college dreams, I'd just be happy to get in after my struggle with math.

"I'm not sure other than we'll be together."

"Hell yeah, we will," he agrees with a smile, lifting my hand to his mouth.

I was worried the ceremony would take forever, but all too soon, the final students make their way up to the stage and we're listening to Hartmann close the ceremony.

"I can't believe my last baby will be up there next year," Mom muses as we make our way down to go and find the graduates.

"Don't go getting all emosh on me, Mom," I joke, earning an amused smirk from Kyle. We both know I was the one fighting with my emotions the last hour.

"I'm not. I'm good," she lies. "I'm so proud of you all, you know that, right?" she asks, pulling me to a stop, forcing others to swerve around us. "I know I've been hard on you all about your education and your future, but it's only because I want you to have all the options that your father and I didn't have." Dad stands awkwardly behind us, obviously hearing Mom's words.

"We know, Mom, and we appreciate it." I reach out and squeeze her hand when I see a little sadness creep in.

She's worried about Letty, we all are after her radio silence the past few weeks. It's not like her and the longer she ignores us, the more concerned I'm getting.

She was more than just my sister when we were kids, she was one of my best friends and I can't help feeling abandoned. It's ridiculous, I know. She's probably just off living her best life, but there's a heaviness in my gut that tells me it's not that at all. Her Instagram is empty, whereas before it was full of nights out and her laughing with her new college friends.

Something is wrong. I know it is.

We take off again, searching for Zayn through the crowd.

Unsurprisingly, Poppy is the first to spot him and she flies at him. He catches her and spins her around with a wide smile on his face before slowing to a stop and planting his lips on hers.

"They're not going to cope well, are they?" Mom mutters, clearly having similar thoughts to me earlier.

"They'll be fine. Plus, it's only for a few months then she can join him."

"And what about you two?"

"We're going together," Kyle states, wrapping his arm around my shoulder.

She shakes her head at us and turns back to congratulate Zayn.

The others surround us, all the seniors have wide smiles on their faces as the team and the squad congregates together, the guys all pulling their girls into their sides.

"We fucking did it, motherfuckers," Jake booms over our group as a round of cheers sound out.

"Time to fucking celebrate," Ethan adds, slamming his lips down on Rae's and crushing her against his body.

"Too fucking right." Amalie is the next to be molested

before Mason drags Cami into his arms, and Shane rubs his hand lovingly over Chelsea's bulging stomach. She's due any day now and I swear she's never looked more beautiful.

I look around at my friends, that lump back, clogging my throat as I think about having a year here without them all. I glance at Justin and Rich who are both laughing, I'll probably even miss those idiots.

"You okay, Kitten?" Kyle asks, pressing his front against my back and wrapping his arms around my waist.

"Yeah," I force out as Ash and Ruby join us. "It's just the end of an era, you know."

"It is," Ruby agrees. "But next year is our year."

"Fucking right it is," Ash booms. "We've got it in the bag. Rosewood High doesn't know what's about to hit them."

We watch the celebrations unfold for a few more minutes before everyone begins to disperse to celebrate with their families before the party at Ethan's this evening.

Excitement races through me as I think about the wild night we've all got ahead of us.

"Right, I've got him, let's go," Mom says, dragging Zayn along behind her.

We head to Zayn's favorite restaurant for a meal to celebrate, just like we did two years ago for Letty.

I glance at the empty chair, a heaviness I'm beginning to get used to pressing down on my shoulders.

She should have been here today, and although Zayn hasn't said anything about her absence, I know it's hurt him. I can see it in his eyes.

"To Zayn," Mom says, dragging me from my thoughts and holding her drink up in a toast. "Congrats, baby. I can't wait to see what the future holds for you."

Dad sits awkwardly at the other end of the table not saying a word as Zayn reaches over and takes Poppy's hand under the table.

"Thanks, Mom. For everything. We couldn't have done any of this without you."

"Always." She nods, her own eyes looking a little glassy.

"Now let's eat before you all want to leave to get drunk." She rolls her eyes in mock annoyance.

The food is incredible, and both Zayn and Kyle eat more than I thought possible.

We say goodbye to Dad in the parking lot, all of us promise to come and visit soon. It's been a few weeks since we all ventured back to the Creek and I feel bad about not seeing him more, but the truth is, all of us hate that place, and aside from big events like this, he refuses to leave. It makes things hella awkward.

The drive back with Mom and Kyle is in silence. Tension comes off her in waves showing what an effort she's put in to appear so positive and put together in front of my dad.

She'd never admit it, but I'm pretty sure she still loves him deep down. Hell knows she begged him enough to start this new life with us.

Kyle squeezes my hand in support, and I smile over at him, glad he was able to come today.

My mood instantly changes though when Mom pulls up to the house beside a car I feel like I haven't seen in forever.

"Letty is here."

I fly from the car and toward the house as Zayn pulls in behind us and screeches to a halt before he also jumps out, following me inside.

There are bags in the hallway and I take off toward the kitchen when I hear a noise but I soon come to a grinding halt when I get a look at my older sister.

She's got tears cascading down her cheeks, and when I drop my eyes down her body, I find her thinner than I think I've ever seen.

"Letty," I gasp, racing toward her as Mom steps into the doorway.

"Scarlett, what's wrong?"

"I'm so sorry, Mom," she sobs as Mom pushes past Zayn to wrap her oldest daughter in her arms. "I'm so sorry, I've totally let you down."

Lifting my head from Letty's shoulder, Zayn and I exchange concerned glances as Kyle comes to stand beside him watching Letty break in our arms.

Guilt covers his face but somehow I don't think this has anything to do with Kane. Or at least, I hope not.

Letty & Kane's story is coming in my upcoming Maddison Kings University series.

Start with the prequel, The Mistakes You Make

ACKNOWLEDGMENTS

I can't believe this is it. The end of an era!

This series means so much to me. It was totally unexpected, Jake and the boys we're totally unexpected to me. But when Jake popped into my head, he would not freaking leave, no matter how much I begged him. And am I so glad he stuck around!

I hope you enjoyed the final book in this series and Harley finally getting her HEA. I've had their story in my head for a long time, I always knew her boy wasn't going to be Kane, sorry to those of you who were gunning for him.

But, as you may have guessed, this isn't the end for Kane, or many of our boys because in only a few months, we're heading to Maddison Kings University.

I'm giving you a whole bunch of new characters that I know you're going to love along with some of the ones from Rosewood that you already know and love.

I can't wait to bring you these stories.

So there's only one last thing to say, THANK YOU for still being here with me. The fact you've read this entire series and invited my boys into your lives means everything to me.

Here's to what comes next...
Tracy xo

P.S. Don't worry, I may just have a plan for Stella too!

ABOUT THE AUTHOR

Tracy Lorraine is a new adult and contemporary romance author. Tracy has recently-ish turned thirty and lives in a cute Cotswold village in England with her husband, baby girl and lovable but slightly crazy dog. Having always been a bookaholic with her head stuck in her Kindle Tracy decided to try her hand at a story idea she dreamt up and hasn't looked back since.

Be the first to find out about new releases and offers. Sign up to my newsletter here.

If you want to know what I'm up to and see teasers and snippets of what I'm working on, then you need to be in my Facebook group Tracy's Angels.

Keep up to date with Tracy's books at
www.tracylorraine.com

ALSO BY TRACY LORRAINE

<u>**Falling Series**</u>

Falling for Ryan: Part One #1

Falling for Ryan: Part Two #2

Falling for Jax #3

Falling for Daniel (An Falling Series Novella)

Falling for Ruben #4

Falling for Fin #5

Falling for Lucas #6

Falling for Caleb #7

Falling for Declan #8

Falling For Liam #9

<u>**Forbidden Series**</u>

Falling for the Forbidden #1

Losing the Forbidden #2

Fighting for the Forbidden #3

Craving Redemption #4

Demanding Redemption #5

Avoiding Temptation #6

Chasing Temptation #7

<u>**Rebel Ink Series**</u>

Hate You #1

Trick You #2

Defy You #3

Play You #4

Inked (A Rebel Ink/Driven Crossover)

Rosewood High Series

Thorn #1

Paine #2

Savage #3

Fierce #4

Hunter #5

Faze (#6 Prequel)

Fury #6

Legend #7

Maddison Kings University Series

TMYM: Prequel

TRYS #1

TDYW #2

TBYS #3

TVYC #4

TDYD #5

Ruined Series

Ruined Plans #1

Ruined by Lies #2

Ruined Promises #3

Never Forget Series

Never Forget Him #1

Never Forget Us #2

Everywhere & Nowhere #3

Chasing Series

Chasing Logan

The Cocktail Girls

His Manhattan

Her Kensington

THE MISTAKES YOU MAKE
SNEAK PEEK
CHAPTER ONE

Letty

"For the record, I think this is a really bad idea," Harley, my little sister, moans from my passenger seat.

"It'll be fine," I grit out through clenched teeth. It's not the first time she's said similar words to me today, and I'm fed up with hearing them.

She scoffs at my response and folds her arms over her chest.

I know she doesn't want to be here. I know she doesn't want to go to this party.

"I told you, you could have stayed at Dad's."

"And leave you alone? Nah, I don't think so."

"I don't need my kid sister tagging along for support."

She turns her narrowed eyes on me.

"He's not going to be there," I assure her for the millionth time.

"It's a Harrow Creek party. They will be there," she warns.

My stomach flips and I fight to keep my expression neutral.

"I've been assured they won't. And if they show up, then we'll just slip out unnoticed."

Harley's eyes burn into the side of my face, but I refuse to look at her and keep my eyes on the road as we make our way to Skylar's house.

It's her birthday weekend and her parents have stupidly left her the house. They think she's having a quiet night with some girlfriends. They have no idea that almost every teenager in Harrow Creek is about to descend on their home.

I haven't been back here to see our dad or my old friends in months, and I'm desperate to rediscover the old me.

It's no great secret that I hate the place, but unfortunately, when Mom found us a new life in the neighboring town of Rosewood, we were forced to leave some of those we love behind—mainly our dad, who for some crazy reason didn't want to leave his beloved trailer and shithole of a place behind.

Harley's knee continues to jiggle nervously in the passenger seat as we drive down the street lined with cars, indicating that tonight's party is well underway.

I eventually find a parking space and kill the engine, but I don't rush to get out.

Butterflies flutter in my belly as all of her concerns about tonight race to the surface.

I need to believe what my friends are telling me and that I'll be able to enjoy my night without looking over my shoulder and being ready to run at any moment. But Harley is right, the chances of him being here are high, and my decision to try to have a normal night with my old friends could be one of the biggest mistakes I've ever made.

"It's not too late to turn around. We could order a pizza, watch a movie," she offers.

I know she doesn't have a lot of interest in this party. She was only thirteen when we left this place, it was easier for her to leave her friends behind and start over. But at sixteen, I was turning my back on possible lifelong friends. Friends I didn't want to leave behind.

I glance down at my little black dress and suck in a deep breath.

"No. We're going to enjoy our night."

He has ruined enough of my life in the past. I am an adult now. I'm a college student. I should not be running scared from the boy who tried to make my life a living hell.

"Okay," Harley concedes, pulling the handle and shouldering the door open.

A second later, I follow. Locking the car behind me and smoothing down the front of my dress.

I felt good, and I didn't need the looks from a few of the guys loitering outside of Skylar's house to tell me that I looked good. The dress I'm wearing clings to my curves like a second skin, my hair is sleek, hanging down past my shoulder blades, and my makeup is dark, accentuating my gold-flecked dark eyes.

I pull my leather jacket around my torso a little tighter as I catch up with Harley on the sidewalk.

"Ready to party, lil' sis?"

She glances over at me, concern still evident in her eyes, but she forces it down and plasters a smile on her face. She's sixteen now, most would probably say too young for the kind of debauchery happening under the roof of the house in front of us. But we're Creek kids. We grew up surrounded by this. She's already seen worse than what might be happening here tonight. Hell, I was up to all sorts of shit I don't want to even consider Harley getting involved with when I was sixteen.

Shaking my regrets from my head, I take her hand in mine and together we make our way through the crowds to find Skylar and my old group of friends.

Music booms from the speakers someone has set up in the living room, making the floor rattle as we make our way through the kitchen.

"Here," I say, handing Harley a Solo cup with a weak vodka orange inside. Mine, however, isn't so weak. The prospect of bumping into the enemy forces me to splash a little extra alcohol in mine to help take the edge off my nerves.

I drink half down in one go, reveling in the burn as the vodka slips down my throat and begins to warm my belly.

My muscles ache to join the crowd that I know will be in front of the speakers and let go.

College is great. New York is fantastic but still, you can't beat a Creek party.

"Come on, I know where they'll be." I take Harley's hand once more and we push our way through the mass of people toward the living room.

Most pay us little attention as we pass, but a few recognize us and nod or smile in greeting.

There would have been a time when everyone would have spoken to us, but we gave up that right when we packed all our shit and moved.

We're outsiders now, and I feel it more and more every time I come back here.

I see a flash of blonde on the other side of the living area that's been turned into a makeshift dance floor for the night, and I head that way.

"Letty," Skylar squeals the second she sees me, she steps away from the guy she's dancing with and throws her arms around my shoulders. "It's so good to see you." The slur in her voice indicates just how much she's had to drink already, and when she pulls back, I notice her eyes are blown too.

"You too, Sky. It's been too long. Happy Birthday."

"Come on, let me introduce you to the guys." She threads her fingers through mine and drags me toward her group of friends. Most I know from school but there are a couple of new additions, including the guy who quickly drags her away from me and wraps her in his arms.

Jealousy burns through me at the way he stares down at her. So much love and adoration it makes my chest hurt.

"This is Matt," she says, happiness laced through her voice.

I know all about him. When we've spoken recently, he's all she talks about.

Hearing how happy she is back here is about the only thing that makes me homesick. Not for Harrow Creek, but for those I love.

"Sky says you're at Columbia. Impressive."

"T-thanks," I stutter. "It's pretty awesome."

Going to college—especially a college like Columbia—makes me an anomaly around those I grew up with. Only a few from the Creek get a shot at college, most don't even graduate. And if they do, it's more likely they'll end up at Harrow Community College, where Sky and Matt are. A few lucky ones get out, I know of a handful who are at Maddison Kings—the closest college to the Creek—but that's got more to do with connections than it has to do with ability.

"Being back here must suck after New York," Sky mutters.

"Nah, it's home."

Truth? This place is hell. If it weren't for Dad or the few friends I still have from here, then I'd never return.

The whole place is depressing.

"How's college?"

"Yeah, it's good. It's Harrow College, doesn't get better than that," she jokes.

Sky always had big dreams to get out of the Creek just

like I did. Only her life and her plans didn't quite go the way mine did.

I have my mom to thank for everything. If we were still here, still living in Dad's damp old trailer, then I doubt that I'd have ever had a shot at a college like Columbia. No doubt I'd be at community college and enjoying it about as much as Sky's face shows she really is.

"I'll go and get you ladies more drinks." Matt nods at Harley who's been standing beside me awkwardly listening to this conversation as if she's a part of it.

"Baby Hunter, how's it going?" Sky asks. "Bry is around here somewhere." She looks around for her little brother but with the number of bodies filling her house, it's no surprise she doesn't spot him.

"I'm sure I'll catch up with him. Happy Birthday."

"Thanks, sweetie."

Matt quickly reappears with some very strong drinks for us and after a few minutes, Flo Rida pumps through the speakers and we forget our shouted conversation in favor of moving to the beat.

Matt pulls Sky's ass into his crotch and they move together in perfect sync while I dance with Harley.

"You need to slow down," I warn. We've only had a couple of drinks but already her eyes are looking a little wild.

"I'm good. Just enjoy yourself."

"I know you're on edge about this, but it will be fine." Discreetly, I look over her shoulder, not feeling as confident with my statement as I should.

Sky assured me that he wasn't going to be here. But looking at this house right now, almost every teenager in the Creek has turned up. Why wouldn't he show his face?

Swallowing down my unease with a large mouthful of vodka. I turn my attention to dancing and enjoying myself.

I'm not scared of him. And I have every right to be here for my friend's birthday.

One song blurs into the next until the back of my neck is hot with sweat and I've got a nice buzz going on thanks to Matt's attentiveness in supplying us and the birthday girl with drinks.

"I need to pee," Harley shouts in my ear. "I'm gonna—"

"I'll come," I say, slipping my hand into hers.

"I don't need a babysitter," she snaps.

"I'm aware." She might be my little sister, but we're all Creek kids. No matter our age, we know how to look after ourselves, and these kinds of wild parties aren't new to us. "I need to go too."

We drop our empty cups in the kitchen before making our way toward the upstairs bathroom in the hope there's less of a line.

There's not.

"Ugh," Harley complains when she sees the length of it. "One good thing about the houses in Rosewood... the extra bathrooms."

She's not wrong. Everything about our lives in Rosewood —the next, more wealthy town over—is a world away from this place.

"Sky seems happy," Harley says, changing the subject. Most people are looking at us as if we don't belong, we really don't need to be standing here obviously discussing the difference between this shithole town and our new one.

Thankfully, the line goes pretty quick, and not too long later we're back with Sky with fresh drinks and Bry in tow when Harley literally bumped into him on the way to the kitchen.

He smiles at her like she's the most incredible thing he's ever seen. It's no secret that Sky's little brother has always had a crush on my little sister. Sadly though, the feelings are not mutual and Harley friend-zoned him a long time ago.

But thanks to the vodka pumping through her veins, she

allows him to pull her into his body and they dance together effortlessly.

I push aside the fact no one has made a beeline to dance with me and immediately push the thoughts of one person from my head. He's not going to be here tonight, in-person or in my imagination.

I down my drink and focus on the music.

I'll be out of here tomorrow afternoon and heading back to New York. I can put this place, all my memories and mistakes behind me and continue with my new life as if this little visit never happened.

We're still dancing when a couple of guys descend on Matt, one immediately locks his eyes on me. I've never seen him before, which is unusual for a place like the Creek. Maybe he's been unlucky enough to move here.

"Hey, beautiful," he says, taking my hand and lifting my knuckles to his lips.

Yeah, he's so not from here.

"Hey."

My body heats as he obviously checks me out, his eyes lingering on my chest for a little longer than should be allowed for two strangers.

"Dance with me, beautiful."

He doesn't wait for my agreement and steps into my body anyway. The second he does, the scent of alcohol on his lips hits my nose and I understand his forwardness.

The front of his body burns against mine and I throw caution to the wind and slide my free hand up his chest and wrap it around the back of his neck as our hips move together.

"Whoa, someone's got some moves," he says into my ear as his hands land on my waist. His voice is so low and rough, it sends shivers skating down my spine, causing warmth to bloom in my belly.

With his spicy scent and heat surrounding me, I lose

myself in him. So much so that I don't notice anything has changed until Harley slaps my shoulder, dragging me from my own drunk head.

"What?" I snap at her, annoyed that she's bringing me back to reality.

She tips her chin to the other side of the room. "The Harris twins just walked in."

My stomach drops into my toes.

"He told me himself. He's not coming. Got other plans." Sky's words from our conversation when she invited me to this party come back to me.

My mouth goes dry as I watch them step farther into the room and look around as if they own the place. I fight the urge to swallow and to appear unfazed by their appearance.

So what if they're here. It doesn't mean he is.

"Are you okay?" the guy whispers in my ear.

"Umm..." Unlike when we first started dancing, my body doesn't react to his closeness or his breath racing over my neck.

I'm numb.

Numb and scared. Not that I'd ever admit that.